# DANCING IN THE FIRE

BY SHIRLEY LATESSA

Waverly Press
P.O.B. 20624
Columbus Circle
New York, New York 10023

This novel is a work of fiction. All references to historical events or to real people, living or dead, and references to existing localities are for the purpose of giving this novel a historical setting. All other names, characters, places, and incidents are the outcome of the author's imagination. Their resemblance to any place, incident, or to anyone, living or dead, is entirely coincidental.

Book and Cover design by Susan Handman

Cover illustration by Jacqui Morgan

ISBN: 0-9657922-1-8   U.S. EDITION

Copyright © 2000 by Shirley Latessa

All Rights Reserved

Printed in the United States of America

January 2000

First Edition

## *Acknowledgments*

There are many people to whom I would like to express gratitude for their invaluable help with the many drafts of this book.

First and foremost I am indebted to my daughter **Gina** for allowing me to use an incident from her life that is the basis for this novel.

Then I'd like to offer a very special thanks to **Yael Gani** for her careful editing, reediting and proofing of this book, for her valuable suggestions, and for all the help she gave in guiding this book through its production.

And my heartfelt appreciation go to those who were willing to read the various manuscripts of this book, and who spotted the weaknesses and mistakes in the content of the novel. They have helped, it is hoped, to make this a better and more accurate story. Many thanks to **Wendy Ran**, **Gershon Segelman**, **Rebecca Schacht**, **Jon Hilton**, **Rochelle Fang**, and **Annette Stollman**.

And thanks to those people in Israel who were so free with their advice when I traveled there for background material. I hope they'll forgive me for any mistakes or misrepresentations of their fascinating and unique country.

And last, but not least, I'd like to thank **Jacqui Morgan** for her wonderful cover and **Susan Handman** for her beautiful book design.

In memory of my father

PHILLIP PESACH STOLLMAN

## Dancing in the Fire
### by Yehuda ben Yehuda

To look for God
Or perhaps His likeness
To seek His name
He Who is Unnamable
Not believing
Yet trusting belief

How shall we do it?

We shall strip off
Our old, worn garments
Toss shirt and shoe
Prayer shawl and book
Into the cleansing flame.

We shall grow wings
Of purified desire
We shall be bold, be daring
We shall set sail for home
Leap on its hallowed ground
And dance like humans dance
Like ranks of angels dance

We shall dance, yet long to dance
Naked in the fire.

Shirley Latessa

The entire novel takes place
in the months of
October and November
1993

## 1
*Monday afternoon*
## CHARTRES

Elizabeth Layton was standing in the Chapel of Saint-Piat in Chartres Cathedral, captivated by a delicate thirteenth-century sculptural fragment of the Nativity, when it happened. A forgotten memory rose up in her with all the impact of an explosion. It nearly blew her off her feet. Nothing in the scene Beth was looking at prepared her for it. The little sculptural scene was so tranquil, so enchanting. And she had been standing there peacefully and contentedly admiring it, thinking how right Eric had been in telling her not to miss this piece among so many spectacular things to see in and around the cathedral. Yes, she liked it very much. Lying on a straw cot, Mary was reaching down, ever so gently, to stroke the child in a corn crib below her. In a gesture of comfort to his wife, Joseph was leaning across the foot of the cot, while an ass and ox looked on. It was turning into another lovely afternoon. She had looked at the stained-glass windows, the labyrinth, the marvelous choir, the Virgin of the Pillar. She would leave a little time to buy some postcards for her daughter Becky, and to walk around the famous porticos outside. But she didn't want to leave this chapel yet. Beth glanced at her watch. Forty-five minutes until she was to meet Eric at the train station. She turned back to the charming scene and felt drawn into it, welcomed into it. Husband, wife, child. A circle of love large enough to take in the common barn animals, and all who stood there admiring the sculpture.

That's when it happened. Abruptly. Without warning. Beth was sitting in the room of her old New York apartment overlooking Central Park. It was twenty-some years ago, a few days before Christmas, and she was leafing through a book of art she had just unwrapped, a gift from her sister, Merle. It was a beautiful book, filled with quality reproductions of treasures from the Vatican's art collection. Beth was admiring the Caravaggio painting called *The Deposition*, when Alicia came bouncing into the room and climbed into her mother's arms. Alicia was not yet seven, but even then her black hair was thick and reached below her shoulders. Beth carefully placed the book on the coffee table and returned her daughter's hug.

After a moment, Alicia slid out of her lap, moved to the coffee table, and stood staring at the book still open to the Caravaggio. "Mmm, mmm," she began to hum a nervous little tune, then walked away, but immediately returned to stand in front of the book again. "Mmm, mmm," she sang, and then with a pudgy forefinger she pointed to the print and asked, "What's this?"

Beth had seldom taken her two daughters to church. She had long ago given up Christianity, had hated going to church when she herself was young, knew that her mother had made the family go because it was the proper thing to do, and because her father was a doctor, and because they were respectable members of their community. But when she married, Beth vowed that she would never teach her children things that neither she nor Matthew believed. So no regular church for the children, no Sunday School with stories about sweet Jesus who somehow became God. She had hated the idea of a suffering God, a God whose agony took the anguish away from humanity. When had that ever happened?

Beth was uncertain what she should tell Alicia. But

as a dutiful mother who had been asked a question, she stared at the painting that showed Christ being taken down from the cross, and tried to formulate an answer. Jesus' mother was there and the other Marys, also Nicodemus and St. John the Evangelist.

"That man is dead. His name is Jesus. You've heard about him. He's the one that was born in a manger and that we remember on Christmas. Well, when he grew up he was a very good man, but some bad men had him killed. His mother and his friends are taking him down from the cross and are going to bury him." Simple. Factual. Honest.

Alicia continued to hum, "Mmm, mmm." Then she pointed to the man who was John the Evangelist and asked, "Why is that man gasping?"

Beth leaned forward and stared at the picture. The man's mouth was open in an expression of dismay. She had to admire her daughter's use of such a sophisticated word as *gasping*. Indeed, one could say John was gasping. "He feels very sad at what's happened to Jesus."

"Mmm, mmm," Alicia continued to hum and to stare at the print. Then she turned to her mother, her large eyes opaque and obsidian black, and said, "We were there, you know. . .before we came down the last time. And we gasped too. And when we went home that night, we couldn't sleep."

Her daughter's comment and matter-of-fact tone startled Beth, and her own mouth, like John the Evangelist's, dropped open. But Alicia had turned back to look at the print again. After a moment, she bounced out of the room saying, "I hear Becky waking up. I'm going to teach her to play *Chutes and Ladders*."

That evening when Beth mentioned the incident to her husband, Matthew said, "Oh, she's probably heard stories about Jesus from her friends and from her teachers, including the Crucifixion."

"That's probably it," Beth answered.

"Children have vivid imaginations. Remember all the little people Alicia used to pretend lived in her blanket?"

And that had been the end of it. Beth forgot about it. She had not thought of it again until this moment.

It was her feet she saw first, coming out of the memory, her feet in her comfortable sport shoes standing on the marble floor of the chapel, then the frieze of the Nativity again with its graceful figures. Beth needed to sit. She could feel her legs trembling. She walked out into the cathedral and sat down in one of the pews. The many-hued light pouring in from the stained-glass windows made the cathedral look tenuous and otherworldly.

Why had she remembered that incident just now, here in Chartres, standing in front of a Nativity scene? She had totally forgotten it. Like useless water, it had drained away from her memory, never to return in all Alicia's growing-up years, in all the years of Alicia's struggle with leukemia and in that terrible, sorrowful year after her death. But suddenly here it was. Why? Why now?

The large cathedral felt cold and clammy, filled with old air, old memories. Beth wanted to run out of there. But her legs were too wobbly, her knees too weak. Just breathe slowly, she instructed herself. She needed the sun. She needed to go to the bathroom, needed also to get something to drink to steady her nerves. Beth rose, found her legs under her, and with great concentration, walked to the restroom. She then left the cathedral.

On a side street heading toward the train station she found a café, went inside and ordered a café noir. Strong coffee would ground her, bring her back into the present, into reality. Beth didn't think about the postcards she had forgotten to buy for her daughter Becky, nor about the porticos she had neglected to look at. She thought about that odd, odd memory.

Alicia had said that the two of them had stood at the cross, at Christ's Crucifixion.

". . .before we came down the last time. . ."

Beth's hands shook as she raised the cup to her mouth. Could Alicia really have remembered something from a past life? If the child in her had remembered it, the growing youth must have forgotten it. Alicia had never mentioned it again. But how was it that Beth had forgotten it? And why had it suddenly surfaced today? In front of a Nativity scene? And with such an impact? To whom could she speak? Where could she go for an answer?

Paul.

Paul would have some thoughts about this. Yes, when she returned to New York in a few days, she would telephone her friend Paul Burrows in Gloucester, Massachusetts. She might even arrange to visit him. Paul, a widower in his late seventies, believed in reincarnation. Yes, that's what she would do. And she would call her friend Mathilda Jones in California. Like Paul, Mattie was a different sort of believing Christian. Mattie would have something interesting to say about this experience of Beth's. Beth glanced at her watch. Twenty minutes till she had to meet Eric. She carefully lifted the cup and swallowed the cooling liquid.

Reincarnation.

There it was again. That uncomfortable idea coming up in her life once more, after she had finally reconciled herself to setting aside all spiritual ideas that she couldn't prove. Eric had helped her with that. Good, kind, practical Eric.

She ordered another cup of coffee, drank it, then walked the few blocks to the train station.

## 2

*Monday afternoon*
## CHARTRES

Beth was standing in the station waiting for him, when Eric Halsey arrived only minutes before the train was due to depart. For a moment he stood in the crowd—just to look at her. Over three years, and still the sight of her made something flutter near his heart. It wasn't that she was beautiful, it was that her face was so expressive, and it was the way she gesticulated, so gracefully. Her hands positively danced when she talked. And the figure was darn good, a little fuller than when he had first met her. But she had been so thin then, so stressed. Now she was happy. With him she was happy. And so was he.

Beth was waiting near the gate, a pensive look on her face. Eric was familiar with that look, something was going on inside her fertile and active poet's mind. Chartres Cathedral, he thought. It's set her off. It can do that to people. He hurried forward, gave her a big hug, and took Beth by the arm.

"The man I saw was an absolute charmer," he told her as they walked out onto the train platform just as the train pulled into the station, "funny and full of marvelous stories. Unfortunately, his work. . .his sculpture, is second-rate. Nothing the Barry would want."

Beth nodded but said nothing as he helped her into the train.

"What's the matter?" he asked, as they found their seats.

"You look. . .well, bothered. Don't tell me you hated the Cathedral."

"Oh no, it was wonderful, really quite wonderful."

He smiled, relieved.

"But the strangest thing happened to me there." And as the train pulled away from the station, past the town and out into the countryside, Beth described her experience in the Saint-Piat chapel.

Eric listened without interrupting her. When she finished, he said, "Is it so strange? Great art touches us so deeply, it often draws long forgotten memories out of us, don't you think?" He put his hand over hers lying in her lap.

"Weird that I should have forgotten something like that."

"Why weird?"

"Because I remember so many things. I have a very good memory. It's one of my faults, as you well know."

"Good for your poetry. . ."

"Granted, but the shadow side is that it's hard to let go of things. And it's the way this one hit me, a bolt of lightning flashing up out of the unconscious, and nearly knocking me off my feet." Beth shook her head and withdrew her hand from under his. She ran her fingers through her short gray hair. "It's not just the memory, Eric, it's the way it's shaken me up. I barely made it to the café, my legs were like jelly."

Eric sat quietly, his wide shoulders hunched slightly forward, his arms on his knees. "Well, it's an interesting idea to contemplate," he finally said, "if one can take a child's imagination seriously. At that age they don't yet distinguish between reality and fancy."

"But why did the memory come suddenly like that and. . .and rattle me? I was having a marvelous day,"

Beth's voice began to tremble. "I've had a marvelous six weeks. I've been so happy, so content traveling with you..."

"You're a poet. You were looking at art and consequently open."

"Maybe," and then she lapsed into silence and turned to stare out the window.

## 3

*Monday afternoon*
## EN ROUTE TO PARIS

Beth caught the wary, puzzled look in Eric's eyes. Frankly, she didn't like what she saw there, so she turned to look out the window. What didn't he understand? Did he think she was blowing up an incident out of all proportion? Was she?

Three and a half years ago, she had been talked into going on an art tour to the Aegean by her family. Their purpose had been to keep her from mourning Alicia's death. It was on that trip that she had met both Eric Halsey and Paul Burrows. But in her fragile state, in foreign places, suffering from irreconcilable losses—the untimely death of first her husband and then her oldest daughter—Beth had gone through a crisis, had somehow crossed a line into another reality. But was it another reality? Or was it madness? Whatever it had been, she had come out of it cured. Her sense of sorrow, futility, and anger had vanished. For a short and definitely euphoric time, she had resolved to keep her natural skepticism about the non-rational at bay. She was in love with Eric, and he with her. She was writing and writing well. And that's all that seemed to matter. But, of course, that complacent attitude hadn't lasted, couldn't last. And when she began, once again, to question just what had really happened to her, Eric, with simple wisdom, said, "If there's another reality, we'll all find out when we are dead. Be content with this life. You're here now, babe, in this reality. That's all we can know, so make the most of it. That's the best any of us can do."

Trees blurred alongside the train's path, hiding everything. Myself, she thought. Hiding myself. And then there was a sudden opening into sun-filled fields. An announcement, she thought, an annunciation. Of what, Beth? What was the significance of that memory that had so shaken her? Alicia's memory? Her memory? Reincarnation. But wasn't Eric right? Reincarnation was something one couldn't prove, not really, not scientifically. And that's what mattered. That was the crux. But what was it Paul Burrows had said? That for most of us, our present physical/psychical constitution blocked our pre-birth memories. Was he right?

Trees again, occulting everything. Outside. Inside.

For Paul reincarnation made objective sense. For him it seemed perfectly reasonable. But for Beth it was an interesting, even curious, albeit an uncomfortable idea. One without proof. And truth be told, she wasn't sure she liked the idea. The thought of life after life after life fatigued her.

The train pulled up to a station. Where? She hadn't seen the sign. But people. Here were people. Leaving. Coming.

But her likes and dislikes shouldn't enter into her reasoning. As a good academic, she knew that wasn't helpful. Yet no matter how she looked at reincarnation, and she had tried for a time to entertain it, she always came back to the same question. A question that stood there like a wall she kept banging into: How can you believe what you don't actually know? "There is more than one way of knowing, my friend," Paul had said to her. "You want to know things only with your brain, and your brain, after all, is limited to this world and to this one sense-oriented life."

But she had no other way of knowing, therefore how could she believe what she didn't know and couldn't prove? Today that retort was not giving her comfort. It was no longer an answer she could hide behind.

Is that what she had been doing?

The train leaving the station sounded a warning. Beth glanced over at Eric, a French newspaper was in his hands and he was apparently reading it. She turned back to watch the train move out of the station. They were soon past the village and in the countryside.

Was that what her complacency had been, a way to hide? Had she been hiding?

Trees again. Dark trees of the mind.

Had she simply been afraid to pursue non-sense-perceptible ideas, afraid to shake herself up, to make herself uncomfortable? Was she afraid now? Had the courage she had found for herself over three years ago disappeared? And what if Alicia had indeed remembered a past life? Was it possible? Was it genuine? And had Beth forgotten that childhood episode because she had not wanted to entertain, had feared to entertain, the idea that there might be some truth to what the young Alicia had said? Was Beth afraid? Afraid of what? Change? Had she driven the memory away because of fear, a beast she loathed, a beast she was willing to fight, if she was aware of it, if she could experience it rising into her consciousness? Had fear lived and worked that unconsciously in her? It was an unbearable thought. She began to breathe deeply again, audibly.

Eric put his hand on her shoulder. "Are you all right?"

"Fine," she said, but the thoughts she was thinking rattled her and she had to work to calm her breathing.

But wait, she told herself, this sudden déjà vu is something more than just a window cracking open, giving a view into a past life. This wasn't just any memory. Little Alicia had placed herself at the Crucifixion. And her mother with her.

Oh, my God!

No wonder she felt rattled. And chilled. Beth buttoned the coat she was wearing with shaky hands. Again Eric looked questioningly at her, but she simply shook her head. Hold on, she told herself. Now hold on a minute. *If* that memory were true. *If* Alicia's memory was a true one. That's a very big *if.*

But *if* wasn't good enough.

*If* was like a stone in her belly. How would she live with it?

She had to find out.

## 4
*Monday night*
## PARIS

That night at dinner, to Eric's disappointment, Elizabeth was still distracted. They were at their little Russian restaurant, not far from their small but elegant hotel near the Boulevard St. Germain. Eric had picked that restaurant for their special night. It was a funky little place that had delighted Beth no end when they had come upon it a week ago. They had come back once before and at that time Beth had made witty comments about the decor, which was Disney-like, and the staff, who were dressed in seventeenth-century costumes. The food, however, was excellent and expensive, fit for a czar—and for rich tourists.

But tonight Beth was unusually quiet and after the first course Eric himself had lapsed into silence. He kept fingering the antique watch in his pocket that was his present to her. Thursday they would be on their way back to the States and he had hoped, had planned, to talk to her again about marriage, to raise it once again. Beth had agreed to make a decision at the end of this trip, and the trip was winding down. They had been so content together these six weeks—but looking at Beth's troubled face, the words he tried to speak, like dry bread, kept crumbling in his mouth.

A few hours ago, after they had returned from Chartres, Beth had immediately put in a call to their friend Paul Burrows, but had not found him at home. Her need to make that call had disturbed Eric. It's not that he wasn't fond of Paul, he was. But Eric was afraid of what that phone call, all the way from Paris to the Boston area, augured. It was Alicia again, rising up like a ghostly phoenix, in that memory at Chartres. It was the inability of Beth to accept her daughter's death cropping up again.

But why now? She had gone through that crisis over three years ago, had even written a marvelous novel about it. Eric liked to think that he had helped her through that crisis when they were on that trip, but he had to be honest. His advances then had only awakened fear in Beth—the fear of trusting love, and loved ones, to support her in life. After all, didn't loved ones leave? Either by choice or taken by death? And Beth had been left by both her husband and her daughter. "Half her family," she had often said. Two deaths within a few years. Though Beth had claimed that she was reconciled to the losses now, Eric wasn't all that convinced. Even though Beth said she loved him, she had as yet been unwilling to commit to marriage. What else could it be but fear of loss? Something in her psyche wasn't reconciled, no matter how often Beth protested that it was. And now that memory. That blasted, silly memory.

Eric watched her face as Beth toyed with her *blini*. He fingered the watch in his pocket. He had wanted to give it to her as an engagement present. He must have sighed audibly because Beth looked up.

"I'm sorry, Eric." She put her hand on his. "It's just that incident in Chartres, don't you see. I can't shake it's impact. A little goofy, huh?"

"Not goofy, hardly that. But what do you propose to do about it, babe?"

"What can one do about it?" she shrugged. "I'd like

to talk to Paul. Maybe I'll try again when we get back to the hotel." She glanced at her watch.

"We'll be home in a few days."

"I know."

"Can't the phone call wait?"

She slowly shook her head.

"Why?" he asked.

"I don't know. That memory came with such power, you see. I can't shake it. Like something insisting on being answered."

"How can you make yourself believe in reincarnation, Beth?"

"I don't know. I'm not sure."

But there was something in her eyes that belied her words, and it made Eric very uneasy.

When they returned to the hotel, Beth tried to get through to Paul once again, but there was still no answer.

In bed, a little while later, Eric reached for Beth. She moved closer but still seemed absent. He rolled over on his back. "Beth, let's talk about this. What are you thinking? You're thinking something. What is it you're thinking?"

Beth sat up and hugged her knees. "I have to do more than contemplate whether Alicia's memory was true. I have to find out."

"But how can you do that?" He suddenly felt cold.

"I'm not sure, but I have an idea." And she rested her chin on her knees.

"What kind of idea?" He sat up.

"I think I'd like to go there," she finally said, without turning to face him.

"Go where?"

"To the Holy Land, to Palestine, Israel," she said. "Where it all took place."

He could feel the tension, a sudden chill, misting the air between them. "Okay," he said without enthusiasm. "Why not? I've always wanted to see the place myself. They have some wonderful Byzantine mosaics." Byzantine art was a passion of his. "Why not plan to go there. . .on our honeymoon in a few months?" Those words came out unplanned. Still she had promised to give him an answer before they left France.

She turned to look at him then, ignoring the reference to marriage, "I can't wait. This has to be resolved now."

He pulled the blankets back, got out of bed, and moved the few feet to the tall windows. He drew back the drapes and a gold-gray light flowed into the room. There was no one in the street. Everybody at home, in their own beds, sleeping with their loved ones.

"Why?" Eric asked. The word cracked through the tightness of his throat.

"Because it's so terribly important, don't you see?"

Eric turned to look at her, making out her darker shape in the shadowy room. "Frankly, Beth, I don't. Let's say, for the sake of argument, that reincarnation is true, and that you were indeed living in the time of Christ. That's two thousand years ago and over. Why is it so terribly important to find out now? Why can't it wait a few months? It's waited two thousand years and all of this lifetime, what's the big rush suddenly?"

"Because it changes everything. Everything gets changed," she said. Her voice was filled with passion.

But Eric was hearing what he didn't want to hear. "Everything? Us too?"

"Oh no, I didn't mean that."

"Didn't you?"

"I meant. . .I only meant one's whole world view,

one's life, how that really is." She climbed out of the bed the two had shared for a week, her face a crosshatch of light and shadows. "Maybe Paul is right," she said. "Maybe there is another world, a supersensible world. Maybe Alicia is there, waiting somewhere." She came toward him and stood in front of him, a pleading look on her face. "Don't you understand? The memory returned to me just now, and that has to mean something, because it came with...with power. That's never happened to me before."

Eric was silent, waiting for Beth to go on.

"That means it needs attending right now. Surely you can see that?"

"What do you intend to do?"

"I want to go to Israel now. I don't mean right now, but as soon as our time in Paris is over. In three days."

"But I have to be back in New York, Beth."

"That's okay. I mean, I know *you* do...but I don't. Look, my novel is in the stores. I've completed the book tours. There's no reason I have to rush back." He felt a terrible ache behind his eyes. "Eric, please don't look at me like that, this hasn't anything to do with you and me."

"Doesn't it?"

"Ten days," she said, "that's all I want. Just ten days. I want to walk around those holy sites and...and just see if anything happens. See if I can experience anything familiar, a déjà vu kind of thing, that's all."

"Beth, do you want to marry me?" He had to ask her, didn't want to ask her like this, it was all wrong, not the way he had planned it. What had he done with the watch?

"Why are you asking me that now?" He could hear the frustration in her voice.

"Because that's what we promised each other. We said we would decide about marriage on this trip. And this trip is almost over."

"I can't think about that now. Look," she said, with effort, "let me go off on this little adventure, then the day I get back, I'll give you my answer."

Beth, don't treat me like this, he wanted to say.

"You think I'm planning this so I don't have to give you an answer now?"

Beth, why is this so hard for you, why is yes or no so hard for you? But he kept silent.

"You do, don't you? You think I'm deliberately putting you off with an elaborate charade."

"I think, Beth, that your subconscious is creating a scenario that gives you an excuse to postpone deciding whether you want to marry me or to give me up." He was saying words. Did he believe them? Acting like a magazine psychiatrist.

"Give you up? Has that become the choice now?" her voice was loud. "Marriage or separating? Nothing in-between?" She moved to the chair a few feet from him and flung herself down in it. "Why are we talking about marriage when I'm talking about something else, worried about something else?"

Beth, he wanted to say, don't run. Don't run from me. Wait. We can do this together if it's so important.

"Eric, you've understood me better than any man I've ever known, please be understanding now." Her voice sounded tense and weepy. She was pleading. "Ten days, that's all I ask. If nothing happens, then I'll let go of it. Okay?"

He walked over to the chair and took her by the hands and pulled her up toward him. He embraced her. "Come to bed, Beth." He could feel her taut body within his arms. "Okay, Beth, okay, okay. Don't cry. Ten days. You can have your ten days. Come to bed."

## 5
*Wednesday morning*
## BIG SUR, CALIFORNIA

Mathilda Jones was sitting at the wheel of her station wagon, heart pounding, unable to turn the key.

Why was she doing this?

She opened her large purse for the fifth time and fingered the airline tickets, then reached into the envelope, pulled out the tickets and itinerary and looked carefully through them. One round-trip ticket to New York, one round-trip ticket to Israel. All paid for.

How much money could she get for them if she decided not to go? Right now, at this moment, decided not to go? Surely something.

She could do that, she didn't have to do anything that she didn't want to do.

She peered out of the car window at her cottage. Why was she abandoning it? Why was she leaving her home, leaving the careful security she had built for herself? Why was she deserting her haven for an open-ended adventure—without perimeters, without guidelines, the road uncertain, the end unknown?

Mattie stepped out of her car and looked out at her hill, at the forest surrounding her little house, at her opulent garden that she was relinquishing to someone else's care. Years ago she had moved here, after her husband and son had died. And she had been reasonably content. Didn't she have everything she needed here in these hills, in the nearby town, in her garden, in her books, and in her work? Wasn't she comfortable living a life that had few surprises, where little broke through the dependability of her days? How had she gotten herself into this mess, making a trip to unknown parts, for goals that were less than clear?

Mattie walked to the door of her cottage. Perhaps she had not turned off the coffee pot. Had she pulled the plugs out of all the electrical appliances? Had she turned off all the lights? She stood at the door, keys in hand. And hesitated. She knew she had taken care of it all. Of course she had. She had walked through the house half a dozen times checking everything.

She returned to the car.

She knew perfectly well why she was going on this daunting trip and leaving the protection of her life behind. So she'd better get on with it.

Mattie climbed into her car and turned the key in the ignition. She drove slowly down the driveway and onto the road, finally onto the highway that would take her to San Francisco and her nephew's house. A couple of days' visit with Doug, whom she adored, and then on to New York. And finally Israel. She was terrified right down to the tips of her toes. But she was going. This trip had to be the medicine she needed for whatever it was that ailed her.

If not, the patient would die. Period.

## 6
*Wednesday afternoon*
## PARIS

The line through security was long, and Gidon ben David used the time to look around him at the other passengers who would be flying that day. It was an old habit from his days in Israeli military security and from his years in what the men who worked there euphemistically called the Prime Minister's Office.

It was easy to recognize the Israelis going home. They were burdened with shopping bags filled with goods from Europe, arguing with their spouses or trying to keep toddlers under control, and dragging along oversized carry-ons. Right after Gidon had left the Intelligence Service to take this job as trade representative for a consortium of collective settlements, he too had returned from each trip loaded down with goods for the family. After all, it was for the money that he had left the Service. That and the hope that a better life-style, as his American relatives called it, would improve his marriage and make his children happier. But on this trip, as on so many the past couple of years, Gidon had only small gifts in his check-in luggage, a little something for his parents, widowed mother-in-law, his wife, and his two teenage children.

Gidon felt rested. He had taken a couple of days off in Paris after nearly three weeks in Northern Europe trying to find markets for the products he represented. And there was a girl in Paris. That always made things nice.

His eyes strayed to a couple standing against the wall not far from him, talking intensely. He watched them because he knew they were lovers, not married, he was sure, but lovers. Gidon liked to study lovers, particularly those around his own age or older. The man was just under six feet, broad shouldered and in his fifties. He was partially turned away from Gidon, had a strong body, a good profile and a well-groomed head of hair. American, no question. New York, probably. And well-to-do. He could see it in the man's stance, in the cut of his coat, the way it fell open. The woman was lean, had a nice figure, was of medium height. Her hair was gray and worn short, very stylish and very Parisian. She had an interesting face, expressive, not really beautiful, but definitely attractive. She was wearing expensive wool pants and a cashmere sweater that suited the end of October weather in Paris and she was carrying an all-weather coat. A small carry-on was at her feet. The woman was either in her forties or fifties, it was hard to tell. At first Gidon thought she was French until he saw the sport shoes. Older French women seldom wore shoes like that. She too must be American.

The woman was talking heatedly to the man. The man looked unhappy. They are definitely lovers, Gidon decided. Only people in love can look that hurt, he thought, and felt a twinge of jealousy. The woman suddenly broke away from the man. The man picked up the carry-on and followed her. They moved into the line somewhere behind Gidon, just as it was his turn to pass through the security checkpoint.

Gidon wandered through the duty-free shops, drank coffee, and when his flight's departure was announced, entered the plane. He found his seat in Business Class and watched as the large plane filled up. It was a slow process and the line began to back up. Too many bags to stow away, too many children to accommodate. He was about to take out his book and read when to his surprise the woman he had been watching with such interest near the security check-in entered the plane. She was alone.

She stopped next to Gidon, "I think I'm sitting in the window seat," she said. "Oh, do you speak English?"

"Here, let me help you," he answered, in his slightly accented English. Gidon rose quickly and took the case and the coat from the woman. His seat had been changed at the last minute. He had argued about it at the check-in counter. But now he was glad.

"Thank you," she flashed him a grateful smile. "Oh, wait, let me get my book," she said. She retrieved her case. Gidon glanced at her well-groomed hands—no polish and no wedding ring. As she was lifting her book out of her carry-on, the two of them were suddenly crushed against each other.

"Sorry," Gidon said.

"Worse than the New York subway," she retorted, blushing slightly, which Gidon found charming.

Finally, she moved into her seat and he stowed her things in the compartment above them.

"That's a terrific book of poetry," Gidon said, lowering his tall frame into his seat. He gestured at the book that was lying in her lap.

"Oh, do you know it?" the woman turned to him with interest.

"I do," he answered, "Mathilda Jones is a wonderful writer. You're in for a marvelous adventure."

"You've read it?"

"I have."

"Me too, many times. And I agree with you. Truth is, the author's a friend of mine."

"Mathilda Jones? Really? What is she like? Sorry, I

don't mean to pry, but I've often wondered what kind of a woman she was. Her poetry has such depth, so many layers."

"That's just like Mattie, lots of layers."

He nodded in appreciation.

"Well, she's also very astute, very intense, enormously bright, a great listener. A great friend. And she can be didactic and at the same time terribly shy, if you can imagine such a combination. And when she's focused in on something, forget it, you could set off a rocket near her and she wouldn't hear it."

They stopped talking to watch the flight attendant tell a woman, in no uncertain terms, that she could not stow her carry-on luggage in Business Class when her seat was in Economy. In a moment they were arguing in Hebrew. The flight attendant won out in the end, and the woman finally moved up the aisle complaining all the way into the next section, with several other people scolding her for holding up the line.

Gidon shrugged his shoulders, "Don't mess with our Israeli stewardesses. They win every time." He turned to his seat partner with interest, "I fly a lot, mostly for business, but this is the first time I've ever sat near someone who reads poetry. We're a rare breed, I'm afraid."

"Very rare," she said, then laughed, "but not extinct, I hope. Whenever I travel I carry a book of poems with me. One I'm familiar with. I find it comforting, like traveling with an old friend."

"Really?" Gidon pulled a book out of the seat pocket in front of him. "Here is the book of poetry that I've been carrying all over Europe for the last three weeks," and he showed her a book written in Hebrew.

"You too?" She shook her head, "I'm afraid I don't know Hebrew."

"It's by a veteran Israeli writer called Yehuda ben

Yehuda, a collection of his works."

"I know ben Yehuda's work. He's a wonderful poet. Extraordinary perceptions, and beautiful images, don't you think?"

"Yes, I do. And in Hebrew there is also the sounds, the rhythm. He has a good, good ear. Ben Yehuda is sort of our Walt Whitman."

"What a wonderful comparison," she said.

The flight attendant came around with orange juice and a while later the announcement came to buckle up.

"Where did you learn to speak English so beautifully?" she asked as the plane pulled away from the gate.

"American parents. They immigrated to Israel before I was born. But I spent a lot of time in America when I was young, almost every summer with my grandparents when they were still alive. My parents wanted me to be bilingual so they spoke English to me. Still," he smiled, "I have a slight Israeli accent that I can't get rid of. It comes from the soil, I think."

"And the interest in poetry?" she asked him.

"I don't know." He shrugged. "Who understands these things? I guess I've always loved poetry. I've read quite a bit of American and English poetry, and a little French, though I'm not as fluent in French. And of course, Israeli poetry. It's hard to describe why one likes poetry, isn't it?" he asked her.

"Very hard. You either have a passion for it or you don't."

"For me, poetry is one of the reasons to love the unlovable human species. That the human mind can create poetry, that for me is a reason not to despair." He suddenly laughed. "I didn't mean to get so heavy. Sorry."

"But you said that so well, and life is pretty heavy, isn't it?" She was looking at him with genuine curiosity.

"My name is Gidon ben David," he said, and extended his hand.

"And I'm Elizabeth Layton," she shook his hand.

"You're not the poet, Elizabeth Layton?"

"Yes, I am."

"Good God!"

"But don't tell me you've read any of my books?"

"I have. Well, I hardly know what to say. And to think I made a fuss when they changed my seat at the last minute. Now I'm afraid I won't give you any peace on this trip."

"Well, I have a few questions I would love to ask an Israeli. This is my first trip to your country."

"And you're traveling alone?"

She lowered her eyes for a moment and then looked up and smiled at him, "Yes, yes I am."

So where was the boyfriend? Had something gone wrong between the two of them?

He closed his eyes and began to recite:

*"Where were you when the gilded days*
*of October ended? When the last thin*
*flower cut through the hard cold soil?*

*And where were you when the blood*
*red rose fell on the stone steps like a wound?*
*And birds abandoned the yard?*

*Will you come only with winter to stalk*
*and blow and stride like death through my valley?"*

He opened his eyes and found her staring at him in astonishment.

"I love to memorize poems," he said.

"Why that one? It's...it's so..."

"Bitter?"

She shrugged. "I was going to say *slight.* It's part of a long sequence poem.

"I know. Was that sequence poem written from life?" he asked her.

"In some way or other all poems are from life. Even the invented ones."

He didn't press her.

Before long they were airborne. The two began to talk like old friends. Gidon asked her a lot of questions about American poetry and about some of the current poets, many of whom she knew personally. In turn, Elizabeth plied him with questions about Israel. When he asked her the purpose of her trip she hesitated for a moment, then said, "Oh, just a tourist who wants to look at the Christian sites."

"Are you religious?"

"No, not really. I just had this urge to see where it all began, the tradition I was born into. What part of Israel are you from?"

"Tel Aviv," he said, and told her about his wife, Avigail, and then about his daughter, Rinat, and son, Geel, who were both in high school. "My son has one more year and then off to the army."

"Well, hopefully this new peace initiative will succeed, and your son won't get drawn into a war," Beth said.

"We have to try," Gidon answered.

Over wine at dinner, Gidon asked her where she was staying. She told him Jerusalem and mentioned a small hotel not far from the King David Hotel. She said that she was a widow with a married daughter, then revealed ever so casually that she was seeing a man and that they had just traveled in Europe together.

"Why didn't he come with you?"

"Oh," she said, after a slight hesitation, "he had to be back in New York. He acquires art for for the Barry Museum there."

*Where were you when the gilded days/of October ended?* Trouble in Paradise, Gidon decided, and the thought gave him a slight sense of satisfaction.

A neighbor of Gidon's, who worked at the airport, had driven Gidon's car to the airport that day. He had parked it where he always parked it when Gidon was expected back from a trip. So when the plane from Paris arrived in the early evening at Ben Gurion Airport, Gidon offered to drive Elizabeth to Jerusalem.

"But I thought you said you live in Tel Aviv," she said.

"I do, but I have to be in Jerusalem in the morning, so I'm going to stay at a friend's house overnight." It was a lie. He didn't want to end the encounter. And he was in no hurry to get home.

Gidon wheeled their luggage to the car, then drove Elizabeth Layton to her hotel in Jerusalem. Just as they were about to say good-bye, he pulled out a business card and offered it to her. "Look, I don't know who else you know in this country, but if you need any help or just a friend, give me a call."

She took the card without looking at it. "Thank you for everything," she said. "I've really enjoyed our conversation. And thanks so much for the lift."

He knew then that she wouldn't call. She had a lover and she wouldn't call. Gidon was married and she wouldn't call. With a twinge of regret he watched her follow the porter who was carrying her bags into the hotel.

As he drove his car away from the curb, Gidon looked into his rearview mirror. A man got out of a

Mitsubishi and went into the hotel. Curious. That Mitsubishi had been behind them all the way from the airport. Out of habit, as he had driven away from the airport parking lot, Gidon had checked his rearview mirror to see if he was being followed. To his surprise, he was. It was obvious now that it wasn't he who was being followed, but Elizabeth Layton. What was going on? Gidon felt that old familiar excitement in his solar plexus.

Was the woman in trouble? Was she here to meet someone? Had he inadvertently interfered?

Why should she be followed?

Critical times, and there were many enemies—both Arabs and Jews—wanting to disrupt the peace negotiations between Rabin and Arafat. But what could this woman have to do with any of that?

Probably nothing.

If she was in trouble she would no doubt be safe tonight. Hadn't she said that she was going to unpack, order up some supper and go to bed early? And if she wasn't going to stay in, if she had a liaison with someone and didn't want him to know about it? Well, it was none of his business.

Nevertheless, some old instinct made him drive around the block. As he passed the hotel, Gidon saw the man who had followed Layton come out of its front door and return to the Mitsubishi. Gidon circled around the block once again. As he passed the hotel for the second time the car was still there with two men inside. One was reading a newspaper and the other was watching the hotel entrance. If they knew he was observing them, they seemed unconcerned. Gidon drove once again around the block and parked up the street, several cars behind the Mitsubishi. He waited there an hour, but nothing happened. Neither of the two men went back into the hotel.

And Elizabeth Layton did not come out. Gidon pulled out into the street traffic, drove past the Mitsubishi and the hotel, once again unremarked, and finally onto the street that would take him to the Tel Aviv highway.

This is none of your business, he told himself again.

But all the way back to Tel Aviv he thought about the woman.

## ❧7❧
## *Wednesday evening*
## JERUSALEM

Beth pulled off her shoes and lay back on the bed in her hotel room. She barely took in her surroundings except to notice that everything looked new, clean and unexceptional. She would unpack in a few minutes. Eric had wanted to book her into the King David, but it had been full, so the King David had recommended a small but good hotel down the street.

And here she was. In Israel. In Jerusalem. Without Eric.

Now what?

Driving from Ben Gurion Airport up into those ancient hills where Jerusalem was located, rushing through the dark, shadowy October evening, Beth had scarcely listened to Gidon ben David's running travelogue. Her heart had been pounding too rapidly. Not until she was in the car with the friendly and attractive Israeli had it occurred to her that she had come to his country on a rather wild adventure. Talking on the plane to the man had postponed the moment when she had to decide how she was going to go about achieving her mission. And their conversation had kept her from thinking about Eric's disapproval. In Paris she had fought for her right to make this trip, but driving up into the hills toward the ancient city, the certainty she had felt, like snowmelt, began to seep away.

This undertaking was a little nuts. Really, a bit crazy. Stop it, she scolded herself, sat up, and swung her feet off the bed. This is getting you nowhere.

She would make a start tomorrow by walking around the Christian sites in Jerusalem. Then take it from there. As for Eric—after all, she hadn't asked for the moon. Ten days is all she wanted and ten days is not a big deal. She would make it up to Eric. She knew him. He wouldn't stay mad for long.

Or would he?

Eric had not called. Tomorrow he would be on his way from Paris to New York. Without her.

This kind of thinking was not helpful. Best to let it go. She unpacked, took a shower, ordered food from room service, watched the English international news on the TV, and then went to sleep.

## 8
## *Wednesday night*
## TEL AVIV

Gidon ben David was still awake when the phone call came.

He was lying next to his sleeping wife thinking about his arrival home. His daughter had greeted him almost shyly. His son coolly. Later, after TV, he and his wife had made love. It was perfunctory, passionless. Staring at the ceiling he thought about the girl in Paris with a sense of loss. Young, beautiful, uncomplicated Corinne, with her cropped black hair and her long, slim legs. When they made love it was light, easy, filled with laughter, with sensuality, adventure even. Not so routinized as it had become with Avigail.

Headlights danced along the ceiling and then disappeared. It was close to 1:00 a.m. He thought then about the woman he had met on the plane. Elizabeth Layton, gifted American poet. Was he interested? He wasn't sure. It seemed clear she wasn't. She had subtly let him know she had a boyfriend. Still, he had enjoyed talking to her, had enjoyed her intelligent questions, her sense of humor, the way she listened with her whole body. Maybe he would have left it alone, wouldn't have given it another thought, if that damned Mitsubishi hadn't followed them...her. Oh, what the hell. His interest was piqued. Old habits die hard. Gidon couldn't sleep. He listened to Avigail's steady breathing and thought again about his wife. How could one know someone as long and as intimately as he had known Avigail and yet with each encounter find her more and more a stranger? He would leave on a trip, stay away two weeks or three, come home, but at each reunion it was as if a little more of the intimacy between them was gone, rubbed away like dead skin cells while he had been traveling. His own parents seemed to get closer and closer as they grew older. He and Avigail were going in opposite directions and he didn't know how to stop the slide downhill. Or even if he wanted to stop it. He wondered then if this woman who shared his bed was as imperturbable with her lovers as she was with him. Best not to think about that. There were places his mind shouldn't go.

He thought then about his kids. After a day or two, following each return, his daughter, Rinat, would warm up and there were hugs which he so needed and so loved. But Geel was angry with him and he wasn't sure why. It was deep and cutting and Gidon was afraid to probe it, probe him, afraid that something would be said that would cause his son to be lost to him forever. If he left it alone, perhaps his son would grow out of it. Perhaps. Was he away too much? When he had left the "Prime Minister's Office" he had told himself that it was because the job was hard on family life, impossible for family life to survive it—the separations, the tensions because of the dangers, his preoccupation with his work. Gidon had told his bosses that he was leaving the Service because he wanted to be home more. And then what had he done? He had leapt at a job that had meant traveling as much as he had traveled for his old one.

Why had he done that?

He knew why. He rolled over and stared at his wife's back. It was a wall. He turned to stare at the ceiling. If things got worse, he could always take the job his parents had offered him, managing their restaurant in the Galilee. They were thinking about retirement. But he knew he wouldn't take their offer. At forty-three he was too restless. He should settle down, find a job that kept him in the country. Would Avigail like that? Would he? Coming home every night? What would that be like? What would happen to their carefully nurtured freedom? What kind of a question is that, Gidon ben David, for a married man to ask? Well, these were modern times. He couldn't expect to have a marriage like his parents. Wasn't sure he wanted one.

Then the phone rang.

He picked it up. Avigail turned over but she didn't open her eyes.

"Gidon?"

He recognized the voice. After four years. Two syllables and he still recognized the voice.

"Yes."

"A blue Peugeot will pull up in front of your building in fifteen minutes. Get in. We need to speak with you." Without waiting for an answer, the man on the other end of the phone line hung up.

There was that familiar rush of adrenaline. There was that answering reaction, I don't have to do this any more. But above all there was curiosity. He rose and dressed quietly and quickly.

Gidon was waiting in the shadows of his apartment building when he saw the car pull up. Exactly fifteen minutes had passed. He walked up to it, yanked open the door and got in. The car slowly moved away, out of the quiet neighborhood street and into traffic. Gidon knew the driver, Dov. The man had at one time been part of his team.

Dov drove out of traffic and down another quiet street, past apartment buildings with their dry grass and the browning plants. Almost November and still too hot with no rain in sight. After circling around for a while, automatically making sure that they were not followed, Dov parked the Peugeot. Gidon waited.

"Making money?" Dov asked him.

"Yeah, a little."

Dov studied him for a few moments. Finally, he said, "You know what's going on?"

Gidon hazarded a guess. "You talking about the peace process? Arafat talking to Rabin? Negotiations? Land for peace?"

"You know how nervous everyone is. Israelis divided. The Palestinians divided. The whole country a powder keg ready to go off if someone strikes a little match. Paranoia is running rampant in both Tel Aviv and Jerusalem."

"Yeah, and which side of the issue are the big boys in the office coming down on?" Gidon half-smiled.

"What do you mean?" Dov opened his arms in an innocent gesture, but his eyes were wary. "Our office stands behind its Prime Minister. You know that."

"Sure," Gidon answered, "I know that. What do you want, Dov?"

"The woman you sat next to on the plane. Did you get a chance to talk to her?"

Gidon turned so he could view his companion better. "Is that why my seat was changed at the last minute? I should have guessed."

Dov ignored the question. "The woman had return reservations for tomorrow from Paris to New York. Two days ago she cancels her reservations home and makes reservations to Israel. Why?"

"Why not?"

"I told you everyone in the office is paranoid. They are looking at anyone or at anything that might interfere in the peace process."

"A poet? Or do they think she's a terrorist?" Gidon couldn't keep the sarcasm out of his voice.

"She's more than a poet. She's written articles. She's traveled to Muslim countries and has written extensively about conditions there.

"So what's the problem, that should be good for us, they're lousy."

"Have you read any of her books?"

"A few."

"She champions the cause of women against men and against their governments."

"In underdeveloped countries. And most are repressive governments. That doesn't make her a terrorist. That makes her courageous."

Dov ignored the derision in Gidon's voice. "Could you tell if she's anti-Semitic or anti-our government?"

"Oh, for God's sake. What if she is anti-our government? So is more than half our population. Suppose she goes home and writes negative articles. What can she do to any of you?" He emphasized the word *you* .

"Probably nothing. You're right. Probably nothing. But right now anything and everybody out of the ordinary are being looked into. You happened to have been on the plane with her, so we thought we would take advantage and arrange the seating."

"Great."

"So what did you talk about?"

"Poetry."

"Poetry?"

"She *is* a poet."

"We know she's a poet. Damn it, Gidon. Be cooperative."

"Dov, I don't like being used without my knowledge."

"It's the bosses. They get off on secrecy," and Dov rolled his dark eyes. "No harm done. No danger. Don't be stubborn."

"What do you want to know?"

"Why did she come, just now, to Israel?"

"She's a Christian pilgrim."

Dov just stared at him.

"That's what she said."

"Did you buy it?"

Gidon hesitated a moment. "Why shouldn't I buy it? She's Christian, a poet, and curious. Why shouldn't she come and look for her roots?"

"Suddenly? At the last minute?"

Gidon had no answer to that, so he said, perversely he knew, "You've been at this stuff too long, Dov. Haven't you ever done anything on the spur of the moment, unplanned, just for the hell of it?"

"It's the timing, that's all. At another time we wouldn't have paid attention. So did she say anything interesting, anything we should know about?"

"Nothing."

"Are you going to see her again?"

"Why should I see her again?"

Dov shrugged his shoulders. "Well, if you do and she says anything interesting, you know how to get in touch with me." He started up the car again and drove Gidon home in silence.

His hand on the door handle, about to get out, Gidon asked, "Are you going to tail her all over Israel?"

"Why?" Dov's voice rose slightly. "Someone was following her?"

Gidon turned around, his blue eyes narrowing. "Don't you know? We were followed by a black Mitsubishi all the way from the airport. A man, one of two, got out and followed her into the hotel. Was he or was he not one of your people?"

Dov hesitated, "I don't know."

Gidon stared at him for a moment and then got out of the car.

## 9

*Thursday morning*

## JERUSALEM

At seven the next morning, Gidon ben David was sitting at the café across from Elizabeth Layton's hotel. He had a good view of the entranceway. An unread newspaper was in front of him along with a cup of coffee. Gidon had risen early, after only a few hours' sleep, and had left a note for Avigail to tell her that he had a breakfast meeting in Jerusalem. In Jerusalem he had phoned his office in Tel Aviv to tell them he would not come in until tomorrow, that today he had personal matters to take care of. Then he had come to the café across from the hotel to watch and wait.

He wasn't sure why he had come.

Yes, he was.

Somehow he had been dragged into this little escapade. He had been set up by his old bosses, and he had made the connection with the woman. Being used irritated him. But now his curiosity was engaged. No doubt that had been anticipated too. Well, to hell with them. Elizabeth Layton had been followed while she was in his car. His car. That made him a player.

If he wanted to be.

And Dov had seemed genuinely surprised about the tail. But that didn't mean that his bosses hadn't set it up. Yet what if it wasn't them? Then who was following her?

There were many cars parked along the street, but

the black Mitsubishi was gone. After parking his own car near the hotel, Gidon had walked up and down the block before finally settling himself at a table in the café. There were several people sitting in cars. Probably guides waiting for their customers to come out of the hotel. Well, he would wait too.

A few minutes after nine in the morning, Elizabeth Layton walked through the entrance of the hotel. She hesitated momentarily, looking around her with either curiosity or concern. When the doorman gestured at a cab, she shook her head, glanced at the map she was carrying, came down the few steps to the sidewalk and turned to her left. She was going to walk, that would make things easier. Gidon watched as a man got out of a blue Fiat parked just up the block. The man—short, wiry and dark—took off after the woman. The Fiat moved away from the curb and disappeared down the hilly street. Gidon could feel the rush of tension and excitement. The American woman was still being followed.

Gidon left the café and started after her, keeping the man following her also in view. Though Gidon didn't recognize him, he could still be one of theirs, one of the new ones. Or not. It was hard to tell. The man was wearing jeans and a cotton shirt, innocuous and international.

Elizabeth Layton was dressed in tan slacks, a white T-shirt, with a sweater tied across her shoulders. She obviously didn't know the Israeli weather. It would be unseasonably hot all day. Gidon recognized her sport shoes and smiled. She stopped at the corner to look at her map, and then moved determinedly to her left again. She had some goal in mind. She didn't stop to look in the shop windows. She did stop to look out at the occasional vista, but she was assiduously following the map. He thought he knew where she was going. After several blocks, he was sure of it. She was heading for the Old City. She was going to enter the Old City by the Jaffa Gate. Layton crossed the busy street, then walked up the long incline, along Suleiman's wall toward the gate. The man who was following her was closer to her now. Did they have a rendezvous? Or was she unaware of him?

As Layton approached the gate, Gidon hurried to close the distance between them. It was always crowded inside the Jaffa Gate and he didn't want to lose her. Of course, he ran the risk of her noticing him and it was too soon. He didn't want to interfere in any meeting. Only if she was in trouble. If she did notice him, he had his story ready.

As Gidon entered the gate, Layton was standing a few yards away staring again at her map. Gidon, keeping to the cover of the crowd, casually moved away from her, careful not to draw attention to himself. Then he looked around. The man who had been following her was nowhere to be seen. From across the crowded square he saw someone approach her, an Arab. Gidon moved in a little closer. The Arab spoke to her. Layton shook her head and after a few more cajoling moments the man moved away and approached another solitary walker. Okay, that one's only a self-styled tour guide. Layton paused to look at the Citadel and the Tower of David, then moved on down the street. There was traffic, and quite a few pedestrians, not unusual for a weekday. Gidon kept his distance and tried to locate the man who had been following her. He didn't see him. Layton turned into the Street of the Chain. Once again, she stopped to consult her map, and once again an Arab man approached her. After a few minutes of argument the man moved away and Layton continued down the street. They were skirting the Jewish quarter. Layton entered a store that sold silver candlesticks. From outside the small shop, Gidon saw her point to her map. The Jewish man came to the door and gesticulated. She thanked him and continued on her way.

Moments later she was overlooking the square in front of the Western Wall. The Western Wall, or Wailing Wall, was of vast importance to Jews. However, it was also part of the wall that had surrounded the temple where Christ had preached in his final days. The temple, of course, was long gone, destroyed by the Romans in A.D. 70. On the sacred hill, where once the Jewish temple had dominated the city, were two Islamic holy places, the Dome of the Rock and the El Aqsa Mosque.

The Temple Mount, the ancient Mount Moriah, was not a bad place to begin one's sightseeing, and not a bad place for an assignation. It was always busy, full of tourists, but few Jews. Was Elizabeth Layton heading there?

Layton walked up to the barrier that cordoned off the section where the Jewish orthodox men were praying against the Western Wall, books in hand, their prayer shawls draped about them, swaying and murmuring their prayers out loud. She stood for a while watching them, then moved toward the women's section to watch the more decorous women, heads covered, whispering their prayers. After a few minutes she started up the walkway toward the two famous Muslim holy places. There were many visitors that day and Gidon had no difficulty following her unobserved. Finally, he thought he spotted the man who was following her.

Once inside the Dome of the Rock area, Layton moved first to the El Aqsa Mosque. She stopped and stared at it. What was she thinking? Gidon watched as the man following her walked past her and into the El Aqsa.

However, Elizabeth Layton did not go into the Mosque. That was interesting. Gidon wondered if he had been mistaken about the man. Instead Layton walked across to the Mosque of Omar, the Dome of the Rock. Its familiar golden dome, undergoing renovation, was gray now and covered with inelegant scaffolding.

Did she have a meeting with someone inside?

But Layton just stood there, staring at the fountain outside the Dome where worshippers washed their feet before entering the shrine. She didn't go in. Instead she circled around the famous shrine until she came to the Golden Gate. It was a sealed gate through which no human could intrude, but through which the Messiah was to enter when he came, as the Jews still hoped, or when he returned, as the Christians expected.

There was a group of tourists there listening to their English-speaking guide. Layton moved in for a moment. When she left the group to continue around the Shrine, Gidon noticed a tall, gray-haired man walking after her as she headed south along the inside of the Western Wall. Completing her circle of the Temple Mount, Layton walked back to the gate and out. The man hurried after her. And Gidon followed the two of them.

Outside the Temple Mount, seemingly oblivious to the two men behind her, Layton consulted her map once again, then crossed the square, climbed some stairs and plunged through a doorway. She was entering a very confusing part of the Old City. And hurrying after her was the gray-haired man. A rendezvous, Gidon wondered, as he followed the two?

It wasn't long before the trio were wandering through the enclosed and twisting Byzantine streets of the Old City where Arabs hawked their wares from small shops and kiosks. Clothes, antiques, jewelry, food.

Layton stopped now and then to refer to her map. Each time she did, some young man approached her. Each time she shook her head. The young men would argue. But Layton would move on.

It was possible that she was genuinely lost, that she didn't know about the man following her. If so, where had she intended to go? To the Church of the Holy Sepulcher? Then she was making wrong turns. She was now in the Muslim quarter, heading away from the famous church. From her body language, she looked as if she was lost, or else she was an accomplished actress. This wasn't a great area to be in, particularly alone. With the attempted peace negotiations, there were hotheads on both sides looking to make trouble. If Layton had followed the Israeli news, she would be aware of that. Usually a person traveling to a country knows a little about the current situation.

But if she had come here to meet someone, he wanted to give him or her a clear field. Was it the gray-haired man who was moving casually behind her, ostensibly staring into the tiny shops of the Quarter? Or was it some other?

As Layton hesitated near an intersection, a young Arab came toward her. He began to argue with her and the gray-haired man stepped out in front of them. He gave Layton a courtly little bow. Gidon couldn't hear them, but he could see her body relax with relief. The Arab man backed away. After a few moments of conversation, Layton showed the man her map. The man pointed to a spot on the map and then the two walked away together.

Gidon followed them.

The man was taking her through narrow, twisting alleyways, leading the woman deeper into the Muslim quarter, talking all the time. Gidon could hear their occasional laughter. The more he watched the two, their body language, the more convinced he became that Layton did not know this man. Gidon suddenly had a strong sense of foreboding. Layton was in danger.

He mustn't let the man get her into a house or a building.

Not while Gidon was alone. And unarmed.

He didn't question himself.

There was no time.

He was going to intervene.

## 10
*Thursday morning*
## SAN FRANCISCO

"You look like you're going to a funeral instead of a wedding," Doug said to Mattie over a cup of cappuccino in the dining room of his house.

"You know I hate traveling."

"That's because you never go anywhere interesting. An occasional poetry reading in some dusty, midwestern university town is not the south of France."

"Since Jack died, I've never had the desire to return to Europe."

"You're afraid you might meet some gorgeous hunk there who'll make a pass at you, and horror of horrors, you might even get laid."

"Oh, shut up, Doug," she said, but her tone was mild.

"Sex is good, my pet."

"At this point in my life a man would only clutter it up."

"Wonderful, I highly recommend it."

"Doug, are you going to get off my case?"

"Absolutely not. All this living alone is making you dotty. You should move to San Francisco and live near me."

It was something Doug said to her at least five times a year. Doug was the son of Mattie's half sister, Alice, who was the daughter of her father's second marriage. There were other nieces and nephews, but Doug was the one she loved. Doug was the one she was closest to. Doug was thirty-eight and gay.

Eighteen years ago, Mathilda's husband and her two-year-old son had been killed in an automobile accident. Doug, only twenty at the time, had come up to Portland, Oregon from L.A., to be with her. He had stayed with her for weeks, losing his job in the process, missing a semester of school. Until Mattie was on her feet again, Doug cooked for her, held her while she cried, told her funny stories, read the newspaper to her and poetry. He took her on long walks and to the movies. Doug had finally talked her into selling her house. She sold it and purchased a cabin near Big Sur. After college Doug moved to San Francisco and worked for years in the garment business there. It wasn't long before he was running his own business.

"Get a haircut, for God's sake," Doug told her as he pushed a Royal Doulton plate of miniature muffins toward her. "You look like Alice in Wonderland, and no woman forty-five should look like Alice in Wonderland. That's what comes from living in the woods all alone."

"I have very good neighbors. I can bike to the village, and I like long hair." It was an old conversation and she took no offense. "It feels like me."

"The men are beautiful in Israel. They have that irresistible aura of danger about them. But no one is going to be interested in an aging Barbie Doll."

"Good, then I'll stay an aging Barbie Doll. I'm not interested in Israeli men, good looking or not. That's not why I'm going."

"Why are you going?"

"Netta's wedding. Ruth and Michael want me to come. I've missed the other weddings in their family."

"Baloney."

"What do you mean 'baloney?'"

"I mean, my love, that the wedding is only the excuse, not the reason."

Mattie just shrugged. She would tell him. Of course she would, but in her own good time.

Doug didn't press her, instead he said, "Finish up. I'm taking you with me to the business. We have to get you some decent clothes before you leave tomorrow."

Mattie started to protest but Doug raised his hand.

"No. You are not going to Israel with two pairs of blue jeans and a T-shirt."

"I don't just have. . ."

"No. That's it. I know Israel. I know the way they dress. The days of the pioneers are over, my dear, except maybe for Aunt Ruth. Jeans are okay once in a while, but with a good belt, a terrific shirt, some jewelry. Leave it to me."

Mattie relented. There was no one in the world she loved more than Doug, and for all his bantering and teasing and chiding, he was the one, without question and without judgment, who was always there for her. The one human being who loved her. The one human being whose love she trusted. "Okay, but I have to meet someone at four."

"Oh?"

"An old student of mine. A couple of summers ago. We've kept in touch. Very talented young man."

"Young is good, my pet."

"Sorry, Doug, this is not a romance."

"I'm banking on Israel. The men are magnificent. Trust me. I've been there and I've sampled."

## 11
*Thursday morning*
## JERUSALEM

Gidon hurried after Elizabeth Layton and the tall man who was guiding her through the crowded streets and finally overtook them. "Well," he said, "Elizabeth Layton!" He moved in front of Layton, effectively stopping her, grabbed her hand and pumped it like an old friend. "Isn't this a coincidence?"

"Why, hello, Gidon," Layton said, with obvious surprise. Was there also some uncertainty?

Gidon had made a quick judgment. In the old days he might have taken the gamble, might have risked the woman to procure more information. But he was a private individual now. He could do as he damned well pleased. He smiled at the older man who waited politely. Gidon could read nothing from his face.

"What are you doing here?" Layton asked.

"I finished the business meeting that I told you about last night," he emphasized the words "last night" and watched to see the man's reaction. There was none. "So as long as I was in Jerusalem I decided to take a stroll around the Old City. It's fascinating, don't you think?" His question took in the older man too.

"But an impossible maze. I was lost until this fellow American came to my rescue," Layton turned to the older man, a grateful expression on her face. It seemed innocent enough.

"George Hemmings," the man said, and offered Gidon his hand.  American, but not Arab-American, Gidon observed.  Nevertheless, the Palestinians had many allies in America.

"I'm in Israel on business," Hemmings told him.  "I come a few times a year.  I was shopping for souvenirs for the family when I saw this poor lady.  She looked lost and was being accosted by one of the so-called guides who are everywhere in the Old City."

"Mr. Hemmings was going to point me in the direction of the Holy Sepulcher," she said.

"Really?"  Gidon stared at the man who had led her in the wrong direction.

The man returned his stare unblinkingly.

"Look," Gidon said, "I have nothing to do this morning, why don't *I* take you to the Holy Sepulcher, and show you through it?  I know Jerusalem very well."

"Oh, that might be nice," Layton said, but she sounded tentative.

"So," Gidon turned to the man who called himself George Hemmings, and said, "there's no need to take you out of your way, unless you would like to join us for a tour?"

"Well, that's very kind of you," Hemmings said, with a nod of his head and a pleasant smile.  "I've seen it many times and I do have things to do this morning.  So as long as our lost American is in good hands, I'll bid you both 'adieu.'"  His manner was gracious.  "Enjoy your visit, Mrs. Layton.  Israel is most unusual."

Layton extended her hand to George Hemmings, and he took it.  "Thank you so much for rescuing me.  I hope you find the perfect gifts for your family."

"I'm sure I will.  Nice to have met you.  And you too," Hemmings said to Gidon.  He gave him a cool smile and moved away.

So, Gidon thought, our Mr. Hemmings is not too pleased with my little intervention. He watched the man's retreating back and made a mental note to get Dov to look into this American businessman.

Hemmings stopped a few yards from them, ostensibly to look into one of the shops.

"This is a piece of luck," Gidon said, and he took her by the elbow and steered her in a direction away from the American.

"What is?"

"Bumping into you like this. It must be fate." He guided her down a narrow, deserted alleyway and glanced back. No one was following.

"Do you believe in fate?"

"When it suits me," he said. "Look, since we're in the Muslim quarter, would you like to see the Church of St. Anne, first?"

"The Church of St. Anne?" she asked, and held up her map, as they moved along.

"Yes," he said, "it's very near here, quite beautiful." He didn't break his stride and she followed after him. "It's built over the house where Mary's mother and father lived, Anne and Joachim, according to tradition. And on its property are the Pools of Bethesda. You know what happened there, don't you?" He slowed down.

She wrinkled her brow and then shook her head. "I can't remember."

"Jesus did some healings there. It's all in your New Testament."

"I must confess, it's been years since I read the New Testament."

"Unusual for a Christian Pilgrim. They usually quote the bible to you chapter and verse."

"I'm not that kind of pilgrim," she said.

"Really? What kind are you?"

She just smiled and shrugged. It was a good smile.

Play the friendly guide, he warned himself. And keep your objectivity.

I can do whatever I damn well please.

"After we see the Church of St. Anne, I'll show you the Antonia, it's very near here."

Layton shook her head.

"You don't want to?"

"It's not that. What is the Antonia?"

"It's the place where they brought Christ, after he was arrested on the Mount of Olives. It's where he was examined by Pilate, where he was scourged and where he was given the robe and the crown of thorns."

"Of course, yes, I'd like to see that."

Gidon led her up and down streets, pointing out sites. He knew Jerusalem very well, knew all of Israel well. He had trained himself quite consciously to know the land for which he was fighting.

"From the Mount of Olives, they probably brought Jesus through the Lions' Gate, known to Christians as St. Stephen's Gate. It's just down the street from the fortress that, as you can see on your map, is on the north side of the Temple Mount."

He took the map out of her hand and found the Antonia for her. He could smell the clean faint trace of French shampoo in her hair. Easy does it, he warned himself. "The north was always the weakest side, from a military point of view. That's why the Antonia was there."

She raised her eyebrows in a question.

"The Antonia was a fortress. In the time of Christ the other three sides of the fort had deep valleys surrounding its walls. The valleys are filled in now. There's a church where the Antonia stood, called the Chapel of the

Flagellation. It's the first station of the cross."

"Oh," she said, and nodded.

"From there we could follow all the stations of the cross till we come to the Church of the Holy Sepulcher." He waited.

"But that's terribly kind of you. Are you sure you have the time? I feel like I'm imposing."

"It's very hard to find on your own, you see. These streets twist and turn. And yes I have the time. Unless you would prefer one of these guides that wait for tourists like you?" Despite the lack of sleep, he felt very alert today. A little like old times. A little like his old life.

Elizabeth Layton laughed and her green eyes lit up. She looked genuine and vulnerable. "I don't think so."

"As it happens, I've had my meeting, which luckily was very short, and I'm free as a bird for the rest of the day. I've just completed some work and I'm due a little time off," he told her, not completely fabricating.

In a few moments, Gidon stopped in front of a small door. "Here we are, the Church of St. Anne."

They entered into a courtyard and Elizabeth exclaimed, "But how lovely!"

"The church is a Crusader church, twelfth century. It's one of Jerusalem's oldest standing churches and one of the best preserved. Come, I'll show you the chapel. Then I'll shut up and let you look, okay?"

The look of pleasure at his understanding was all the response he needed. This is a poet, he told himself. Don't forget, this is a poet.

As they walked silently through the church grounds he watched her. She stopped a long time in front of a statue of an old woman, St. Anne holding her baby, Mary. He liked it too. The impossibility of it all. That appealed to him.

He tried to read Elizabeth's responses as they walked

around. Often she looked quizzical. Sometimes she just stood and stared off into space as if she was listening. A few times she said that it was all very lovely, but looked as if there was something she was trying to grasp, and couldn't. Perhaps she was struggling for a poem. If so, she took no notes.

Elizabeth stopped inside the chapel to listen to a group of pilgrims, one of the many church groups that came with their pastors. They were sitting in the pews and singing hymns. Elizabeth watched for a while but did not join in. After a few minutes she left the chapel, with Gidon behind her.

"Where are the pools you were telling me about?" she asked him. He guided her toward an excavation area.

She stared at it. "This doesn't look like a pool."

"Well, this was part of a cistern system. Water was always a problem here in Jerusalem and they had quite a complex method for getting it and preserving it. A pool has to have some source of water. Perhaps it was a ritual pool and therefore artificial."

"I see."

"Some believe that the animals that were to be slaughtered in the temple were first washed here."

"Animal sacrifice," she said, "yes, I should have remembered that."

"It was here that Christ healed a cripple."

She looked at the elaborate dig for a time and then said, "Thank you."

They walked back to the entrance.

"You probably know," he told her as they walked toward the Chapel of the Flagellation, "that none of these churches can be certain that they are on the holy site they commemorate. Except maybe the Antonia. That's a pretty good bet, at least for Christ's examination and imprisonment. Even the Holy Sepulcher can't claim for a certainty that it's built over the place where Jesus was crucified and buried. There were no churches in Jerusalem until the fourth century."

"Really? Why is that?" she asked him.

"War and destruction. A terrible period for both Jews and Christians. Christianity didn't see itself as a separate religion outside of Judaism so early on, but as its fulfillment. Jerusalem was destroyed in A.D. 70. by Rome."

"Yes, I remember that from my college studies. Though, I have to confess, I was never a good student of history."

He waited for her to go on, but she didn't. So he continued. "So after A.D. 70 the state of Israel was no more, until '48 of our century. There were terrible battles back then and Christians suffered alongside the Jews. Jerusalem was totally destroyed and most of its surviving population, those who weren't sold into slavery, fled. It was Constantine's mother, the Empress Helena, in the fourth century, who had the Church of the Holy Sepulcher built. This was the beginning of the Byzantine period in the history of our country. Helena found Christian anchorites living in caves around the city. They had preserved, by word of mouth, the knowledge of where the events in the New Testament had taken place. On the basis of their memories, Helena built many memorials in the city."

"You know a lot," Elizabeth said. "I don't know New York this well."

"Yes, I made a point of it," he told her.

She looked into his face, her eyes crinkled in interest.

Yes, he thought, she would be interesting to talk to. . .if. . .

They entered the Chapel of the Flagellation. He watched as she walked through, noticing again how often she just stopped, even closed her eyes as if she were listening for something. For what?

After they left the Antonia, they followed the stations of the cross.

At the fourth station, Gidon said to her, "This is where Jesus met with his mother. It's a small oratory now. I think the lunette above the entrance is beautiful. The bas-relief was done by a Polish artist."

Elizabeth paused to look intently at it for several minutes, then said, "Thank you for pointing that out."

"The last five stations are in the Church of the Holy Sepulcher. The Franciscan Fathers, from the Monastery of the Flagellation, take this walk every Friday carrying a cross," he told her. "Many people like to follow them."

As they climbed down the steps to the Church of the Holy Sepulcher, he said, "I'll point out where events allegedly happened, and then I'll keep quiet."

She nodded, so he went on. "You know that this church is controlled by several religious denominations, six actually. Each controls it's part of the church."

"Really? I didn't know that."

"Yes, so be prepared, this will not look like St. Peter's in Rome."

She looked up at him, again a spark of interest in her eyes. "You've been to St. Peter's?"

"I have. Have you?"

"Yes," and she moved inside the church.

They stopped just inside the door at the Stone of the Anointing, a long slab of polished pink limestone, with its eight lamps above it and candlesticks around it.

"This is the spot where Jesus was laid after he was taken from the cross," Gidon said. "This is where Mary cried over his body."

"So this is the place. The place of the Deposition,

where Mary and John the Evangelist and the other women took him down from the cross," she said, and her voice sounded hollow. "There's a marvelous painting by Caravaggio of that scene. Do you know it?"

He shook his head.

"But," she looked baffled, "wouldn't this spot have been in the countryside back then?"

"The city grew, you see, and swallowed up what was once outside it."

Elizabeth turned halfway around. "And where would people have stood to watch the Crucifixion, do you think?"

"Maybe where we stood before we descended down the steps to the church," Gidon offered. "Or maybe from below this hill."

She sighed.

"What?"

Elizabeth wrinkled her brow and shook her head. "It's as impossible to imagine that scene standing here inside this church as it was back home sitting in my living room, and yet this is supposed to be the place."

"By tradition," he reminded her. What an expressive face she had.

"Yes, by tradition."

"Actually, the place of the Crucifixion is above this place. On another hill. Come, I'll take you there."

He led her up some stairs to the three altars where the Crucifixion allegedly had taken place. "Three different churches have their altars here," he told her and stood back to watch her. He had seen pilgrims weep at this sight. Elizabeth Layton did not weep. She just looked, her head often tilted as if she was listening, and stood for a long time in front of each altar.

Finally, she said, "Thank you."

"Let's go see the tomb where Jesus was buried, and according to your religion, resurrected. I hope there isn't too much of a line. It's quite small, so only a few people can enter at one time."

The line inside the rotunda to the tomb was short and soon the two of them stood inside the small room with its fragment of rock. Here an angel was supposed to have announced the Resurrection to the frightened women followers of Jesus. All of this Gidon explained in a whisper as they stood there, the scent of her barely noticeable perfume making him feel heady and...and...

Step back, he told himself.

But there was no room.

They moved then inside the chamber that housed the coffin itself, the last station of the cross. A marble slab covered the rocky casket. The room was candlelit. There were flowers. There were icons. One showed a sorrowful Mother Mary. Elizabeth stood for a while staring down at the coffin. And Gidon observed her sensitive face, the way her eyes seemed to be listening, and allowed himself a sense of pleasure. An icon herself, he thought.

As he watched her, some lines from a youthful poem by Yehuda ben Yehuda came into his mind:

*I have seen your garden, my love*
*those careful blossoms*
*watered by the tears*
*of countless generations*
*carried in your blood. But, love*
*those specters are gone*
*lost in Sheol's great shadow.*
*I understand, but come away—*
*Come away*
*lift up your eyes*

*to my eyes. And see.*
*See what blooms*
*there in the deep.*
*Irises to fill the heart*
*with never-ending light*
*planted here in the ground*
*of my immutable love.*
*Come away, Beloved. Come.*

"Four different Christian churches watch over this tomb," Gidon told her as they left the two small rooms.

"Four?"

"Come, let me show you something." He took her by the arm and walked her around the Holy Sepulcher. "The hill the tomb was part of has long ago been carved away to allow the sacred tomb to stand freely," he said. Directly behind the tomb was a little chapel. A priest sat near the altar there. Gidon took a coin out of his pocket and handed it to her, "Give it to the priest."

She did. As she started to leave, the priest rose up and in a foreign language said something to her. He handed her a small metal and wood cross and a card with fluted edges. Pasted on the card, under a cross and the word *Jerusalem*, was a dried flower. It said, "Flowers from the Holy Land." And under that were the words, Coptic Orthodox Church in the Holy Sepulcher. Elizabeth showed both items to Gidon.

"It's their little piece of the church."

"Coptic, that's originally Egyptian?"

"Correct."

"Thank you. This is somehow very touching," she said, looking at the little dried flower, then she put both tokens in her pocket.

Gidon led her through the church, past various

chapels watched over by different denominations, upstairs and downstairs, past the tomb of Joseph of Arimathea, past the Holy Prison where Christ was supposedly kept, through the Crypt of St. Helena.

As they were leaving the church, he said to her, "It's after one. Let me take you to lunch."

"Oh no, really. I couldn't impose. . ."

"It's not an imposition, really not. I hate to eat alone. Let me show you that Israel is not all past and monuments. I'll take you into the new city to a very good Middle Eastern restaurant."

"Are you sure?"

"My pleasure," he said, and gave her his best smile.

## 12

*Thursday afternoon*
## SAN FRANCISCO

The young Israeli carefully read through the memorandum he had written. It would be in the diplomatic pouch on the late plane to Israel and on the proper desk by Friday morning.

> Mahmud Aziz met with a woman this afternoon in a coffee bar near the waterfront. She has long, dark blond hair, is about 5'6" and slim. She looks to be in her forties. The two spoke for about an hour. The conversation was intense. And sometimes intimate. I couldn't tell if they were lovers or not. But it was no casual meeting. At one point he handed her a thick long envelope. The woman seemed reluctant to take it. But finally did. She put it in a large purse. My guess is that it contains money. But it could be a manuscript of some sort. I am enclosing photographs of the woman. We will see what we can find out about her on this end.

He signed it carefully and gave it to his superior to read.

## 13
### *Thursday afternoon*
### THE ATLANTIC

Eric was seated in First Class. The seat next to him was empty. Beth's seat. It was like a sign, a symbol, an emblem of reproach. Absence. Bare. Uninhabited. Something missing. Someone.

Eric was drinking scotch and soda, trying to get some warmth into his icy heart. All the old sentimental love songs were right. His heart felt frozen, his belly tense, his world suddenly lunar, barren, with little sign of life. No matter how he tried to reconcile himself to Beth's sudden departure, it felt like she was slipping away. If felt as if his body was a house and she were moving out, slowly emptying it. He thought of a poem of Beth's that she had written when her husband, Matthew, had been alive. Alive, but having an affair with a younger woman.

> *She is letting go of him*
> *the way the dignified let go of life*
> *one quiet breath*
> *and out into the ether*
>
> *the way trees let go of leaves*
> *stripping them away*
> *growing used to*
> *their weightlessness.*

*He is moving out of her fingers*
*her eyes, the ribs hiding*
*her heart. She can feel him*
*taking shape*
*on the other side of her skin.*

*When she sighs*
*he slips away*
*moving across her tongue*
*taking all his promises.*

*As she opens the door*
*to look at the cold winter sky*
*she feels him running past her*
*down the white street.*

*Only the snow follows.*

Beth was convinced that Matthew would have left her—if he had not died so suddenly of a heart attack. She had never published that poem. But she had shown it to Eric, had given him a copy. Why had she done that, he suddenly wondered? To warn him? But it was she who was leaving, she who was slipping away, running past him "down the white street."

To run off to Israel, to so suddenly need to explore the idea of reincarnation. And right at the time when they were going to decide about marriage. No, incorrect, *she* was going to decide about marriage. He had already decided, long ago. This was the woman he wanted to be with for the rest of his life. He didn't want to keep two apartments, barely using one. For what reason? In New York they were known and accepted as a couple.

It was fear. Well, he understood fear. He had run

like crazy after his own marriage had broken up. But now? They were so good together, so good for each other.

Beth was running.

She had looked at reincarnation before, but it was an idea one couldn't prove. It hadn't taken her long to see that. She had written so eloquently about the dilemma of *knowledge* versus *belief* in her novel, of *dream* versus *reality*. It had apparently touched the hearts of many readers, because she had received a lot of mail about those conflicts. If there was a world beyond the sense world, she had written, it was the world of the imagination. That was a world she was familiar with. For an artist the realm of the imagination was the *something else* other people longed for. Cultivate that, she had concluded, and be satisfied.

But now this! To suddenly remember the comment of a child of seven, and then to give it so much credence that she had to change her travel plans, had to go off on a wild-goose chase—it made no sense. Beth was running, was postponing decisions, was falling back into old worries, into old griefs. And where did that leave him? Where did that leave *them*?

Eric ordered another scotch and soda and when it came he took three large gulps. The truth was he was angry. Beth was pulling away from him and didn't have the guts to see that's what it was. She was leaving him the way his father had left his mother when he had been a teenager. No, not that way. He swallowed another mouthful of scotch. His father had left his family for another woman, one who had made him very happy—which had angered his mother and confused him. But his mother had stayed angry and bitter all her life, was bitter now after forty years. Yes, he could understand that bitterness. He was feeling it now.

And if Beth's need to search was genuine, then why hadn't she wanted him to come with her? Or why hadn't she been willing to wait a few months and go there on their honeymoon? After all, it had waited two thousand years, what was this sudden rush? It didn't make sense. None of it made sense. He drank the last of his drink and ordered another. It was not making him warm. It was not taking the edge off his bitterness. He was building himself a cocoon of resentment, fear, and anger. And, you know what? It was very satisfying. It just shows you what three drinks before lunch, or whatever meal they were eating, could do.

## 14
### *Thursday afternoon*
### JERUSALEM

There was an array of Middle Eastern salads on the table in front of them, and a pile of pita bread. Beth and Gidon were seated in a plant-filled restaurant in the new part of Jerusalem. It's inhabitants seemed to be a combination of Israelis and tourists, all intent on their own conversations.

During the early part of the meal, Gidon, to Beth's relief, kept the talk light. He talked about Israeli food and restaurants, claiming to be somewhat of an expert because his parents were in the business.

Frankly, she was a bit confused. How had she acquired this charming guide? He was charming, no question. But why was he bothering with her? What did he want?

Early on in life, Beth had decided that she was plain, that men wouldn't look at her, then rush to her side across a crowded room. That had left her free in a way, free from self-consciousness, free to be who she was. Even with her late husband, Matthew, she had never felt beautiful. Smart, yes, clever and gifted, yes, but never beautiful. Then Eric had entered her life. He had made her self-conscious in a rather marvelous way. He loved her gestures, her eyes, gazed at her as if she were the Mona Lisa.

But this one, talking about restaurants and paying her so much attention, what did he want? Okay, she had a slim figure, and a youngish face, no wrinkles and a smooth jawline. These attributes she owed to her mother. What was this attention about? He loved poetry. All right. They had that in common. But what else? He couldn't be interested, could he? He was very handsome with his blue eyes and his light brown, curly hair, with his broad shoulders and his tall trim figure, taller than Eric. And younger. Younger than herself, too. She must be what—eight, ten years older than this man? No doubt, if he wanted to stray from his marriage, he could get young women easily. So what was this all about?

Stop it, Beth. Stop thinking of him that way. Accept the lunch and thank him, then go on your way.

"So why haven't you signed up for some guided tour if you wanted to see the holy sites? Wandering around by yourself in Israel is not the easiest thing to do, nor the safest." Gidon offered her a plate of eggplant salad.

"It was an unplanned trip," she answered.

He raised his eyebrows and looked at her with his head slightly cocked. It was an appealing gesture. "So what caused this sudden urge to go in search of your roots?" he asked.

What should she tell him? She spoke slowly, not looking at him, "Oh, there I was admiring Chartres Cathedral. . ."

"Extraordinary cathedral."

"There are so many depictions of Christ's life there. It made me wonder what the beginnings were actually like." She could feel an echo of the shock she had felt when the memory lifted up into her mind, when was it . . . ? Just a few days ago? A lifetime? Yesterday?

"Are you all right?"

"Yes." Beth swallowed hard, smiled at Gidon, and then looked away. At the plants. At the people lunching. At the waiters. Just beyond their table was a young couple having a quiet but rather heated argument. She felt sorry for the young man who seemed to be getting the worst of it.

"So just like that you decided to come?"

She turned back to Gidon, "I was already in Europe and as I had nothing special to hurry home for, I decided, 'why not?'"

"Are you always so spontaneous?"

"No. Usually I'm a great planner, but just before I went to Europe I had finished a book tour to publicize my novel. I'm between books now." Why did she feel the need to elaborate?

"And your boyfriend, he couldn't come with you?"

Oh, dear, what to say? "He would have liked to," that at least was true, "but he had to be back at work. So I decided to come here alone."

He gave her an odd look.

She turned away and pointed to a dish on the table. "What's that?"

"Humus, it's made from chick peas."

"Oh, of course. I've eaten that before." She helped herself to a portion. "Where did you go in Europe?" she said. She was not going to talk about Eric. "Tell me about your last trip."

And so he did.

Over coffee, Gidon asked her, "Do you do something else or do you write full time?"

"Book reviews. Articles—about poetry, about places I've been. And I've taught in various colleges. But the past few years I've concentrated on the writing. Now that the novel is done, I'm working on poems for a new book."

"That's great. Perhaps Israel will inspire you."

"Perhaps."

"You mentioned a married daughter."

"Yes, she's married to a Philadelphia lawyer. She's a French teacher in a college there." Beth paused only for a moment. "My eldest daughter died of leukemia four years ago."

"Oh, how terrible! Sorry."

"Thank you. It's all right. As you can imagine, it took some doing, but I've come to terms with it."

"I didn't mean to pry."

"That's all right, really. It's a fact of my life. There must be many mothers who have lost children in your country, Arabs as well as Israelis."

"Yes, the bountiful gift of war, thousands of bereft mothers, widows and orphans."

"And fathers?"

"Yes, fathers too."

"And still we make war," she said.

"Yes, still we make war," he answered. "So tell me, have you seen the Temple Mount, Mount Moriah?"

"You mean the Dome of the Rock?"

"The other names belong too."

"Yes, yes, of course they do. I went there this morning. I was following. . .that is I had hoped to follow Christ's last days. But without you I wouldn't have been able to." She looked up at him, and then to her consternation, blushed. So she looked across at the quarreling couple who were now eating in stony silence. "I didn't know it would be so hard to get around on my own. I've been to other Middle Eastern cities and should have known better. I don't know what I expected. Something more western I guess for the beginning of Christianity."

"Are you disappointed?"

"I'm not sure. Anyway, there I was trying to follow my map, but maps aren't much good in the Old City, I obviously got turned around."

"Jerusalem is not like Paris."

"No, it's not like Paris," she smiled.

"Jews, that is, religious Jews don't go up on the Mount."

"Why?"

"They're afraid of stepping on the spot where the Holy of Holies once stood, the inner sanctum of the Temple. So they go only as close as the Western Wall of the old temple grounds, the so-called Wailing Wall. Mount Moriah is also the place where Abraham almost sacrificed his son Isaac."

"Gruesome idea," she said, with a shudder.

"It was for him a question of faith."

"So why did the Muslims build their holy site on just that place? A sort of thumb your nose at the Jews? 'My God is bigger and better than your God' reason?"

"Maybe a little of that, but also Abraham is an ancestor of the Arabs, and Mohammed was supposed to have ascended to heaven from there. Did you go into either of the two Muslim shrines?"

"No, I saw enough Mosques in Istanbul a few years ago. I didn't come here for that. I just wanted to walk around the place where Jesus preached. Hard to find any trace of that, though."

"Everything changes."

"Except hate," she said, "that seems to last forever."

"Human nature."

"Human nature is better than that."

"Only when it makes art," Gidon said.

"Tell me about your name. Gidon. What does it mean?"

"Gidon was a Biblical hero, a warrior. He saved his people from the Midianites. Judges 6:14. You would call him Gideon."

"Oh, yes, of course."

"I prefer the Hebrew pronunciation. Gidon ben David. My parents' last name is Silver, but my dad's first name is David. So I changed mine into a Hebrew one, ben David, son of David. It's old-fashioned. But I like it. So, are you serious about this man you sent home to New York?"

Beth was momentarily startled. "Yes, I am serious."

"You're divorced?"

"Widowed."

"So if you're serious, are you going to get married?"

"I haven't decided yet." Hadn't she?

"Why haven't you decided yet?"

She hesitated only for a moment. "Fear," she said, knowing then that it was still there. "One bad marriage. Two deaths in my little family. Fear of more losses."

He nodded. "If you don't commit, maybe the pain will be a little less if things don't work out." She saw the corners of his mouth tighten ever so slightly.

"Just that," she answered.

When the check came he took it and refused to take her offer of money. "Before I let you go," he said, when the waiter returned with his change, "I want to take you to the Garden Tomb."

"The Garden Tomb?"

"Yes, it's the rival location for where Christ was buried. It's quiet and beautiful. People go there to think or meditate. Even Jews. We'll drive there. It's quite close. Then I'll drop you off at your hotel."

She said yes.

Why not?

## 15

*Thursday afternoon*
## JERUSALEM

The Garden Tomb was, as Gidon had said, quite beautiful. They walked through what looked, not like a graveyard, but like a formal English garden. For a while they followed an English guide and heard a short lecture on how in the last century this garden had come into consideration as an alternate burial site for Jesus.

Gidon was quiet while they walked through the garden.

He's not intruding on my encounter with what's here, Beth thought, and was touched by his consideration.

She was impressed by the place. So much nicer to create a garden to commemorate a holy event than to build a church over it. Of course, the place where Christ had been buried couldn't have been as lovely as this. It was the wrong ambiance for so tragic an event.

All day long Beth had tried to imagine Jerusalem as it was two thousand years ago. But she couldn't feel deeply into its past. Well, that had always been her problem, hadn't it? She had always been impatient with the past, with history, had seen it as getting in the way of the present. Had she expected too much of herself, rushing here to Israel? Had she expected to acquire inner wings and suddenly fly into a remote time, and find. . .what? Herself? But everywhere that she had been today she had sensed some prejudice or judgment in her that had come between her and what she was seeing and trying to experience. Was she getting in her own way? Beth moved on to the next bed of brightly colored flowers and sighed.

"What's the matter, Elizabeth?"

She just shook her head and smiled at the Israeli who seemed so solicitous of her. "Please call me Beth, won't you. All my friends do."

"Beth, yes, thank you." And he looked pleased.

What did Gidon think of tourists like herself, she wondered, glancing sideways at him? She had come to Israel, a country in the midst of a crisis, a country striving for enormous and far-reaching changes, and she was, like many before her, more or less indifferent to all of the present struggle.

"The flowers are quite wonderful here, don't you think?" he said. "The English church group that cares for the place has done a good job."

"Yes. The English do love flowers."

"It's one of *our* best businesses," he told her. "We actually rival Holland."

She felt a twinge of embarrassment for her indifference toward his new homeland, embarrassed for others like herself. But she deliberately drove the feeling away. Modern Israel was, without question, very interesting, but she had come here with a purpose and it had little to do with what was happening presently in this country.

"Would you like to see the burial cave they think is Jesus'?" Gidon asked her.

"Thank you, yes."

So he led her to, and then into, the small cave tomb hewn out of the rocky hill, and they stood for a while looking at where the body would have been laid. "You're in the anteroom where the mourners sat and where, according to your Gospels, the youth, or the angels, were found on Easter Sunday." Beth stood inside for a while and carefully observed the ancient tomb. She noted where the body would have been laid, where the mourners would have sat. Was there something here? If there was, she couldn't feel it. People were buried in caves. Sometimes many people. But this seemed like a cave for one.

"This must have been a rich man's cave," she said.

"Yes, that's the point. Jesus was buried in Joseph of Arimathea's tomb."

"Right." And if this were the one? What did she want to happen now? Some memory to awake in her? What? To see an angel, a youth, a body, abandoned clothes, Mary Magdalene, John, what?

When Beth indicated that she was ready to leave the cave, Gidon said, "I think there is more scholarly weight on the side of the Holy Sepulcher."

"Perhaps, but more poetry in the garden, don't you think?"

"Yes," he said.

"Well," she said, "I haven't come here to find poetry."

"No, then what, Beth?"

"The truth," she said, and saw him look at her in a quizzical way. "Though I'm not particularly religious. . . still, I was raised Christian and in a fairly Christian country. I hope your American parents would understand why I said that."

"Oh, they would understand perfectly. That's why they immigrated to Israel."

When they arrived at the hotel, he said, "Look, it's still early. Let me take you to Bethlehem. It's not a long way by car and seeing it as the sun goes down can be a special experience."

Her hand was on the door handle. Just a few steps

and she would be in her hotel, safe. She was amazed when she heard herself answer, "I'd like that."

What was she doing?

What the hell was she doing?

She didn't look at him. She clasped her hands together primly and put them in her lap.

Gidon put his foot on the gas pedal and soon the car was gliding past the hotel, and safety.

## 16
*Thursday evening*
## SAN FRANCISCO

Mattie left the following message on Beth's New York answering machine:

"To the best of my recollection you are due back from Europe today. I hope I'm not mistaken. I'll be in New York tomorrow afternoon around four just for overnight. It's a long story but I'm on my way to Israel Saturday evening. Can we get together for a meal or for coffee? I need to talk to you. You've been away too long. Oh, and welcome home and hello to Eric."

## 17
*Thursday evening*
### BETHLEHEM

The fact that Elizabeth Layton had said *yes* to Bethlehem made Gidon feel intoxicated. Just a little. Why not?

There was something about her. Was she dangerous? Was she in trouble? And the woman was attractive, not really beautiful, but the way she moved, the way her thinking lit up her face.

He could pull back from these feelings, if need be. It was just a pleasant attraction, nothing serious, not enough to keep him from losing his awareness, his objectivity. Simply put, he liked being with her. Corrine, in Paris, was young, fun to have around, to make love to, and easy to leave. But this one was...well, bright, and a grown-up, an adult, which had an appeal all of it's own. Gidon wanted to keep talking to her, to prolong their time together. And if going to Bethlehem also kept him from going home, from thinking about his marriage, for which he had no solution, and wasn't even sure he had a problem, was that so terrible?

"You are about to go into a part of Judea that we took from the Arabs in one of our numerous wars," he told her. "We fought hard for that piece of land. Jews couldn't go to their holy sites when the Arabs were in control."

"Are you against the peace negotiations?" She glanced at him.

"No. We have to try," he said. "We cannot send our young people to die in war every generation."

"Sad," she said.

"More than sad," he said, "tragic."

As they pulled away from the hotel, a green Renault slid away from the curb. They had picked up a tail again. And that too was interesting. For a moment Gidon wondered if he missed the old work—the adrenaline, the rush, the sense of purpose, of secret power. He kept the Renault in sight as he drove out of Jerusalem, as he chatted about the sights they were seeing on the road toward Bethlehem. He spoke about the new housing, the solar heating that was now mandatory in Israel, the agriculture, the Bedouin Arabs that the Israelis were encouraging to settle down. And he watched the Renault.

Elizabeth listened attentively to his narration, and asked questions. When they passed a small, white-domed structure with an Israeli soldier standing guard, she asked, "What's that?"

"That's the tomb of Rachel, Jacob's second wife, the mother of Benjamin and Joseph, two of the twelve sons who make up the twelve tribes of Israel. People, mostly Jews, go there to pray. Four thousand years ago Rachel lived in Bethlehem. They say she still weeps for her children, Israel."

"The lot of mothers everywhere, it seems," Elizabeth said.

They passed a checkpoint where Israeli soldiers asked for documents. Gidon showed his papers and she her passport and the car moved on. It was a warm autumn evening, still early. The sun was beginning to set, casting a coral light all about. Soon Bethlehem was in sight. Gidon thought that for such a heralded place it was an ugly town—poor, unkempt, unaesthetic. He watched

Beth's face as they drove through it to get to the Church of the Nativity.

"Bethlehem's hillier than I imagined," was all she said.

Gidon pointed out some hills covered with buildings. "Those are the so-called Shepherds' Fields," he said. "There are still shepherds in the hills around the town, but Bethlehem is not quite the sleepy rural town that it was when David was alive three thousand years ago, nor when Jesus was born two thousand years ago."

But Elizabeth was silent, staring out of her window.

Gidon waited, then asked, "Shall I tell you something about the Church of the Nativity?"

"Yes, please."

"What you're about to see is a twelfth-century Crusader church built over a Byzantine fourth-century church that is built over caves where the birth of Christ is supposed to have taken place. Again it was Constantine's mother, the Empress Helena, who first put a church here. It was partially destroyed in the sixth century during the Samaritan revolt and then rebuilt. It looks like a fortress from the outside."

She turned to him with a questioning look.

"Wars," he said, "so everyone ran to the church."

"Like in Collioure," she said. "It's in the south of France," she added. "My daughter Alicia and I once vacationed there, not long before she died." When he waited, she said, "Please go on."

"The church is Greek Orthodox, except for a small chapel that is Armenian. Next to it is a Roman Catholic church, St. Catherine's, fairly new. It's from there that they broadcast the Christmas Eve Mass. The two churches are connected by a series of caves. People hid from persecution in the caves under the churches as recently as the Roman occupation. That was fairly customary in times of persecution. Your St. Jerome lived in a cloister where St. Catherine's is now located, while he translated the bible from Hebrew into Latin."

"You certainly know a lot about this."

"A hobby of mine," Gidon said. "I've read your New Testament and I've read the Koran. It's a small country and we get many visitors. Israelis know a lot about their country. They take pride in it. They fought hard for it."

He carefully pulled out into traffic, and passed the car ahead of him. "Conflict," he said, as he tucked in behind a truck, "is the way of the world. It's simply a given. So you pick your side of an argument—it doesn't matter if others pick a different side—that's expected. And you fight like crazy for your side. That's the way it has always been, and probably that's the way it will always be."

"Do you really believe that?"

Gidon glanced over at her. "I'd like to believe something different, but I see no evidence for it, neither in history nor in the world today. Do you?"

Her eyes narrowed in concentration as she listened to him.

"Even the pagan gods, if they existed somewhere other than in the collective imagination," he went on when she did not answer, "fought each other. So can the peoples be any different? Humankind has always fought over things, over territory, for instance. So you identify with something, some cause, some people, some country, and you teach yourself to love that people and that country. Then you fight with all your might against anyone and everyone who want to take that land away from you, or anyone who wants to deny you your history or your right to exist. You make a stand in this conflicted world. You have to make some sort of stand. Then you find things to love about the human spirit, poetry for one, and music for another."

"That's a very bleak view of the world. Are you such a pessimist?"

He laughed, "Probably. But mostly I think the world is so complex, so unfathomable, that none of us will ever be able to understand it, never be able to untangle all the threads and the knots that tie humans and countries together. Can any of us, for instance," he took a deep breath, "understand just one other human being?"

"Maybe that's the beginning of something better, understanding just one other human being."

"Have you? Can you?"

Elizabeth just shrugged.

Gidon parked near the church, and by the time they were out of the car, the Renault had stopped down the block. Gidon and Elizabeth walked to the entrance called the Door of Humility. "It's called that because you have to stoop to get in," he told her, "but the truth is that they made the entrance small so the Muslim soldiers wouldn't ride their horses into the church. You can see the old Crusader arch above it, all filled in."

He watched her while she walked around the church looking at the reddish-brown Corinthian columns and the remains of the twelfth-century mosaics. Once again she seemed thoughtful, as if she was trying to figure something out. After a while she said, "Can we go into the older church?"

"Yes, the Grotto of the Nativity is below the main altar. Come, I'll show you."

He led her down some stairs into a crowded enclosure. Just before they descended the last step into the room, and while they could still see above the heads of the people there, Gidon pointed out the spot where the birth of Jesus was alleged to have taken place. It was marked by a fourteen-point silver star on the floor, with fifteen lamps hanging above it. He then gestured toward the Altar of the Manger, a few feet from the birth spot, and opposite it, the Altar of the Magi. An American church group was in the small space with its minister. The minister was reading from the Gospel of Luke, and Beth moved in closer to listen. Gidon stood aside and watched her as she listened to the birth story. Those around her looked joyful, exuberant even. But not Elizabeth Layton. After the minister finished his reading, the group sang, "Oh, Little Town of Bethlehem," then "Silent Night," and finally "Joy to the World." Though she listened, Elizabeth did not join in the singing. When the American group finally went up the stairs, she walked up to each of the altars and stared at them for a while.

Finally, she said to Gidon, "Thank you."

"Follow me," he said, and led her deeper into the caves. He pointed out storage places, other altars, and then led her up some stairs and into the more modern and impressive Church of St. Catherine. There was a Mass going on, so they watched for a few moments and then left, stopping first to look at the statue of St. Jerome in the courtyard.

As they walked back to the car, Gidon asked her, "Do you want some postcards or a book or anything?"

She shook her head.

When they were in the car and heading out of Bethlehem with the Renault a few cars behind, he said to her, "You don't look like you enjoyed that very much."

She turned to him with an expression of surprise on her face. "Oh, I'm sorry, really I am. I'm very grateful to you for taking me. . ."

"That's not what I meant," he said. "What I meant is that you don't seem to be finding what you're looking for."

"No? Well, I guess you're right. It all seems so silly."

"The churches, the altars?"

"Oh no. I mean my coming to Israel. I don't know what I expected."

"What are you looking for, Beth?"

She turned to him. Her eyes, filled with moonlight, looked huge. He saw her make some sort of decision.

"The past. . . some personal connection to the past that will make the present comprehensible, myself understandable." He could feel her struggle. "I guess I'm giving God another chance."

Gidon raised his eyebrows and she laughed.

"A chance to let me know if he really exists. God and a host of angels. I guess it's just not possible to know." She smiled. "Maybe mine is a silly quest. Maybe you're right. Maybe it's all about choosing sides. Maybe for a moment back in Europe looking at all that Christian art I suddenly caught the disease of optimism. Frankly, right now I feel rather foolish."

"Why? Nothing you've said is foolish. Jews come to Israel for the same thing. And Jews who live in Israel travel about to their own holy sites looking for the same thing. Why would I think you foolish?"

"If you knew me better you would know how foolish. None of this is like me. I'm a fairly practical person, not given to chasing after impossible dreams. But that's what I'm doing. It makes me feel adolescent, a college sophomore searching for the meaning of life. . ."

He waited but she didn't go on. So he said, "You're not religious, but you're hoping that there might be some transcendent meaning to life. That's an honorable quest."

"I don't know. Maybe it was shortsighted of me, but for most of my life I didn't care, not until...until..." she was staring out the window away from him.

"The losses?" he said.

"Yes, the losses—one husband, one child, half of my family. Before that the present had been enough to worry about. I was really a bit irritated with the past, impatient. And the same with religion. I thought it imprisoned people."

"And now?"

"Now I'm not so sure. Watch out!"

He turned his eyes back to the road in time to keep from sideswiping a passing car. "Sorry."

"You must think there's some lack in me, because you Jews base your claim to this land on the past. And you'd be right."

"Most Jews wouldn't know how to deal with life without this rootedness in the past," he said. "For those who have lost the ability to believe, perhaps it takes the place of true religious feeling. If you can't believe in God, you can surely believe in history, in the Land, in the Jewish people."

"Yes, I can understand that. I still don't know how to deal with the past. Some screw missing in me, I guess. Over is over, I used to think. We have only today. Use it. Make the best of it. Maybe that's very American. I don't know what to make of the idea of God, or as you put it, something transcendent. But I know people who do, who think life is fraught with meaning. People I love and respect. Mattie, Mathilda Jones, the poet you like, for one. My elderly friend Paul Burrows, for another. Two very bright people, both quite religious in their own way..."

"But not you?"

"I don't know. I guess I'm such a show-me person. I need proof, you see."

"Proof?"

She nodded. "I do believe in something," she said.

"And what is that, Elizabeth Layton?" He could feel the faint, delicate heat of her face as he turned to look at her.

"I believe in the life of the imagination. Which I believe can be mighty and without perimeters. That for me is the *something* transcendent. But something objective? A supreme deity? Or angels? That's hard. So I've come here to look. But all I see in the holy sites is the long ago past, and there it remains, covered up by churches and monuments. An odd, oriental, and therefore unfathomable past, one that is completely inaccessible. And here is the present, and never the twain shall meet." She laughed.

"So you've come here to Israel to run around the holy sites looking for proof of God?" He shook his head. "You think proof is possible?"

"I never did before. But suddenly, there in the cathedral in Chartres... My boyfriend thinks my coming here is..."

"Is...?

"Something else." She twisted her hands in her lap and stared at them.

"To avoid some commitment? Marriage?"

She raised her head in surprise. He knew he had hit a nerve. But she answered him. "To avoid a decision, he thinks. But it's not true. That can't be true."

"Are you in love?"

"Yes, yes I am."

"You believe in exclusivity?"

She hesitated, then said, "I believe in loyalty, if that's what you mean."

They drove then in silence. Occasionally he glanced

over at her. She was staring out the passenger window, either observing the scenery or thinking.

When they reached the suburbs of Jerusalem, she spoke, "And what about you, Gidon ben David, do you believe there is an over-arching meaning to life, to modern life?"

Gidon slowed down, allowing the cars behind to pass him. The Renault did not pass. "I don't know. As you say, where is the proof? The truth is, I would like to think so, in spite of what I said in Bethlehem. Some significance to all the suffering of the human race. Yes, that much I admit. But not like our religious here. Something, well, more inclusive, if you know what I mean."

"Yes."

"But if there's no way of finding out. And if we can't really *know*, shouldn't we do something else?"

"And what is that," she said, "choose a side and fight for it? How can that be more inclusive?"

"That's the modern dilemma, isn't it? We want to be citizens of some special nation and citizens of a world community all at the same time."

"And individuals. Don't forget our need to be individuals.

"Yes, that's a struggle here in Israel. We like to think we are individualistic, but, like leaves off the vine, we wither when we become detached from the group, from other Jews. Is that good or bad? I don't know."

Elizabeth looked at him with interest.

"So what are our choices?" he picked up the thread of the previous discussion. "It seems to me that we have to imbue our lives with meaning if we are going to stay human. Isn't that what you do as a poet?"

"Maybe."

"Maybe that's all the religious really do. I know it's not

a new idea, but it's the only viable one that I can see." They were driving through the streets of Jerusalem now.

"And how have you endowed your life with meaning, Gidon?"

He liked her very much at that moment. And yes, she was beautiful. "Have dinner with me," he said, impulsively, "and I'll tell you."

She didn't say anything.

"It's still early, barely eight o'clock."

"I've had a very nice day. . ."

"So have I."

"I don't think it's a good idea."

He didn't argue. "Okay."

They rode again in silence. When they pulled up to her hotel, he said, "Are you going out tomorrow to continue your sightseeing?"

Her words sounded reluctant. "That's what I came for."

Gidon fished in his inside jacket pocket and pulled out a pen and then a card. It had his office number on it. But he turned it over. "I'm writing down the telephone number of a very good guide with a car. If you intend to go out to look at the Christian holy sites, it's not a good idea to go alone. He's very reliable and not too expensive." Gidon finished writing down the number and handed her the card. "Please call him. Israel can be dangerous for those who don't know where, or where not, to go."

Elizabeth took the card from him. "Thank you. I really had a very nice day and I'm grateful to you."

"I enjoyed it too." He offered her his hand.

She took it, opened the door and got out, then turned back a little uncertainly, "Well, good-bye. . ."

"Good-bye, Beth."

And she walked into the hotel.

## 18
*Thursday night*
## JERUSALEM, TEL AVIV

Before Gidon left Jerusalem he made a call to his cousin, an ex-army hero, who was a licensed guide with a car and took individuals or small groups of tourists around Israel. "If she calls you, Aryeh, drop everything and take her around."

"Who is she, the Queen of England?"

"No, but I think she's in trouble and I don't know if she knows it." He then explained about the tail.

"Don't worry about her. If I'm with her, nothing will happen to her." Aryeh was hooked. He loved intrigue.

"Thanks, Aryeh, I owe you one."

"I know. But what are cousins for."

When he returned to his home in Tel Aviv, Gidon dialed the number Dov had given him. Within minutes Dov returned his call.

Once again they met in Dov's car. Once again they drove to a quiet street.

"See what you can find out about an American man who calls himself George Hemmings." Gidon described the man to him. Dov listened very carefully, but said nothing.

"And, if that's not one of your people following her in a green Renault, get someone on her case tonight."

Dov didn't say yes. Instead he said, "Tell me about your day with her and don't leave anything out."

So Gidon told Dov all the facts and anything pertinent in the conversation.

"Why didn't you wait until you saw for sure where Hemmings was taking her?"

"It wasn't to the Holy Sepulcher."

"If you had waited to see where they were going, we would have more information than you just gave me."

"And what if the woman was in danger? I was alone and unarmed. Do you want an incident, just now, with an American target?"

Dov didn't answer.

"I don't think she's up to anything, frankly. I think she's trying to work out some personal religious problem."

"Except that there's someone following her."

Gidon's eyes narrowed. So it wasn't one of theirs.

"How do you account for that?" Dov's tone was mild.

"I can't. Unless..."

"Unless?"

"Unless it's her boyfriend checking up on her."

"You think that's possible?"

"How should I know?" Then he relented. "I doubt that would explain George Hemmings."

"Maybe not. Gidon, we would like you to continue to see this woman."

Gidon looked at Dov coolly. "And what if the woman doesn't want to see me?"

"How can that be, such a good-looking fellow like you?" Dov was not known for his sense of humor."

"I have my own work."

"You don't have that much to do. You can finish what's important in a day or two."

They had been checking up on him.

"I don't work for you any longer."

"We know that. Right now, with everything that's

going on, we don't have people to spare for this. It's not priority. But it is interesting. All we are saying is continue to see the lady and then if there's anything to report, you'll report it."

"This is stupid."

"Someone is following her."

Gidon was silent.

"At least if she's with you, she'll be safe. She's a poet. Take her to see your uncle."

That was an appealing idea. Gidon's great-uncle, the poet-statesman, Yehuda ben Yehuda, was quite old now. He lived in a kibbutz with his wife, not far from the port city of Ashdod. That might indeed interest Elizabeth, give him an excuse to call her. "I'll think about it, Dov."

When he returned home his wife was asleep. The night was warm and the air conditioner was droning loudly. He looked at his wife's back, that formidable partition in the middle of their bed, and he turned away and lay on his side thinking about Dov's suggestion.

## 19

*Thursday night*

## JERUSALEM

The first thing that Beth did after returning from Bethlehem was phone Eric. She reached his answering machine. "Hello, darling. Welcome home. I hope you had a smooth and uneventful flight. Israel is very interesting and very small. I've already seen quite a bit. I'll tell you all about it when I reach the real you. Oh, and the hotel is fine." Then she gave him the phone number of the hotel, which he had, and her room number, which he didn't have, and asked him to call as soon as he was able. She hung up the phone, sat down in the chair with her notebook, her journal. Writing in it daily was a habit she had acquired when she was in college. She wanted to record some of the impressions of her first day in Israel before they vanished, so she curled up in the comfortable chair and wrote:

"The death and birth of Jesus, that was my first day here in Israel. I think I've already seen the most important sites that I came to see. Maybe there's little reason for staying on...The Church of the Holy Sepulcher is a strange place. Supposedly built on the hill where Christ was crucified, you descend to enter it in the middle of the walled city. An unruly place with six different Christian denominations laying claim to it. Architecturally, I couldn't figure it out. It seemed to make no sense. Try as I might, I could get no impression of the monumental events alleged to have happened there. The Garden Tomb, it's rival for the interment of Jesus, was beautiful, an English garden, but nothing. I say nothing. What did I expect to happen? Some sense for those momentous events? Here is an unrecognizable Christianity, an Asiatic Christianity, a long way from my Protestant roots, or even from the great Catholic cathedrals of Europe. And Bethlehem, dreadful town, hardly a place for the birth of a God. Am I being too cynical? Probably. Caves? Yes, one can experience something there. What? Simple, primitive beginnings. Can something that began in so exotic a place as this country, this city, Jerusalem, and that Middle-Eastern poor town, Bethlehem, have anything to say to us today? I don't know, I really don't know. Maybe this was a foolish quest, a wild-goose chase. And Eric was probably right."

Beth put her pen down. Why couldn't she have waited for him? Why couldn't she have come back with him at a later date? What was the hurry? *Was* Eric right? Was her rushing off like that simply a way to postpone giving him an answer about marriage? She felt a sudden longing to be with him, to have his sensitive and attentive self by her side, to feel his strong, muscular body next to hers. She stared at the large hotel bed in which she would sleep alone again tonight.

Beth jumped to her feet. What was the matter with her? She was no quitter. She was not going to rush back home just because Eric hadn't called her. She had come to Israel with a purpose and she was going to follow through. She was not going to give up just because one day of sightseeing had produced little.

Beth looked for the room-service menu, found it, selected a light dinner and phoned in her order. She cleaned her face and took a quick shower. As she waited for her dinner she thought about what to do next. All right, this was going to take more work than she had expected. Perhaps the problem was that other than the Gospels, she knew little about Jesus' life and little about the times and milieu he had lived in. Surely one can't expect to have any kind of insightful experience if one doesn't do a little work first. She had gone to several countries hoping poems would come out of her visits. And they had. But would they have, if she hadn't prepared herself before each trip by familiarizing herself with the country, some aspects of its history, and its unique culture? So what made her think she could come to modern Israel in search of ancient Israel and what had happened nearly two thousand years ago without doing any research? Well, she would have to remedy that. Tomorrow she would find a bookstore, one that had books in English, and she would read as much as she could at night. An Israeli man knew more of Christian history than she did.

And speaking of an Israeli man, what was she to make of Gidon ben David? She had to admit, she really enjoyed his company. His knowledge of the sites had helped her enormously. But why was she being "taken up" by a very appealing, very attentive young Israeli? Seven, eight years younger, at least. And why did it make her feel guilty? Was it because she found him attractive? Just because she was in love with Eric Halsey didn't mean that her senses were dead to all other men. And besides, she would probably never see Gidon again. She had not encouraged him to call. And that gave her a small pang of loss. It was nice to be on the receiving end of all that attention.

There was a knock on her door. Her dinner had arrived. Before she sat down to eat, she pulled out the card Gidon had given her and dialed the number he had written on the back. She would have an escorted tour tomorrow.

## 20
*Friday afternoon*
## NEW YORK

When Mathilda Jones arrived at the Hilton Hotel in New York City, there were no messages for her waiting at the desk. As soon as she had hung up a few of her new clothes, she dialed Elizabeth Layton's number. Again she reached Beth's answering machine. Mattie left another message, stating that she would go out for a little walk and then be back by six. To please call her. Or had she mistaken the date of Beth's return from Paris? Mattie was leaving tomorrow evening for Israel and was anxious to speak to Beth. "I'm in room 2106."

It was a warm October day and Mattie headed up to 57th Street and then east, looking in store windows, staring at the amazing number of people in the city. Actually, she liked New York. One could be anonymous in New York. That suited her. But the amount of things to look at and people and traffic were tiring. After less than an hour she returned to her hotel. There were no messages. She went up to her room and ordered dinner in.

## 21

*Friday evening*

## TEL AVIV

The following evening, Gidon received a phone call from Aryeh. He described minutely what he and Elizabeth Layton had done that day.

He had taken her for a ride through the Hebrew University, past Hadassah Hospital, then over to the Mount of Olives. They had walked down to look at the Church of Dominus Flevit, the Church of All Nations, the Garden of Gethsemane, walked past the cemeteries, then they had driven over to the Coenaculum so she could view the place of the Last Supper. After that, Aryeh had taken her to Yad Vashem, the Holocaust memorial, and then over to the Israel Museum to visit the Shrine of the Book where some of the Dead Sea Scrolls were exhibited. Finally, he had taken her to a large bookshop where she bought half a dozen books on Israel and on Jewish history.

"She's a very nice lady. She listened to everything I said. She's smart and asked lots of questions."

"How did she react to Yad Vashem?"

"She asked if she could go through it alone."

"You let her?"

"Don't get so excited. I followed her. She seemed particularly moved by the Children's Memorial."

"That doesn't surprise me."

"Did anyone follow you?"

"Not that I could see. But I'm no expert, Gidon."

"I know."

"However, there was one interesting encounter."

"An encounter?"

"Yes. After we had seen the Shrine of the Book, we stopped at the Museum coffee shop for a drink. A man came up to us and sat down with his coffee for a while."

"Describe the man."

"Tall, with thick gray hair, probably in his sixties, an American."

"Go on."

"He introduced himself as someone she had met in the Arab bazaar in Jerusalem."

"Name."

"Wait a minute. . ."

"Name."

"I've written it down. Here it is, 'George Hemmings.'" Gidon was silent so Aryeh went on. "It was nothing special. He asked how she was doing, what she was seeing, where she was from. You know, small talk. They spoke for a while about the Dead Sea Scrolls, and Hemmings recommended that she take a trip down south to see Qumran."

"What did she answer?"

"She said that she probably would."

"Did she say when?"

"Not then."

"What do you mean, 'not then?'"

"I mean she spoke to me about it later."

"Did Hemmings ask for her phone number?"

"No, but he did ask what hotel she was staying at and she told him and he asked how she liked it."

"Anything else?"

"Nothing else. It was all small talk, nothing special."

"Did the man say where he was from?"

"He told her he was from Chicago and in the import-export business. And that he came a few times a year to Israel. Oh yes, he showed her a picture of his wife, his two sons and three grandchildren. Why? Is this something?"

"I don't know, Aryeh. You said something about Qumran?"

"Yes, tomorrow we are going to Qumran and to Masada and the Dead Sea."

"She hired you for tomorrow?" Gidon's mind was working quickly.

"I just said that."

"Skip it."

"What?"

"Skip the date tomorrow. I'll take her to Qumran. Take the day off and take Rina out. I'll pay you for the day."

Aryeh was quiet for a moment. "Should I call and tell her?"

"Definitely not. Let me handle it."

"Okay, but too bad, she was a great tipper and a nice lady."

"Maybe another day, Aryeh."

"Probably not. Not if she thinks I'm in collusion with you. You sure she wants to see you?"

"This is business, Aryeh, not pleasure."

"I thought you were out of that business."

"You're never out of that business. Thanks, Aryeh," and he hung up the phone.

He made one more phone call that night.

## 22
*Friday night*
## JERUSALEM

Friday night, just before she climbed into bed, Beth phoned Paul Burrows in Gloucester. Today's outing, with the amicable Aryeh as her guide, had been interesting, but had brought her no nearer to the breakthrough she was seeking. Paul had helped her through one turbulent time, now she asked him once again for his aid, his thoughts. Two or three times she had tried to reach him while she was still in Paris, with no luck. She reached him now.

"There is a western approach to reincarnation that is right for our times," he told her on the phone.

"Is that different from the eastern approach?" she asked, realizing how little she actually knew about the whole subject.

"Oh yes, definitely, yes. Reincarnation, and along with it, karma, is a vast and profound subject. One could study it for years and never come to the end of it."

"That's encouraging," she said, and sighed audibly.

"Sorry, but you do ask questions for which there are no simple answers. Do you want the spiritual world to be less complicated than your computer?" he asked with a chuckle.

"Frankly, yes," she said, and Paul laughed again. "So tell me something about this western approach."

"Different peoples have had different tasks over the ages," he said. "This current western approach has to do with an evolution of consciousness, something you and I have talked about before. Karma and reincarnation are also in evolution, and therefore much change has come about over the centuries. As humanity has changed, the nature of karma has also altered. And especially in our times when the human being has acquired so much freedom. But this is hardly something that one can discuss over a long distance phone call. My dear, this must be costing you a fortune."

"I don't care, Paul. This is important to me." She then briefly recounted her experience in Chartres to him. "Do you think Alicia's memory could be one of those false memories we talked about once when I visited you?"

"Of course it could be, my dear, but it could also be genuine, given the fact that it was such an early memory, one Alicia had crossing over from babyhood to childhood. Yes, without a doubt, it could be a genuine memory."

"Hmmm."

"And then she forgot it?" Paul asked.

"Yes, and so did I."

Paul promised her a long letter then, which he would fax to her hotel, answering some of the questions she had posed to him. Talking to Paul had steadied her. She would stay on course. She would not give up her search too quickly. No, definitely not.

Beth picked up her journal and began to write. "Three and a half years ago Paul helped me come to terms with my sense of loss, hopelessness, and anger at the death of my loved ones. He helped me understand that the threshold I had crossed, when I was so devastated and in mourning, was a crossing into the world of my imagination. Now here is the crux and where Paul and I are divided. Paul insisted—no, insisted is too strong a word—Paul suggested that the world of my imagination has not only a subjective reality but an objective reality as well. He said that each individual realm of the imagination opens up into an objective spiritual realm—a real world that borders on this world. Without denigrating his beliefs, I cannot follow him that far...

"That said, I must confess that the result of that 'imaginative' battle was that I came through my crisis, my seeming madness, to the other side, to sanity and health, and yes, even to peace. But in the months that followed, all through the writing of my book, I was never able to go along with Paul's thinking, with Paul's explanation, as intriguing as it was. To do so would have meant taking a leap of faith—which I could not take. I am such a show-me person. How could a rational person accept as a certainty that the world of our inner imagination opens out into another world, inhabited, not only by the one imagining, but by other beings—spiritual beings and the dead—unless one experiences for oneself those beings, those dead?

"And reincarnation, well, at that time, before that experience in Chartres, reincarnation seemed even less plausible. It certainly was, and is now more than ever, an intriguing idea. But what can I do with an idea? I need more than the desire or the wish for it to be true, I need proof, something concrete. Like Jonah, I need a sign. Is that asking too much? Am I missing something?"

After writing in her journal she climbed into her bed with her new books spread out around her on the the blanket. She spent an hour browsing through the lot, and then decided to read the book she had purchased on Jewish history in the time of the Second Temple.

That was the time when Jesus had lived.

## 23

*Friday night*

## NEW YORK

Mattie was lying on her bed in the New York Hilton on the twenty-first floor thinking about fear.

"Fear," her mother had told her when she was quite young, eight or nine, "comes to distract you from something very significant. It's like an elf, but this one is more evil than mischievous. This elf wants to pull your attention away from some marvelous gift you are about to receive."

"What kind of gift, Mommy?"

She could still hear her mother's voice—how it dropped to a whisper. "Maybe from hearing a special secret, or seeing a marvel never seen before. Or fear wants to keep you from recalling a long, deep, and very wonderful memory, maybe one from the time when you were still living with the angels in the heavens. Fear always wants to hide from you some great treasure. If you overcome your fear, just for a moment even, you can find this treasure. And if you find this treasure, you will carry it with you all your years on earth."

But she hadn't found the treasure and fear was still with her, still a destructive enemy.

The problem was that Mattie didn't always know when she was afraid. So how could she overcome it, even for a moment? Somewhere below her consciousness it played itself out, no doubt affecting everything she did and all her choices.

She rolled over and looked at the clock. It was a little after one in the morning. In the evening she would be on her way to Israel. She hadn't been able to get hold of Beth and that was a disappointment. She felt the need to talk to her, to explain to her why she was going to Israel, to hear her response. But Beth and Eric must have decided to stay on in Europe for a while longer. If Beth was in New York, she would have returned her call.

Mattie turned over on her back and stared at the dark ceiling. An unfamiliar room in an alien city at the beginning of a unpredictable trip. She felt as if she were locked in a tower, twenty-one stories high, and tomorrow the executioners were coming. No prince would save her. Her long blond hair was not long enough for him to climb up on.

And besides, these windows didn't open.

And there were no princes.

Later she would be on her way to Israel. And the simple fact was, she was afraid. Inexplicably. Not just of change, and she was afraid of change. Not just of traveling, and she hated and feared traveling. Not just because she was away from her little cottage, and she always felt rudderless and less herself when she was away from her home. She was afraid of Israel.

And that was a new revelation. That fear had lurked in her below her consciousness—for how long? All this life?

Lying in Doug's charming little guest bedroom, Thursday night, surrounded by half a dozen Ralph Lauren pillows, with her own poetry books on an exquisite little antique table, a cup of cocoa on the bed stand next to her, the buried fear had risen up in her in all clarity. Just like that. No particular reason. Suddenly, there it was.

Every time Mattie had been invited, urged, by her half brother Michael and his wife, Ruth, to come to Israel for a visit she had demurred, had found excuses, had thought it merely her reluctance to leave home and travel. Doug, too, had urged her to come with him on his several trips there, but she had always declined. She had ignored the numerous bar mitzvahs and weddings over the years, had allowed the family to think of her as a recluse, even as peculiar. Had allowed herself to think so too. Everyone, including herself, had forgiven her her peculiarities because she was a poet, a well-regarded poet.

How is it that she hadn't known before that moment in Doug's house that she was afraid of Israel? What was it about that distant land? Since she had family in Israel she had kept up with events there, even subscribed to *The Jerusalem Report.* And it wasn't fear for her life, no, that wasn't it. She wasn't afraid of terrorists or the outbreak of another war. Nothing like that. This fear went deeper. If only she could speak to Beth. But Beth was not in New York.

Mattie reached over and turned on the light next to her bed. She picked up the book she had brought along to read on the plane. And opened it. She probably wouldn't sleep much that night. Fear was a restless bed partner.

## 24
*Saturday morning*
## JERUSALEM

After eating an Israeli breakfast of salads, cheeses, rolls, and coffee, Beth returned to her hotel room, put a small notebook in her purse, and came down to the lobby to wait. Aryeh was due at eight. She glanced at her watch. Ten minutes to go.

Beth had returned to her hotel just before dinner yesterday. But Eric had not phoned. She left a message with the desk that she would be in the dining room for dinner if she should get a call. But none had come. And none had come all that long evening. This morning she was more than hurt, she was angry. But she was not going to allow Eric and his silent reproach to color her day. She was looking forward to this trip to the Dead Sea and Qumran, to being out in the countryside on this, once again, warm day. And so she pushed Eric out of her mind.

Her thoughts strayed to Gidon. She wondered if he would think her mad if she told him the truth, told him about her déjà vu in Chartres. Why hadn't she? She suspected that he liked her, that he might even be interested in a little extramarital fling. That was flattering, and frankly, she had taken pleasure in his company. He was bright, interesting, and sensitive. And he loved poetry. But it probably wasn't a good idea to keep seeing him, even on a platonic basis.

Why? Because Eric wouldn't like it?

Well, she wasn't married to Eric yet.

She felt a momentary shock. I'm still free, she thought, and Eric right now is acting like a prig.

At that moment she looked up and saw Gidon enter the hotel. Her mouth opened and her stomach did a flip flop. Still, she resisted the urge to call out to him.

Gidon stopped a few feet inside the hotel entrance and looked around expectantly. When he saw her, he smiled, and walked over and lowered himself into a chair near hers.

"You look very nice this morning," he said by way of greeting.

"What are you doing here?" she asked. "Back in Jerusalem on business?"

"No, pleasure. I hope." He smiled.

He was quite handsome. Really very appealing. And she wasn't married yet. "You hope?"

"It's up to you."

"Me?"

"My cousin, Aryeh, couldn't make it this morning, so he called me and I said I'd fill in for him."

Her eyes widened and her heart started thumping loudly.

"I hope you don't mind. I'm really a very good guide."

"What about your job?"

"It's Saturday, the Jewish Sabbath."

"Oh, yes, sorry."

"I know this country quite well, as well as Aryeh. You won't miss anything. What do you say?" Gidon cocked his head, his eyebrows raised in a question.

"I. . .I don't know what to say."

"Say *yes*," he said. "Besides I've planned a very big

surprise for you after we see Qumran and Masada and the Dead Sea. So you can't refuse. I promise you, you'll love this surprise. So are you willing to let me be your guide today?"

"Okay," she said.

He gave her a big smile and led her out of the hotel.

Now what is this all about? she asked herself, and wondered why she felt such pleasure.

## ⊰25⊱

*Saturday morning*

## JERUSALEM, THE JUDEAN HILLS

"First I want to take you to a spot where you can get a panoramic view of where we are going today. It's in east Jerusalem," he said.

"Okay," she said.

He drove to an apartment building and parked in front of it. "Aryeh and his family live in this building. He lent me the key. Can you climb a little?"

She hesitated a moment.

"We're just going up to the roof. Aryeh would have brought you here, too," he added.

So she got out of the car and followed him.

They climbed five flights, and then Gidon opened the door to the roof and led her to it's east side. "Look," he said. "Aryeh's very proud of this view."

It was a stunning view. Stretched out east and south of the city, beyond it's green belt, was a vast golden desert.

"The Judean wilderness," Gidon told her. "And see that little speck of blue?"

She nodded.

"The Dead Sea. Or as we Israelis call it, the Salt Sea."

"Extraordinary," she said. "Stark and rather scary."

"Is it?"

"Harsh and bleak. But beautiful."

She stood staring for several minutes, and then Gidon said, "Okay, that's where we're going."

"Thank you, Gidon, and thank Aryeh," she said as he led her back down the stairs. He dropped the keys in Aryeh's mailbox.

Gidon, playing his role as guide, talked as they drove out of Jerusalem. He showed her where the lines were that had divided the city after the founding of Israel. He told her about the War of '67 when Jerusalem was reunited, of the shock when the Israelis saw the destruction to the old Jewish section of Jerusalem and to its holy sites.

Beth paid close attention to everything he said. Still, she was wondering how it had happened that she was about to spend a day in the country with a very attractive, seemingly interested Israeli. And how it was that she had blithely said yes?

Oh, well, she'd figure it out later.

"Which war did you fight in?"

"The Yom Kippur War."

"The same one your cousin Aryeh fought in," she nodded in recognition.

"Every generation has fought."

She heard nothing in Gidon's voice, no pain, no anger, no sentiment of any sort. A kind of neutrality. Where had he learned that detachment, in the army? Or was that a folk characteristic of Israelis?

Soon they were on the road descending through the hills. Gidon pointed out the new settlements that had sprung up in the recaptured land, perched on the hills outside Jerusalem. With her eyes she followed where he gestured. The natural land was barren, the sand bleached almost white by the sun. Only where people lived was there any green. Tenacious, she thought. To live here you had to be tenacious and stubborn.

"The trees you see are planted on the northern slopes of hills because they get more dew there and less sun. When you see natural vegetation, it is usually at the lower spots, at the wadis. A wadi is a dry river bed. They run in winter, which is our rainy season. We are looking for rain to come soon and break this hot spell."

"That would be welcome," she said. "It is definitely too hot. I was wearing woolens in France."

"It will only get hotter where we're going, I'm afraid," he turned to look at her, "but you're dressed for the heat today."

Beth was wearing white cotton pants and a striped red and white T-shirt. But she carried a cardigan sweater. Just in case. She watched the heat shimmer in the air as they descended through the hills and thought, looking at her sweater, Beth, you are a cautious woman. And she stole a glance at Gidon who was maneuvering around a slow truck.

"We are descending through the Judean wilderness, a drop of forty-one hundred feet by the time we get to the Dead Sea."

"Really?"

"Really. In Jerusalem the rainfall is from twenty-one to twenty-three inches a year. But at the Dead Sea, which is only fifteen kilometers aerial distance, there is about one inch of rain."

"Extraordinary," she said.

"People escaped to the desert throughout the country's long history—criminals and revolutionaries, religious zealots, or people driven out by war. The hills are filled with caves, as you probably know."

She listened with interest as he told her about the Bedouin Arabs, those nomadic sheep and goat herders that crisscrossed the lands of the Middle East. They were passing a tent and tin-shack camp situated along the water pipeline.

"Israel hopes to settle more and more of them into permanent villages. Bedouins don't recognize borders. That's hard on security."

Beth asked many questions. She realized now that to have any success with her quest, she would have to know a lot more than she had come here knowing. And Gidon, without hesitation, answered them all—questions about history, geography, the political and cultural situation, without however revealing his own predilections. She was getting, as Gidon had promised, a guided tour of the area. And much else besides. He certainly knew a lot. And that impressed her. Definitely an interesting man.

"To your right is the village of Bethany, known in the New Testament as the home of Lazarus, Mary, and Martha. The Arabic name of the village is Elezariah. Elezariah in Hebrew is Elazar. In English Elazar is Lazarus."

For the most part, Gidon spoke to her factually. But now and then, she would hear a note of pride creep into his voice. Then he would return to his objective narration.

Later, he said, "We're passing the Good Samaritan Inn. There used to be inns every ten or twelve miles so people could purchase supplies and rest themselves and their animals. This is halfway from Jerusalem to Jericho."

"It's so barren, this Judean landscape."

He glanced over at her, "Do you find it ugly?"

"Not ugly. . ."

"But?"

"But not welcoming."

"After the war I came here often, to the desert, to camp out, to be alone, to think."

She looked at his profile. He was concentrating hard on the road at that moment, trying to move past some cars. He has strong features, she thought. A good face, nothing of vacillation in it. She waited for him to go on, but he didn't.

They came to a crossroads. "That road goes to Jericho," he said, pointing to a ribbon of asphalt unrolling to their left.

"So some of this will belong to the Palestinians soon," she said, gesturing out at the land.

"Yes, if the peace process is successful."

"Will it be?"

He shrugged. "We have to try. Now look carefully. At the lowest part of the valley is the Jordan river, between here and the Moabite hills across. The River is the border between Jordan and Israel, as I'm sure you know. It's situated in what is called the African-Syrian rift. The river is very narrow, not like the great rivers of America or Europe, so you can't see it yet. But look to your right. There. Can you see the Dead Sea?"

She followed where he pointed, and there it was peeking through the hills, a milky blue lake. Beth felt a wave of excitement. They were drawing near to the lowest spot on earth.

"Now look to your left, that's a Monastery named after John the Baptist. He wasn't born here, he was born in a village close to Jerusalem called Ein Kerem which is now part of Jerusalem. But he baptized in the river near here."

Gidon pointed out a kibbutz they were passing. "The climate here is almost always summer so they grow crops all year around, melons, palmellos, grapes."

"They irrigate, no doubt."

"They definitely have to irrigate. Finding water was always a life issue in Judea. Our ancestors...my ancestors were very inventive."

He pointed out a factory that produced table salt from the Dead Sea.

Before long they were on a highway running along the Sea. There were date palms along the way.

"They look like giant pineapples," Beth said.

"Israel has the most productive date trees in the world. When the State came into being, in '48, there were no date palms in Israel. We got the first trees from Iraq... somehow." He smiled. "Then we improved the varieties, made the fruit larger, made the pits smaller. We get about four times the harvest on a single tree as do our neighbors. You should try them. Quite delicious. Israel is first in agriculture in the world. We get more output per acre than any other country including the U.S. Well, here is Qumran," he said, and turned the car to the right and began driving up the short distance to the dig.

## 26

*Saturday morning*

## THE JUDEAN WILDERNESS

Gidon pulled the car into the parking lot. The Fiat that had been following them from Jerusalem would no doubt pull in also. But there was a black Renault down the road. He hoped the second car would also turn into the parking lot. He drove past several tour buses and parked his car. As he got out, the Fiat and the Renault pulled into the parking lot, one after the other.

Checkmate, he thought, with some satisfaction.

"Do you have a hat?" he asked Elizabeth.

She shook her head.

Gidon reached back into the car and pulled out a backpack. From it he removed a floppy white hat with a large brim and gave it to Elizabeth.

"My daughter's," he said.

Elizabeth put it on. He put a cap with a visor on his own head, then hoisted a large thermos with a strap onto his shoulder. "Water," he said. "We Israelis carry it with us everywhere. It's hot and very dry here. You can get dehydrated before you know it."

Gidon led her through the small excavated community of Essenes, describing what was known about the legendary sect that had taken itself off to live in isolation—to pray, to work, to study and to prepare for the Messiah. He told her how the scrolls had been discovered, how Israel had purchased them, told her about the current controversy—

after forty years all the texts had still not been made public. She listened with her head tilted in a way he had come to find attractive. If she knew any of this or all of this she didn't say, so he told her about the excavations and about some of the theories surrounding the site and the community.

And as he spoke he kept his eyes open for those who were following them. But there didn't seem to be anyone who was paying them much attention. Perhaps their followers were sitting in their cars watching each other.

That morning, driving to Jerusalem, he had wondered how Elizabeth Layton might feel seeing him again. Would she be angry? Would she perhaps resent his interfering so often in her life? If curiosity was a hallmark of his nature, so was suspicion. He wondered if she had made plans to meet someone at Qumran. George Hemmings? He would like to think she was just what she said she was, a pilgrim trying to reconcile some religious issues. And most of the time when he was with her he did. But there was this little niggling doubt. How could he not doubt? There was someone following her. Still she hadn't seemed too distressed when he had offered to be her guide today. And that had made him inordinately happy.

As he narrated the story of Qumran and of the Dead Sea Scrolls, Elizabeth Layton listened attentively. She asked questions and looked at everything he pointed at. She didn't seem interested in the other people there and that made him more relaxed. She managed the heat fairly well. He insisted she drink and they shared the single cup and that was nice. They walked around the site for about forty minutes, then returned to his car.

"Shall we stop somewhere along the Dead Sea?" he asked as they pulled away.

"Oh yes, please," Elizabeth said. "I'd like to put my feet in the water."

"We'll stop down the road where there is a public park and public swimming and where we can get a cold drink."

"I'm enjoying this, Gidon. I can't thank you enough."

Gidon felt a quiver of pleasure. Easy, he warned himself, not for the first time that day.

It was a late October Saturday and the desert beach was crowded. Gidon parked the car. The two automobiles trailing them parked theirs, but the drivers once again did not leave their vehicles. Good, Gidon thought, as he led Elizabeth down the path to the shore, let them watch each other. The sea was filled with swimmers who had come to cool off on this unseasonably hot day. The air rang with laughter as people tried to get under the heavy salt water without much success. When Gidon and Elizabeth were close to the shore, the two removed their shoes and put them near a rock.

"Don't worry," he told her when she looked uncertain about leaving her shoes, "this is not New York."

They rolled up their pants and started toward the water. But the beach of rocks jabbed at their feet, and soon Elizabeth took hold of Gidon's hand. She was giggling as she tried to get across the slippery stones into the water. They finally made it and stepped a foot or so into the sea. But there were rocks there too and Elizabeth held onto him.

"Oooh," she said. "I don't know if I like this. This is the most peculiar water I've ever been in. It's almost oily. I heard that it was completely dead."

"Not really," he said. "There's algae and lots of bacterial life." She had a firm grip, but the skin on her arm, which he had taken hold of, was smooth and soft under his fingers. "Full of minerals and very healthy. People come here from all over the world to bathe in the waters and to bake in the sun."

"Really?"

"Really. There's something about the sun around here. It doesn't have the harmful rays that cause skin cancer. So you can sunbathe here without worrying. This combination of sun and water is good for arthritis and psoriasis and a few other things. And the mud. This mud we market."

"You're joking."

"Honest. We sell this stuff. If you don't believe me, I'll take you to a cosmetic factory and you can see for yourself."

"Now you *are* being a good tour guide."

After they had put their shoes back on and finished their fruit-juice drink, Gidon said to her. "Let's go on to Masada. We'll have lunch there first and then take the cable car up to the top. That's quite a hill, with quite a history."

## 27

*Saturday*

## NEW YORK

Mattie couldn't reach Beth that morning, nor was there a message after she returned from a visit to the Guggenheim Museum. She had lunch in the hotel, and then tried Beth again. Still no answer. So Mattie opened up her address book and found Eric Halsey's number. She left a message on his machine. When she returned to her room late that afternoon from visiting the Metropolitan Museum, she found a message from Eric. She called the number he had left. After speaking to him, she made an overseas phone call to Ruth and Michael.

## 28
### *Saturday afternoon*
### THE JUDEAN WILDERNESS

When they were sitting in the large cafeteria below Masada, Gidon asked Beth, "So what do you think of Israel?"

The assortment of salads lay barely touched on her plate. It was too hot to eat, so Beth contented herself with drinking fresh orange and grapefruit juice. "To tell you the truth, Gidon, it's too early for judgments. I haven't seen very much of your country. This is only my third day."

"So give me some surface impressions."

"You mean about modern Israel?" She realized it mattered to him. "That would be unfair. I came here knowing little about your country except what I read in the newspapers and what you've told me in our conversations. And I'm grateful for that information. But I haven't digested it yet." She stopped, but he said nothing, only watched her out of what now seemed cool and impassive eyes, so she said, "Do Israelis hate that? All us Christians coming for something that happened two thousand years ago. . . ?"

"And paying little attention to the miracle we have wrought in this land? Why should we resent that?" Was his tone a little sarcastic? "We have a great respect for history. Ours after all is over four thousand years old in this land." No, ironical. "We who were born here are also fascinated with our past and particularly with the history of this land. Every time you put a shovel into the earth, you find antiquities"

"And you, Gidon, are you intrigued with your long history?"

He stirred his lamb stew and took his time answering. "I've taught myself to be interested."

"What do you mean, taught yourself?"

She watched him as he struggled to make a decision. He doesn't really trust me, she realized, and found that rather interesting, even appealing.

"I was born in this land. I feel secure in that, in who I am..." his face was thoughtful now.

"And who is that?"

"I'm an Israeli."

"I know that, but..."

"No, that's not as simple or obvious an answer as it might seem."

"I didn't ask for a simple answer."

"I'm not sure you'll find this interesting."

"Why? Because I'm not Jewish?"

"Okay. But this might not make much sense to you."

"Are all Israelis convinced that no one in the world understands them?"

"Yes. You've caught something of our character already."

Beth smiled, "So?"

"So, do you think parents can pass their ideals on to their children?"

She thought about it for a moment. "Probably not."

"No. They can't." His tone was unequivocal. "Not even their fears. Well, to a certain extent their fears. For those of us who were born here, for me, life is clear-cut. Israel is home, this is what we know. We are, well, we are Israelis. We are what our parents had hoped we would be when they came to this land. Normal. Neither exemplary nor terrible, interested in everything that people are interested in all over the world, what we are going to do as adults, how we are going to earn a living, the opposite sex, having a family, a home. Our parents wanted us normal, but now I think we disappoint them." He stopped and pointed to her dish. "You're not eating."

"I'm listening, Gidon." But she lifted up her glass and took a sip.

"For my parents and their generation and those who came here before them, this being Israeli is not just a question of citizenship. It resonates in them in a way that is hard to explain. To be an Israeli. That has layers and layers of meaning, of nuances for them. For them, it carries with it thousands of years of painful history of not being Israeli."

"You said your parents were Americans?"

"They came to Israel from America not long after the Second World War. First generation Americans. Their parents had immigrated to America from Russia. But my mother had uncles who had come to Israel even earlier than that. They had this dream. They had lived in the Diaspora. They had lived with fear and uncertainty—and they were right to be uncertain, and right to be fearful. After all, along came Hitler and six million Jews were murdered. That earlier generation came here, not as Israelis, but as Jews."

"And there's a difference?"

"That's what I'm trying to explain."

"Sorry."

"They came looking for a place that they could call home. Jews have been the eternal wanderers, always in exile, living as tentative guests in countries, never sure when they might be persecuted or driven away, even after generations. They wanted a land of their own where they could be normal, do all the normal things every other people has done. For hundreds and hundreds of years Jews dreamt about coming back to the land of Israel."

"Why didn't they then?"

"A few did. But many were still waiting for the Messiah, who for them had not yet come. Then the great return would happen, that was the belief. But some young Jews at the end of the last century and at the beginning of this century got tired of waiting. Europe was in upheaval. The First World War, the Russian Revolution, later the Second World War. So there were organizations formed, Zionist organizations, for the return. And people began to come back here, to buy land, create new cities, new farming communities."

She watched his face as he spoke. Once again it showed that cultivated neutrality. His words sounded quite dispassionate. Did Israelis usually hide behind a seeming disinterest? Or this Israeli? "Those who came here with that dream were courageous. They made enormous sacrifices to rescue this backwater land from centuries of neglect, from swamps, from desert. Homeless for centuries, they came to create a homeland and to fight for their independence. They were willing to die of diseases and war. And they did. For them this land is like a precious scroll, something sacred, something to be cherished. My dad says he never felt so at home, so at one with the land, and he was born in America." Gidon hesitated.

She didn't know if he was going to go on, so she said, "You still haven't answered my question."

"Haven't I?"

"I asked why you had to teach yourself to be interested in your long and rather remarkable history.

You've told me about your parents, their dream, you've given me a lesson on Zionist history..."

"Sorry." He jostled his glass and water spilled on the table.

"No, no, I find what you've told me very interesting." So much for dispassion, she thought. She reached across the table and touched his arm. Then quickly withdrew her hand. "I didn't mean that the way it came out. I'm sorry. I don't know enough about your land and your struggles. I feel remiss, somehow."

"That's not necessary. You're not..." With his fork he began to doodle on the table with the spilled water.

"...not Jewish?" she finished the sentence.

"You must find me very insular."

"Not insular, defensive, perhaps. But I am curious about you, Gidon ben David." She blushed suddenly, "And about your generation, those who were born here. You asked me how I felt about Israel. I'm more interested in how you feel about Israel?"

"It's not so..."

"...so simple. I know, but tell me anyway."

"Perhaps you don't value something you haven't longed for in the way, say, my parents longed for this land."

"But you fought for this land, you and your generation," she said.

"Yes, and almost each generation has fought for this land since independence in '48. But still it's different."

"How could you do that if you didn't value this land?"

"Sometimes life presents you with situations and you simply react. That doesn't mean that you've given it a lot of thought."

"But you've thought about it since?"

He nodded. "There's something else going on with my generation, really our generation," and he made a gesture connecting the two of them, "not just in Israel, but all over the world. The world is so small now. There's a world culture. I'm not saying it's a good world culture but it's definitely there. We know a lot about one another. We're no longer so isolated—one country from another, one people from another."

"I agree with you. You feel this as a conflict?"

"Yes. Well, sometimes. Are you finished with your lunch?"

She nodded.

"You didn't eat much."

"It's too hot to eat."

"Then lets go. You're here to see Masada, not to hear about me."

"But I'm interested, Gidon," Beth said as she rose from her chair.

He gave her an enigmatic smile. But the conversation about him had ended. She was sorry about that, sorry that he found her incapable of understanding him. Was she? Was his story, his Israeli story, beyond her? Was the fact that she wasn't Jewish an impassable barrier between them? Was she pleasant company but ultimately an outsider? She felt a little saddened by that thought and looked regretfully at the tall figure leading her out of the dining room.

They took the cable car up to the plateau that was Masada. The Snake Path wound below them with its few stalwart climbers. "Masada is 1345 feet above the Dead Sea," Gidon told her, once again the tour guide. Beth tried to turn her attention away from their conversation at lunch to what she was seeing. "The sides of the mountain are very steep and it makes it nearly impregnable to attack from below. The plateau is 656 yards long and 350 yards wide. It has no natural water supply and therefore an elaborate cistern system had to be developed. Not like New England, right?"

"Not at all like New England," she said, and stared out at the barrenness that they were suspended over. How lonely it looked, how could people live without green? She had been raised near water, in a land abundant with water, in a land where the sun was kind and a giver of life. Here the sun stole life, sought it out where it stood and burned it or dried it into dust. What kind of people had this land nurtured? What kind would it nurture now? She stared at Gidon who was looking out at the approaching plateau. A combative people, ready to take on the world? King David's people, always on the lookout for Goliath?

As they stepped out of the cable car, Gidon told her that all the excavations at Masada had been done in an eleven-month period in 1964 and 1965. "The finds here were tremendous and they've helped historians know much more about the Second Temple period, the period in which Jesus and his apostles lived. Do you know anything about that time?"

"I'm reading about it now," she told him.

He glanced at his watch. "We have about two hours. I'll show you everything, just as Aryeh would have. Let's start with the Western Palace and then move around to the northern slope."

"Lead on," she said, "I'm in your hands."

"Before the Jews made their final stand here and held off the Romans for five years, it was a Herodian Fortress. Herod was always afraid that the Jews would rise up and kill him or that Cleopatra would come storming out of Egypt in an attempt to conquer him. So he built this place."

They walked around the fortress in the heat. The flies were annoying and Beth swatted at them and wondered what on earth the flies lived on in this desolate place. She found Gidon's narration very interesting. But often her thoughts strayed to the man himself. Why had he chosen to spend his free time with her? She was glad about it, that she had to admit. But what was it all about?

Or was the answer the most obvious and simple one in the world?

They looked first at the excavations at the northern end, then stood above the camp from which the Romans had launched their final assault. "Fifteen thousand soldiers against less than one thousand Judeans. In A.D. 73, it fell. But the Jews, rather than face slavery and conversion, chose to die."

"What do you mean, chose to die?"

"Lots were drawn and ten men were chosen to kill all the others, then to set fire to the fortress, and then to kill themselves."

"My God!"

"And that's what they did. A few women and children survived to tell the tale." He turned to her then and asked, "Do you think it so terrible, this mass death?"

"Yes," she answered firmly, and then added with a small laugh, "and no. I'm trying hard not to judge another time by the standards of our own. If I did, then I would have to think that they were part of some mad cult like those terrible cults in our century where people committed suicide on the sick advice of some charismatic leader."

"You think that was the case here?"

She hesitated, and then said, "Their religion and their freedom were important to them, maybe in ways we can't begin to understand. Ours is, after all, a terribly secular age."

"I agree. The alternative was to be sold into slavery and to convert. Their faith was something that for many was worth dying for. Our whole survival, Jewish survival, has depended on zealots of some kind or another. Otherwise we would have gone the way of the Phoenicians, the Philistines, and scores of other nations."

"It must have been extraordinary to have believed so implicitly."

Gidon nodded. "Bones were found during the excavations. They were given a military burial. The last defenders of the last Jewish State. We're very proud of this place, Beth. Mass suicide is horrible, yes. But the obstinacy and the unwillingness to submit to slavery, that we admire. My generation in Israel was not raised to be obsequious. We were raised proud. Jews were murdered in so many Diaspora communities without raising a finger to help themselves. But not Israelis."

He was staring down at the camp below, not looking at her, talking, she suspected as much for himself as for her. "On some level we are fearless and yet there is much to fear. On another level we fear terribly. We, and more important, our loved ones are never out of danger. Is there a future for us and for our children? But alongside that fear, that uncertainty, there is also courage, pride and strength. We know we will defend ourselves."

Beth watched his profile as he stared down at the once Roman camp. The burial of those defenders of their faith after so many centuries, and a military one at that, was somehow very touching.

"We take both the danger, the uncertainty, and our courage as a matter of course. But it takes its toll. It forms who we are as Israelis. Many don't like us, say we're brash, arrogant, impolite, self-promoting and self-involved. Living at the edge does that to one, but it makes life precious, you see, every single day, precious, every single encounter, precious." He turned to her and gave her a small smile.

She reddened a little. "And you like living on the edge?"

He shrugged. "I have imagined myself elsewhere, yes. I love London, for instance, the solidity of it, the civility, but..."

"But?"

"It wouldn't work. I have decided to throw in my lot with this country and this people."

"That doesn't sound like something you were born into. That sounds like you made a conscious decision somewhere down the line."

"Yes, I did. Sitting in the desert as a young soldier, healing from both physical and psychic wounds, from losses children should not have to face but too often do in this hard world, I made that decision." Then he looked at his watch. "Come," he said, "we have to be somewhere. My big surprise." He turned and started walking toward the cable car terminal.

"Where are we going?" she asked, hurrying after him.

"You'll see," and he gave her a big grin. The guided tour was over.

## 29

*Saturday*

# NEW YORK CITY

It was too early to be up, after such a late night, but Eric Halsey was still on European time. Last night he had gone to an opening at the Steinroe Gallery. Mark Steinroe was an old friend of his, and the Barry was interested in the artist the gallery was exhibiting. It was an installation piece by a young woman who was very hot right now. She was a self-promoting type and had spent a lot of the evening courting Eric. But he hadn't fooled himself about the reason for her attentions. Still, one more glass of wine, and who knows what would have happened.

Rubbish, he told himself. Who are you kidding?

Eric walked into his kitchen and opened the refrigerator. Nothing there but brie, bread, coffee, and milk. He took out the coffee, prepared it for brewing, then went to his front door, opened it, and hauled in the New York Times, which contained some of the Sunday features. But he didn't feel like reading. Last night everyone had asked about Beth, and his simple answer had been, "She's in Israel looking for background for a book of poetry." He hoped he had been convincing. Eric poured himself a cup of the half-brewed coffee and laced it with milk. Good. Just what he needed. He mopped up the drips on the counter with an old rag and shoved the coffee pot back under the dripping apparatus.

What would Beth have felt watching Lyla Brown, their guest of honor, throw herself at Eric? Would she have been jealous? He tried to imagine the scene, but couldn't. Of course, no doubt, Lyla would have been more subtle in her advances if Beth had been there. He walked into the living room and stood looking out of the window at the park.

He hadn't called Beth yesterday. He wasn't sure why. Was he still mad? Was he still trying to nurse the hurt he felt at her taking off like that? Eric had found her message waiting for him when he arrived from the airport Thursday evening. The voice on his answering machine sounded like the old Beth, his Beth. It sounded like so many messages he had received from her when she had been on the road promoting her book, or like the messages he had received when he was traveling—reassuring.

Eric hadn't gone over to her apartment yet. He might today. He wanted some of his clothes that were there. But he wouldn't stay there, even though he had stayed there most of the last two years. His own apartment seemed less lived-in now, though everything looked almost the same. It was as if something, not someone, had moved out, some semblance of life, even of memory. It was as if he had collected all that life and memory and had moved it into Beth's place. His center was no longer here. Only his periphery inhabited this space. Even the pictures he liked the most, of his two boys, were at Beth's.

Eric poured more coffee into his cup, walked back into the living room, unlocked the door to his patio and walked outside. He had a great view of Central Park. That was one of the perks of a successful career, a dynamite apartment on Fifth Avenue with the park spread out before him, and a decent-sized patio from which to appreciate it. The air was cold. Definitely not the time of year to be having breakfast outside. But he welcomed the cold, crisp air. How was he feeling? He had wanted to stay angry, but that anger was slipping away. He missed Beth, that was how he was feeling. He loved Beth and he missed her. He realized that last night, when he had behaved with all the correctness of a married man in response to Lyla Brown's obvious flirtation. And Lyla was a great-looking girl—too young for him really, but great looking. Why did he want to stay angry? What was Beth doing that was so terrible? Why had he made such a fuss?

Eric brushed the leaves off the metal chair on his patio and sat down. Was it his own insecurities? A divorced man who was the child of divorced parents? Had he purposely refused to understand? Had he been so fearful that she wouldn't say yes to marriage that he had precipitated a crisis? Was this a crisis? Did he lack trust? His ex-wife, whom he had never loved, had left him, the way his father had left his mother. Had he imbibed his mother's lack of trust?

Why had he taken Beth's decision so hard? Hadn't he told Beth to decide on marriage now or to leave him? That was the ultimatum he had given her. God, could he be such a fool? Instead of making things easier for Beth, hadn't he made them more difficult? She was looking for something, some belief system, and he had refused his support. He had let her go off with cold words, showing his lack of confidence in her. Had he not implied that she was emotionally unstable? What an idiot. Who was emotionally unstable? He loved Beth. And Beth loved him. Why couldn't he let her have her ten days, and see if she could resolve her dilemma? Why had he thrown boulders in her path, like some monstrous troll, when she had come to him for understanding? What a fool. When would he grow up?

Eric rose from his chair. Carrying his cup, he moved back into the living room, and went to the telephone. He was about to pick it up when it rang.

"Mattie," he said, after the caller had identified herself. "Where are you calling from?"

## 30

*Saturday afternoon*
## THE SHEFELA

Yehuda ben Yehuda was dreaming, but this was no ordinary dreaming, this was a dreaming that had come to him slowly in old age. He was not really sleeping. He was lying on the bed. He could hear his wife, only a few feet away, in their small kitchen preparing the coffee they always took at about three in the afternoon, after their nap.

"Yehuda," Malkah had just called, "wake up. Five minutes and it's ready."

"Yes, yes," he had answered. "I'm awake."

But he was not awake. His eyes were closed and he was watching the two angels on the hill out past his garden, across the road, and beyond the fields. The blinds across the bedroom window were closed against the light and against the unseasonable mid-afternoon heat. But he could see them. They were arguing as they always did. He couldn't hear the words. He never heard the words. But it was about him, he knew. Once again they were arguing about him. He would like to hear the words. He knew that if he listened hard, he could. But he was afraid. Perhaps one of them was the Angel of Death coming for him. He was afraid if he made himself hear, then he would die. Was he so afraid of death? Sometimes. But sometimes not. It was his insatiable curiosity, he had long ago decided, that made him reject the idea of death. He was after all eighty-five years old and had led a full life, a marvelous life.

"Yehuda, are you awake?"

"I'm putting on my shoes," he called out, but he didn't move, didn't open his eyes. He watched the angels.

One was young. And one was old. He was attracted to the young one, to his vitality, the way his body moved, the colors that fluttered away from him as he sometimes danced around the hill, gesticulating wildly with his arms, causing his wings to undulate madly, beautifully.

The other was quieter. When he gestured it was less like light and color, more fluid, like a river. Yehuda was reminded of water moving gently over stones. He was more afraid of that one, of what the stillness implied, of the sad face that sometimes seemed transparent with grief. Did Death grieve? Or was the youthful one, full of zest and joy, was he in reality Death? Yehuda didn't know, couldn't be sure—unless he listened. And he didn't dare listen.

He dreamt about the angels often now, that dream and the other, the one about words. In the word-dream, it was he who was standing on the hill, but alone. In the dark. Stars everywhere. Magnificent. Clear. And then the stars would begin to move, begin to fall—a shower of descending stars. Only they weren't stars. They were words and, as they fell about him, he knew they were heavy and opaque. Millions of words whose meanings were closed to him. He was terrified. Not that the heavy words would hit him, injure him, maybe kill him, but that he understood none of them, that he had lost his capacity for understanding words, and with it the whole meaning of his life. Standing in terror under a black sky with hills of darkened words all about, he would open his eyes.

"Yehuda, wake up," his wife was shaking him by the

shoulder. "They will be here in a little while. Come get your coffee."

Yehuda allowed the angels to fade away and opened his eyes. He sat up and swung his legs off the bed. "I was watching the angels again," he told her, feeling with his feet for his slippers.

"You should have the courage," she said, heading back to the kitchen, "to walk up that hill and ask them what they want."

That was Malkah. Ten years younger than he, she had enough courage for the both of them. The only times he had ever seen her afraid was when their son had been at the front, and then the grandchildren. For herself, never. For him, she wouldn't allow it.

He caught up with her in the kitchen and picked up the tray to carry it the few steps into the dining area. When he had worked for the government, first in Tel Aviv, and later in Jerusalem, they had lived in spacious homes. Compared to those places, their kibbutz quarters were small—a living room, with a corner for the dining room table, a kitchen that opened into the dining area, a bedroom big enough for their bed and a dresser, and of course the bathroom with its shower. Still, with the space the kibbutz had provided him for his work and for his papers and books, it was enough.

"What's this cake?" he asked her as he set their food on the table.

"Mirik made it." Mirik was their granddaughter. "It has raisins in it. She brought it over while you slept. You only get one piece now. The rest is for the company."

"Ah, yes. I'd almost forgotten. The company. An American poet." He pulled the seat out for her and then sat opposite her. "Gidon's friend."

"That's right," his wife said, pouring the coffee.

"Tomorrow, when that delegation from the Knesset comes, Mirik will bake you two cakes."

"They think I have some magic solution, something that will make this peace initiative between Rabin and Arafat work better."

"Do you?"

"Keep talking, that's what I'll tell them. If we can learn to settle with words and not guns and bombs, we will finally be a light unto the nations."

"They know all that."

"I know they know, but when they hear it from me they will either think it is new and is magic or else they will think, ah, we're on the right track. Do you have a better solution, *ketzeleh*?"

She shrugged. "Gai is in the army now." Gai was a grandson.

Yehuda stared into his coffee. "This is how I see it," he said.

"What, my love?" Malkah asked.

"Dreams," he answered.

"Tell me," she said, lifting the cup to her mouth and watching him with wonderful, listening eyes.

"I think we dream all day long. Part of us dreams and dreams. Only because our minds are so busy, we don't notice it, except sometimes, when we write poetry, for instance."

"Yes, go on."

"I think that in old age, however, we begin to notice those dreams."

"Why is that, Yehuda?"

"I'm not sure why. Why in old age does our memory improve? I mean the memory for those lost days of childhood?"

"A quieter mind, perhaps."

"I don't know about a quieter mind," he said, and put a forkful of cake into his mouth. "My mind feels full. I'm still interested in everything. How can I not be with all the phone calls and visits I get. I know what's going on in Israel and what's going on in the world. I think it's a quieter body. A freer body. The urges, passions, instincts, quieter." He winked at her and reached for her hand and squeezed it, then leaned back in his chair. "But there is also this dreaming. I walk around. And sometimes I dream. And dreams, too, interest me. It is a miraculous thing, this old age."

"Yes," his wife said, "when the bowels are working, and the arthritis is not too bad for a walk in the orchard."

"Do you dream, Malkah?"

"Perhaps."

"Then tell me."

"Yehuda, you are the poet. I have no poetry in me. I have only these," and she lifted up her hands to show him. "I dream about the sweater I shall make for Mirik's son, or about the flowers I will plant and perhaps live to pick. I dream. . .dream. . ." she paused.

"Yes?"

"Of peace," she said firmly. "Come, let's clean up and prepare for your guests."

## 31

*Saturday afternoon*
## THE SHEFELA

"This part of Israel is called the Shefela," Gidon told Beth and looked into his rearview mirror to make sure they still had their escort. They did. "There are many villages and kibbutzim here," he told her, gesturing with his head at the rolling hills.

"Gidon, will you please tell me where we are going?" They had been driving for over an hour now and were in a very different part of the country. The sudden changes in topography took her breath away. The country was so tiny, yet every few miles the geography changed.

"All right, if you can't wait."

"I definitely can't wait."

"On the plane we spoke of an Israeli poet called Yehuda ben Yehuda..."

"Of course, I remember. You were carrying a book of his. Don't tell me..." Her mouth parted, her eyes got large.

Gidon nodded. "He's my great uncle, the brother of my maternal grandmother. My grandmother went to America with her new husband in the twenties. My mother was born soon after. My grandmother's brothers came to Israel at the same time, bringing with them Yehuda, only a teenager. That was in 1923. Yehuda was an ardent Zionist, you see."

"How long was he in the government?"

"Years," Gidon shrugged. "He held several different Cabinet positions. After that he was part of the Knesset, our Congress. He was quite a renowned figure, greatly admired, even by those who were not of his party. He fought with the world for Israel's right to exist and often fought with Israel when he thought it had strayed from its moral path. He was always, I guess you would call it, a voice of the people."

"What's he doing now?"

"He's returned to his old kibbutz with his wife, Malkah." Gidon turned the car into a narrow road. "This is it. He's eighty-five and has gone back to a more simple life. He still writes poetry, works every morning, also on his memoirs, and organizing his papers. His papers interest him less, but his publisher has insisted on their historical importance, so Yehuda has reluctantly agreed. The kibbutz has given him an office, a room for him to work in."

"Oh, Gidon, this is a wonderful gift." Ben Yehuda was a very famous poet even outside of Israel, she told him. She had taught a course in twentieth-century poetry in translation and Yehuda's poetry had been among her favorites.

"He knows your work, too, Beth."

"You're joking. But my work has never been translated into Hebrew."

"No, but he reads in several languages and English is one of his favorites. Remember the British were here between the two world wars. He particularly likes the books you wrote on women in third-world countries. He admires your fire, your commitment."

"Oh, my God."

"Don't tell me you're nervous."

"Are you kidding? Of course I'm nervous. Yehuda

ben Yehuda is a living legend. It's like meeting the Walt Whitman and the Abraham Lincoln of Israel all rolled into one."

He found himself terribly attracted to her then, to her enthusiasm, to her humility in the face of a fellow poet. She was pretty successful herself. But a warning voice rose up in him. Go easy. Hold back. She has a boyfriend, and you're on the job.

Who cares?

He could feel whatever he damned well wanted to feel. And right now he was enormously attracted to this American woman.

## 32
*Saturday afternoon*
## The Shefela

"Unfortunately," Beth was saying, "it's a small and rather academic movement in America. It has little influence on what goes on politically or economically. We poets often have an inflated idea of what our work signifies for humanity." She was sitting on the sofa in Yehuda ben Yehuda's small quarters. Next to her was Gidon. To her right, in a straight-backed chair, sat Malkah, Yehuda's wife, a strong and large-featured woman, familiar from so many photographs. She, like Golda Meir, had been a favorite of photographers. And in a soft chair opposite her the legend himself was sitting. He was a small man with white hair like a tonsured monk. His eyes were a steel blue, still lively and penetrating, his face round and cherubic.

"Here it is different," Yehuda said. "In Israel, if you are a poet, everyone knows you, recognizes you. Even if they don't read your poetry. Everybody knows you and is proud of you because, as an Israeli, you belong to them."

"The advantage of a small country," Gidon said. "Small and nosy. Everything that happens here, good or bad, people know about. We have TV, and too many newspapers and too many magazines."

"Still, no poet has ever become President or Prime Minister," Yehuda said. "They were smart when they made Havel president of Czechoslovakia. A playwright, a writer is what they needed. When the country broke in two, at least it was peaceful. That's the power of the artist."

"My uncle will never forgive his party for not electing him Prime Minister," Gidon said with a grin.

"They were fools," Malkah said, "and I am very grateful to them."

"You didn't like public life?" Beth asked her.

"It is hard on family. But we both did our duty. We have nothing to be ashamed of and nothing to regret. Israel is here to stay. And Yehuda had no small hand in it. We are proud of our country and we are proud of our culture," Malkah said. "Why not? For a small state we have produced much. In science, too, we are very good."

"You have probably noticed," Yehuda's eyes twinkled, "that Israelis...how do you say it...blow their own horn at every opportunity."

"Why shouldn't we?" Malkah said. "Look what we have achieved in a few short years."

"So you met my nephew on the plane," Yehuda said.

"Yes, a happy coincidence."

"Did he tell you he was a spy?"

"Uncle," Gidon said, "you know very well what I do, I work for a consortium of kibbutzim." His tone was barely chiding.

"Our kibbutz is part of that consortium," Malkah said, and smiled at her nephew with unabashed pride.

Beth turned to look at Gidon with new interest.

"But before that you were definitely a spy. I was in the government. I have ways of knowing about these things." And Yehuda winked at Gidon and Gidon wagged his finger at him. "This lovely lady needs to be put on guard with you," Yehuda said.

"Don't pay any attention to him. Before this job I worked in the Prime Minister's Office."

"A euphemism for Intelligence of a very special kind."

"Uncle."

"It's not a secret. Everybody in Israel knows it. And before that he worked for Military Intelligence."

"My uncle has never forgiven me for leaving government service and takes every opportunity to rub it in," Gidon turned to Beth. "He himself stayed in government until he was over seventy-five."

"They needed me. The fools in Jerusalem needed me," and Yehuda laughed. "And now they don't need me."

"Nonsense," Malkah said. "Then explain to me why a few times a week government officials of all ranks come down here to talk to you. It's not for my coffee or Mirik's cake. If they asked him to run for the Knesset again, he would do it."

Yehuda ignored that and said to Beth, "Did Gidon tell you he was a poet himself?"

"Uncle, enough."

Beth raised her eyebrows questioningly.

"I assure you, Beth, I write strictly amateur verse. . ."

"Not so amateurish. . ." Yehuda countered.

". . . which is for no one but myself. My mistake was ever showing him," he jerked his head in the direction of his uncle, "my stuff. I must have been drunk."

"So with all his various talents," Yehuda ignored Gidon's reproach, "he chooses not to be in government, which could use him. . ."

"Oh, for heaven's sake," Gidon stood up and walked into the kitchen area and poured himself another cup of coffee.

"...and not to be in the arts which the world needs almost as much as it needs air, but to be in commerce." Yehuda said *commerce* as if it were a dirty word.

"My family has a right to eat as well as other Israelis and to have clothes on their backs, and my children have the right to go to the University..." Gidon called from the kitchen.

"...and to have two television sets and a big house and go off on expensive vacations skiing in the Alps..."

"Yehuda," Malkah intervened, "leave Gidon alone. He has his own life to live." She turned to Beth, "One of our sons is in the insurance business. It's a miracle Yehuda still talks to him. Not everyone can be like you, Yehuda."

"Who wants him to be like me? But a merchant?"

"He's doing Israel a service."

Gidon returned to his seat. "My uncle wants all of his family to either live on a kibbutz, be an artist, or work in government."

"There are enough merchants among the Jews. And more are arriving every day. We need more Zionists and more idealists."

Beth listened to the exchange between nephew and uncle with fascination, trying to understand what being an Israeli meant to the two generations.

"All right, children," Malkah stood up, "you will have to stay for supper."

"Oh, we couldn't do that," Beth said, "that would be too much of an imposition." She looked at Gidon for instructions.

"But you are giving Yehuda a wonderful afternoon," Malkah dismissed her protest. "You can't leave us so soon."

Gidon said, "I have the time if you have the time, Beth."

"Well, yes then, but only if I can help with the meal."

"No help needed," Yehuda said. "Gidon will help Malkah bring the supper from the *cheder ochel*, the kibbutz dining hall, and you and I, my dear, will take a walk through the kibbutz. I will show you some of our little community," he said.

"It's dark, Yehuda," Malkah reminded him.

"So, a moonlight stroll with a beautiful lady, what could be so terrible?"

"Be careful," Malkah shook a forefinger at her, "Yehuda will no doubt lecture you. He feels he has to instruct everyone younger than he, Jew and Gentile alike, on the marvels of our little country."

"How can you say such a thing?" Yehuda threw his hands up in mock denial.

Beth turned to Gidon.

"Go, Beth. Yehuda has been dying to get you alone so he can ask you all sorts of questions. And he accuses *me* of being a spy."

"Do you see what I put up with in my own family? No respect," Yehuda smiled. "Ah well," he shook his head and took Beth by the arm and led her to the door.

"One hour, Yehuda," his wife said. "Supper will be on the table in one hour."

The night was warm but there was a pleasant breeze. The sound of insects droned in the moist air. In the many trees of the kibbutz, night birds chirped or called. Above in the cloudless sky, the brilliant stars seemed to lean toward them as if they were waiting for some word, some recognition, something from the human who had neither the wherewithal nor the inclination to give it.

A seed for a poem, Beth thought. "Is the sky always like this?" she asked.

"Why not? This is Israel."

Beth and Yehuda began their walk past the small

housing units with their individual gardens.

"Everything is dry now, but—can you feel it—any day the rains will come and turn everything green. Malkah loves to garden. For a Jew to garden, to put her hands in the dirt of her own country is a marvelous thing. History has been hard on us. And it's been a long history. Am I walking too fast for you?" the elderly man asked her.

"No, not at all."

Beth seldom thought about her own history. There was an aunt, her father's sister, who was interested in the family tree. But other than the fact that she knew her ancestors had come from France, Germany, England, Scotch-Ireland, and Italy, she herself was not interested, did not feel the pull of the generations behind her.

Yehuda went on, "There are two things that lie deep in the Jewish psyche," he said. "I say *psyche* because Americans don't like the word *soul.*"

Beth laughed.

He went on, "That's because it has no economic value. You can't weigh, count or measure it. Anyway, there are two things that lie deep in the Jewish psyche," Yehuda started again. "The first is a profound sense of guilt and the other is the need for the community of other Jews. Now the guilt I'm speaking of is a special kind of guilt..."

"What kind of guilt is it?"

"A terrible fear of doing wrong and suffering for it. Guilt gives to the Jew an unusual fear of retribution, either from God or from life."

"You think that kind of guilt is unique to the Jews?"

"I didn't say unique, I mean they feel it in an especially intense way." He nodded sagely, and took her arm as he directed her down a tangential path. "The other thing that lies deep in the Jewish psyche is a need for community. Guilt I could do without, but community I love.

A Jew is never comfortable when he removes himself from the folk, from the fellowship of other Jews. And I don't care how many Jews assimilate. Deep down they feel uneasy for moving away from their roots. They feel guilt."

"So guilt serves then."

"Not well enough," Yehuda said. "In the past when a Jew severed himself from the community he feared the retribution of God. When so many Jews in the modern era stopped believing in God, if they were not to disappear altogether—and the *goyim* were not going to let them assimilate so easily, they needed something else to hold the community together."

"And what was that?"

"Israel. The State of Israel. Here I don't have to be a believer in God to feel pride, to love my people, my past. I must confess something to you, my dear. . ."

"What is that, Yehuda?"

"I am in love with my people. Maybe a fellow poet will understand me if I say without equivocation that I am in love with this land. No, more than in love, I am entranced by this land, caught in its spell. If she were a lover, I couldn't be more mesmerized. I think it troubles the older angel." Yehuda stopped talking and his step slowed.

"Pardon me?"

He resumed his pace. "One of the two angels who haunt my dreams," he told her. "He disapproves of me, I think. I feel it. But not the young one. The young one is quite content with me."

"Do you believe in angels?"

"Not really," he laughed, "but I do believe in dreams."

"Yes, dreams can be something special."

"Come, I will show you the schools for our children."

Soon they were walking past a group of buildings with playgrounds around them. "Those are the kindergartens. My wife taught kindergarten for years, before we moved to Tel Aviv and then to Jerusalem."

"That's when you were in the government."

"Good years. Hard years."

"Do you miss it?"

"'There is a time for everything under the sun,'" he said, "a time to govern and a time to be governed." He pointed to the buildings they were passing. "The grade school used to be only for our kibbutz children, but now we are taking in children from surrounding villages. The same with our high school up ahead. Children come from all over. Some board here, some come here daily by bus. The school is quite large. Even some of the teachers don't live on the kibbutz." He sighed, "The kibbutz has changed since Malkah and I first came here with others to found it. We lived in tents then."

"When was that?"

"In the early thirties. It's too dark to see the fields now but all this land was purchased from the Arabs."

"Do you mind the changes?"

He didn't answer her right away. They walked on heading toward the high school, passing people who nodded to them. Finally, he said, "That's a difficult question for an old man to answer. I have lived for most of this remarkable century. When I was a child I couldn't have dreamed of the marvels that have come to pass, nor of the tragedies. Yes, to answer your question, there are many things I miss about the past. I would be lying if I told you different. But change means progress. Nothing stands still. So I can say, no, I don't mind the changes. That is to say, I understand them. But I do miss some of the old ways."

"Such as?"

"Such as the smaller closed group—I speak now only of what has changed in the kibbutz. I miss the greater sense of community. We are very open now. Children and teachers come to our schools from the outside. We have a store that sells pottery and ceramics, some made in our own factory. All day long cars and buses come into our kibbutz bringing people, looking or buying. Some of our members work in other parts of the country and come home only at night or on the Sabbath. Children are no longer raised in children's houses but in their parents' houses..."

"Is that wrong?"

"Not wrong, only different, in my opinion, less revolutionary. And in my day we were very revolutionary. It is marvelous to be a revolutionary when you are young. We wanted to change everything, not to be like our parents, slaves to the almighty ruble or dollar or shekel. We wanted to be different, to be an example for the world. When children slept in the children's houses, women were as free as men to participate in the life of the community. And they did..."

"And now?" They were walking past the high school with its large sports field.

"And now they participate less. As couples they participate less. But it was just that generation that was raised in the children's houses that wanted the changes. They wanted their children home with them. You should hear my granddaughter, Mirik, on the subject."

"It's very peaceful here," Beth commented, breathing in the damp evening air. And then she remembered all the enemies around the tiny country.

"So how do you like Israel so far?"

"It's fascinating, I must admit. But I'm not sure I can find what it is I'm looking for."

"And what is that, my dear Elizabeth?" and Yehuda patted her arm that was laced through his.

And suddenly Elizabeth was telling him, first about

the loss of her husband and daughter and then about her museum trip three years ago. "On that trip I went through a crisis. I crossed over a threshold, real or imagined. But somehow I was able to release my daughter from the prison of my pain. Was it real? Was it a dream? How can I answer that? But as crazy as it sounds, that experience seems the most real thing that ever happened to me. It changed my life. It didn't make a believer out of me, but it opened a door that I cannot close and. . ."

"And what?"

". . . and cannot go through." She sighed.

"Sounds like my two angels, my dear friend."

"Tell me about your two angels."

"A long story. But you go on with yours."

It was a relief to talk. Yehuda reminded her of Paul Burrows. Well, not really. Paul was a tall man with a full head of white hair. And Yehuda was short with a shiny bald spot on the crown of his head. And Paul was a Christian who believed in reincarnation. And Yehuda was Jewish, ardently so, and maybe even an unbeliever. But they were both wise in their own ways with something wonderful gleaned from full lives. So she went on. "After that experience I felt freer than I had ever felt in my life. The ground beneath my feet was less stable, but just that instability opened up the world for me in a new way. It broke down some hard wall I had built around me, a wall of intolerance, of fear, really. I even managed to write a rather autobiographical novel."

"You have? Brava for you. When is it due to come out?"

"It came out six months ago, and miracle of miracles, it's been well-received."

"Then you must send me a copy when you return home. Will you do that?"

"Oh, but I would love to."

"Now finish your story so I will understand why you have come here to my homeland."

And then, just like that, as they were walking down the paths of the kibbutz, a gorgeous sliver of a moon above them, and stars like spilled salt crystals everywhere, Elizabeth Layton told him about her experience in Chartres. When she had finished her tale, they were standing on the steps of a very large building.

"Shall we go in?" Yehuda asked her.

"Yes, please."

And they walked into the building. Yehuda found the light switch. They were in the lobby of a theater. On the walls were paintings and wall hangings. "These were all done by members of this kibbutz," Yehuda said. He showed her the auditorium, then led her down some stairs to look at the large hall where weddings, bar mitzvahs and festivals took place. And then he led her out of the back door and through the terraces and gardens.

Yehuda then picked up the thread of their previous conversation. "So you now believe in reincarnation and have come to Israel to look for your own past."

"Not quite accurate, Yehuda. It's more accurate to say I am, for the first time, seriously considering reincarnation. No, wondering about it is the accurate thing to say. And as my daughter placed both of us here at the time of Christ's Crucifixion. . . Oh, dear, I hope I haven't offended you?"

"How can you offend me, Elizabeth? Wasn't Jesus one of ours?"

"Yes, of course." They walked in silence for a while, then Beth said, "In some ways, Yehuda, it is a foolish quest. In most ways."

"My child, no quest is foolish. Does not the human being long to understand what is not understandable?

Does not the human being long to escape the limits of his own skin, his own small mind? I would do exactly what you are doing. I would rush to find out *if* I could find out," and he laughed.

Then he stopped walking and an odd look crossed his face.

Suddenly Elizabeth began to recite:

*"To look for God
Or perhaps His likeness
To seek His name
He Who is Unnamable
Not believing
Yet trusting belief*

*How shall we do it?*

*We shall strip off
Our old, worn garments
Toss shirt and shoe
Prayer shawl and book
Into the cleansing flame.*

*We shall grow wings
Of purified desire
We shall be bold, be daring
We shall set sail for home
Leap on its hallowed ground
And dance like humans dance
Like ranks of angels dance*

*We shall dance, yet long to dance
Naked in the fire."*

"Interesting," Yehuda said. "Whose is it?"
"Yehuda, it's yours! Don't you recognize it?"
"Say it again."
She did.
"Yes, of course. But the translation. All the sound is gone."
"Isn't it any good?"
"A young man's poem. Yes, good enough. It captures the idea."
"*Dancing in the Fire.*"
"Who among us wants to dance in the fire anymore?" he asked. "Now we want to become merchants and go skiing in the Alps." Yehuda glanced at his watch. "They are waiting for us. We'd better go back. Let me say only one thing to you, child, don't be afraid to search, to long for something, to seek change, because...because if you become afraid, then in old age you will not retrieve your courage and you will become less than...less than, what shall I say?..." He smiled and took her arm again, "...less than a human being. So, yes, dance in the fire. Come, we'll go by way of the Dining Hall. You need to see that. It's the heart of our community."

As they were approaching Yehuda's apartment, Beth asked, "Yehuda, why is Gidon...why is Gidon taking me around like this?"

Yehuda looked up at her, his face soft and wise in the moonlight. "Don't you know? A lovely woman like you?"

"But he has a wife and children."

"They have, what is it called, an open marriage. You know what that is?"

She nodded.

"It is no marriage, if you ask me. Not that men have ever been saints. But it is different now. Marriage used to be a rock. Something you could depend on. Today it is merely an institution, like schools or government, a place to raise the children, a business arrangement. And who is happy, tell me? Not my nephew, no, not my nephew."

With that, they were back at Yehuda's apartment.

## 33
*Saturday night*
### OVER THE ATLANTIC

Mattie hated the idea of flying at night.

Well, at least it would be a short night since she was flying toward the sun. She ran her fingers through her long, blond hair and stared out the airplane window at the impermeable night sky. Somewhere beneath them was the Atlantic, another dense blackness. If there were stars, she saw none. This darkness is the mouth and throat of a beast, she thought, a whale—Cetus perhaps, and they were flying into it, were being swallowed up by it. When they landed they would be in the belly of the beast, exit with their carry-ons into alien territory where everything she knew and relied on would be of little use.

Mattie pulled the shade down.

She would stay awake the whole time. She would read quietly so as not to disturb her fellow passengers. If the plane was going to crash, she wanted to be awake for those last minutes. Being plummeted into death while asleep was an intolerable idea.

Mattie had requested a window seat because it was away from the constant movement in the aisles of the plane. A family in the two rows in front of her were returning to Israel. There were four children under five and the mother, who seemed terribly young to Mattie, undressed, diapered and covered each one with a blanket before finally settling down in her own seat. The woman's husband helped. They talked to their children in both English and Hebrew, passing food about and bottles and water, oblivious to the stares of those seated around them. Would the children sleep, Mattie wondered? It didn't matter. She herself intended to be awake and she didn't care if there was noise to help her pass the night. Between Doug and that girl in the poetry class she had taught at the "Y" last summer, she was not feeling too good about herself. And that wasn't like her. She never spent much time worrying about herself. It wasn't very interesting, certainly unproductive. But the comment of that girl—what was her name—had somehow gotten to her. Louise Taybury. Why that particular girl? The summer was long over and still she wondered about it. Mattie had taught poetry classes for years, at various conferences, summer workshops, and at the "Y." Her policy when she taught was simple, never be harsh, never be unkind, but always be honest. And not everyone had been happy with her for that honesty. Yet no one had gotten to her like this inept poet, Louise Taybury.

The young woman was furious at Mattie's comments on her work. But the truth was the girl was a poor writer. Her poems were sloppy and poorly crafted. They were, admittedly, very intense and very erotic, but that didn't make them good. And Mattie had been critical. So on the last day of classes the Taybury girl had stormed into her office. She called Mattie a repressed bitch, whose own poetry was bloodless, dry, without emotion or humanity. She accused Mattie of writing the same poem over and over again, told her that she was in a rut, that her sixth book of poetry was exactly like her first book. She told Mathilda Jones that the best thing she could do for herself was to go out and get laid, then maybe she would find something else to write about other than seeds, rocks, and mountains. Maybe then she wouldn't be so threatened by explicit love poetry.

No denying it, the woman hit Mattie in a vulnerable place, calling Mattie's poems bloodless, and implying that she was simply repeating herself. Frankly, Mattie had begun to worry about it herself. After all hadn't Sally Goldberg, an editor with whom she had worked for years, subtly suggested that Mattie consider traveling more, or had Mattie thought of "maybe writing a novel?" Then there was that New York Times review of her last book, *Shifting into Acorn*. It criticized her for the sameness of her subject matter, yet praised her for her skill and style and masterly craft.

That had been the moment Mattie decided to take the trip to Israel, to say yes to her half brother and his wife's invitation. She needed a change, needed new vistas.

But she was filled with anxiety—as she knew she would be. She despised her anxieties, knew she should fight them. She was doing this trip as if it were medicine, and that was not a healthy attitude. There was after all so much to see in Israel. But it was hard to be away from her cabin in Big Sur. Like being naked in public. Her life creed had been that in a grain of sand the whole world existed, that all it took was penetrating that grain, really seeing it. That contained in her own garden and the surrounding hills was all she needed from the world for a lifetime's study and work. How had that belief suddenly failed her? Was she now to be thrust out into the world without a rudder or an anchor? If her poetry deserted her, what would she have? If her poetry was bloodless, without passion or life, what could she count on? The thought was unbearable. More unbearable than her fear of traveling, her discomfort with strangers, her dislike of unpredictable adventures. She knew she had to do something, and coming to Israel for a visit with her oldest half brother and his wife was something. That was all she could manage now. Thank God that somehow Beth was visiting there. It was a good thing that she had put in a call to Eric. Beth in Israel! It was like a providential sign that she had made the right decision. Yes, that was definitely a good sign.

Change or die, she repeated to herself. Over and over again, change or die. Did it matter what Louise Taybury or her editor or Doug said, or what that reviewer in the New York Times wrote? No, none of that mattered. What mattered was that she, herself, knew she needed to change.

Bottom line. Period.

Mattie brushed her hair out of her eyes and thought, but everything doesn't have to change. My hair is still my hair, and some part of me is still me. She closed her eyes and thought, maybe I'll just rest for a few minutes.

## 34

*Saturday night*
### JERUSALEM

Elizabeth and Gidon spoke little on the drive back to Jerusalem. Gidon didn't try to break into her thoughts. She seemed content to watch the shadowed scenery and to think, and he was content just to be in her company. Now and then, he looked into his rear view mirror. No cars followed them back to Jerusalem.

As they approached the city, Gidon asked her, "Would you care for some coffee before I take you back to your hotel, or perhaps a drink?"

"Yes," she answered, "I think I would. Coffee."

Gidon took her to a favorite night spot of his where they served both drinks and coffee. There was a Russian piano player, a new immigrant, a concert pianist really, exquisitely playing quiet songs. Hebrew and Russian, some American, no rock.

They ordered *café filter* and some apple cake for Gidon. Elizabeth seemed suddenly shy. They sat quietly listening to the music for a while.

"I'm so grateful to you, Gidon," Beth began, "for taking me to meet your uncle...for the whole day, really."

"He took quite a liking to you," Gidon said.

"He's very kind..."

"He can be, but he can be also very tough. He doesn't suffer fools gladly, I'll tell you that. And he liked you."

"Are you really a spy?" She tried to smile.

"I'm not a spy," that was true now, "and I'm not a poet."

"But you write."

"Occasionally I write."

"Why?"

"Doesn't everyone who loves poetry want to try their hand at it?"

She nodded.

"So I try. That's all. It's not serious."

"What is serious for you, Gidon?"

He looked at the way her green eyes seemed to deepen and darken when she was listening.

"You said at lunch today that when you were sitting on a hill in the desert after you left the army you came to some sort of decision—to throw your lot in with your own people, I think you said, to be. . ."

". . .to be an Israeli." Gidon could feel the tension between them, the attraction. He could see by her sudden discomfort that she was aware of it too. "Does that sound like a lot of *Sturm und Drang* to come to something that should be obvious?"

"I don't know. I ran around all over the world, in my younger and not so younger years, sure that I could see, and tell others, mostly women, what their problems were. It finally dawned on me to stay home and look at my own country, to be an interested American. My last book of poetry came from that experience. So tell me your story."

"It may not be too interesting."

She wagged a finger at him.

"Then, okay." He half-smiled and took a deep breath. "For years growing up I thought some vital element in me was missing. Finally, when I was in the army, I realized that what was missing in me was missing in many of my generation. I tried to explain some of it this afternoon."

He waited while the waitress served the coffee and cake. When she left, Gidon went on, "You met my uncle, perhaps you might meet my parents. For them, being Jewish is like a gene. It's in the blood. You're born with it like the color of your hair or your eyes. You don't have to question it. But, and this is key, it's not only a fact of heredity, which is easy to accept, but in them it seems to work like a force of nature." He stirred sugar into his coffee. "But for me it was, yes, obviously a fact. I am Jewish because my parents are Jewish. But it didn't work in me in this, how shall I call it, this elemental way, this powerful and instinctive way."

"How did it work?"

"It didn't. That's the point. In some ways I could have gone anywhere to live. I felt as much a citizen of the world as I felt like an Israeli, so. . ." he paused and cut into his cake with his fork.

She waited and when he didn't go on she said, "So?"

He could see that she was listening hard and because of it he tried to explain, "But I was born here, and this country has a need, a great need to be defended and cared about and helped into the future. Remember I told you that if some transcendent meaning to life is not obvious to you, then you have to create your own meaning?"

"Yes."

"That's what I decided to do. I decided, an act of will I guess, to throw in my lot with this people I was born into."

"And that was a hard decision?"

He loved that she didn't pretend to understand. "Yes, in some ways, because you have to back it up with something."

She shook her head.

"You've commented more than once on how much I

know about this country. Well, that's because I made myself learn all about it. I made myself travel every inch of the land, made myself study its history, its geography, all its outpouring of culture, the different peoples who have settled here..."

"Quite an undertaking. I did something like that, too."

His eyes questioned her's.

"For a few summers, when my girls were older, I traveled all over my country. I just got in the car and went, no plan, no particular goal, just to see America and to speak to Americans."

"I understand that," he felt mildly relieved. "However, this land is small..."

"But it's roots go deep."

"Yes, very deep. So I decided to love this land and its people."

"And you didn't before?"

"That's hard to answer. Yes, in some ways, but not in the way my parents and Yehuda did."

"Yehuda said he was enchanted by this land, 'mesmerized' I think is the word he used."

Gidon nodded. "I think it's just in the blood of that generation. They simply love this land. For them it's a bit like giving birth to a child. They loved it before it was born. But I didn't feel it in my blood."

"That's the part in you that was missing?"

"Yes. Is it so odd?"

"I don't think so. How many things do we start off loving? Most things we have to work at. We're not always successful."

He liked her very much at that moment. "So I taught myself to love this land. It was a conscious decision on my part."

"That's not easy."

"No, it's not easy. I found out that you can't force yourself to love. But you can make yourself interested in something."

"Yes, yes, that's true," Elizabeth said. "That's just it."

"And when you really get interested, get involved, eventually you begin to love what once you were only interested in."

"And you did it?"

"Yes, I did it." He looked into her admiring eyes and then he thought about his marriage and wondered why he had failed there at loving. Had he been interested enough? But then relationships were different, he told himself. Two people are involved.

"What do you think would have happened to you if you hadn't made yourself interested in your homeland?"

Gidon shrugged, "I might have gone off to America like others before me, like one of my brothers, or I might have moved to London—I adore London, or Paris."

"You like big cities?"

"I do. I like the culture of big cities. When I hear music or read..."

"Poetry?"

"Yes, poetry, or see theater, or dance or opera..."

"...then you believe in the worth of the human species."

"You remember."

"Yes."

"Does this all sound like nonsense, a sort of tempest in a teapot?"

"Not at all, not any stranger than my rushing to Israel to...to..."

"To what, Beth?" he put his hand over hers.

She paused only for a moment, and then said, "To see if reincarnation really exists." She gently pulled her hand out from under his and picked up her cup.

It was an answer he hadn't expected. Still he barely blinked. "Reincarnation? And does it? Have you found your answer?"

She looked at him with a grateful expression, "Not yet."

"Tell me about it."

"When I was visiting Chartres I suddenly remembered something I had long ago forgotten."

"Go on."

"I remembered a day when my daughter Alicia, she's the one who died, told me that the two of us had witnessed Christ's Crucifixion, 'before we came down the last time,' she said."

Gidon tried not to look too startled. "Tell me what she told you."

And so she told him the story of seven-year-old Alicia's déjà vu.

He let out a deep breath when she finished, "That's quite a story, very curious."

"Especially given the fact that we were not a religious family and that we had not taken our children to church nor told them bible stories."

So now he understood why she had come so spontaneously to Israel. He felt a huge sense of relief. She was not here on some devious mission. His instincts had been right all along.

But then why was she being followed? That seemed even more ominous now.

"You think reincarnation is true?" he asked.

"I don't know if it's true, but the experience there in Chartres really shook me up. It came so potently. A dead memory suddenly rising up like a specter...no, that's too tame an image...like a volcano. It simply erupted out of my subconscious. I knew I had to find out. So coming to Israel and walking through the holy sites seemed a way of at least trying to see if any of them said anything to me."

"And have they?"

She sighed, and rested her chin on her clasped hands. "No, not really. But then I came here so ignorant. I'm sure that doesn't help. And everything is so built up...and I never had much luck with the past."

Gidon now understood Beth's reactions at the various places they had visited. "It's important to you now?"

"Yes, it's important. It would change everything if I found out that it was true."

"It would make you believe in God?"

She was watching him now, no doubt wondering if he thought her crazy. Did he? No, not really. What would he have done if his daughter had said something similar. He didn't know. Perhaps he would have done what Beth and her husband had done, dismissed it as childish fantasy.

But perhaps not.

"Yes, probably. Something like that," she said.

"Yes," he agreed, "that would change everything." He wondered if she included in that her relationship with the man she claimed she loved. He didn't ask her that, instead he asked, "What are you going to do next?"

"I don't know," she told him.

"If I can help in anyway, please let me," he told her.

"Thank you, that's very kind," but he heard her voice tighten as she said those words.

When they arrived outside the hotel, Gidon spotted both cars that had been following them that day parked along the block.

"Gidon," Beth said, "I've had a wonderful day, I can't thank you enough..."

"Beth, can I come up to your room?"

She didn't look at him but removed her hand from the door handle and shook her head. "You're terribly nice, Gidon. And very attractive. But I can't be... Gidon, what do you want from me, with me?"

"Whatever you're willing to give me." God, that sounded stupid.

"I'm involved with another man. This timing is all wrong, don't you see. If I were free..."

"I'm not free," he said.

"Yes, but I can't do what you do. I can't be involved with two men at the same time. I couldn't handle it emotionally."

"You love this man?"

"I thought I told you I do."

"But you don't want to marry him."

"I didn't say that."

"What did you say?"

"I said I was afraid."

"Okay."

"Okay, what?"

"Then I'll respect your feelings, but..."

"But?"

"But I would like to keep seeing you?"

"Why?"

"Why? Because I'm forty-three years old and jumping into bed is not everything. I like you. I enjoy your company. I'd like to be your friend. Is that so ridiculous?"

Beth slowly shook her head and once more reached for the door handle.

"Can I call you tomorrow?" he asked her.

She didn't turn around but she said, "Yes."

He put his hand on her arm. "Sleep well."

"You, too." And she got out of the car and walked into the hotel without looking back.

Gidon drove his car slowly down the block watching his rearview mirror as he did. Neither of the two cars followed him.

# 35
## *Saturday night*
## JERUSALEM

When Beth entered her hotel room she saw the light on the telephone blinking. A message. Her heart began to beat rapidly. She hoped it was from Eric. But before she could retrieve it, the phone rang.

"Hello, is this Elizabeth Layton?" It was a woman with an Israeli accent.

"Yes?"

"Do you remember me? This is Ruth Jones, Mattie's sister-in-law. We met in New York."

"Of course, Ruth. Eric and I talk often about that wonderful day the four of us spent together in New York. How is Michael?"

"Michael is fine. We heard you were in Israel. You came but didn't phone us?"

"Well, I would have sooner or later," Beth said. Why hadn't she contacted Mattie's brother and wife? "I've been so busy sightseeing."

"Tours, they show you all the obvious things. You'll come to us. Michael and I will show you an Israel that they don't show you on tours."

"Where are you calling from?" Beth asked.

"From home, from our kibbutz. We're in the Emek, the Jezreel Valley. It's north of Jerusalem, not far from the Sea of Galilee."

"Ruth, how did you know I was in Israel?"

"Mattie called to tell us."

"Mattie, but how. . .?"

"She called Eric when she arrived in New York. She couldn't get hold of you so she called Eric. He told her that you had come to Israel. She's coming."

"Who's coming?"

"Mattie!"

"Coming here?"

"Of course here, where else?"

"She is? When?"

"Tomorrow she arrives. That's why I called."

"Mattie? Coming here tomorrow? How did that happen?"

"After all these years, Michael finally talked her into it. Our granddaughter Netta is getting married in a week, and so she's coming."

Beth was astonished. Mattie, who hated to travel, was coming to Israel? She could hardly believe it. And just at this moment—when Beth was here. What a piece of luck!

"We want to invite you also."

"What?" Beth came out of her reverie.

"We want to invite you to the wedding. It's in a week."

"But wouldn't that be an imposition. It's already late to bring in extra guests. . ."

"It's a kibbutz wedding, one more guest means nothing. You're in Israel, you have to come."

"I'm afraid I'll be gone by then."

"You'll change your ticket. Mattie said we should keep you here. She is excited to see you."

Beth's thoughts were going a mile a minute. Mattie coming to Israel. She had to see her, to talk to her. "When does her plane arrive?"

"Tomorrow morning. We are taking one of the kibbutz

cars and meeting her."

"Is she going back to the kibbutz with you?"

"She wants to spend a few days in Jerusalem before she comes to us. So we're driving her up to Jerusalem. Afterwards she will come to us."

"What hotel will she be in?"

"We put her in your hotel, that's what she asked."

"I can't believe it. I can't believe she's coming."

"Michael says it's a small miracle. This is our third grandchild to get married. We were never able to get Mattie to come before. The next thing is I'll believe in God. Now, this is the plan, if you agree, Beth. We would like in a few days to drive up to Jerusalem and bring you both back for a visit with us and for the wedding. There is very much to see in our part of Israel. It is more green, more beautiful than the area you are in. Of course, Jerusalem is something special, don't you think?"

"Yes, of course."

"So what do you say?"

"I say yes. . . if I can change my ticket." It would serve Eric right for being so damned pig-headed.

Ruth told her when Mattie's plane would be landing and when they would arrive in Jerusalem.

"I'll be waiting for you at the hotel," Beth said.

"Good, see you tomorrow. Michael sends you best wishes."

"And a hug for Michael. And thank you so much for the news and the invitation." She hung up the phone.

What marvelous luck. Mattie coming to Israel.

Beth threw herself back on the bed and sighed contentedly, then remembered to call the desk for her phone messages. There was one. It was from Eric.

"Shall I read it to you or send it up?"

"Read it."

"Okay. It says, 'I love you, baby'. . . no, it says, 'babe, I love you, babe,'" the clerk corrected herself, "'take all the time you need.'"

Beth laughed, "Thank you. I think you'd better send the note up. But please wait a half hour." She stripped off her clothes and turned on the shower. This had been a wonderful day. Gidon, Yehuda, Malkah. And Ruth and Michael. And that lovely note from Eric—wonderful, wonderful Eric. She knew he would eventully come around. Eric was too good, too kind, too understanding to stay mad for long. She loved him dearly.

And he wasn't pigheaded.

And now Mattie was coming and they would have a few days together in Jerusalem. The tide was turning and somehow her quest didn't seem so foolish after all.

She thought about Gidon. She thought of the day Gidon had given her. It had been a marvelous day. But now, after Eric's note, she felt a slight twinge of guilt. Toward whom, she wondered with amusement? Because of whom? Gidon had agreed to be just a friend. So it was all right. No need for guilt. And she thought about Yehuda's words about Jewish guilt. Interesting, but she was sure guilt was universal.

Beth climbed into her bed and wrote in her journal for over an hour, then put her notebook down and turned off the lights.

## 36
*Saturday night*
## Tel Aviv

It was after eleven-thirty when Gidon arrived home. His children were in their rooms, but his wife was waiting up for him.

She didn't ask him where he had been but said, instead, "I'm going away for a week."

"When?" Gidon asked, as he put his jacket in the closet.

"Tomorrow."

"Tomorrow? You're leaving tomorrow and you wait until tonight to tell me."

"What does it matter, Gidon?" Avigail answered with a shrug. "You won't be inconvenienced in the least. My mother will come a few times to shop and make the suppers. The kids are old enough to take care of themselves. She'll sleep over if you don't intend to be home. You have nothing to worry about. The children are in school all day."

"I'm not worried," he said, moving into the living room. "Where are you going?"

"Kuşadasi."

"Turkey?" Kuşadasi was a resort town near the ancient site of Ephesus. "You're suddenly interested in archaeology?"

She shrugged.

"Who are you going with?"

She looked him in the eye. "I'm going with Hagai."

"You're still seeing Hagai? I thought that was over."

"It was, but now it's not."

"I see."

"Anything else?"

"No." Gidon turned to walk down the hall to their bedroom. He saw his son's door close quietly as he passed it.

## 37

*Sunday morning*
## Tel Aviv

Gidon watched his wife step into a taxi from his living-room window. He couldn't see the man inside the taxi, but he knew he was there. It was seven in the morning. He went into the kitchen to make himself a cup of coffee. His son came in, said nothing, but reached into the cupboard to take out the corn flakes.

"Where's Rinat?" Gidon asked him.

"She left early."

Gidon nodded. He watched his son sit down at the table, pick up a piece of the morning paper and begin to read it. Suddenly, Gidon found himself talking, "Geel, I want you to take the day off and spend it with me."

"The boy looked up startled. "What?"

"I want you to miss a day of school and spend the day with me."

"Miss a day of school?" Geel was an excellent student.

"That's what I said."

"Why?"

"Wait and see."

"I can't miss a day of school."

"Yes, you can."

The boy was silent. Then, "What do you want to do?"

"Let's go for a ride."

"Where?"

"It doesn't matter where. Let's go for a ride and talk."

"You want to talk?"

"Yes."

"I shouldn't miss a day of school."

"One day. I want this, Geel, I want you to spend a day with me."

"You never asked me before."

"I'm asking you now."

"Let me make a phone call to Ayelet, and then, okay." Ayelet was Geel's girlfriend and classmate.

Before Gidon left the house with his son, he made two phone calls from his bedroom. The first he made to Elizabeth Layton, but she didn't pick up, so he left a message saying he would call her that night. The second he made to Dov to tell him that he would not be spending Sunday with Elizabeth Layton and to be sure their men covered her as she would be on her own today. He asked about Hemmings. They were still looking into his background. As far as they were able to tell, he was just what he said he was, an American businessman importing goods from Israel to Chicago. Gidon insisted that there had to be more. Dov assured him that they would continue trying to find out.

He left a note for his daughter and his mother-in-law saying that he and Geel were together and they would be home by evening.

## 38

*Sunday morning*
## BEN GURION AIRPORT

The minute Mattie stepped off the airplane into the Israeli morning sunlight, she felt a whoosh of elation. She had done it. She was here. In Israel. She had taken hold of her life, was acting instead of reacting. Her old, protective cocoon was about to unravel. If that left her feeling a bit naked, it also gave her an unanticipated sense of satisfaction. She didn't expect to find herself miraculously turned into a butterfly, nothing so marvelous, but some old tattered binding was about to shred away. She had taken the first step. She was in Israel. Israel!

Mattie ran her fingers through her hair. Yes, it was there—long and silky and familiar. And there were Michael and Ruth waiting for her as she came through the gate after passing through customs. All grins and hugs and scolds for never having come before. Yes, they had found Elizabeth Layton. Yes, she was waiting for them in Jerusalem. Yes, she was coming to the wedding.

During the ride up to Jerusalem from the airport, Mattie interrupted their narrative on the state of the, by now, sizable family, to ask questions about what they were passing. As they drew nearer to the ancient city she felt a rising sense of excitement. Without doubt, she had made the right choice coming here to Israel, a country and a people always living on the edge. It was something she needed to be a part of. She wanted to throw herself into this land's desperation. She wanted to soak up some of it's vitality, it's ability to cope. She wanted to live, if only for a few weeks, a life without certainty, without guarantees. Something would happen here to turn her around. In that first hour in Israel, she had no reservations whatsoever. Some unconscious fear that she had harbored for years about this country was dissolving, melting away in the unexpected sultry heat of late October.

She turned a glowing face toward Ruth, and said, with high emotion, "I am so happy to be here."

And Ruth answered, "Well, it's about time. You will fall in love with Israel. How could you not?"

Mathilda Jones just nodded. She was feeling exhilarated, jet-lagged, and ready for adventure.

## 39

*Sunday morning*

## THE JUDEAN WILDERNESS

Gidon hadn't planned it, but he was driving toward the Judean wilderness. His son hadn't said a word for the last half hour. He sat there, stony and uncommunicative. At the start of their drive, Gidon had asked him questions—how was school, what subject did he like best, how was it going with Ayelet? He had gotten grunts or one word answers. Now it was silence.

Why had he decided to do this? What did he want to ask Geel? He wasn't exactly sure, but that feeling had come, that feeling that had served him so well when he was in the field. Call it intuition, but he had suddenly known, that morning, that if he didn't break through the silence that existed between himself and his son, it would be there forever. There was no time to wait. He had to act now. And Gidon knew how to act. There was a question he had to ask his son, but he could not grasp it, could not take hold of it. Okay, he told himself, it's there, don't stab at it, it keeps moving away when you do that. Do something else, talk about something else, and don't push it away. Then it will stand still. It won't be poised to run. Then you will take hold of it. That question.

Gidon began to describe to Geel his last trip, the places he had been, the people he had met, what he had accomplished. He was good at describing minutely. He had been trained for that. Geel asked no questions but he could sense him listening.

"I hope someday you can see Paris, maybe even with Ayelet after you both get out of the army. It's a city for lovers."

"What's so special about Paris?" Geel finally spoke, his voice gruff, his tone registering disinterest.

"Maybe the architecture. The city is designed so artistically. . . it's as if it was built to encompass the whole range of human emotions. It has wide, grand boulevards with monumental buildings, but also narrow winding streets with charming shops and cafés. Maybe it's the people, well-mannered, civilized, tolerant of lovers. . ."

"What do you know about it?"

The anger in his son's voice shook him. After a moment, Gidon answered, "Well, I've been there, you see, and I walk and watch."

"Yeah, sure."

And then there was quiet again.

By now Gidon knew where he was taking them. There was a hill he wanted to climb, one he had climbed often when he was only a few years older than Geel. He was content to drive without talking now. He turned the radio on.

"Play whatever station you want," he said, and was not surprised when his son found a station playing the heavy metal music his father detested.

Finally, Gidon parked the car at the foot of the hill.

"Let's go," he told Geel.

Geel got out of the car reluctantly. "I don't know what we're doing."

"We're going to climb that hill."

"What for?"

"Because I say so, or is it too hard for you?"

Geel gave his father a sour look and started up the

hill. They climbed without talking for half an hour and finally arrived at the spot Gidon had been aiming for. Yes, there it was, nothing had changed. There were the remains of an old campfire where others too had come to be at peace and to think. Gidon sat down and looked out over the vista. He could see the Dead Sea, and endless pale gold sand, and hills on both sides of the border. Here and there was a patch of green, a town, a village, a settlement, an oasis.

Geel stood there, hip thrust out, looking away from his father.

"Sit, Geel."

Geel didn't move.

"Geel, please sit."

Geel exhaled, shrugged his shoulders and finally sat a few feet from his dad.

Gidon knew the question now. It had come to him the moment he had stepped onto the small plateau that was the top of this mountain, Simple, unmysterious, the question that had plagued him for months.

"Geel, why are you so angry with me?"

"Who said I was angry with you?"

"Geel, answer the question."

The boy's face went through a series of changes. Right now it was ugly with hostility. "Why? Why? You don't know?"

Gidon shook his head.

"You can't be that stupid," the boy almost shouted.

"Apparently I can be. So tell me."

"Why do you let her do it?" he said, his voice loud with rage. "And why do you do it?"

Gidon's heart began to race. He could feel his stomach knot. "What? Do what?" his voice shook only a little.

"What kind of an example are you for me. . .or my

mother for Rinat?  I'll tell you what kind, no kind, a terrible kind."

"Tell me."

"Why can't you be more like grandma and grandpa, *your* parents.  Look at them.  They're happy together.  They do everything together.  He still holds her hand when they sit and when they walk he takes her arm. . ."

Gidon understood now.

"When Ayelet and I get married, we're not going to be like you and mom, no, not like that.  God forbid, we should be like that.  We're going to love each other and stay faithful and not go our own separate ways and each sleep with whomever we want."  And to Gidon's shock his son began to cry.

Gidon didn't move, didn't try to comfort his son.  He couldn't, even if he had wanted to.  After a few minutes he asked, "What do you want me to do, Geel?"

"Leave her.  Or are you too weak?"  Another shock.  "Why should you two stay together?  Can you give me one good reason?"

Gidon's words moved across his tongue with barely any air to guide them.  "We never wanted to break up the family."

"The family!  You call what we have a family?  You're hardly ever home.  Mom's mind is never where we are, always somewhere else, with someone else. . ."

"That's not quite true.  We wanted you kids to have everything. . ."

"Everything!" Geel spat out the word.

". . .not just things, but stability, two parents. . ."

"Two parents who can't stand each other, a house where there is no love, only duty.  You're preoccupied.  She's preoccupied.  When Rinat first got her period, did she go to mom?  Did she go to you?  No, she came to me, for God's sake. What kind of home is that?"

Gidon hugged his knees and stared down at his boots. "People make decisions. They think it's for the best, but. . ." he had no more to say.

"Are you finished? Can we go home now? I have homework and I want to see Ayelet tonight." Geel got to his feet.

"Wait, Geel, wait a few minutes more. Sit please. If we leave like this, maybe we won't have the courage to speak again for years."

Geel hesitated, then sat down again.

"Geel, I don't know if I can say this and make you believe me. I love you. You and Rinat are the most important people in the world to me."

"Yeah, sure."

"Yeah, sure, Geel. I tell you this and ask that you believe me. If I can't convince you of that, then I've lost half my life. For you and your sister are half of my life. The best half, really. Let me say something in defense of your mother and me. We thought we were in love, maybe we were, but like so many of my generation, we were afraid to give all for fear of losing all. I don't know if you can understand that. And, too, we were a new generation, different from our parents, *sabras*, a free generation, making new rules and breaking old ones. We thought that if we lived openly, without the rules that excluded loving others, we would keep our own love forever alive. . ."

"Did you?" his son's voice was less bitter.

Gidon sighed, "The honest answer to that is *no*. Others have managed, those who've experimented with marriage in the same way we did, some of them, but not your mother and I. Why? I don't know. Maybe we didn't love enough to begin with. Maybe it was the times. Maybe and maybe. The truth is, Geel, I don't know. I simply don't know."

"Then why do you stay together?"

"We always thought it was for the sake of keeping the family a family."

"Some family." And now Geel's voice was without rancor.

"Yeah, I see we fooled no one except. . ."

"Except?"

"Shall I use a cliché and say 'except ourselves'?"

Gidon stood up. He offered his hand to Geel and Geel took it. He pulled Geel to his feet. They started down the mountainside toward the car. "Geel, thank you for telling me."

"What are you going to do now?"

"I don't know what I'm going to do. I do know that I'm going to think about it."

"Good."

Gidon touched his son's arm. "You and Ayelet will do better, much better."

Geel nodded vigorously. "You're damned right we will."

## 40

*Sunday afternoon*

JERUSALEM

Mattie was shaking her head, "Unbelievable. Adventure seems to follow you wherever you go, Beth. How do you do it?"

The two women had lunched a few hours earlier with Michael and Ruth. After lunch Michael and Ruth had driven back to their kibbutz up north, and Mattie had returned to her hotel room to take a nap. But she couldn't sleep. So she phoned Beth who was reading in her room. They met and were now sitting at a table on the terrace of the King David Hotel drinking coffee.

"You're here only days and already you've met an attractive man who seems to be interested in you..."

"For the duration of my stay, don't make too much of it. And besides, I'm involved with Eric."

"...and you've met Israel's most famous poet."

"You'll get to meet him too, since Yehuda invited me for another visit."

Mattie flung her hair back with both hands, "Things just seem to happen to you, Beth. I must say, I envy you."

"Don't, they're seldom the things I want to happen to me. One relationship is all I can handle, but that's not why I came here."

"Why did you come here?"

"Eric didn't tell you?"

"No. He was very mysterious."

In great detail, Beth told Mattie what had happened to her in Chartres.

Mattie didn't interrupt, but when Beth finished her story, she said. "That's extraordinary. Curious and rather marvelous, don't you think?"

"More troubling than marvelous, Mattie. It's all so bizarre, so... so interfering. There I was, doing just fine, writing again, stable again, and falling in love again. Do I need this?" She threw her hands up in a despairing gesture.

"But there it is again, Beth. That same, same thing. Life just breaks in on you. Look what happened to you in Crete. And now in Chartres."

"Life? Is that what you call it?"

"What would you call it?"

Beth shrugged. "Craziness. Weirdness. Believe me, I don't look for it, didn't look for this."

"That's the point. Then why does it happen to you? What triggers it?"

Beth sighed and rolled her eyes.

"Perhaps it's because you travel. You pursue things." Mattie squinted thoughtfully in the late afternoon sun. "That's got to be part of it. And I've never done that. Until now." Mattie twisted the strand of hair, that was hanging down her face, into a coil. "Well, I have to change. The only question is, how?"

"Why do you have to change, Mattie?"

"Because I do," Mattie said.

"Who's been putting that nonsense in your ear?"

"It's hardly nonsense, Beth," Mattie shook her head. "Let's face it, I'm dull."

"Dull! You've amazed and edified thousands of poetry lovers. What's got into you? You're the most sensitive soul I know, Mattie, and probably the best poet writing in

America today. What's going on with you?"

"Sensitive! The best writer! Utter rubbish! You just said it, Beth. I edify. Is that what poetry is for? To edify? To be pedantic? To pontificate. . .?"

"You're exaggerating. . ."

But Mattie held her hand up and Beth stopped speaking.

"Truth is, I'm a stale and finicky writer, forty-five years old, in a state of near panic, come here to Israel hoping to find something that will stimulate me to write a novel." And Mattie plunged into her story about Louise Taybury and the others who had hinted or simply told her that she needed to move toward something new.

"Who the hell cares about what they all feel?" Beth said after Mattie had finished. "What matters is what you feel."

"Terrified for one thing. Beth, I think they've hit the nail on the proverbial head," and her voice became low and husky, "because. . .because I feel myself drying up. Over and again I turn inward for insight and inspiration and find only an empty well. Frankly, I'm scraping the bottom and I'm scared to death."

"Every writer has a dry period, Mattie. It always causes panic."

"This is something more than just a dry period. This is go forward or die. Grow or die. Really, Beth. I kid you not. I'm desperate."

"My God, you're really serious."

Mattie nodded.

"So you've come to Israel?" Beth's eyes held a question.

"A land I've always been terrified of, and didn't know it. But I had to start somewhere, so why not here? I have family here and a wedding and that's reason to come here, to start here. And then there is something about this country—always on the edge. Will it survive, won't it?"

She looked down at her plate and her hair fell around her like a waterfall. "All I know is that I have to do something different. I've been too reclusive, depending on inner resources that seem to be deserting me?"

"No. . ."

"Truly, Beth. It's not enough to have technique and skill and a way with words. I want. . .I need inspiration. Something new. Something breaking in on me, the way destiny breaks in on you. Because, Beth, if my writing ever leaves me, I might as well be dead. Maybe I am, maybe I'm half-dead."

"Don't say that, Mattie," Beth reached out and put her hand on her friend's arm. "Your writing will never leave you."

"I don't have that certainty any longer." Mattie yawned then. "God, I'm tired. I think I've been up for days."

Beth waved at the waiter.

"Well, I'm going to begin with Jerusalem's holy sites. I hope you're willing to go back to them and look again."

"I'm way ahead of you, baby. I've already booked us a guide. I'm looking forward to revisiting the sites with you. Maybe you'll see what I haven't seen."

"Don't get your hopes up. You have a wonderful eye."

"With a big mote in it now."

And the two laughed.

They paid their bill, then walked back to the hotel. Neither of the women noticed the men who were following them, and who entered their hotel only moments after they did.

## 41

*Sunday night*
## Tel Aviv

The call from Dov came at eleven that night. As soon as Gidon got into the car Dov lit into him.

"So you think this Layton woman is straight, a gifted poet, a charming woman, and a Christian pilgrim?"

"What's up, Dov? Something happen?" Gidon was careful to keep his voice neutral, but his gut tightened into a small hard knot.

"There is a lady that has just arrived in Israel. She takes a flight out of San Francisco to New York, then takes a plane from New York."

"Okay."

"Before she leaves San Francisco she meets a man, a Palestinian. Do you remember a man named Mahmud Aziz?"

Gidon shook his head.

"After your time, probably. He's a writer and a suspected terrorist. He fled the country a few years ago and we lost sight of him. However he showed up in San Francisco a couple of years ago. He writes a lot of inflammatory articles that are printed there, which are then smuggled into the territories and circulated. He comes from Nazareth. Around thirty."

"Okay."

"Well, Aziz shows up in San Francisco at a meeting of some group we've been keeping an eye on. From then on, we started keeping an eye on Aziz."

Gidon waited.

"Last Thursday he meets a woman in a coffee bar in San Francisco and hands her a thick envelope, probably containing money. The following day that woman goes first to New York and then gets on a plane to Israel."

Dov paused and stared meaningfully at Gidon. But Gidon stared back without expression and waited.

"So our lady arrives in Israel. We don't stop her. We want to see who she gives the money to. She is met at the airport by two Israelis. . .we're checking them out now. . .and guess where they take her."

"How should I know?" but he was beginning to draw an inference.

"They take her to Jerusalem, to the same hotel where your lady friend is staying. . .Elizabeth Layton. Okay, that could be a coincidence. But, no, my friend, it is no coincidence. She is met in the lobby by your lady friend. A big hug, a big greeting. They lunch together. They have coffee together."

"What's this new lady's name?"

"She's another one of your American poets, can you beat that coincidence? Suddenly we are invaded by American poets. Her name is Mathilda Jones. Ah, I see you know the name."

"Yes, I know the name."

"She is well-known?"

"In poetry circles, very well-known. Do you know what her connection is to Aziz?"

"Not yet. But we will soon."

"So what now, Dov?" Gidon asked. "I take it that now you're very interested and will pick it up from here."

"No."

"No? You're not interested?"

"Now we're very interested, but we want you to stay with this."

Gidon stared out of the car. Only a few lights were still on in the apartment windows all around. Why, he wondered? Couldn't sleep? Personal problems? No doubt, personal problems, he decided. Not this stuff.

"You've made the connection. You took Layton to see your uncle and she is no doubt very grateful. No, you're still our best bet."

"I have another job, Dov. I'm not sure I want this one."

"These are crucial times, Gidon."

"The times are always crucial."

"You know what I'm talking about, Gidon. Don't be so hard-assed."

"I got out of this business for a reason. I don't want to do this."

"You like this lady?"

"Yes. It's not what you think. She seems...seemed like a nice lady..." he left the thought hanging.

"Maybe you've lost your edge."

Gidon didn't answer.

"You don't have to do anything dangerous. We'll be around. All you have to do is see them as much as possible, talk to them. And report back to us. Nothing difficult. Pretty straightforward stuff. You could do this with one eye shut."

Gidon had the urge to punch this desk-hero in the face. He had never liked the man, but instead he said, "I've another job, Dov. I've taken off enough time since I came back from Europe. I have reports to..."

"How long before you can wrap up those reports?"

"Two, three days. Look, I have personal problems right now. My kids..."

"We'll talk to your boss. It'll be okay. Everyone understands National Security, particularly in these days. So. . .?"

Finally, Gidon asked, "What do you want me to do?"

"Stay with them. Befriend them both, hang out with them. Your wife is away?"

Gidon looked up.

Dov shrugged, "News gets around. You have a nice mother-in-law. She's always ready to help you out. So pretend you're interested in one of the poets. If it could be this Jones lady, that would be the best."

"I really don't want to do this."

"So what?" Dov said. "What does that matter?"

"Let me think about it."

Dov took that for a yes. "Good. It won't be too hard. Just see how much you can tag along."

Gidon sat for a long time in the thick, soft armchair in his living room. It was an expensive chair. So was the sofa. And all the tables. For such luxuries he had left the service. And now was he back in? Granted the times were very unsettled—Rabin and Arafat negotiating, and half the country and half the Palestinians against it. No more wars was a great goal. Could it happen? Did it have a chance?

He thought about Geel. His son. They had reached across a great divide today, had closed a gap. He didn't want to see the gap open wide again. Geel. He would be in the army soon. Gidon wanted peace, peace for his own son and for every other father's son. Even if it was only a small chance, they had to take it.

He knew what he was going to do, had known it the minute he walked away from Dov's car. Everything else in his life could be unraveling, but there was one thing he had won for himself, he was an Israeli. That's who he was. Lousy father, lousy husband, but a good Israeli, an exemplary Israeli.

He would do what was asked of him, what was needed from him.

He thought about the woman, Elizabeth Layton. Was she simply lying, even about that reincarnation thing, was that all just hokey stuff? Dov and his bosses seemed to think she had another agenda. But yesterday he had spent a whole day with her and he couldn't believe she was so duplicitous. He may have been out of the work for a few years but there was one thing one never lost, the ability to read people.

He watched the reflection of the traffic lights slide slowly across his ceiling. Still, why had Beth not told him about Jones' pending trip to Israel? They had spoken about Jones often enough. It would have been natural to say, "Oh, by the way, Mathilda Jones is coming to Israel. We're going to meet here." But she hadn't.

Gidon ben David, you're a fool. You think you can read people but you can't see past your infatuation. Was that what it was? Had he allowed himself to get entangled emotionally with a woman he was 'observing' as an antidote to looking at his own untenable marriage? And was he really entangled emotionally? Or simply seeking a distraction?

And how come he hadn't admitted to himself that his marriage was a failure, not just a comfortable, workable arrangement, but a failure? Geel had seen it. How could he, who was such a student of other people's lives, be so blind when it came to his own? And why had he settled? For seemingly so little? Was he so enamored of his own freedom? And was that what he had really? Freedom?

He thought about his wife. What was she doing at this moment? Probably rolling in the sack with Hagai. The thought made him angry. How come he hadn't been able to see what his kids had seen all along?

How come he hadn't seen his kids?

## 42

*Monday morning*
## JERUSALEM

". . . so I'm going to be pretty busy for the next few days... No, Gidon, no, don't think that. I do want to see you again and I do want you to meet Mathilda Jones. I know how much you admire her work and I owe you that much after you introduced me to ben Yehuda. . .that came out wrong, I would want her to meet you anyhow... Dinner? Well, I think that could be arranged. Could it be tomorrow, Tuesday evening? But I insist I take you this time... Fine. Then we'll wait for you in the lobby at seven tomorrow evening... Me, too."

## 43

*Monday morning*

JERUSALEM

The two women were standing in front of a large draped coffin, the tomb of King David. It's big enough for a giant, Beth thought. She ran her fingers over the black wrought-iron fence that kept the eager visitors from getting too close to the tomb, with its red drapery embroidered with the stars of David. Above it were several silver crowns, decorations for Torah scrolls, in remembrance of the kings of Judah who had succeeded David. So many kings, so many years of history.

"You should remember," an old man told them in English as they entered the holy room, "Jews were not allowed to enter here until 1948, when we fought for our state." He looked at the two women and added, "Christians neither."

Standing next to Beth, Mattie was lost in thought, her hair hanging like crimped ribbons down the side of her face.

Beth tried to make herself feel as she imagined Mattie was feeling, to hear through the space, but she couldn't overcome her critical thoughts, and her thoughts right now were saying that this couldn't in reality be David's tomb. And all the old men standing around eyeing them coldly, while quietly mouthing their prayers, disturbed her. Her mind kept going back to Florence and to Michelangelo's magnificent statue of a youthful, naked

David, with a slingshot in one hand, exuding life. That was the David she wanted to think about, capable, a conqueror, a poet and a lover, a man who had done much and suffered much. This tomb was a place of death, of a long ago past. Nothing here spoke to her.

When Mattie was ready, the two women walked up the stairs to the Coenaculum, a large, rather attractive room in the Crusader's church where Jesus was supposed to have celebrated the Last Supper, the Passover Feast, with his disciples. Beth had been here with Aryeh, and she liked this room.

"Obviously, this is not the actual room where the last supper took place, but built where the room was supposed to have been," Mattie said, running her hand down one of the columns, and staring up at the beautiful ogival arches. "This is very likely the location. Wonderful things were said here. Do you feel it, sleeping in the air?"

Beth shook her head.

"Go back and read John. Christ's farewell discourses. Marvelous. Deep. And here the Whitsun experience took place. That's what you need, Beth, a Whitsun experience," she laughed. "Then you'd find what you're looking for. Me too. Both of us. A wake-up call out of mourning. Speaking so others can understand." She sighed then.

"You already speak so that others can understand, Mattie. You're too hard on yourself," Beth said, moving leisurely around the marble and stone room. Nice to be alone in the room for a few minutes, just the two of them. "I wish I had your background in all of this," Beth stood looking out one of the windows.

"This was turned into a mosque after the Muslims conquered Mount Zion in the fifteenth century," Mattie said.

"Mattie, you believe in reincarnation."

It was a statement, but Mattie answered it.

"I do."

"How come we never talk about it?"

Mattie shrugged. "You never seemed interested. It's not something one can press on another. I leave people alone who find the idea untenable or foolish."

"And that's how I always seemed to you? Even after my epiphany in Crete?"

Mattie nodded.

That hurt...a little. Beth thought she had genuinely changed since her adventure in the Aegean, that she had somehow become more open, less rigid in her beliefs. How come she hadn't convinced Mattie of her newfound openness? Hadn't her novel shown Mattie that? She looked at her friend who was watching her with an expression of genuine affection, and she shook those thoughts away and pursued her question. "How did you come to a belief in reincarnation, Mattie?"

"I've always believed in it."

"You mean you were taught it when you were young?"

"I don't remember that I was, but yes, probably," she answered. "It always made sense to me. It just seems self-evident."

Beth shook her head, "It never made sense to me," then she laughed, "so you were right about me. However, my daughter Alicia believed it, and my young friend Hank. Not Becky, though. She's more pragmatic, like me. My friend Paul, also a Christian, believes in it. But how? I just don't understand it? How did you...can you come to such a belief? Do you have to be taught it as a child? Did you ever doubt it?"

By now the room was filling up and their conversation

stopped. The two women started down the stairs. As they were leaving the building on Mount Zion and walking to where they had left Aryeh and the car, Mattie said, "I never questioned the validity of reincarnation, not even when I went off to high school and met all those mainstream Christians. My mother had a teaching certificate, so I was taught at home until the ninth grade. But you know all that."

Beth nodded.

"It wasn't until I met other children and started to socialize with them, that I realized reincarnation was not a principle of Christianity."

"Not in the church I grew up in," Beth said.

They found Aryeh and got into the car. They settled in for the drive to Bethlehem.

Mattie picked up the conversation, "One life, only one chance to do it right, never made much sense to me. How do devout people believe in that? How do they believe in a compassionate God when that compassionate God doesn't give an equal chance to everyone to make it in this world? Or how condemn millions of people to hell when they have never even heard of Christ? Maybe reincarnation is what's missing in mainstream Christianity. Maybe it needs to be added, or perhaps reinstated, if one is to feel real compassion for others, if one is not to become egotistical in one's beliefs. Repeated earth lives just makes sense. My faith in reincarnation was never shaken. Not even when I gave up Christianity as a belief by the time I was in college."

"But you came back to it again?"

Mattie nodded. "When my mother got sick I was halfway through college, but I returned home and lived with her and cared for her those last two years of her life before going back to finish my degree. I've told you about that."

Beth nodded.

"I read the bible out loud to her every day, doing for her what she had done for me when I was growing up. Struggling with and through her illness, all our talks... I don't know, Christianity made sense to me again. She was a remarkable woman, my mother—serious, deep, a woman who lived with books better than she did with people. I miss her."

Their conversation stopped as Aryeh began pointing out sites of interest as they left Jerusalem. When he stopped speaking for a time, Beth asked Mattie, "You never in all your life stopped believing in God?"

"Never."

Beth sighed. "That's remarkable. Faith. I don't know if I ever really believed in God, not even as a child. My mother was, what I call, a social Christian and so we belonged to a church. And my father, well, my father adored my mother. By the time I was in my teens I was pretty turned off by Christianity. That's why this mission of mine is so weird, almost ludicrous."

"If I had been brought up in one of the denominations, I probably would have been turned off too. It shouldn't be so sectarian, so exclusive. Somewhere it seems to have lost it's esoteric core, its deep heart."

"But, Mattie, I'm not looking for a philosophy or a religious point of view in this. Is that really necessary? Can't we start more simply? What I want to know is not that complicated. Is it possible to come to a belief in the existence of reincarnation? That's it."

"You think that's simple?"

"Frankly, yes. Repeated earth lives. Have I lived before? That's a simple question."

"With profound repercussions if it's true."

"I grant you that. But the question is straightforward.

Is reincarnation true? Can I find some proof, here in this land, because it's not self-evident to me? I'll sort out the different religions later."

"You should go to Safed," Aryeh piped in. "There you'll find the kabbalists. They believe in reincarnation. Of course," Aryeh grinned at them in the rearview mirror, "they won't tell you that because it's supposed to be a secret, and only those who have studied for years get to know about it."

"I don't have years," Beth laughed

"That's okay," Aryeh said with a grin. "They wouldn't teach you anyway because you're a woman. So go to the Druze. They have a secret religion and they believe in reincarnation."

"So, you see, Beth, reincarnation is not such a crazy idea," Mattie said.

"The Druze believe in reincarnation," Aryeh continued, "and that when one person dies, somewhere a new baby is born, and that person has returned again."

"Immediately?" Mattie asked. "No rest for a while, no sojourn in spiritual regions?"

"That's what they believe."

"How exhausting," Beth said.

"But one thing is good," Aryeh said.

"What's that, Aryeh?"

"If you are chosen to be trained to be one of their priests or what are called the Smart Ones, it's all right to be a woman."

"Well, thank heaven for that. Some progress being made," Beth told him.

After having visited the Church of the Nativity, the two women were standing in front of the statue of St. Jerome in the cloister of the Church of St. Catherine in Bethlehem. "I'm not sure I can help you, Beth, in your quest," Mattie picked up their earlier conversation. "You're looking for proof. And proof in spiritual or religious matters is not something that one person can hand over to another. Like faith, it can't be given away."

"I don't know if what I need is proof, exactly, though that's what I thought at first. Maybe what I'm looking for are some tools, some help in finding the experience for myself. Maybe that would be enough, a beginning anyway."

"Well, you had that fabulous episode in Crete, did it change the way you look at things?"

"Yes, without question, it changed my outlook. It caused me to look deeply at this thing we call *the imagination*, but also to leave the door open to other. . .what shall I call them. . .states of consciousness? Look at the saints, for instance," and she gestured toward the statue of St. Jerome. "Something happened to them that caused them to completely change their lives, to become new people. They came to. . .to. . ." She hesitated.

"What do you think they came to?"

"Certainty," Beth said. "Yes, that's it. I want that, too. I want certainty. I had an experience, crossed over a threshold some would say, but it didn't give me certainty. And that's what I want, maybe even need."

Mattie sighed, "Maybe that isn't what the modern person is supposed to have. It can make you too fixed, too rigid, too intolerant, incapable of change, of genuine freedom. Maybe uncertainty is good. It keeps things open and fluid. Maybe your uncertainty is healthier than my certainty."

"For some reason that scares me," Beth said, as they started out of the cloister. "Yet it also appeals to me. Since Crete and the crisis I went through there. . .no, since I lost both Matthew and Alicia, I have learned to live without the ground so firm under my feet. But it makes me often. . ."

"Afraid?" Mattie asked.

They started to walk toward the car.

"Yes, and that makes me mad. It's the one thing I thought I didn't have—fear. But in the last several years I've had it in abundance. Fear of more losses, fear of commitment, fear of. . ."

She stopped talking because Mattie was looking around her with an intensity that made her pause mid-sentence.

"What is it, Mattie?"

Mattie flung her arms out in a wide open gesture. "Forgive me, Beth, I didn't mean to shut you off. But it's this, it's Bethlehem, and Jerusalem, it's everything. . ." Her face glistened with what could only be described as joy.

Beth turned to look around her. What was Mattie seeing? Beth had been here before, to Bethlehem before, to this church before. She had felt disappointment.

But Mattie went on. "It's so different. It's so wildly different that it just feels right to me, as if that was the way it had to be. Beth, I've been excited from the moment I walked off the plane. I don't know how to explain that because I was scared to death to come here. I was doing it like medicine, like penitence, and I've been in a state of high excitement ever since I arrived here. Everything just speaks, doesn't it? The hills, the sand, the air, it's so vibrant with history and memories. Just looking out, in any direction, leads one back, back, back to a time when everything was different, when we thought differently, felt differently, acted differently. That gives me such a sense of satisfaction. To sense, to feel that, yes, something totally new came into the world here. It wasn't understood then and it isn't understood now because we are still changing.

But are we changing for the better?"

There was a hint of despair in her voice, but just for a moment. "We still don't understand the events that took place in this land two thousand years ago. We still haven't grasped that mystery. We've trivialized it. If I had come here and the Church of the Holy Sepulcher or this church had looked like the little churches in America or even the big cathedrals of Europe, or the towns here like the towns back home, I would have been devastated. But they don't. It's not the same. Thank God, it's not. There is an *otherness* here. Something that suggests a totally different and incomprehensible beginning to Christianity. But not only to Christianity, to the whole world."

They were at the car then, and the conversation ended. Evening had come and the stars were out.

"I'll take you for a drive through the Shepherds' Fields," Aryeh said. "Of course, they're not the original Shepherds' Fields, but there are sheep and there are hills. No tour is complete without such a drive." And Aryeh started the engine and drove them out of the city.

Beth sat in the car, shaken, thinking more than looking. When she too had seen the otherness of this town, of Jerusalem, of all that she had witnessed so far, she had been disappointed, put off, had disliked the fact that there was something here unrecognizable. She was looking for sameness, and Mattie was rejoicing in difference. She suddenly saw her own quest as an impossibility if all she was hoping for was to find something that felt familiar and therefore something she could connect to. But that wasn't the right approach, was it? Had she done that her whole life? During all her traveling? She had observed many different cultures, but had she exalted in them? Had she tried to penetrate their differences? No, she had gone looking for something recognizable in the lives of the women there, something she could relate to and consequently bring solutions to. She had always wanted to see what unified peoples, but had she missed the other half? The differences? Even the *glorious* differences?

Beth felt a kind of despondency, felt incapable with her present attitudes, her present faculties, to approach her quest. But then the old, what was it, stubbornness?—yes, stubbornness—then the old stubbornness reasserted itself. And she was damned if she couldn't learn. She would pull back from too much judgment and watch Mattie. Mattie at this moment was like a gift from heaven and she was going to make use of it. If Beth would not only see details, which was her forté, but penetrate those details, maybe that would lead her closer to her goal. It wasn't enough just to listen and look. One had to do it without meeting every perception with a preconceived judgment. Now that would be an interesting task.

## 44

*Monday night*

## JERUSALEM

"They had a typical Christian pilgrims' day, Gidon... Yes, they talked a lot, what do you expect from two women?... Religious stuff, mostly. Your lady friend is interested in reincarnation and the other one believes in it... You ask my opinion, two harmless ladies... Mostly about the sites they saw... No, no one talked to them... Well, I didn't go inside all the places with them because they asked me not to... I'd say she is just what she told you. What are you worried about?... You're kidding... Well, I spotted one car... I'm no expert Gidon... Yes, I'll be with them tomorrow... I can't go in places with them if they don't want me... Okay, okay, but it's not going to be easy... If it's important then I'll do it... Don't worry, I have it on me... I'll call you tomorrow... You too."

## 45

*Monday night*
### JERUSALEM

"Sorry, Eric, that you were not in to take this call. I keep missing you and have to talk to your damned machine. But I was so glad to get your message. Mattie is here now, staying at this hotel. We'll spend two or three days in Jerusalem and then we'll go up north to where Michael and Ruth live, in the Jezreel Valley. There's a kibbutz called Kfar Hayam twenty minutes away from them that has a guest house and we're being put up there. It's right on the Sea of Galilee. I'm looking forward to this. And yes, I will stay on a little longer, now that Mattie is here. And Ruth and Michael have absolutely insisted I come to their granddaughter's wedding. I have so much to tell you, but I don't want to use up all your tape. I'll call you from Kfar Hayam and give you the number. I love you."

> I seem to phone at all the wrong times, so I'm faxing you this note. First, I'm sorry. Second, I love you. Whatever you need to do there in Israel, do with my blessings. Of course, stay for the wedding and as long as you want. I'm off to Santa Fe day after tomorrow for three days, then to Albuquerque for another four. Then two days in L.A. If I let her, Mrs. Barry will keep me on the road for a month. Leave messages on my home machine. I'll check in every day and I'll keep trying to get you on the telephone from wherever. I love you. Eric.

## 46

*Tuesday evening*

## JERUSALEM

She could hear herself talking, babbling on and on. "I didn't start to write seriously until I was in college. Well, a little in high school, yes, but not yet poetry, some short stories. I had a very encouraging English teacher. But, there were the diaries, all through my growing-up years, my mother saw to that . . ." Mattie paused.

"Tell me about your diaries," Gidon ben David said.

Mathilda Jones was sitting with Gidon and Beth in a Chinese restaurant in Jerusalem. She stared down at her plate and her hair cascaded to the table. She flung it back with both hands and looked up. The Israeli, sitting opposite her and leaning toward her, was very attractive. "Gorgeous" is what Doug would have said. The Israeli was listening intently to her and she was so unnerved by him that she couldn't do anything else but talk and talk. Mattie was sure she was talking too much. The man had penetrating blue eyes that seemed at the same time rather neutral, non-committal. What was he thinking? God, she felt stupid and unattractive. Thank heaven for the pantsuit that Doug had insisted she take from his showroom, so she was probably dressed okay.

"Well, I was educated at home, you see, and my mother started me off writing diaries when I was about seven while I was learning my letters. I learned to read at home through writing. I still have them," she said. "Vain of me to hold onto them, I suppose, but there they are, scores of notebooks, stored away in my attic back home, along with my mother's German-language library. I don't know why I keep them."

"They're your life history, of course, that's why you keep them," Beth said. "I wish I had written diaries, instead of poetry and nursery rhymes and little stories that had nothing to do with life, my life, when I was a child."

"Oh no, writing poetry would have been better for me, more true, I think." Mattie shook her head, and was appalled at the way her long ash blond hair spun about her face like agitated furies. But she kept talking. "When poetry is good, really true, then it has a certain individualized stamp, like...like a fingerprint. No one else could have written it and no one else would have seen the thing you are writing about in just that way." She was being pedantic. God, could she stop being pedantic? Boring.

"You are convinced that each human being is so unique?" Gidon asked her. He smiled and his words weren't challenging, but his eyes were cool, yes, definitely cool.

He doesn't like me.

"I am. Absolutely. Each individual is unique, a world in herself or himself," Mattie stated, staring at her plate, and then blushed slightly. "Of course, you can disagree." Dumb and getting dumber.

"Thank you," he said.

"If you get Mattie started, Gidon, you'll get a lecture on the singularity of each stone, each grain of sand, each star, each snowflake," Beth said. "Extrapolating from that, each human being."

"Such a viewpoint could make one an anarchist," Gidon said.

"An anarchist?" Mattie said. "Really? But that's

politics. Definitely out of my line. I'm simply talking about people and the amazing world we live in. Of course," she added, "it's important to support the struggle for freedom everywhere and the chance to express one's true self."

"How do you feel about the struggle here?"

"In Israel? I'm certainly happy to see these negotiations. It's all so complicated though, isn't it, when the same land is claimed by two peoples?" Why didn't he talk to Beth, and take his eyes off her?

"Very complicated."

"I'm glad I don't have to make the decisions," and Mattie flushed and began to laugh uncomfortably.

"Mattie has family here," Beth said, and Gidon turned to her, much to Mattie's relief.

But then he turned back to Mattie, the look still indeterminate. "I didn't know you were Jewish."

Mattie sucked in too much air and began to cough. "I'm not."

Beth said, "Mattie has a half brother here, whose mother was Jewish. Her father married three times." And Beth explained Mattie's family to him.

"My great-niece's wedding gave me an excuse to visit here," Mattie added. "Ruth and Michael live in Sde Gedalia. That's a kibbutz in the north."

"And this is your first visit to Israel?"

Mattie nodded.

"Why?"

Mattie just blushed and shrugged.

"Sde Gedalia, I know that kibbutz," Gidon said. "It's a very lovely, old kibbutz. Has your brother been here long?"

"He came not long after the Second World War, a few years before I was born, and met Ruth here."

"Long time. So do you know any Palestinians living in Israel?" Gidon asked her.

She shook her head. Then to her relief Beth began to tell Gidon about the two days the women had spent together.

But over coffee later, Gidon again turned to Mattie. "So what did you like the best in Jerusalem?"

"That's a hard one. Everything is so astonishing. . . Well, maybe the church they built over Anna and Joachim's house. That's Mary's parents. It was so peaceful. Yes, I loved the serenity there. That must be the house of the parents of the Mary in the Matthew Gospel. I guess one would have to go to Nazareth to visit the house of the parents of the Mary in Luke."

"What are you saying, Mattie?" Beth asked. "Mary had two sets of parents?"

"I'm saying that there were two sets of parents for Mary because," Mattie turned to her, "there were two Marys and two Josephs and two Jesus children. At least, that's what's in the bible."

"What are you talking about?" Beth asked.

"I'm not making this up," she said, then glanced briefly at Gidon who for once was looking at her with unguarded interest. "I hope you don't think I'm making this up? Read those two birth Gospels, Matthew and Luke," Mattie turned back to Beth. "They're two different stories. Except for the names, two very different stories. Read them. That can't be a mistake."

"Really? Two different stories. Okay, I'll read them tonight and see just how different," Beth told her." She turned to Gidon. "Mattie knows the bible backwards and forwards. . ."

"My mother read it to me, everyday until I went away to college. From Genesis through the Apocalypse. Over and over again." That sounds like an apology. Get a grip on yourself.

"She must have been very religious." Gidon said.

"We never set foot in a church in all the years I was growing up."

"Mattie's mother was a bit of an eccentric, a literate recluse, if you can picture it, but wise," Beth told him.

"Yes, very wise", Mattie said. "I never thought in terms of religion. God, Jesus, a host of angels, were just part of the world, of history, of life. My mother never commented on the bible. She just read it out loud and read it and read it. And let it go at that. When she got sick and I went back to live with her I read the bible to her every day." Why was she talking about her mother? This man couldn't be interested in her mother. "She went to college in Germany, but came home because of Hitler. She was terribly ashamed of her German heritage. I think that shame accounts for her reclusion. Of course, I could be wrong." Mattie coughed and took a few swallows of water. Forget your mother, Mattie.

"We also learn the bible in our schools. Here too it is taught as our history and our tradition."

"The New Testament too?" Mattie asked.

"No," Gidon answered. "Not the New Testament."

"I loved the Church of the Holy Sepulcher. Of course," Mattie said, easing back into the discussion of Jerusalem, "the Garden Tomb was lovely, a sort of English garden, an English sensibility in the middle of Jerusalem. But it does stretch one's credulity, I think."

Gidon agreed, "There's more weight on the side of the Church of the Holy Sepulcher. How did you like walking around the Old City?" he asked her. "Did you meet any interesting people? People are always bumping into people they know from back home, or making new friends."

"No, we didn't meet anyone we knew, or talk to

anyone really. We were too busy talking to each other," and Mattie turned to give Beth a warm smile. "To answer your question about Jerusalem, I found it very interesting, utterly fascinating. But also a little heavy, a little dark, as if it had always been serious, as if there were little laughter in this city."

"Really?" Gidon said, "Yes, I can understand the heaviness. The weight of history, but why dark? Why serious?"

"The solemnity of stone, if you know what I mean. And the desert all around, waiting. And so much tragedy, so much evil done here."

"You mean to the city or the tragedy of Jesus' Crucifixion."

"Both."

"You believe in the divinity of Christ?"

"I do," Mattie said, and nodded, and then looked down at her coffee.

"So then," Gidon asked, "did you get a feel for how it must have been in the time of Jesus?"

"Not really. I couldn't think away all the modern people. But I hope to spend a little more time here after my niece's wedding."

"You find the people in the Old City modern?" Gidon asked. Once again the guard dropped from his eyes.

"Two thousand years ago people must have been very different, don't you think?"

He just watched her, waiting for her to go on.

"I mean humanity must have changed tremendously over the centuries and certainly over the millennia," she knew her tone was didactic again, but as he was listening and staring at her with concentrated attention she plunged on. "Both inwardly and outwardly. That should be very obvious to you living in this ancient land. If you read the writings from the past, the poetry, if you study the way hierarchy and art were integrated into life then, you get a feeling for the changes. I guess I always wondered how people could believe in an evolution of the species physically, but not in an evolution of the soul and mind."

"These are the things Mattie worries about on cold winter nights in the Californian mountains," Beth smiled at her friend.

"And simple people, whom the trappings of civilization have passed by, aren't they the same as their ancestors way back?" Gidon asked her.

"Shouldn't one make a distinction between simple people living today in primitive conditions and those who lived in past ages?" Mattie asked.

"You sound like my friend Paul Burrows," Beth said.

"So you see I'm not so off base. It's what we were talking about before, Beth. It's differences again. Not just differences stretched out over space but differences stretched out over time. We can hardly understand the people who lived at the beginning of this century, who didn't think in psychological terms the way we do, who didn't stir around so much in their own psyches."

"Go on," Gidon said.

Mattie turned back to him. He was watching her thoughtfully. "Is it so strange to think that what we call primitivism was the natural state for all peoples in pre-history? It was where the whole human race was. We know that their outer lives were primitive, we know that from archaeology, but we don't know how rich their inner lives might have been to compensate."

"All right," Gidon said, "I can grant you that."

"But that's no longer true today. Primitivism is decadent, and by decadent I don't mean bad, I mean, beyond it's time, and though primitive peoples retain some of that earlier consciousness, and a lot of old traditions and practices, they still carry alongside it our own present inner impoverishment." Mattie whacked at her hair. Really, she would have to tie it back.

"I'm sorry, I don't mean to sound so irascible," she said. "But we moderns make the wildest assumptions about people back then, and I hate that. We think that they thought like us, felt like us, experienced their inner life the same way we do. If they did, they would have come up with modern science and modern technology long before this century, wouldn't they? And we moderns would have come up with another bible or something to equal the Vedas. But they didn't and we haven't. Even a stone changes over time. If a stone can change, why not us?—I'd better stop this. It must be the jet lag. I am going on and on."

"You're a very interesting and bright woman, Mattie," Gidon told her, and she reddened, lowered her eyes and turned to stare out the window.

"Mattie's here to write." Beth told him.

"Oh, what?" Gidon asked.

"I'm really here for a wedding," Mattie said, turning back to him. Again that calculating look. She felt totally confused.

"Actually, we're leaving Jerusalem tomorrow afternoon for the north," Beth said. "Aryeh's taking us."

"So soon?" Gidon said, and now he sounded concerned, disappointed even.

"We're staying at a kibbutz guest house," Beth told him.

"My family at Sde Gedalia has too many guests for their kibbutz to accommodate, so they've put us up at a guest house in a kibbutz on the Sea of Galilee, at least until after the wedding. The kibbutz is called Kfar Hayam."

"What will you be doing up there, besides going to a wedding?" he asked.

"Sightseeing," Mattie and Beth said simultaneously, and laughed.

"Well, this is a wonderful coincidence," Gidon said. "I'm going to be driving my uncle up there in a few days." He turned to Mattie. "Perhaps you've heard of my uncle. He's a poet. Yehuda ben Yehuda."

"Yes, Beth was telling me about her visit with him."

"Well, he has an older brother in a kibbutz up there. . ."

"An older brother?" Beth said.

"Yes," Gidon turned to Beth then, "believe it or not, up in his nineties, and, like Yehuda, he still has all his faculties. I'm taking Yehuda for a visit. It's too much of a trip for Yehuda back and forth in one day so we'll spend the night at my parents' home," he said. "Did I tell you that my parents live just north of the Kinneret, the Sea of Galilee?"

"I think so," Beth said.

"My parents have a restaurant up there," he turned to Mattie, "and Yehuda is very fond of them and of their American menu. Hamburgers, hot dogs, fried chicken. Perhaps we could all get together. It's very close to Kfar Hayam."

"But that would be great," Beth said. "I've been telling Mattie about your uncle and was hoping we could arrange to see him. Oh, Gidon, thank you so much."

"I'll take you to lunch at my parents' restaurant," Gidon smiled warmly at Beth. "I've told them about you."

He really likes her, Mattie decided, and she felt her stomach twist into a knot of disappointment. Well, that's the way it is.

"Isn't this marvelous?" Beth turned to Mattie who managed a smile.

"My parents' place is not a bad place to stay at, either. They have cabins to rent, and horses to ride. Very nice, very rural. My uncle and I will spend the night there."

"Ah, Mattie," Beth said, "we must be making progress with the man. He's taking us home to meet the parents."

And Mattie just nodded.

## 47
*Tuesday night*
## Tel Aviv

Gidon found some juice in the refrigerator, poured it into a glass, and took it into the living room. He didn't turn on any of the lights. Both his children were asleep, and his wife... his wife was sleeping in another man's bed. Okay, okay, he wasn't going to think about that now. He wanted to think about his evening and what he had just reported to Dov.

He wasn't too happy with himself. He had sounded too much like an interrogator at dinner, not like a man relaxed, enjoying the company of two attractive, talented and interesting women. But too much was going on right now. Geel. His wife. His life. Where was he in his life? And now this assignment which he didn't want.

That was untrue. He did want to see Elizabeth Layton again. Beth seemed to him a genuine seeker after some deeper dimension to her life, a person who faced her fears when she recognized them, a person capable of being deeply disturbed when some part of her life's viewpoint wasn't working any more.

And Mathilda Jones seemed too shy and reclusive to be much of an activist. Didactic, yes, even brilliant, but involved in anything covert? That seemed less likely. That she could believe and fight for her beliefs with words, yes, that he could imagine. But nothing covert. No, he just couldn't see it. The package? An innocent favor for a friend.

That brought another possibility to mind, one that had been circling him for days. He finally wrenched it out of it's circuitous path and looked at it square in the face.

Kidnapping.

It's what had worried him in Jerusalem, when he had interfered in the meeting between Hemmings and Layton. An incident to stop the peace process, a kidnapping of one or perhaps now two American poets. Something that would make the international news.

He probed his own feelings, sifting through them for weaknesses that would color his assessment, looked for an overabundance of sympathy that could blind him to what was really going on. He felt attracted to Elizabeth Layton, but it was not the dangerous feeling one could drown in. He was curious about both women. And curiosity always pulled him back to some objective place, some mountain-peak vantage point where he could survey at will what was going on. He had been trained—and trained well—to watch for telltale signs that indicated someone was prevaricating, or holding back, or keeping secrets.

The women had explained how they both came to be in Israel at the same time. A happy serendipity. Did he believe it? It certainly fit in with what Beth had told him about why she had come to Israel. Hers was a unique and interesting story, yet plausible.

Mathilda, well, she had been less forthcoming, but they had only met once, and she was a naturally reticent creature, unless she was being academic, or hiding behind a rather interesting set of beliefs. The wedding, a reason, or an excuse? This was her first trip and her brother had been here forty-some years. That in itself was odd. But not criminal. However, she was bringing something into the country, and it was possible she was being used by Aziz. Yes, he could see that. He'd have to find out.

He wanted to go immediately up to the Galilee—but no good. That would make Elizabeth uneasy. It would look as if he were pursuing her. If he was too obvious, she might decide to avoid him. For the next couple of days, he would have to let Aryeh and Dov's men take care of the situation.

No matter which way he turned the subject over, which way he asked the questions, the answers came up the same. He felt the women were more in danger than dangerous. And he wanted to do something about that, was going to do something about that.

## 48
*Wednesday morning*
## JERUSALEM

"Okay," Beth asked Mattie, when they met the next morning at breakfast, "so what did you think of my Israeli spy?"

"I could believe it, but why do you say he's a spy?" Mattie said as she placed her plate of salads, herrings and croissant on the table opposite her friend.

"Yehuda ben Yehuda said he was."

"Make an interesting story, wouldn't it? And he's perfect casting for the role."

"Maybe for Hollywood, but for real life?" Beth said.

"I don't know about real life. I never met a real spy. Well, maybe once."

Beth eyes widened.

"I'm just guessing, I don't know for sure. But to answer your question, he's very nice, very. . ."

"Very what?" Beth asked as she bit into her croissant.

Mattie blushed slightly, "Very handsome."

"Yes he is and very bright and also married."

Mattie just nodded and looked away.

"Mattie? Are you interested?"

"Don't be silly? Besides, anyone can see that he is smitten with you?"

"Oh, tosh. Last night at dinner he couldn't take his eyes off you."

"That's ridiculous," Mattie exclaimed, the color

rising to her cheeks again.

"If you hadn't been looking everywhere else but at his face you would have seen that for yourself. He was quite taken with you and besides he loves your poems. And I think he's available at least for the duration of your trip. He's got some sort of open marriage. Well, why not, Mattie? You wanted adventure."

"Beth, stop it."

"Okay, okay, but quit acting as if no man could find you attractive. They can and do. Now let's move on to something just as controversial."

"What?"

"I've read the two Gospel stories."

"Oh, do you see the differences?" Mattie sounded relieved to be away from the subject of Gidon.

"Some. So they complement each other. What's wrong with that? But, okay, you tell me."

"In Luke, the angel appears only to Mary and announces the birth. In Matthew, the angel appears only to Joseph."

"So they both were announced to, why not?"

"In Luke, shepherds. In Matthew, the three wise men. No shepherds in Matthew. No wise men in Luke."

"Hmmm."

"In Luke, the birth is in a cave or stable. In Matthew, it's in a house." Mattie looked at Beth and waited.

"Keep going."

"In Matthew an angel comes, once again to Joseph, and tells him to flee, that Herod is after them. And so Joseph flees with wife and child to Egypt where they reside until after Herod's death. In Luke, there is no such trip to Egypt. The child is taken to Jerusalem and presented at the temple as was the custom with the firstborn son. But in Matthew there is the flight into Egypt and the massacre of the innocents. In Luke no mention is made of a massacre or worry of a massacre. The couple travel blithely to Jerusalem with their newborn. We can no longer be talking about the same story. The Luke Jesus must have been born a few years after the child in Matthew and after Herod's death when there was no longer any threat."

"Interesting."

"But do you know what's the most interesting?"

"What?"

"The genealogies."

"I saw them, but I didn't pay much attention to them, all those names."

"Well, you should have read them. From Abraham to David, they are both the same, but after David there are two different genealogies.

"You're joking."

"Go back and read them. In Matthew, the line passes through Solomon all the way down to Joseph. Notice it is Joseph's line they are speaking of in both gospels."

"Joseph? Hmmm, but what about the virgin birth?"

"Maybe a virgin birth meant something else in those days, or why have the two Josephs' genealogies in the bible? They have to be significant. A kind of open secret for those who could understand. Anyway in Luke the line goes from David through another son, Nathan, a priest, and from there on it is different all the way down to Joseph."

"But that's crazy. Are you telling me that none of the church fathers or ministers or scholars of Christianity ever noticed this discrepancy?"

"Oh, they noticed it all right. And perhaps in the first centuries after Christ they understood it. But the Gospels are canon now, so they explain it away or pay no attention to it."

"But later on we are surely dealing with one Jesus?"

"Yes. They must have become one somehow."

"One! But that's impossible. How?"

"I don't know how. But if one takes as a supposition that the farther back in history we go, the less like us our ancestors were, even down to the physical body, then other things become possible."

"The transmigration of souls?"

"In special cases, why not?

"The virgin birth?"

"Language has changed so radically and it might have had a hidden meaning that we have lost. If the genealogies of both Josephs in the two birth stories were important enough to include in the Gospels, I don't think we should dismiss him as the earthly father of Jesus. Poor man, he's never been given his due."

"Okay, I'm trying to reserve judgment, trying not to say this is all nuts," Beth said. "After all, in Greek mythology, it was possible to be the son of a man, say a king, and also of a divine being. For instance, Theseus was the son of King Aegis, but also the son of Poseidon."

"Right. And both fathers were considered important, not just an honorary father, if you know what I mean. And in those early days, both concepts were understood. An earthly father and a spiritual father for significant individualities. Both fathers important and both genuine."

"Did your mother teach you about two Jesuses?" Beth asked.

"No, I just listened to the bible over and over again. From hearing the stories it never occurred to me that there was only one Jesus child. That is, until I went to high school, then I realized how radical my thoughts were."

"I can imagine."

"But, I always believed that the bible was not only history but history given in metaphor, like poetry. And that something else stood behind the words. The bible was to be believed literally, but not literally, if you know what I mean. It was like, well, like poetry, where one picture stands for another. Those who had ears to hear, heard."

"Frankly, this is giving me a headache."

"Yes, I can understand that."

"Mattie, if you patronize me, I'll hit you over the head with this croissant."

"I'm not patronizing you. Am I?"

"This is getting harder than I thought. I'm not sure I like all these complications."

"It's you who came here chasing after her own past lives. What did you expect, that it would be easy? Do you want a spiritual world that is simpler than, say, a computer? What were you hoping to find, some evidence of Elizabeth Layton laid out in mosaics on some floor somewhere—same nose, same hair?"

"Hardly that."

"What then? What would constitute evidence for you?"

"I don't know. I'm hoping I'll know it when I see it."

"'Repent', John the Baptist said. That meant, in the Greek, 'change your way of thinking.' Think like a poet in this, Beth. Be the marvelous observant poet that you are. Come at everything with the openness of a child and not with your educated skepticism. You can always be skeptical later. 'Unless you become as little children you will not see the kingdom of heaven.' I don't think it so odd that you might have a connection to this land at the time of Christ. Someone was there, why not you?"

"Now I am getting a headache. Let's go. Aryeh will

be here soon. If you want to see the Dead Sea Scrolls at the Shrine of the Book and the Holocaust Museum, before we drive up north, we'd better get moving."

Mattie stood up. "Oh, by the way, did you know that the Essenes believed in two Messiahs?

"What?"

"It's in the scrolls they found near Qumran. A kingly Messiah and a priestly Messiah. Just like the New Testament genealogies." And she grinned at Beth.

Beth picked up the croissant that was lying half eaten on her plate and flung it at Mattie. Then she put her arm around her friend's shoulder and walked out of the dining room with her, ignoring the disapproving stares.

## 49
*Wednesday afternoon*
## JERUSALEM

"I think there were two cars following us, Gidon. They don't seem to be hiding, at least not from each other... No, the women were unaware... No, no one approached them, no one at all... No, I haven't seen him... Nothing out of the ordinary. Well, we did go back to the bookstore... Mrs. Layton bought some more books. Mrs. Jones helped her pick them out... Mrs. Jones? She bought some books of Israeli poetry and some Israeli novels, in English, of course... They're having lunch now at the hotel... Yes, I'm driving them up there. We're going first to Jericho, then along the Jordan River through the territories up to Bet Shean, then on to their kibbutz... I always carry it with me, Gidon. Don't worry, nothing will happen to them. Not while I'm with them. I'll call you tomorrow when I get back... You too."

## 50
*Wednesday evening*
## THE GALILEE

"My dear Mrs. Layton, but this is a remarkable coincidence," a vaguely familiar voice called to her from across the lobby.

Beth, who had arrived with Mattie on the shores of the Sea of Galilee only an hour earlier, was standing at the desk in the reception hall of their guest house with the intention of booking a local car for a tour the next morning. She turned around to see who had called her name, and was amazed to see George Hemmings coming toward her.

"Mr. Hemmings. This is a surprise," she walked toward him and extended her hand. "I thought you had left Israel."

He shook his gray head and sighed, "Unfortunately, no, a call from the office in Chicago. I have to extend my visit for a while. But what brings you north? That's a stupid question. Of course, you're here to see the holy sites. And they are marvelous here near the sea, really quite marvelous, not so built over as they are in Jerusalem."

"Yes, an American friend has joined me, and I was just about to hire a car to take us around the lake tomorrow."

"Oh, you mustn't do that."

"I beg your pardon?"

"You mustn't hire a car. You must let me take you around. I have my own rented car, you see, and I've done this several times. But I never miss an opportunity to do it again, the Mount of the Beatitudes, Tabgha, Capernaum, all those places where Christ walked and preached."

"Oh, we couldn't impose. . ."

"Nonsense, you'd be doing me a favor. I'm all alone in this foreign country you see, and I could do with a little company."

"Are you staying at this guest house?"

"Yes, yes I am. I could stay in Tiberias, of course, at one of the big hotels, but I've had enough of big hotels. It's so noisy there and so quiet, so peaceful here. Now, can I persuade you and your friend to come with me tomorrow? I have, alas, only the one day with no appointments."

"I think that would be lovely," Beth smiled.

"Oh, thank you so much. You've positively rescued a fellow American. Shall we meet after breakfast here, say, at eight-thirty."

"Perfect," and Beth extended her hand. "Thank you so much for the invitation."

## 51
*Wednesday night*
# TEL AVIV

It was nine o'clock, Wednesday night, when Gidon climbed into the car with Dov.

"Your Mr. Hemmings is staying at the Kfar Hayam Guest House with your two American poets."

Gidon sat thoughtfully for a moment, then asked him, "What are you going to do?"

Dov shrugged. "Stay close, for the time being. How long before you can get up there?"

"Saturday."

"Perfect."

Gidon raised his eyebrows.

"Hemmings is taking them on a tour tomorrow around the Kinneret."

"They agreed to go with him?"

"Layton agreed. He offered and she agreed."

"Are they both going with Hemmings."

"Those are the plans."

"And so now you'd prefer that I don't interfere again."

But Dov didn't bite the bait. He merely said, "Hemmings knows you."

"Hemmings told Layton that he would show her the Church of the Holy Sepulcher and then led her off in the wrong direction. He could be dangerous, or lead them into danger."

"Don't worry. They won't be alone. Right now we're taking this seriously. We'll see they are well covered."

"What are you doing about Jones and the package she's carrying?"

"Waiting. We want to see whom she passes it on to."

"Did it ever occur to you that it might be a present for her, some money he owed her?"

"It might be. And it might not be."

"Maybe I should just stay out of this altogether, Dov."

"No. If things don't come to a head in the next two days, we want you there no later than *Shabbat*."

Gidon didn't answer. He stared out of the car window at the large apartment building they were parked in front of.

"Gidon, okay?"

He nodded. "Okay."

## 52

*Thursday morning*
## SEA OF GALILEE

Mattie was standing at the edge of the Sea of Galilee waiting for Beth to call her for their day's excursion. She was transfixed by the water, by the simple fact of it. She could hardly believe that she was looking out over this archetypal sea, one on which Christ had sailed, around which Christ had taught and lived.

It was a clear day and she could see across to the Israeli settlements on the other side, to the Golan hills that had once held guns aimed at the communities along this side of the sea.

Mattie had been thinking for days about what Beth had confided in her. How seven-year-old Alicia had remembered standing at the Crucifixion of Christ, with Beth, in another life. It had been a startling story, a deeply moving story. But slowly Mattie's thoughts had turned from Beth and Alicia to herself. If Beth had been living in the time of Christ, why not Mattie also? After all, people came down with the same karmic circle over and over again. So why wasn't it possible that she too had been alive in Christ's time? Had she possibly been a witness herself? Had she felt fear and horror at the way Jesus had died? Is that why she had been subconsciously afraid of this land?

Once the thoughts came she couldn't stop them. Had she heard Jesus speak? Had she suffered persecution as one of his followers or had she been one of the persecutors? If it had been a painful incarnation, surely deep in her unconscious she carried that pain, and she might also want nothing to do with this land. Might even fear it. Her thoughts were running on and on, perhaps without a modicum of logic. Perhaps all she was doing was creating the greatest fantasy of her life. But was it possible? Had she, too, a connection to this land?

When she was in high school, her mother had again spoken to her about fear. That time she spoke not in images, as she had when Mattie was a child, but in concepts. "Fear comes when you stand at an inner precipice, at the edge of true knowing. Fear occults something that can come to you from beyond the threshold of death or from beyond the threshold of birth. By that, I mean a spiritual world. Fear, which you may not recognize is there, makes you turn away at that threshold. It closes your eyes and ears, squelches the memories that want to rise up in you—perhaps from an earlier life, or from that life we live between death and a new birth. Or hides something that wants to come to you from the future, for that is also possible. Fear, a terrible, cruel enemy, is a tool of the opposers. Fear makes us turn back from the path we inwardly long to pursue. And in our times, for more than a century now, Fear comes to all modern human beings in a special and harmful way."

Mattie was not going to speak to Beth about this, about the possibility that she too had been in this land at the time of Christ. Mattie didn't want Beth to feel that she had usurped her mission. She would look and listen and quietly struggle with her own questions. She, at least, didn't have to prove to herself that reincarnation existed. For her it was self-evident. The only question was when and where, not if.

## 53
*Thursday morning*
### THE GALILEE

Beth entered the lobby of the Guest House at 8:25, Thursday morning. But George Hemmings had not yet arrived, so she sat down and waited. It was fifteen minutes before he showed up, a little red in the face, a little short of breath.

"Oh, my dear, I am so sorry to be late." He came at Beth, his arms extended. He took her hand in both of his and pumped it vigorously. "My car. It seems it won't start. I was positively devastated. I've phoned and raised holy hell. But they won't have a new car for me until late this afternoon."

"Oh, I'm so sorry," Beth said.

"No need, no need. New plans have been made. A driver from Tiberias had just dropped off a passenger here, saw my plight, and offered us his services for the day. So we can go on with our plans. I don't think there's too much to worry about. I'm sure he'll try to do more than just drive. He'll probably try to play the guide as well. His car seems quite clean, so I think we'll be all right. Where's your friend?"

"She's sitting down by the shore watching the birds. I'll just go fetch her."

"Good. Then we'll be on our way."

The driver's name was Uzi. He was still in his twenties, a blue-eyed young man with red hair and an easy smile.

As soon as the two women were seated in the large back seat, and George Hemmings in the front next to the driver, Hemmings turned to the women and said, "I've planned a full day, if that's all right with you. First to Nazareth and Cana, then to Megiddo, then back to Tiberias for lunch. After lunch we'll drive around the Sea of Galilee, stopping at the Mount of the Beatitudes, Tabgha, and finally Capernaum."

"Lovely," Beth said. "Are you sure you have all this time to spend with us?"

"Oh, my dear, you are saving my life, positively saving my life," he said. "I don't have any appointments until tomorrow and I was about to travel all by myself, till you came along."

"Then, we are both delighted, aren't we, Mattie?"

Mattie nodded.

"Excuse me," Uzi piped up from the front seat. "It would be better to go around the Sea this morning and then do Nazareth and Cana in the afternoon." He had turned around and was grinning at the women cheerfully. "I saw many tour buses going out of Tiberias to Nazareth on my way here."

"And no doubt there are lots of tour buses heading for the Mount of the Beatitudes too," George Hemmings said. "No, we will keep to our plan. Nazareth is where it all began, so let us start there."

Uzi shrugged his shoulders and turned back to the wheel.

As the car pulled out of the parking lot, George Hemmings turned around and gave the ladies a self-satisfied wink.

Uzi drove them along the lake toward lower Tiberias, then into the hills and upper Tiberias where the view of the sea was magnificent. It wasn't long before they were in the hills of the lower Galilee. There were few trees, except near houses or settlements, and Mattie asked about that. "Once the Galilee was filled with forests, before the Turks," Uzi said, and explained how the trees had been cut down during the reign of the Turks because "the Turks taxed landowners on each tree. All the trees you see are new, planted by the Jewish National Fund this century, over two hundred million trees. Building construction is not of wood here but of stone. Stones we have plenty. Wildlife is coming back now that we have trees. With rainfall the trees will help to keep the soil from being flushed down the hills. Trees change the climate too."

"I didn't know the Sea of Galilee was below sea level," Beth said, noting a sign on the side of the road that indicated they were just now at sea level. "Yes, it is, but we'll be much higher soon," Uzi told them. "Our Israel is full of surprises, don't you think?" And without slowing down, he turned around and grinned at the women.

"Pay attention to your driving." Hemmings' tone was sharp.

Beth looked out of her window, contentedly. The hills were still brown, the rainy season not yet come, but she felt at peace. She was sure that she was going to love this day. She was with her good friend and with a kindly escort, and they seemed to have a knowledgeable guide. She had spent the previous evening reading about the area and felt a bit more prepared for her tour than she had been in Jerusalem. And it was so nice to be in the country. Relaxed, open, she was ready to give herself over to what the day might bring.

"That hill is called the Horns of Hittin," Uzi told them, pointing at some ruins in the distance. "The Horns of Hittin is where the last battle took place between the Crusaders and the Muslims. Saladin defeated the

Crusaders. They lost the battle because of the summer. The Crusaders were dressed in heavy armor and the Muslims were dressing very light, so that's how they got defeated. July 1st, 1267. Some traditions say that the Beatitudes took place there too. There's always more than one tradition."

They passed several Arab villages. "These are Israeli Arabs. You know it's an Arab village because you see the minarets."

"This area gives me an inexplicably nice feeling," Beth whispered to Mattie.

But Mattie didn't hear her. She was staring out her window with a look of concentration that Beth envied.

"Since we're passing Cana of Galilee first, should we stop there first?" Uzi asked.

"Might as well," Hemmings said, "unless the ladies object," and he turned to look at them.

The ladies did not object.

"What's special about Cana of Galilee—that will be that first miracle performed by Christ, turning the water in jars into wine," Uzi told them.

The little town of Cana looked prosperous, and by the headgear of the men, Beth saw it was an Arab village.

They parked the car on a main street and began walking up the hill, past houses with courtyards to what, Uzi explained, was the newer Catholic church that "is built to expose the older church below it. According to tradition this church is built over the house where the miracle took place. You will see, when we go below, some jars like they used back then for water."

"Thank you, Uzi," Hemmings told him, "I think we can manage on our own..."

"Oh, do let him give us the tour," Beth said, touching Hemmings' arm. "I must admit, I'm a poor Christian and

I know so little about all of this."

"Certainly, my dear, if that's what you would like," Hemmings smiled at her and let a grinning Uzi lead the way.

"Most of the holy sites are coming from the tradition of the Byzantine era," Uzi told them as they entered the church. "Maybe memories of where events happened. So below you will see a house with the church on top. The Franciscan church is new this century."

They looked at the upper church and then their guide took them down to look at the ruins of the house with clay jars in several rooms. "The large jars were for water, wine and oil," Uzi said.

Beth was drawn to the small jars that "were for perfume or sometimes for tears. Such jars were found in many tombs," Uzi told her. Beth found everything very interesting, but she could find no sense in the story of turning water into wine. What significance did it have? It made Jesus seem a bit of a magician. She would ask Mattie about that later. Now her friend was totally absorbed in what they were seeing. Differences, that's what excited Mattie. But because Beth was unable to find a link to the familiar, did that make her unreceptive, shut down her poetic perceptions? The thought of it was very disturbing.

Mattie walked alongside Uzi and occasionally asked a question. Behind them like a shepherd guarding his flock was George Hemmings, seemingly more interested in them than in the church they were visiting. Beth hoped she hadn't offended him by suggesting Uzi take them through the church. Had he wanted to do the guiding? Well, she would have to make it up to him somehow.

Half an hour later they were standing outside the church. Not far from it was a large store selling souvenirs. "They sell the local wine here," Uzi told them. "Most pilgrims love to buy the wine as gifts or souvenirs. Wine from Cana."

## ⋈54⋈
### *Thursday morning*
## THE GALILEE

Uzi waited to see if the women wanted to buy any of the Cana wine. It was a favorite with Christian pilgrims well-read in the bible.

But it was George Hemmings who made the decision. "You must let me buy you each a bottle of Cana wine. No, no, I insist," he said, as the two women started to demur.

So while George haggled over the price of the wine, Beth and Mattie selected postcards. And Uzi stood by and watched them all. So far nothing unusual had taken place. The women seemed genuine enough, really interested in the holy sites, but the man, that was a more curious story. George Hemmings had looked around the sites with only desultory interest. Mostly he watched the women, Layton in particular. Uzi's bosses had asked him to see what the connection was between the women and the man, and to see if any packages changed hands. There was also a secondary concern he had been told to be aware of—the possibility of kidnapping. "Stay with them," were his instructions. "We're nearby. But not close enough to be noticed. Use your best judgment," he had been told. "If something comes up, it will be your call. What we need to know is, are the women dangerous or in danger."

When they returned to the car, Uzi said, "Nazareth

is not far, just over a few hills, not many miles," and he gunned the motor.

"Listen," Mattie leaned forward. "I wonder if we could make a short stop here in Cana, before we go on to Nazareth?"

Uzi turned his head in time to see the startled look in Hemmings' eyes, and to see Layton turn to her friend with raised eyebrows.

Mattie handed Uzi an address, with a hand-drawn map on it. "I'm told it's quite easy to find. It shouldn't hold us up for more than ten minutes." Her tone was both apologetic and firm.

Uzi stared at the address and map. He had his instructions. "Okay, I can find this. No problem."

"How intriguing," George Hemmings said, with what Uzi thought was forced cheerfulness, "you have friends in Cana?"

"Well, not really," Mattie said, and she sounded reluctant, "friends of a friend. I have to drop a little something off here. It won't take long." She then sat back, her mouth a firm line and turned to stare out the window.

Uzi pulled the car out into traffic, but watched the women through his rear view mirror. He could swear that this unscheduled stop was a surprise to Elizabeth Layton. He could see it in her face, see the perplexity there, see the question play around her mouth. But she remained silent. All very interesting.

It was a small town and it wasn't long before Uzi pulled up in front of a door in a narrow street. Mathilda Jones got out of the car. Uzi was about to ask her if she wanted him to accompany her when George Hemmings said, "I don't think you should go in there alone, especially as you don't know these people," and he began to open the door on his side of the car.

"No," Mattie's words were curt. "I'd rather do this alone. I won't be gone more than five or ten minutes. I promise," and she walked away from them without waiting for a protest or answer of any kind. She knocked loudly on the door. Uzi observed George Hemmings' face as he slid back into the seat next to him. Definitely not pleased.

In a few moments the door opened a crack. Was that a young woman standing there? It was hard to be certain. Jones said a few inaudible words, the person stepped back, opened the door, let Jones in, and then closed and locked the door behind her.

The three occupants of the car were silent, but all eyes were on that door.

Eight minutes later, the door opened again. Mathilda Jones walked through, turned around, reached back into the dark opening, and shook someone's hand. Uzi thought it was the hand of an older woman. Jones then came directly to the car and opened the door.

"I hope I didn't keep you waiting too long," was all the explanation that they got.

## 55

*Thursday morning*

## THE GALILEE

Beth only glanced once at her friend as they left the town of Cana. Later, she told herself, accepting the fact that Mattie did not want to talk about her little adventure in the presence of two strangers. Well, it could wait. Beth was here for something else. She turned to look out at the hills surrounding them as they drove toward Nazareth. They were old hills made of limestone, hills that had witnessed much, had been through much.

When Beth saw the sign pointing to Nazareth, she felt moved. There's something here, she thought, and observed her friend who was watching and listening. Be a poet, Beth, she told herself. Be Beth.

"In most countries, main roads will lead to cities. In Israel main roads often lead to the holy places."

Uzi told them that Nazareth was not an Old Testament town, that it must have been a tiny village in the time of Jesus, that its importance comes from the Christians who settled there and kept the memory of Jesus' childhood alive.

However, the present town of Nazareth seemed quite sizable. But because of the surrounding natural hills, Beth could sense at least a little of what it must have been like when Jesus was a boy. Which one was this Jesus? Luke or Matthew? The priest or the king? Or were there two boys living here? Mattie had certainly complicated things.

They were descending through what seemed a rather prosperous town toward the main section below them. Uzi slowed down. "We are passing a place called Mary's Well. You see, it's like a little fountain. It used to be a well. That's a Greek Orthodox church over there called St. Gabriel."

A little farther on, Uzi parked the car and they walked through a marketplace that seemed to sell everything—shoes, clothes, food. Uzi told them as they maneuvered their way through the crowds that they were going to see a modern church funded by many nations and built from 1959 until 1969. The new church was built over Mary's childhood home, "by tradition," Uzi told them, where the Angel announced to Mary that she was carrying a son who would be called Jesus. It was built over the ruins of an eleventh-century Crusader church which was in turn built over a fifth-century Byzantine basilica which in turn was built over an earlier Jewish-Christian synagogue-church. "We have a lot of history here in Israel," Uzi said, with a laugh. "You have to have a very good memory."

"You Israelis seem to have that in abundance," Beth said.

Uzi grinned at the two women. "The Crusader church was destroyed by the Berbers in 1263. In 1620, this place was turned over to the Franciscans who take care of it to this day."

Beth loved the facade built of stone with bands of writing in Latin and depictions of the four Gospel writers carved shallowly into the stone. At that moment she wished Eric was with her. He would love this, and she felt a twinge of guilt at having insisted that she come to Israel alone. Why had she done that? But if she hadn't she would not have met Gidon nor Yehuda ben Yehuda and she felt suddenly uncertain. Never mind, she told herself sternly. You are here with a purpose. Pay attention.

The church inside was very large, with great concrete pillars, built less like a church for worship, Beth thought, and more like a shrine. In front of the altar, there was a railed-off area open to the level below. From there one could peer down into what was the house of the girl Mary. Another house of Mary's parents, Beth thought and looked at her friend who was staring down at it with an earnest expression on her face. Beth could hear singing.

"That's from the church above, where the actual praying is going on. Various groups come with their own ministers or priests," Uzi told her. "You can see all around, on the walls of the church, plaques from the different countries donating to the construction of this church. The United States is the third one from here. Take a walk around and look at the plaques."

So Beth did. Each plaque was of a different style. The one from the U.S. was of a woman whose body and clothes were cut with machine-like angles, very hard-looking, against a colorful metal background. How very American, she thought. What would Eric think of this? Maybe she would bring him back here for a visit. Maybe they would come here on their honeymoon. That thought startled her. But she was going to marry Eric. Of course she was. Then she thought of Gidon saying, "Whatever you are willing to give me." And then of her friend, Mattie, who, she knew, was interested in Gidon. She shook those thoughts out of her head and walked around and looked at each plaque.

Beth was impressed with the Church, but other than finding it a wonderful commemoration of the event, and loving the feel of the Galilee, she didn't sense any particular connection to it, well maybe just a little longing.

She looked around for Mattie and found her once again staring down at the place of the Annunciation. And then she caught sight of George Hemmings. He was watching Beth with cool, even calculating eyes. It gave her a start. He waved at her then, smiled, and his expression changed.

They finally descended into the caves. "People were living underneath, under the ground, in the rocks," Uzi told them. They walked for a while through the cave-like Grotto of the Annunciation with its altar and crosses. They saw the baptistery of the older church, and then they ascended.

"Come, we will go to the church built over the carpentry shop of Joseph. It's just a few feet from here," Uzi said.

## ⊰56⊱

*Thursday morning*

## THE GALILEE

After they left the two churches, Mattie walked with Beth and the two men back through the marketplace. Beth saw a scarf that she wanted to buy for her daughter, and Uzi bargained with the merchant for her. George claimed that he had bought all the souvenirs he needed in Jerusalem the day he had met Beth. Mattie bought nothing, she was too filled with this day. With her little adventure too.

It was very hot, and Uzi insisted that they all buy bottled water for their trip to Megiddo. They then returned to the car and soon were traveling down through the hills into the Valley of Jezreel.

"Didn't you say your brother's kibbutz was near here?" Hemmings said to Mattie.

"Not far. Sde Gedalia. Beth and I are going there Sunday for a wedding," Mattie nodded, trying to feel warmth toward Hemmings. "I'm looking forward to seeing their kibbutz." The truth is, she resented Hemmings being here, resented his having invaded their little party. She wished it had been just herself and Beth. Perhaps she should have told Beth. But she hadn't. Now she warned herself to be nice.

"Oh, you've never visited there before?"

"No. This is my first trip to Israel. After the wedding we'll move over to my family's kibbutz. They're full up with wedding guests right now, and besides, we wanted to sightsee, particularly the Christian sites." She was in the Holy Land, and she was being chatty. She didn't want to be chatty. She was in the Holy Land and she wanted to stare in silence out of the window toward these hallowed hills.

Be nice, Mattie. Change. Share.

"Your first trip and already you have friends, not only Israelis, but Arabs," George said.

"Friends of a friend," Mattie said. She was not going to say more. She was certainly not going to explain about Mahmud to a stranger. She had had a little adventure and she was feeling good about it. Very good about it. And now it was over. And now she could turn her attention to this day. If only she could go off by herself and let the places she had been to reverberate in her. If only she could let her imagination have free rein. Had she been here before? If only she didn't have to make polite conversation, to listen to others. And then she took herself to task. She was here to learn to be with others, to let go of her own need for isolation and solitude. Observe now, she told herself. Recollect in tranquillity later.

There was something about this area. Something about Israel. She was being drawn into it, back, back into it. How could she not? The sheer magnitude of what had happened here thrilled her. You could pierce through the air and again and again come to layers of history. She was an archaeologist, only her soil was the atmosphere around her, and her tools were words and imagination. She ached to dig, to find the hidden strata, to uncover, to discover, to see and then to write. She envied Beth her quest. To have lived here before. Yes. Yes. But why only Beth? What about others in Beth's circle? Yes, why not she herself?

Take it easy, she warned herself. Let it come to you. Don't force this issue because you want Beth's déjà vu. This may have nothing to do with you. But she didn't believe it. Something was here and it was familiar.

If only she didn't have to make polite conversation.

Oh, well, that was part of it, too. Part of her reclaiming herself just as the Israelis had reclaimed this land. She would be nice to Mr. Hemmings. She would try to be nice. But right now...

How beautiful the Galilee was. Despite all its wars, there was a quintessential peace here, as if the world had begun here, from this land, had taken it as its model. And, oh, there was so much to see and experience, and she could stay in this land as long as she wanted. Before leaving this country she would rent a car and come back to this area alone. Yes, yes, that's what she would do. She felt elated as if old burdens and fears were about to drop away with just the tiniest bit of a nudge. This land is magical, she thought. And I need magic.

Uzi picked up his narration, "We're heading south through the Jezreel Valley, then west toward Megiddo. West, not too far, is the Mediterranean. You can go from the Sea of Galilee to the Mediterranean in not much more than an hour, depending on the traffic of course, which by the way, can be pretty terrible."

"Do you know what Megiddo is famous for?" Uzi asked them a little while later.

"Not really," Beth said

"The final battle, Armageddon," Mattie said.

"It's a fortress town built by King Solomon," George Hemmings said.

The Jezreel Valley was fairly flat and filled with prosperous-looking farming communities. "This is one of Israel's main agricultural areas," Uzi told them. "Over there," Uzi pointed to a hill that stood alone, "is one of the sites where some say the transfiguration took place. It's only one of the places. Another is Mount Hermon. The town in this valley is Afula. You can see the mountains of Gilboa east, and over there south are the Samaritan Mountains," Uzi continued his narration as he drove them through groves of olives, freshly turned soil, and cotton fields.

The land of the bible, Mattie thought, gratified. And I'm here.

## 57
### *Thursday morning*
### THE GALILEE

Beth listened contentedly to Uzi's narration. She liked this place far better than the Judean wilderness. She was not a desert person, had to work to see a desert's stark beauty. But she could see herself living in this area. She didn't sense that she had once, but this modern Beth would rather live in the Galilean hills than in the dry Judean hills, with its moon-like landscape. She tried to imagine that she had once lived here—why not?—and had gone to Jerusalem with hundreds of others on a pilgrimage for the Passover celebration and had witnessed the Crucifixion there. Perhaps it was why she felt a touch of antipathy for Jerusalem and its surroundings. She was amused that she could think these ideas today, without feeling the least bit crazy.

"This valley was all swampland seventy-five years ago. The original *chalutzim,* the pioneers, came here and drained the swamp and planted the land. Many died of malaria and other sicknesses," Uzi said. "But they carved out our homeland."

As they approached Megiddo, Uzi told them, "Megiddo is very famous as a dig. It holds the record. It has twenty-five cities being built one on top of the other, more than any other known place. The most interesting level is the city built by King Solomon three thousand years ago. And that is the fifth layer and the sixth layer.

It means twenty layers had to be taken off to get to it. Actually, Megiddo dates as far back as the stone age, five or six thousand years before your Jesus. The name of the city, Megiddo, comes from one of the kings that fought against Joshua."

They went inside a modern building first. There they stood around the model of King Solomon's city and heard a talk. Then they began their walk around the plateau. The valley stretched out below them and Beth could see why Megiddo was strategic. So this is the place of the Last Battle, the battle between good and evil. Looking out over the valley gave her an eerie feeling. And despite the heat, she had a sudden chill. Mattie was standing not far from her, also looking across the valley, a dark expression on her face. She feels it too, Beth thought. Whatever *it* was.

"This is one of the city-states that Joshua conquered," Uzi told them. "David's time was a time of war, of conquest. Solomon's time was one of peace, so he built towns and cities all over the country. Solomon never lived here, maybe one of his vassal kings. Still, Megiddo was rebuilt here on his authority and large numbers of his horses and chariots were stabled here."

Beth was glad that they had brought the water. George Hemmings looked hot and she began to worry a bit that this trip was too much for him. She asked if he was all right.

"Fine, fine," the man said, "I'm enjoying myself immensely, couldn't enjoy it more," he said. But he didn't look like he was and Beth felt a little uneasy.

They saw the Canaanite temple, palaces, storehouses, the famous stables of Solomon, then walked around the plateau, listening to Uzi's explanation of Megiddo's water cisterns.

"Come," Uzi told them. "You must see this. This is very special."

He took them to the edge of the plateau and led them into a cave, actually a long descending tunnel, carved out of the rock. It was dimly lit and there was a formidable set of wooden steps. Beth couldn't see the bottom. She was suddenly hit with a sense of foreboding as she stared into the blue light and down the endless stairs. The rocks on either side looked menacing, as if they were waiting to clutch or crush her. She shivered, wanted to protest and turn back. Ridiculous, she told herself. This is not like you. It's just a touch of claustrophobia.

"Come, friends," Uzi said. "I promise you it is much cooler inside." He took Beth by the arm and led her rather rapidly down the steep steps.

Down, down, they headed, but Uzi was walking much too fast. They were leaving Mattie and George behind. The walls were too close, the lamps too dim above them. Get hold of yourself, Beth told herself. These wooden steps are secure enough. And these rocks have been motionless for centuries.

She loosed herself from Uzi's grip and started to descend more slowly than the sprightly, red-haired young man in front of her. George and Mattie seemed to be falling behind. Well, George was older. And Mattie, she saw, when she turned to look up, was being solicitous. "Wait, wait!" Beth called to Uzi. How could he expect Hemmings to keep up this pace?

"Plenty of time," Uzi called back to them. "This tunnel leads to an old secret cistern where the precious water was once kept. They could descend here and get it during a siege," He was still descending rapidly. "It's a hundred and eighty-three steps down, but the way we're going it's only eighty up."

The steps were very steep and Beth found her knees quivering. This sudden uneasiness is stupid, she told herself, hanging on to the rail with both hands. Still, there was something about the narrowness of the tunnel with its wet stone walls, and the fact that they seemed to be descending into the bowels of the earth and she couldn't see the bottom, that increased her anxiety level. What was the matter with her? She had never been claustrophobic before. And this was not the descent into hell. Only an old watering hole.

Beth tried to breathe evenly and to think about what it must have been like to descend to the bottom during a time of siege and bring water all the way back up to the top, to the fort. But her mind was not feeling the least bit creative. She was too busy willing her legs to move down yet another step. She knew she was walking faster than Mattie and George but she had to stay close to Uzi who was their leader, who would save them in case of anything.

Beth saw Uzi waiting at the bottom for her, just near where the steps led upwards again. She landed next to him with a sigh of relief.

He grinned at her. She was about to scold him for his too rapid descent when he spoke to her in a voice barely audible. "Listen, there is no time to explain. You must be very careful of the man who calls himself George Hemmings. He could mean you harm. Don't at anytime be alone with him. And don't go off with him again. When we go to get the car, we all go together. Don't offer to wait at the bottom of the hill with Hemmings. If both of you women stay with me, you'll be safe. I'm sorry there's no time to say more."

Beth was startled, and her stomach did a flip-flop. Before she could respond, the young man had begun his ascent toward an aperture of light and she could hear Mattie and Hemmings a few steps from the bottom. How did Uzi, whom Hemmings had met just by chance this morning, know anything about him? Beth was both baffled and alarmed.

"Those Ancients did not have it easy," Hemmings said when he finally landed at the bottom. "And now the ascent. I think Israelis like to torture their guests a bit. It's interesting, but I could have missed this part."

"Oh, but it's fascinating, don't you think?" Mattie was breathless. "Beth, what's the matter? You look green!"

"Green?" Beth's laughter sounded hollow. "It must be this crazy blue light. But if you've had enough, let's get out of here." She could see Uzi waiting for them halfway up the stairs.

"Wouldn't this make a wonderful place for the climax of a mystery novel!" Mattie said.

"The rescue or the murder?" Beth asked with a shiver.

"I haven't thought that far yet," Mattie said, with a laugh.

"Let's get out of here," Beth said, and started up the stairs.

"Only eighty-some stairs above us," Hemmings said.

## 58

*Thursday morning*

## THE SHEFELA

Yehuda put the phone down and returned to the table where he was having breakfast with Malkah.

"Gidon wants to go tomorrow to see Asher, instead of Sunday."

"Why?"

"Who knows? Business, he says. On Shabbat, I asked? He said, yes. So I said, 'Of course'." He stared at his coffee.

"What are you thinking?"

"I'm thinking that it has something to do with this woman he likes."

"Your poet?"

"He said she would come to lunch or dinner when we are at Sharone and David's."

"So? He likes the American poet. It's not the first."

"She's a very nice lady."

"Nice ladies have affairs, too, *ketzel.*"

"What do you know about it?"

"Don't be so sure, you old goat?"

"What? You're going to make a confession?"

"Don't be so sure. Women have eyes, too."

"Are you going to take away all my faith in the human species?"

"How much do you have, my love?"

"In you, everything, in others, they are only as good as they have to be."

"No."

"No?"

"No, now you only talk. You love this crazy species."

"I love Jews."

"That's what I meant."

He put down his cup, walked around the table, and gave her a kiss on the cheek. "I'm going to visit Shmuel."

"Good."

Yehuda stopped at the door. "He's younger than me by two years."

"Sickness."

"The two of us will talk."

"You'll talk. He'll sleep."

"It doesn't matter."

Yehuda walked out into the unseasonably hot weather. He didn't mind it. He loved the heat. His childhood home had been cold. Cold colored all his early memories. Russia and cold. Here in his beloved land it was warm. Here the colors were vivid, not pale and gray as in his old homeland. Russia, his homeland? Never! Israel was his homeland. This lush land was God-kissed, no question, if there were such a being.

Shmuel lived about a ten-minute slow walk from Yehuda's apartment. He was the father of one of their members and had lived in America before he and his wife joined their son here, a dozen years ago. Unlike most of the members of this kibbutz, Shmuel was religious, not crazy, not extreme, but religious. When his wife was alive, the kibbutz had provided them with kosher food and she had cooked for the two of them. But she had died last year and now he ate vegetarian, occasionally fish, brought from the dining room. Shmuel was dying slowly—bad heart, bad liver, bad kidneys. The will to live had left him when his wife had passed on. That didn't surprise Yehuda. He couldn't imagine life without Malkah. Thank God, she was younger by ten years. If the angel of death was kind, he would go first.

Shmuel was lying in front of his rooms on a lounge chair in the shade. His walker stood nearby. He seemed to be asleep, wrapped in blankets even though the day was warm.

When you're old, you are always cold, Yehuda thought, especially if there is no longer anyone to warm your bed.

He sat down in the chair next to the sleeping man. He shook him gently by the shoulder. "It's me, Shmuel," he said to him in Yiddish. "Wake up and talk."

The eyes fluttered. "Yehuda?"

"Yes. Yehuda."

"So tell me the news."

Little by little Yehuda went over the items that he had read that morning in the newspaper. Shmuel closed his eyes but Yehuda knew he listened. After Yehuda told him about the latest efforts in the peace process, Shmuel said, "They are going to give away too much."

"You can't have peace without compromise."

"We shouldn't trust them. They will take what they can get and then push us into the sea."

"We have to take risks."

Shmuel opened his watery eyes and fixed them on Yehuda. "This is a peace made by old men. Then they will die and leave their grandchildren to fight for their lives. You'll see, Yehuda, you'll see. You would have done better if you were Prime Minister. A poet's mind is what they need. Imagination is what they need. What else is in the papers?"

"The old Rebbe is still alive. He had a stroke but he is still alive. There are signs all over Israel proclaiming him the Messiah."

Shmuel opened his eyes again and nodded at Yehuda, "Jews are fools. They believe in a dream."

"What dream Shmuel?"

"The Messiah is only a dream."

"You don't believe in the Messiah, Shmuel? How is that possible for a believing Jew? All your life you went to the synagogue."

"Until I came here to God's land. I've been thinking and thinking." Shmuel turned his head in Yehuda's direction and fixed his rheumy eyes on him. "What else is there to do lying here?"

Yehuda nodded.

"Whenever there were troubles we Jews dreamed of a Messiah, but did one ever come? Never, not in all our years of exile, not in Spain, not during the pogroms, not during the Holocaust, not during the War of Independence. The Messiah is only a dream and we have to depend on ourselves. No one will save us. Only ourselves, Yehuda." And he closed his eyes, and Yehuda knew that now he slept.

Walking back to his rooms Yehuda wondered how a religious man could come to the end of his days and no longer believe in the coming of the Messiah, a three thousand-year-old dream of the Jews. "Only ourselves, Yehuda." So he, too, had always believed. But now there were his two angels. What did they think about all of this?

He would have to ask them.

When he got the courage.

## 59
*Thursday afternoon*
## TIBERIAS

He was not happy about this assignment, not at all. This was not up his alley. But he had been pressed into it at the last minute, only a day before he was supposed to leave for home. His wife Betty had been particularly unhappy. He was supposed to be back for their granddaughter's birthday, and now this. But he couldn't say no, considering the request had come from high up. He hoped they would get someone else into the country in a few days to handle the situation. They were definitely understaffed here. Especially now when this peace initiative, with all its ramifications, had used up all available personnel. So it was up to him to stay close to the Layton woman and now, of course, to Jones.

George Hemmings and the two women had just finished a meal of St. Peter's Fish, salad and potatoes. Seated at an outdoor restaurant overlooking the sea in the town of Tiberias, the three were now drinking a dark, rich coffee and eating dessert. Uzi had found some friends, other drivers no doubt, and was sitting several tables away engaged in his own conversation. Hemmings' talk with the women during the meal had revealed little. Trying to be gregarious, he had spoken of his family and about his export-import business. Mathilda Jones had talked about poetry, about life in Big Sur. He imagined her a rather good teacher, a woman easily given over to her work.

And a loner probably. She hadn't mentioned a husband or children. Quite pretty really when she was talking. However, there was something shy and old-fashioned about her—the lack of make-up, the long hair. Was it deliberate, an attempt to be unobtrusive, to go unnoticed? She hadn't been his primary objective, no, that had been Layton. But there was that odd episode in Cana. What did it signify? What was in that package? And from whom had it been sent? He had carefully noted the Cana address, that should be a start.

Actually, Layton had done nothing out of the ordinary in the days he had kept an eye on her, except spend time with Gidon ben David. His people knew ben David had once been the Prime Minister's man, part of an elite group. Had ben David's retirement been a charade? Had the package that Jones delivered in Cana really been a favor done for Layton? And what had gotten into Layton suddenly? She had been so friendly this morning. But during lunch she smiled a lot yet hardly spoke. She looked a bit distracted, a bit pale. Perhaps she had gotten too much sun. It was unseasonably hot in Israel for October. Everybody was talking about it, complaining about it. Luckily, here in Tiberias near the water there was a nice breeze and the view was spectacular. But Layton's reticence made him wary. Did she suspect him? And, if so, how did it happen?

Uzi.

Of course.

How convenient of him to show up just at the moment when his car had failed. And wasn't that mechanical failure also convenient? It seemed likely he was compromised. Well, he would try to get as much information as possible and then get out. He would like to be on a plane no later than tomorrow.

"You must have planned this trip quite a while ago," Hemmings directed his words to Beth.

"No," Beth said, but didn't go on.

He wished he knew what it was he was supposed to find out. If his bosses knew, they didn't let on. "Fish, that's your job, nothing else, nothing dangerous," they had instructed him. "Find out as much as you can about Layton's relationship to ben David. How long has she really known him? Get her talking. Get both women talking. Tape it all. We'll take it from there." And he had tried. However, this wasn't what he had been trained to do. He had never been more than a courier. Well, no use crying over spilled milk, this was his assignment now.

"I've had my tickets for about a month," Mattie said, "but Beth's trip was completely spontaneous."

"Oh?" Hemmings turned back to Beth with what he hoped was a friendly, fatherly smile.

"Nothing out of the ordinary," Beth said, and gave him a small smile in return. "I was in France traveling with a friend and since I didn't have to be home quite yet, I decided to visit the Holy Land."

That much his bosses knew.

"I think it was all those churches we visited in Europe that piqued my curiosity."

"So you two didn't plan to meet here?" Hemmings raised his eyebrows."

"No, that was serendipity," Mattie said, and explained.

"Then you know no one here in Israel?" George asked Beth.

"Well, no one except Mattie's brother and his wife."

"How about the man who found you in the old city of Jerusalem and who seemed so happy to see you?" He knew he was pressing, but he had his instructions.

Beth's face colored slightly. "Oh, him, well, yes, now I know him..." she hesitated for a moment. "He was my seat partner on the plane from Paris, and he's been most helpful to me here." And then she added, "He lives in Tel Aviv with his wife and children."

"A businessman?"

"Yes."

That she was reluctant to speak about ben David was interesting considering the time they had spent together.

"Gidon ben David is the nephew of Yehuda ben Yehuda," Mattie said. "He took Beth to meet him."

"The statesman?" Of course Hemmings knew him.

"And poet. Ben Yehuda's a national icon," Mattie said.

"Of course. I remember him from Israel's early days. He was in the cabinet, if I am recalling that correctly."

"Yes, an ardent voice for Israel to the world and a voice of conscience inside Israel," Mattie flung her hair back.

"What a piece of luck—to have met ben Yehuda. One can't help wondering how he feels about the peace process? Did he by any chance mention it?" Hemmings asked Beth. He was not doing this very smoothly.

"We didn't talk about the peace process."

Hemmings forced a laugh. "I thought everyone talked about the peace process these days."

"We talked about poetry and...and...life."

"He must have been very stimulating."

"Yes, very."

There was a silence which Mattie broke, "I've kept close watch on Israel and its politics from the beginning."

He looked at her with interest.

But Mattie wasn't looking at him, she was toying with her food, "Well, I have a brother here, you see. How could I not? And then nieces and nephews..."

"So you're a Zionist?" George asked Jones.

"No, no, not in any literal sense, if that's what you mean. I've never been active in any Zionist organization. You do know that I'm not Jewish," and she explained to him about her family.

"Well, Jewish or not you must at least be pro-Israel, with so much family here," George said, when she finished her tale.

"What do you mean pro-Israel?" Beth suddenly demanded.

Careful. Don't push the wrong buttons. "I mean," he turned to her, "pro-Israel in these current peace talks."

"Two peoples, both with claims to the same land. They're going to have to work something out," Mattie said. "What other way is there?"

"Your brother feels the same?"

"Of course he does. He's fought in the wars. His children have fought. And his grandchildren are now in the army. No sane person wants to see yet another generation go to war."

"And what about your friend, whom you met on the plane?" Hemmings asked Beth.

"The same."

"I suppose you both will write about your impressions here when you get home."

"I hope to do some writing," Mattie said, "perhaps a novel."

"I didn't come here to write," Beth said.

I wish you hadn't said that, George Hemmings thought. I wish you had said you were here looking for material for a book, or for poetry. That would at least cover up your lack of knowledge of Christianity. No, you are up to something. And it's not being a Christian pilgrim. And I'd love to find out what. He put his coffee cup down, wiped his mouth with his napkin and said, "Shall we go on with our sightseeing?"

"I'm wondering. . ." Beth covered her face with her hands for a moment.

"Beth, what is it? Is it too much sun?" Mattie asked her.

"I am feeling a little funny." Beth said, and then turned and stared George Hemmings squarely in the face. "I wonder, would it be so terrible if we canceled our trip this afternoon?" She touched Mattie's arm, "You and I could go out again tomorrow. Right now, I need a little rest. Of course, this shuts you out, George," she gave him a polite smile, "and I'm so sorry to do this to you after you've been so kind, but I am feeling a little woozy and I'm not sure walking around in the hot sun this afternoon would be the best thing for me. I just hadn't expected it to be so hot in October. Is that so terrible?" The words tumbled out of her.

George Hemmings was taken by surprise. "Of course not." What else could he say? "Foolish of me to try to cram so much into one day."

It had to be the driver. He had definitely found some moment to speak to her. Where?

"Thanks for being so understanding."

In that damned water cistern in Megiddo. Well, how much did his bosses expect him to find out, or to do, with the Israelis hanging about?

"It was such a lovely morning," Beth was speaking quickly, not looking at him. "We so much appreciate your taking us. I hope this doesn't ruin your day and that you will go on with the tour as planned."

"Come to think of it, I'm a bit tired myself," he told them. "Perhaps I'll take the rest of the day off, and see about getting a new car."

"But you must let us pay for this lunch," Mattie said. And she motioned for the waiter.

"But I invited you!" George Hemmings protested a little.

"Now you must let us do something for you, a small token of our appreciation for your kindness today."

George Hemmings acquiesced graciously. "Then I thank you very much."

When they reached the kibbutz motel, they said their good-byes to Uzi. Walking away from the car, George Hemmings said to the women, "Perhaps I'll see you on the beach a bit later?"

"Perhaps," Beth said and extended her hand. "And thank you again."

That finishes it, George Hemmings thought, moving away from the women. They'll have to put someone else on the job. This simply wasn't up his alley. Perhaps if he could get out of Israel by tonight he would make that birthday party tomorrow.

## 60

*Thursday afternoon*

## THE GALILEE

"Elizabeth Layton, what is going on?" Mattie asked her, after they entered their room and after she had closed and locked the door. She plopped down in the armchair and waited for an explanation.

"You're asking *me* what's going on? What was that package thing all about in Cana?"

"Oh, that," Mattie waved her hand dismissively. "I brought some money in for the mother of an old student of mine, a young man who is currently living in San Francisco. A very gifted poet."

"Mahmud Aziz. You're still seeing Mahmud Aziz."

Mattie blushed, then smiled. "He keeps in contact. I'm . . . I'm not interested."

"Because he's only thirty?"

"That, but more than that. Anyway, I saw him for coffee in San Francisco, and he asked me to do him a little favor. I was a bit reluctant at first. . ."

"He asked you to bring money into Israel? Weren't you suspicious?"

"For his family, not for anything else. He promised. It wasn't very much."

"But you're still not sure about him."

Mattie shrugged. "Mahmud's politics are his business, not mine. I merely agreed to do a friend a favor. Nothing special about it and certainly nothing illegal."

"But it made you uncomfortable."

"Actually, I rather enjoyed it. My own little adventure. Sorry for all the Mata Hari stuff today, but frankly, I didn't think it was Uzi's or George's business."

"That was probably a wise decision."

Mattie raised her eyebrows.

"I'm not sure we should trust George Hemmings."

"Not trust George Hemmings? Why, for heavens sake?"

Beth sat down on the edge of her bed facing Mattie and told her what Uzi had said at the bottom of the stairs in the cistern at Megiddo.

"Oh, my God, that is weird," Mattie got up and began to pace around the room. "But that doesn't make sense! How does Uzi know George Hemmings?"

"I don't know. But you should have heard Uzi's voice, Mattie, he sounded positively urgent. It sent ice right through me. Maybe it was that eerie tunnel..."

"So no sunstroke?"

"No, but the wind got knocked out of my sails, it was so unexpected. It started me thinking. I do keep bumping into Hemmings. Funny that he should be here at this little out-of-the-way guest house."

"He did ask a lot of questions at lunch," Mattie said.

"I thought so too. I don't know what to make of any of this."

Mattie shook her head. "Somehow, Beth, things just seem to happen to you."

"You think Uzi might be a little...well, a little nuts?"

Mattie sat down next to Beth. "Maybe just mischievous. Or maybe it's part of the tour package. Give the tourists a little taste of mystery and intrigue. Megiddo was certainly a good place for it."

"Maybe. Hard to think of Hemmings as sinister, or as a spy type."

"Don't think in clichés, Beth. Spies should be as average as possible."

"Well, then Gidon can't be a spy either because he's too obviously typecasting."

The two women laughed.

Beth said, "This is all too ridiculous. I opt for the 'give the tourists a thrill' theory. At any rate, I'm glad for the change in plans."

"Me too. Beth, let's rent a car and drive around the Sea of Galilee ourselves tomorrow, just the two of us, no guides, no kindly or sinister strangers. I enjoyed the guided tour, but. . ."

"Just what I was hoping to do. Why should we worry about George Hemmings? He said he would be busy with business tomorrow."

"Right, and after that he's on his way back to the States. And what can he do if we run into him at dinner or on the beach? Kidnap you and sell you into white slavery?"

Beth started to giggle.

"After all, I'm with you. What could happen to two able-bodied women together?"

"Not a single thing," Beth agreed.

"Oh, Beth, I should have known that hanging around with you would produce all the adventure I needed. I think I'm going to write a novel after all," and she gave Beth a hug, then whacked her hair out of both their faces.

The two women napped, then went to find out about renting a car for the next day. In the late afternoon they changed into swimsuits and walked down to the beach. Beth read her book on the history of Israel during the Second Temple period and Mattie wrote in her notebook.

George Hemmings was not on the beach that afternoon, nor did they see him that night at dinner.

## 61
*Thursday afternoon*
## TIBERIAS

Uzi told his boss, among other things, about Jones' delivery of the package in Cana. He gave him the address.

"What about Hemmings?" his boss asked him.

"He's no Christian pilgrim."

"What was his reaction to the unscheduled stop in Cana?"

"He seemed surprised by it, and quite perturbed."

"Do you think he expected the package to be given to him?"

"I think he had something else in mind altogether."

"Like what?"

"Didn't you say something about kidnapping, about causing an incident?"

His boss was silent.

"What's going on?" Uzi asked. "Layton seemed as surprised by the stop-off in Cana as Hemmings."

"Maybe more than one agenda?"

"That's how I read it. Sorry if my warning to Layton took me off the case, but I felt she needed to be warned. Do you have someone else to take over?"

"We'll find someone."

"Did I make a mistake? Should I have kept quiet?"

"I don't know, Uzi. It was your call. You were the man on the scene. Time will tell, won't it?"

"Yes," Uzi said, and hoped that he hadn't screwed up.

## 62

*Thursday night*

## THE GALILEE

"Somebody got to her, most likely the driver. He was conveniently there for hire when my car was conveniently out of commission... Somewhere on the trip she froze up. Now she's suspicious. Jones on the other hand was very talkative... Small talk... No, it needs to be somebody else... I should think it was obvious... Okay, one more day, but I suggest you hurry. I'm supposed to be in Tiberias all day tomorrow and if they see me... As discreetly as I can.

## 63
*Thursday night*
## TEL AVIV

"The drop-off took place today, Gidon."

"Where?"

"Cana, with Layton, Hemmings and our man all in the car waiting while she delivered the package. Pretty blatant."

"Or pretty innocent."

"She was in the house about ten minutes and then she came out and they went on with their trip, which by the way they didn't complete."

"Why not?"

"Uzi took it into his head to warn Layton off Hemmings. Apparently she listened."

"The Cana house, whose is it?"

"We'll know in the morning. How soon can you get up there?"

"*Shabbat.*"

"Not tomorrow."

"Now you want me up there early? It's not possible. I've made arrangements. Besides, it might put the women off if I come too early. You have someone watching them?"

"Yes."

"It will have to do until I get up there. So is there a connection between Hemmings and Jones?"

"Uzi thinks not. Jones pretty much stayed away from

Hemmings—except in the Megiddo cistern tunnel. But Uzi opted to talk to Layton privately, so he left Jones and Hemmings alone. Gidon, we would like you to find out what's going on."

"I'll be up there Saturday."

"Not tomorrow?"

"No. I've already rearranged this trip once. Best I stick with Saturday."

## 64
## *Thursday night*
## THE GALILEE

The lights were out, Beth was lying on her bed writing in her journal. She could hear Mattie's gentle breathing from the other bed. But Beth couldn't sleep. She was too full of thoughts to sleep. She wrote:

"If I don't put that incident with Uzi out of my mind concerning George Hemmings, this whole day will be lost and that is far more disruptive to my purpose here than any danger old George Hemmings could prove to be. . .

"This day was for the most part quite wonderful. The Galilee is a special region. As different from the south as night is from day, or I should say it the other way around. Because if Judea is the night, then the Galilee is surely the day. Okay, let us have Mary living in Nazareth. And whether there was one child or two, I don't know, but Nazareth is the place for a child to grow up. Yes, let's put Jesus there. I would have to say that Nazareth spoke to me the most today. Not the actual city, which is sizable, but the hills around it. And the light and the air.

"Nazareth was small in Christ's time, that's documented. Mattie thinks it might have been a religious commune, some place that had its monks, or whatever, and a lay community around it. A bit like the Essene community at Qumran. And Jesus among them. That's not documented.

"And perhaps Alicia and I in some earlier life among them too.

"I can't believe I'm thinking this way, but that's what I was thinking this morning moving through those hills. And then on that fateful Passover, perhaps we were among the pilgrims who went to Jerusalem to celebrate the holy days and there witnessed the death of Jesus. Our friend? Our teacher? Who knows? This is of course all my imagination, not a memory. But who is to say, and I should know, that the imagination isn't as real as this sense-perceptible world? And maybe I've been fighting Paul Burrows' ideas for too long and he's right and the imagination is a gateway into a spiritual reality. And a writer, if she enters deeply enough, can come through her own imagination to the other side. One's own personal imagination first, then without hardly noticing it one passes through a door or gateway and one is someplace else, some objective place and only the pictures are one's own, not what stands behind them...

"I know... I know... This isn't like me, but I'm in a room on the edge of a consummate sea and I can think and write these words. Mattie could be right, that the gods, the angelic beings, write their thoughts and pictures into us and our world as metaphor, tell us their secrets as metaphor. Paul thought so too. Surely no poet would turn away from the imagination. Are we as confined to our own individual minds as we moderns like to think? Perhaps there is a world just beyond a threshold that our senses can't reach, and behind the pictures our imaginations create are realities of a spiritual nature, and perhaps Mattie's experience of Nazareth as a small religious and lay community is not so off the wall. And if reincarnation is true, and it is an old and venerable belief, not to be denigrated by the likes of me, where are all those who lived at the time of Christ? Are some of them among us now? Could I be one?"

Beth swung her feet off of the bed, took her notebook, turned off the lights so as not to disturb Mattie's sleep, and went into the bathroom. She drank a glass of water and sat down on the closed toilet seat and wrote for another half hour before she finally returned to bed.

## ⋄65⋄

*Friday morning*

## THE GALILEE

"This is so beautiful," Mattie said, as she and Beth were approaching the Mount of the Beatitudes in their rented Renault. She felt inordinately happy. In front of them were the buildings and gardens of the convent, behind them the sea. "Now I know why they call it the 'sea of seas,'" Mattie said. "It's perfect."

And Beth, after steering the small car around a curve, looked out and agreed. "I don't know if I can find a clue to my past life. Perhaps I expected a little too much from this journey. But I can imagine living here," she said.

"The Galilee is like a little memory of paradise, isn't it?" Mattie said. "And yet the scale is so human."

As the small car chugged up the hill, Mattie read out loud from their guidebook about the Mount of the Beatitudes and the chapel that had been built in 1937 by Antonio Barluzzi. Beth parked the car and the two women got out.

"This landscape must be glorious," Mattie said, with a sweeping gesture, "when the rains come and make everything green, and the wildflowers spring up. What an exquisite spot for the Sermon on the Mount."

"I agree. Oh, Mattie, isn't this much prettier than the Judean wilderness, even than Jerusalem?"

"I don't know. I haven't seen much of the Judean wilderness yet, and a desert does have it's own stark beauty."

"I could do without it," Beth said.

They toured the little octagonal chapel. Above them, circling the fine dome, were eight colored windows inscribed with the text of the Beatitudes. Mattie's eyes turned often to stare out through the glass windows that opened on all sides to the hills, and also down to the Sea of Galilee. She wanted to let her imagination loose, let it fly over the hills, skim over the top of the water, and return. She wanted to imagine herself and Beth sitting on the hillside with many others, listening to the Master, wanted to hear him saying the now familiar words, "Blessed are the beggars for the spirit, in themselves they shall find the kingdom of heaven." She wanted to say to Beth, "Perhaps we were both here, not only you and Alicia, but me too." But she didn't. Like a falconer, she quietly retrieved her imagination, calling it back into the lovely octagonal room.

After touring the chapel, the two women walked the colonnaded portico, circling it. Though there were several bus-loads of tourists, the chapel and porch were serene and quiet. Mattie turned now and again to watch her friend. If only Beth could strive for and appreciate what was different in others, in history, and in ideas. If only she could stop looking for the world and others to mirror back what she already knew and believed, then maybe... But her friend was struggling. And that was good. That was very good. And what right had she to be critical? Hadn't she, for most of her life, built around herself safe walls? And hadn't she let the world go its own way? At least Beth hadn't done that. Well, she wasn't going to do it any longer either. Somehow she was going to let this exotic country with its fantastic history change her. Even modern Israel. Yes, that too was intriguing. And if some of that ancient history belonged also to her, well and good.

When they were finished with their tour, the two women walked back to the car and drove the short drive to Tabgha, carefully following their map.

"This is the place of the feeding of the five thousand," Mattie told Beth when they had parked their car.

"A curious miracle," Beth said.

"Yes, if you think what is meant is physical food and not spiritual food.

"Metaphor again?"

"Makes sense."

"Yes, it does. A spiritual feeding perhaps?"

Mattie nodded. "Wasn't that what the people needed as much as food? Something emanating from the being of the Master and flowing out to his followers like manna from heaven. Only heaven was at that moment here on earth."

They spent a long time in the church in Tabgha, called the Church of the Miracle of the Loaves and the Fishes. It still housed some of the Byzantine mosaics that had once graced a much older church. The mosaics were singular works of art, depicting the wildlife that had once roamed the region. "Aren't these gorgeous!" Mattie said, and she read to Beth from out of the guidebook. "'Modern day Israelis have studied these scenes very carefully, with the objective of bringing back to the region as much of the wildlife as is still in existence.'"

"Eric would be absolutely thrilled with these mosaics. I must bring him here," Beth said, and then blushed.

"What is it?" Mattie asked.

"I told you. Eric wanted to come with me, but I asked him not to. I thought it was because I needed to do this on my own. But I'm not sure now."

"About Eric?"

"Oh, I'm sure about Eric. . .I think. Now why did I

say that?. . ." Beth chewed on her lip and shook her head as if to clear it.

"Are you interested in Gidon?"

"Gidon is a lovely man. . .Oh, Mattie, I'm confused about everything. Life is just too complex. But I don't want to talk about that right now. I want to be what you call a poet. . .and live into this place and into this area and do what I came here to do."

"Sorry."

"Please don't be. It's not you. . . You've done nothing wrong. By coming to Israel you've rescued me from an impossible treasure hunt. I could have done nothing on my own, so much for my arrogance. I'm really so grateful that you're here," and she squeezed her friend's arm.

They left the larger church and walked through the grounds down to the Chapel of the Primacy that was built at the edge of the Sea of Galilee. It was a small building made of the local black basalt blocks over a rock called Mensa Christi.

"'On this rock I will build my church,' Christ said of Peter."

"It could be this spot," Beth said.

"It certainly could be."

"Let's go outside and sit for a few minutes." Beth said. "I need to write."

"Good," Mattie agreed.

Outside, overlooking the sea, the women found a place on the rocks to sit. Each pulled out a notebook and began to write. Mattie was taking notes, a sense of place. She quickly filled up a few pages. When she looked over at Beth, she saw a poem forming on the page of Beth's notebook.

Good, Mattie thought with satisfaction, if Beth can just write. . . see and write. Then in her own way she might find what she's seeking. Wasn't that what writing was after all, a way to break past the senses' barriers and see, smell, touch, hear, taste another world? Or even one's own?

Half an hour later they returned to the larger church and bought some postcards. And each purchased a book that depicted the mosaics of fish, animals, and flora.

"This is my gift to Eric," Beth told Mattie.

Capernaum was their next stop, an excavated town, long ago deserted, but it had been large in its day. "Jesus was said to have lived there during most of his ministry," Mattie told Beth, "possibly in Peter's home."

Over what was thought to be the remains of the house of Peter and his family, a very modern and circular church had been built on great pilings that lifted it above the digs of Peter's house. As the women walked up to it, they could hear singing from the church above in French. Once again a visiting church group was having its own service in a church in the Holy Land.

"This must have been a beautiful town, right here on the edge of the sea," Beth said. "Yes, this is so different from Jerusalem. You really can get an idea of what it might have been like here in the time of Christ."

"There were many miracles performed here by Christ, or as John puts it, many signs."

"Such as?"

"The raising of the alderman's daughter after she was dead, the casting out of a demon from a man in the synagogue."

"Yes, casting out of demons. I can understand that."

"Let's go look at the old synagogue," Mattie said. "Early A.D., not the one where Christ taught, but possibly above the one where Christ taught."

It was a well-restored site with tall pillars topped with fine Corinthian capitals. The walls were made of limestone. There were doorways with Jewish symbols on the lintels and on the capitals of the columns. After walking through the well-excavated synagogue, they moved around the ancient site looking at the various *finds* that lined the sidewalks.

Mattie was loving the morning. She had lost her dread of Israel, lost it the moment she had stepped off the plane. And now she wanted to be rid of the timid lady who had inhabited her psyche since the loss of her husband and child. And, above all, she wanted to be done with the recluse, with the woman who had carefully circumscribed her own life to avoid more hurt and suffering. She wanted to court adventure, to be as open and as wide as the wind, to allow that *something* that had for years been hidden by fear, to cross over the threshold and awaken her. Was she finally waking up? Like the princess who had slept for a hundred years until the prince had come and kissed her awake? Mattie flung her hair back. Well, there was no prince. She was waking her own self up. Wasn't that the modern way?

For a moment she imagined Gidon ben David as the prince. Tomorrow they would be having lunch with him. She blushed at how happy she felt at that thought. And Yehuda ben Yehuda. That too would be wonderful, she reminded herself.

After they returned to their car, they drove around the eastern shore of the Sea of Galilee to the lakeside restaurant in a kibbutz called Ein Gev. They sat on the terrace overlooking the sea and ate a lunch of fish, potatoes and a carrot dish. Beth had been talking about her friend Paul Burrows.

"You say he's studied the philosophy of Rudolf Steiner?" Mattie felt a little quiver of excitement down the back of her spine.

"Yes, it's called anthroposophy."

"That's a remarkable coincidence. Beth, you know my mother's parents were originally German and they sent her to college in Germany. She studied philosophy at the university in Berlin."

"Yes, you did tell me that. What has that to do with Paul?"

"Wait. She came back home when the Nazis came to power. My mother was very ashamed of the Germans, of her heritage. I think that shame is what drove her into living so isolated."

"Yes, we talked about that before."

"Did I ever tell you about my mother's German-language library?"

Beth shook her head.

"She had dozens of books, mostly philosophy—Hegel, Fichte, Leibnitz, Kant, and also Rudolf Steiner."

"You're kidding."

"No, they're all up in my attic. My mother's library."

"Have you read any of her books?"

"I'm fluent in German, so I've read her Goethe books and her complete collection of Novalis, whom, as you know, I adore. But I don't love philosophy and I left those books alone. Consequently, I never read anything of Steiner's. But I must say, I am curious now."

"He's translated into English, so my friend Paul has told me."

"Have you read any Steiner?"

"No."

"Your friend Paul sounds fascinating. When I stop off in New York for a visit on my way back from Israel, will you take me up to meet him?" She caught the amazed look on Beth's face. "I'm serious about all this change business, Beth. I can't hide out in Big Sur for the rest of my life. If you can have adventures, why can't I?"

"You can have mine. I'd gladly give them all to you?"

"Really? Even Gidon ben David?"

Beth looked up at her with a curious expression on her face. Mattie reddened. "Mattie, are you interested in Gidon?"

"Of course not. You found him first..."

"Mattie?"

"No, all I meant is that he sounds like a marvelous adventure. Beth, tell me something. How do you do it? I mean, how did you find Eric?"

"On a museum art tour. I told you the story, Mattie."

"That's not what I mean," she pushed her hair aside in a gesture of frustration. "I mean. How does one attract men when one is middle-aged?" She blushed. Why did this topic make her feel so awkward?

"I'm not sure I could answer that, Mattie," Beth put her hand on her friend's for a moment.

"It was hard enough when I was young, when we were young," Mattie said. "But then it was, well, more natural. Right now, as a middle-aged woman the process, whatever it is or might be, just feels unnatural."

"You attracted Mahmud Aziz."

"That doesn't count."

"Why not?"

"He was in love with my poetry. And I was an American."

"You think that's all it was?"

"Yes...no...I don't know." Mattie shook her head. "Tell me something, Beth, do you believe in love?"

"Believe in love?"

"I don't mean filial love, or the love of a child for her parents or the love of parents for their children, but... but romantic love?"

Beth put down her fork. "Don't you?"

Mattie sighed, "I'm not sure anymore."

"With Jack?"

"What was it, I ask myself? Friendship plus pheromones? It's so long ago. . ."

"And since?"

"Since? Definitely friendship plus pheromones. Sometimes, only pheromones."

And they both laughed.

"Well, is that so bad? Friendship and pheromones?"

"I don't know, Beth. If you study the Victorians or even the Middle Ages, if you read their poetry, the feelings between men and women were so intense, so passionate. People could love for a lifetime. People could die for the sake of their love. Such intensity seems to have evaporated from our society. Now it's more about possession or winning or having someone to take care of you. . .I think we are all much too selfish now. Can you imagine a man willing to die for you, for the love of you?"

Beth thought about it for a moment. "Not really. It's much easier to walk away from someone today, and . . ." Suddenly Beth's eyes widened.

"What's the matter?".

"Look behind you, look!"

Mattie turned around. "What am I looking for?"

"Did you see him?"

"Who, Beth," and she turned back to her, "Gidon?"

"Don't look at me. Turn around."

And Mattie did. "Who am I looking for?"

"George Hemmings. He's gone now. Did you see him?"

Mattie slowly turned to stare at Beth. "You saw George Hemmings?"

"Yes, I saw him leave the restaurant. Didn't you?"

"No, are you sure?"

Beth hesitated. "Well, he was far away. I can't be sure. But I swear it looked like him."

"That's creepy, Beth."

"There are too many coincidences, Mattie, and frankly it's beginning to make me angry."

"What can happen?" Mattie was trying to reassure herself as well. "We are sitting in a fairly large restaurant with dozens of people around us. And besides, if it was him, he's gone now."

"Why was he here? Why wasn't he in Tiberias attending to his business. I don't like all of these coincidences?"

Mattie didn't like them either. "Isn't it possible, if you did see him, that he was here on a business lunch? After all, this is a pleasant drive from Tiberias. Was he with anyone else?

"I couldn't tell."

"Maybe he and his business associates came over by boat and had lunch. Why not?"

Beth thought about it. "That could be so. This is a well-known spot for tourists. You're probably right."

"Most likely Uzi was playing a prank yesterday, giving the tourists a thrill in a dark cave."

"I'd like to wring his little neck. Sorry if I made you nervous. Are you okay?"

"I'm fine," Mattie said, and tried to dislodge the little stone that had settled in her stomach. Well, you wanted adventure, she scolded herself.

"It's far too beautiful today to think of silly things. It might not have been him anyway."

"Right. Do you want to continue on with our tour?"

"Absolutely," Beth told her. "Don't you?"

"I'm not afraid of George Hemmings," Mattie said, and tried to believe it. "Two American girls could take him easily."

And they laughed.

After lunch they drove leisurely around the lake, stopping off at the baptismal site on the southern shore where they watched a group of about thirty Americans go through a baptismal ritual. Then they drove to Tiberias, turned in their car and did a little shopping in town. Mattie kept her eyes open for the omnipresent George Hemmings, but didn't see him. They returned to Kfar Hayam by cab in the late afternoon. The women read on the beach, talked through most of the evening and went to sleep early.

## 66
*Friday night*
## TEL AVIV

Gidon put in a call to Dov that night. He wanted to know what they had learned about the house in Cana before he went up to the Galilee tomorrow. But his phone call was not returned. He waited until past midnight and then went to sleep.

## 67

*Saturday morning*
## THE SHEFELA

It was 5:00 a.m. and very dark. Yehuda had opened one eye to look at his clock glowing out its ever-changing message. It was almost time to get up. Another half hour. Gidon would be here at six-thirty. But he still had time to...to...

Malkah was asleep beside him. The sound of her breathing, the warmth of her body rising and falling gently beside him made him feel safe, safe and comfortable. But why should he need to feel safe? All his life he had fought the good fight, had been fearless, a lion of Judah, no enemy too tough to confront, no job too big to take on. What had happened to him in his old age? He was watching the angels standing on the hill outside his room across the road just beyond the fields. Why was he afraid? Where had this fear come from? If he hadn't been afraid of death in his youth, why should he be afraid of death now?

The old angel was looking at him with reproach. Yes, that was the word, reproach. But why? What had he done? Or what had he failed to do? Had he not served his people well? Had he not won for himself a mention in the long scroll of Jewish history? Had not his poems chronicled, not merely the struggles of a single human being, but also the struggles of a people fighting to be reborn out of the ashes of the Holocaust? Had not his life been one of service, of sacrifice even? Had he not lived each day to its fullest? Why did the old angel gaze at him with such censure? What had he failed to do? And why had the reproachful one come at this time in his life, when it was too late, when he was too old? But too old to do what?

Yehuda looked then at the younger angel dancing about the hill. Shimmering bands of colors wafted away from him and he was a joy to behold. He smiled a smile of approval at Yehuda. Thank God, someone saw his worth, the worth of his life. Why should he bother with the old angel when the young one loved him, adored him, approved of him? He would keep his eyes away from the old one, would look only at the young one. But no sooner had he made his decision than his eyes once again sought the eyes of the old angel. Their light was too intense. It burned him. The angel was searching him, searching through him. What did he want? And as he thought the question, the angel beckoned him. His arm lifting through the air looked like wind on water. His wings fluttered, sending out ripples through the light like waves slipping out to sea. Yehuda rose up. He would go.

"Yehuda," his wife was calling him, shaking his shoulder. "The alarm. You had better get up. Gidon will be here soon. I'll make oatmeal."

Yehuda woke up with a sense of loss.

And of relief. He headed for the bathroom. 5:35. He had time for a quick shower. Malkah would tell him he would catch cold going out after a shower and he would tell her that it was still warm outside and Gidon had heat in his car.

## 68
### *Saturday morning*
### TOWARD THE GALILEE

For the first half hour driving north, Gidon and Yehuda talked about the progress of the peace accord, its chances for success, the merits of the men conducting the negotiations, many of whom Yehuda knew quite well. They talked about the latest terrorist incident involving the kidnapping and killing of soldiers in the Gaza Strip.

"It won't be easy," Yehuda repeated what they both knew. "They will have to work quickly before our people lose their will. That is the danger."

After that they drove in silence. Gidon had much to think about. And he liked the morning hours. He didn't need a lot of sleep and often rose early. But today he was tired. How much sleep had he gotten—four, five hours? But that wasn't it. The conversation with his son a few days ago still filled him with sadness and unease, even presented him with a dilemma. His son had given him permission to...to what? To leave Avigail? Did he want to? That had never been an option he had allowed himself. He and Avigail had an agreement that they both had honored for almost twenty years. The home stayed intact. The two of them could do whatever they wanted in the love department or sex department as long as it didn't destroy the home, the marriage, the institution. But the children for whom the contract had been made hated that institution, that home. And not only the children. He realized that he, too, hated it. It gave him nothing except a dullness where his heart should be. He had ironed out so many human feelings—it had become a habit really—for the sake of his earlier career, for the sake of the children, for the sake of the marriage institution. What did that leave him with? He started to laugh.

"Why are you laughing, my child?" Yehuda opened his eyes and asked him.

"Uncle, I find life very funny."

"So?"

"I'm forty-three and there's nothing about it that I understand."

"That's not good."

"I thought I had figured out everything."

"Yes, no doubt. You did it all with your head, right?"

"Right. I had decided life was simple, that life was a long series of conflicts. My task was to pick which side of a conflict to be on and fight like hell for my side."

"That's the philosophy of a man who has amputated part of himself."

"I'm beginning to think that's just what I've done." He carefully watched the highway. It was early but already the road was filled with traffic, people going visiting or for an outing on this their day off.

"So hear this from a man who is a poet to a man who could also be a poet, think more with your heart."

"Uncle, I wouldn't know how to begin."

How would he begin? He had been trained, and had loved that training, to be self-possessed, imperturbable, objective, to let his mind rule his emotions. Was he too much governed by his head? His marriage had become a thought-out arrangement that his children hated. And, ironically, because of it his son saw him as weak, as a man lacking courage. But to be led by the heart, what would that do for him? Make him a real poet, perhaps, and turn his ordered life into near chaos. Even in his extra-marital affairs he had always kept some part of himself in reserve, had held back, had never promised more than he could deliver. If he ever let go into...into...

"You're going up to the Galil to see this woman, this Layton woman."

Gidon looked over at him. "Am I? Maybe. But didn't I promise to take you up to see Uncle Asher?"

"Tomorrow."

"And didn't you want to see Elizabeth Layton again, and to meet this other poet, Mathilda Jones."

"I did and do."

"And don't I have parents up there?"

"Yes, and even work. But you are going mostly because of that woman. And I'm your excuse. I give you legitimacy."

Gidon almost said to him, in this, too, my head leads me, but I don't know another way. Out loud he said, "I think Elizabeth is in trouble, Yehuda."

"Tell me."

And so Gidon told Yehuda the whole story.

"So they pulled you in again?"

"Yes."

"Israel needs."

"Yes, Israel needs and my assignment is to chase two women all over Israel and see what they are up to."

"Beneath your dignity? Not like rescuing Jews from Ethiopia."

"What makes you think I was in Ethiopia?"

"So where did you get all those Ethiopian rugs and pottery, in the duty-free shop in Geneva?"

"Uncle..."

"Don't fool an old pol, Gidon. You don't like this assignment?"

Gidon shrugged.

"Elizabeth Layton is neither a spy nor a terrorist nor even a troublemaker, though that I wouldn't mind," Yehuda said. "We admire troublemakers, we Israelis. We are all troublemakers."

"I told you she's been followed by some group ever since she set foot on Israeli soil. How do you explain that?"

"It could be something else."

"What do you think?"

"She might be the target of a kidnapping attempt." Yehuda glanced sideways at him.

"That's exactly what I'm worried about. But now things are even more complicated."

"Tell me."

"This other poet, Jones. She has family in Israel."

"Jones? She's Jewish?"

"No, there's a half brother with a Jewish mother."

"Not so complicated. We lose some to assimilation, but we get some back."

"That's not the complication. She's friend to a Palestinian troublemaker, now living and writing in the States."

"Ah. Interesting. You've met this Jones?"

"Yes."

"What do you think?"

"Mathilda Jones is either one of the shiest people I've ever met or a great actress. She certainly seems too timid to be involved in anything covert. However, yesterday, while on a tour of Cana, she dropped off an envelope from this Palestinian at a house there."

"A courier?"

"Perhaps an innocent courier, but we don't know that yet."

"And you think Elizabeth knew about this?"

"I don't know. The women told me that being here in Israel at the same time was mere coincidence. And our operator said Layton seemed surprised by the stop in Cana. Frankly, Uncle, there are more coincidences here than I like."

"And your old bosses? What do they say?"

"They say watch and report, which I will do."

"Still you're glad to see this Elizabeth again?"

"Best not to get involved emotionally."

"The head leading again?"

"In this, better the head."

## 69
*Saturday morning*
## THE GALILEE

Before picking up the women for lunch, Gidon took Yehuda to see his brother Asher in Nive Yuval, a kibbutz Asher had helped found and that now had facilities for the elderly who needed some assistance. Asher, a widower, was the oldest of Yehuda's five siblings. Yehuda was the youngest. The others were dead. Asher had fought long and hard against the changes that the younger members of his kibbutz wanted to institute. He had lost on many counts but not without a good fight. He was, even at ninety-three, still a fighter, and he and Yehuda argued long and loud about the way the peace process was going.

After an hour and a half, it was time to leave the older man and go to Gidon's parents' restaurant.

Asher had declined the invitation to lunch as they knew he would. "It's enough, dragging these legs around this kibbutz with this contraption." He pointed to his walker. "Spare me. And come again soon. If you would only listen to reason, Yehudaleh, you would understand what I'm driving at and then you could talk to your friends who are going to negotiate a stupid peace plan. I had a plan years ago. If you and your friends had listened to me then, it would have meant less wars and we would already have peace. But did you listen? I should live so long..."

## 70

*Saturday afternoon*
## THE GALILEE

The women came out of their motel room to meet him, and Gidon had to admire the way they looked in their full-skirted Israeli cotton dresses and sandals, and with their Israeli suntans. For the first time he noticed what a nice figure Mathilda Jones had. Her belted print dress showed off her small waist and slim ankles. Not bad, he decided, really not bad.

Mattie once again blushed when he took her hand in greeting. Even an accomplished actress would have a hard time getting the pink to rise up in her cheeks.

Well, well, he thought. And was flattered.

"Come, my parents and uncle are waiting for you at the restaurant. I hope you are ready for some hamburgers and french fries, a specialty of the house."

Two cars followed them to the restaurant.

## ⇥71⇤
*Saturday afternoon*
## THE GALILEE

"Oh yes, there are Arab villages all around us, some Druze, of course. We'd rather have it that way, scattered, not in small enclaves of their own where security would be hard," David Silver, Gidon's father, was holding forth. He was a large man, with a full, round face, blue eyes and an open, easy smile.

Beth was sitting at a circular table with Mattie, Gidon, Gidon's mother and father and ben Yehuda. They were in one of the small rooms in a very large, rambling restaurant in the hills north of the Sea of Galilee, eating, as was promised, American food—fried chicken, chili, hamburgers, french fries, cole slaw—and drinking soda. Gidon's father, a big bear of a man, had greeted the women with hugs, then had introduced Gidon's mother, Sharone, a diminutive woman, to them. She has a warm face, Beth thought. She saw from her constant looks at Gidon that Sharone adored her son. And she found that very touching. She felt an instant liking for the woman.

David was saying, "When we finally get things worked out in the West Bank, there are lots of areas that the Arabs are not going to get back for simple reasons of security. For instance Kalkilya, that's one mile outside of Kfar Saba which is eight miles from the sea. We can't have such a narrow strip dividing the north and the south. They could throw a stone across it. They're going to have to accept that some places can't be under their control. There's going to be a lot of shouting and a lot of accusations from both sides, but if at least we keep talking and not fighting, chances are that we will come to a compromise."

It was Mattie who had asked about the peace process. Beth watched Gidon as his father spoke. He was silent. Occasionally his eyes would drift to her, then he would smile and she would smile back. Often she saw him observing Mattie, who was very engaged, asking David question after question, whacking her hair back a dozen times from off her face. Only when she looked at Gidon did her eyes drop to the table and her face disappear under a waterfall of hair. Mattie liked Gidon, that was painfully obvious to Beth. And how did she feel about that? A little uneasy. And she knew she had no right. After all she had Eric. And she had had a wonderful phone conversation with him just that morning. She loved Eric. She knew that. But she had to admit, she was also drawn to Gidon. So what? It didn't have to mean anything. She had let Gidon know that she was unavailable. "Whatever you are willing to give me." It was an offer of friendship which she had accepted. Wasn't that enough?

And how did Gidon feel about Mattie? She saw him observing her. However, she couldn't read his expression. But when he had met them at the guest house, hadn't she seen a look of appreciation, maybe even of attraction, cross his face as he greeted Mattie?

"Many irritations will become of little consequence the minute the economic relationship becomes so strong that it doesn't pay either side to start quibbling," Yehuda said.

"That's right," David said. "Look at the U.S.A. and Canada—their economies are interlocked. You cross the border so easily, nobody cares. When hundreds of thousands of people's livelihoods depend on their having a good relationship with their neighbor, they're not for war. This is what our leaders have been saying. So it's very important," he went on, "to get the economic things going and the ties strong so that it pays for Jews and Arabs to want to fight for peace because of their self-interest and not because of some biblical, fundamentalist ideologies. Everybody's got their own God and their own title deed."

"David," his wife said, "maybe our guests would like their dessert?"

"She's letting me know I talk too much," he grinned. "So, who likes apple pie? New York style apple pie, light crust and terribly fattening. Who cares about fattening, certainly not you two women, I hope. Roz," he called to their young waiter, "a slice of apple pie with ice cream for everyone."

"Oh," Mattie groaned, "I'm not sure I have the room..."

"Nonsense," David laughed heartily. "You're on vacation."

"And what do you think will happen when they start to negotiate about the Golan Heights?" It was Yehuda who once again began the conversation about the peace process.

These peace negotiations are every Israeli's concern right now, Beth thought. There's probably not a household in all of Israel that isn't talking about it. Again she felt a twinge of embarrassment for herself and all the so-called Christian pilgrims who come looking for something that happened two thousand years ago, with little interest in the life and death struggle that is part of the current daily life here.

"Why worry, Uncle? The Syrians will never negotiate," Sharone said. "They'll demand all but they won't negotiate."

"Give them the West Bank, give them, please, Gaza,

but not the Golan Heights. That's too dangerous. That would be suicide," David said, and then turned to Gidon, "What do you think, son?"

Gidon toyed with his knife, drawing circles on the table cloth. "I think peace is going to cost us."

David said, "Sure, but how much?"

Gidon shook his head.

Sharone said, "Next year Geel goes into the army."

David turned to Beth and Mattie, "Ladies, you should see the Golan Heights on this trip."

"Who knows how long we will have it. Or this," Sharone gestured around the room. "If we give up the Golan Heights, they could invade us and all of the Galil would be gone. I don't trust the Syrians. Why should we trust the Syrians? We simply can't give up the Golan Heights, Uncle, and you know that."

Yehuda said, "The Golan is a problem. Not easy."

"It will, as you say, Uncle, all depend on economics," David said. "Enough. We have guests and we haven't found out anything about them." He turned to Mattie, "Gidon tells us that you're one of America's most celebrated poets."

Mattie reddened. "Poets are not celebrated in America. A few academics and their students know us. Poetry creates few stars."

Gidon said, "She's very good."

And Beth observed that Mattie blushed even more and stared down at her plate and her protective hair fell down and hid her face.

"And Elizabeth Layton is also very renowned," Yehuda ben Yehuda said.

"So my son tells me. And how do you like Israel?" David asked the two women.

So all through the dessert and coffee the two women

spoke about what they had seen in Israel.

After lunch, Yehuda rose up and said, "And now before I take my nap, which I'm afraid I need today, I would like to walk a little around the grounds with the two ladies. They should know that you have cabins to rent, and if they ever wanted to come back here they could write undisturbed."

"We have horseback riding, too," Sharone added. "Trail riding or ring riding, we've got it all."

"I'll show them. Come Gidon," Yehuda said, and the two women thanked their host and hostess and followed Yehuda and Gidon out the door.

Once outside, they walked behind the restaurant and up a hill toward the cabins. "I always stay in one, when I come," ben Yehuda told them. "They're very charming, like cabins in the great parks in America's west."

So the four toured the cabin area, which was set among the trees, and the women agreed that it was a bit like the West and indeed very charming. "This would be a wonderful place to come and write," Mattie said.

"You should do that," Gidon told her. "A restaurant nearby and peace and quiet. A perfect place to write. Do you like horses?" he asked the two women.

"I'm afraid I've never been very interested," Beth said, "I adore sailing but was never much of a rider."

"I love horses," Mattie said.

"Good," ben Yehuda said. "Gidon, you take Mathilda to see the stables and I will take Elizabeth for a walk in the woods."

Gidon seemed surprised by the suggestion but agreed. "This way," he said to Mattie and took her by the arm and walked off.

"Shall we go?" Yehuda said to Beth. "I want to talk to you about angels."

## ⇥72⇤

*Saturday afternoon*

## THE GALILEE

There were fourteen horses in two stables and as Gidon and Mattie entered the first, she broke away from him and moved quickly from stall to stall. "Arabians and Appaloosas... oh, how beautiful they are!" She stopped in front of one, reached in and stroked its forehead. "Where did they come from?"

"The Appaloosas from America and the Arabians from this area."

"Oh, I wish there was time to ride," she said.

"Perhaps that could be arranged," he told her.

She looked down at her dress and they both laughed.

"Well, another day, then."

"Oh, I'd really love that," Mattie hugged the horse who seemed quite calm with her. "There's a riding stable only a few miles from my home in California, and I ride at least once a week. The trails lead up into the mountains and it is extraordinarily beautiful there. Have you been to Big Sur?"

"Passing through," he said

"Up in the mountains is a good place to think. I'm sorry I don't have any sugar or carrots. What's his name?"

"Matan,"

"Matan, what does it mean?"

"Present. My mother got him for my dad as a

surprise. I think he's the best of the lot, breeding-wise. He's our prize."

"Do you ride?" Mattie asked.

"I do."

"Do you like it?"

"Yes. When I was in high school, I used to take out groups of riders along the trails. That was nice summer work. I wish my son would like it. It would be good for him."

Mattie turned to look at him. "I had a son once," she said.

"Once?"

"He died when he was two. He was in the car with my husband. A car in the opposite lane jumped the divider and smashed into Jack's car. Jack and Johnnie died instantly. The driver was drunk but he survived."

"Terrible."

"It's been a long time," Mattie said.

"And you never remarried?" They were walking out of the first stable toward the second one.

Mattie just shook her head.

"I have two children, a daughter and a son." He moved toward the fence of one of the paddocks and she followed. "My son is angry at me and I'm not sure it can be repaired."

"Why is he angry, Gidon?" Mattie stood next to him.

"Because he hates the relationship between my wife and myself," and suddenly Gidon was telling her about the conversation he had had with his son. "Geel is certain his marriage will last forever and that it will definitely not be an open marriage." He turned to watch her. She was looking out at the dry grass in front of them. A horse stood at the far side of the paddock and returned their stare. "Why haven't you remarried?" he asked.

She shrugged. "Perhaps no one asked me."

"I doubt that, an attractive, intelligent woman like you...there has to be another reason."

Mattie blushed. "Fear," was all she said, then laughed, and headed toward the second stable. "It's a terrible beast, isn't it?"

"A many-headed life wrecker," he nodded. And then they were in the stable and Mattie was moving from stall to stall, petting the horses, hugging those who would allow it and asking Gidon questions about the animals.

## 73
*Saturday afternoon*
### THE GALILEE

Yehuda and Beth walked through the extensive grounds that belonged to the Silvers. He pointed out the various trees and exotic plants that he saw were unfamiliar to Beth. Finally, they came to a bench in a wooded area. "Let's sit for a few minutes," and he sat down and patted the seat next to him.

Beth sat down.

"So how is it going with your quest?" he asked her.

"Better."

"You are finding proof of reincarnation?"

"Let's say, here in this old country of yours, it doesn't seem so impossible."

"Is that enough for you?"

"I don't know. But I'm glad I came," and she gave his arm a little squeeze, "if I hadn't I never would have met you."

"And Gidon?"

She turned to look at Yehuda. "Yes, I'm very glad to have met Gidon..."

"He has what you call a crush on you," Yehuda told her.

Beth dug into the ground with the toe of her beige sandal. "He's unhappy."

"For a long time now. Some day he will wake up."

"And when he wakes up what will he do?"

"Either change his marriage or leave."

"Which?"

Yehuda raised his hands palms up in a gesture of uncertainty. "Tell me about your friend, Miss Jones."

"What do you want to know?"

"What you think about her."

"A wonderful friend. One who listens. And when she does, it is almost like touch." Beth laughed. "She's deep and sensitive, a bit of a recluse, but who can blame her—considering the losses in her life." Then she told him something of Mattie's life.

"To have lost both son and husband all at once." He *tsked* and shook his head from side to side. "Is she political?"

"She's very interested in what is going on in the world, but, no, I wouldn't call her political. I'm more political than she is. Mattie, well, she's more concerned with—what would I call it—the meaning of life, of the world, why we humans are here. She's more mystical than political, I think."

"In Israel it is hard not to be political," Yehuda said. "She likes Gidon."

"Yes, I think she does. You're very observant."

"What are you going to do about it?"

"What do you mean? What should I do about it? It's not my task to do anything, is it? It's up to them, isn't it? What are you thinking, Yehuda?"

"I am wondering about your young man in New York."

"I see."

"Yes, I'm sure you do. Let's walk some more," and he stood up and began moving up a steep path.

Beth followed him. For a while she was quiet and then she said,

"Tell me about your angels, Yehuda."

"Dreams," he said. "Asleep, not asleep. Sometimes, I am asleep and awake at the same time. But they trouble me. The dreams have nothing frightening about them, but they fill me with fear. Why should that be? I was never a fearful person. Never. It makes me angry, my own cowardice." He looked at Beth and she bobbed her head in understanding.

"Yes, fear makes me angry too."

Then he told her the recurring dream.

"Curious," she said.

"In life I am not fearful. Why in this dream state am I afraid?"

"Does the old one represent death?"

"Once I thought so, but it's something else now," he shook his white head. "Of death I am not afraid. Really. Why should I fear death in old age if I didn't fear death when I was young?"

"Then what, Yehuda?"

He stared down at his feet stepping on the ground. Israeli soil, he thought. My feet are on Israeli soil. After two thousand years. And I helped make it happen. Yes. I helped. Then he thought of the angel and sighed, "I think it's disapproval, reproach."

"Reproach? I don't understand, Yehuda."

"I see it in the old angel's eyes. And it shocks me and it sends fear like waves rushing over me. To have lived so many years, I think a life of accomplishments—oh, not just for my own honor, even though there has been plenty of that, but for my people, for others. I look back, I look around, and I say, I have done something in this world. My life has mattered..."

"It has!"

"...and then I see that angel watching me, and in his face reproach. That is hard, that troubles my days."

"But why reproach? For what reason?"

"I don't know. That is where the fear comes in. I am ashamed to say this, but I'm afraid to find out. I'm afraid that if he tells me, it will cancel out my whole life. And if there is indeed something I have left undone, it is too late to do anything about it now."

"Can I tell you what I think, Yehuda?"

"Why not?"

"I think fear is the worst beast we face in our lives. If we give into it, we become less than ourselves," she struggled, "less than our human selves. I think you have to overcome your fear and face, even reproach, because knowing something disturbing that might be true is better than being dragged down by fear. Does that make any sense?"

Yehuda sighed, "Unfortunately, it does. So you think I should walk up that hill and ask the old angel why he looks at me like that?"

"Don't you?"

"I almost did, almost, this morning. But then my wife woke me. I was relieved, and also a little sad." He stood up. "Come, let's go meet Gidon and your friend. We've been rude long enough." He offered her his hand and Beth took it. He squeezed it. "Thank you," he said.

"For what?"

"For not saying, 'That angel is you yourself and you yourself are dissatisfied with yourself.'"

"That's also a possibility," she grinned.

"I know. So we have had our little chat and it is good to talk to another poet, another dreamer. Especially since you have told me what I already know."

She laughed. "That's the best advice."

He laughed too. "I wouldn't have taken any other."

They found Gidon and Mattie coming out of one of the stables. Together, they returned to the restaurant. Mattie and Beth said good-bye and thanks to Gidon's parents. Yehuda walked them to the car, taking Mattie by the arm. "You know," he told her, "it's a shame that you are not translated into Hebrew. It's a terrible loss for us. You should get this nephew of mine, who is a good poet in his own right, to translate your poems for you."

"Uncle," Gidon said.

"It would be good for you to do something artistic. You can't just fill your life with commerce, your soul will shrivel up. She's here for a while. You two should get together and work on the translations. Listen to an old man, for once."

Gidon smiled and shrugged his shoulders. Mattie just blushed.

"My dear," Yehuda said to her, "you are an extraordinary poet. I have read all your books. Gidon gave them to me."

Gidon colored slightly.

"What I think, my new young friend, is that you must face the world with the confidence of the mind that writes so wisely."

And Mattie just nodded gratefully and pumped his hand.

To Beth, Yehuda said, "We shall meet again, I feel it. Remember the book you promised to send."

"And a letter, too," Beth gave the old man a hug.

## 74

*Saturday afternoon*
## THE GALILEE

Gidon drove the two women back to their guest house and kept his eye on his rearview mirror. The cars that had followed them from Kfar Hayam to his parents' restaurant were still following them. One of Dov's men would be at Kfar Hayam that night and the next, so the women should be all right. Tomorrow, Sunday, the two women were attending a wedding and he was driving his uncle back to his kibbutz. He would be in his own home in Tel Aviv later in the day. As he was dropping Beth and Mattie off, he invited them to go with him to Caesarea Philippi and the Golan on Monday, and they agreed. Tuesday the women were moving to Sde Gedalia to be with Mattie's family. They should be safe there. But he would be around too, somehow.

## ⊰ 75 ⊱
## *Sunday*
## THE GALILEE

It was the early hours of Sunday morning, and Yehuda was asleep in his cabin just north of the Sea of Galilee. He was dreaming his angel dream again. When the old angel beckoned him, Yehuda rose up and walked toward the hill that stood behind the fields of his kibbutz. As he approached the old angel on the top of the hill, the angel turned and began walking down its other side.

"Come," Yehuda heard a voice inside his chest.

And so Yehuda followed the angel. Up and down dozens of hills, through valley after valley the angel strode, with Yehuda struggling behind him.

"Wait, wait," time and again Yehuda called. "Where are we going? It's too far. I am too old, too tired."

And for a few moments the angel would wait, silently. But from his face and hands light would flow toward Yehuda, and with it strength.

After a while, Yehuda would say, "I am ready now."

And the angel would move on again. And Yehuda would labor to follow him.

Once Yehuda called out, "Where are we? We have been traveling so long. This can't be Israel."

The angel only beckoned him and waves of comfort rayed out to him. Yehuda strove onward.

This journey is longer than my life, he thought. But I mustn't lose my life, mustn't leave that behind. Without my life, who am I?

Yehuda stopped and called out. "I can't go any farther. I'm afraid. I don't know this land."

The angel gestured toward him, and Yehuda felt peace rush through him, and the fear was gone. He moved on.

Later, Yehuda looked up. At the top of a grassless, treeless, rocky hill the angel had stopped and was waiting. Yehuda, with a sheer act of will, struggled up the last few yards until he was standing next to the angel. Finally, next to the angel.

The angel gestured toward the valley below them with both hands, illuminating it.

Yehuda glanced down, and felt a wave of shock rush through him. The valley was vast, but blackened by the fire and mud of battle. The discarded tools and machines of war were strewn haphazardly over the entire valley. Bodies of horses and men lay decomposing in the fetid air. No living thing moved there, neither human nor animal. All the trees were burned, stunted by the aftermath of violence.

"Why have you taken me here?" Yehuda cried, and tore his eyes away to look at the angel's.

From inside his chest he heard a voice. "Will you care for this?"

"Where is it? What country are we in? Is it Israel?"

"It is not Israel," the voice inside him said. "Will you care for this suffering land?"

And Yehuda had no answer.

"Come," the angel said inside him, and with great strides the angel plunged down toward the valley.

For a long time they walked through the carnage—tanks and trucks, cannons, guns, bows and arrows, swords, knives, hatchets and hammers. There were thousands of dead bodies—men, women, children, their torn clothes blowing in the wind. The angel walked and Yehuda followed, sickened and in tears, chanting the prayer for the dead that he knew by heart. If there were Jews among the dead . . .

Finally, they arrived at the other side and moved into the trees away from the desolation. In moments they were among mature trees, green-leafed and full. There were peach trees and apple trees and pear trees. There were bushes of blueberries, and raspberries, and patches of strawberries. The war had not come here.

The angel stopped.

He reached into a tangle of bushes and pulled out a basket. In the basket was a baby wrapped in embroidered blankets. The angel picked up the child and handed the child to Yehuda, who took it. The child was beautiful and gave Yehuda a sweet smile.

Once more Yehuda heard the angel speak from within him. "Will you care for this child?"

"Is it an orphan from the war? I am old. Whose child is it? Is it Jewish?"

"It is not Jewish," the inner voice said.

Yehuda looked down at the child. "Why do you ask me? Where are its people?"

The angel took the child from Yehuda, put it back in the basket and returned the basket to the bushes.

Suddenly, the angel took Yehuda by the hand and they were flying up into the air, away from the blue earth and into the star-strewn heavens. They flew quickly past Mars, then past Jupiter. He could hear voices, but they were moving too fast to catch the words. Were they calling to him? They finally circled Saturn where all of human history in a montage of pictures presented itself to Yehuda. But they passed the images too quickly for him to apprehend them. "Wait, wait," he cried, "let me see, let me live in these pictures awhile." But they were heading back to earth again. The angel circled the earth with its azure mantle. And Yehuda peered down. This is glorious, he thought. This is magnificent. He looked for Israel down there and he saw it. No borders, he thought. It blends into Jordan, into the Sinai, into Lebanon, into Syria. He stared at the rest of the earth. Nowhere were there borders. Only land and sea, an occasional cloud, and a cloak of gorgeous blue all around it.

"Will you care for this?" he heard again the question in his chest.

"What are you asking of me?" Yehuda cried.

The angel grasping tight to Yehuda's hand, headed past the moon. Exquisite, Yehuda thought. This is ecstasy. This must be death. They moved beyond Venus, then past Mercury and on toward the sun. He saw angelic beings everywhere, glimmering toward the earth. All were looking toward the earth. Higher and higher Yehuda and the angel flew, until they flew right into the brilliance of the sun. The light was intense. He was breathing light and dazzling sound. Everywhere singing, singing, singing. This is how it all began, he knew, with sound, with singing, a word. They dove deeper into the light. Yehuda listened. And he sensed things he could not put into thoughts, light and colors and shades of color and beings and music. Here was the abode of the archangels, each with his own folk to care for. Somehow he knew that, though there was no speech now, no words. The archangels weaving in light rayed it down to the earth. He felt the love woven into their light. Yet many were weeping. Why? Why? And for a moment the grandeur faded and he felt an indescribable pain. But all too soon they were out of the sun and heading back again toward the earth. The angel landed with Yehuda on a tall, white peak. All around them were snow-covered mountains. But Yehuda was not looking at the snow. He was staring at the stars. They are words, he thought. Yes, unspoken, unutterable words. Each creative and creating. Glory.

"Will you care for this?" he heard the angel ask gesturing at the stars.

"What do you want from me? Who is it you think I am?" Yehuda cried. "I am too old to change now."

Once more the angel took him by the hand and they flew through the air, over mountains, rivers, valleys, and oceans. Finally, the angel set him down on the hill outside his kibbutz. Still holding Yehuda by the hand, he walked over to the young angel, who was waiting and smiling, colors fluttering away from him.

Yehuda heard the old angel say, "He is yours." And with a terrible sound, as if the earth had split in two, the old angel lifted off the ground and disappeared.

And Yehuda woke up. Outside the cabin there was thunder and lightning. The first rain of the season had finally come. He rose out of bed and shut the window. He stood watching the wild storm, the rain pounding on the glass, with tears streaming down his face.

## 76

*Sunday morning*

## THE GALILEE

Sunday morning Mattie shook Beth awake and told her that she was going into Tiberias and that she would return by noon. There were a few items she needed for the wedding, she said. Beth murmured sleepily that she would see her at lunch and rolled back over on her stomach and was asleep again almost instantly.

When the taxi arrived, Mattie asked to be taken to Tiberias' main street. She walked down the street until she came to a hair salon. Inside, she pointed to a picture on the wall and asked the hairdresser to give her that haircut. The shock she experienced looking at herself in the mirror afterwards was great. Her hair was cut to just below her chin, parted on the side with a sweeping bang that feathered down past her ear. Mattie managed to stay calm through the manicure and pedicure. When she walked down the street to the taxi stand, she caught a glimpse of herself in the glass window of a painting gallery.

Who am I now, she wondered?

It will be interesting to find out, she answered.

## 77

*Sunday morning*
### EN ROUTE TO THE SHEFELA

Yehuda was silent as Gidon drove him back to his kibbutz. That was all right. Gidon had his own thoughts to think, his own life to straighten out. But nothing was clear. Geel, Rinat, Avigail. What did he want now? What? And the two American women. He would operate now as if they were in danger. That's all that made sense. He sighed and looked over at his uncle. Yehuda's eyes were wide open and there was a look of profound sadness on his face. Gidon left him alone.

## 78
### *Sunday afternoon*
### TEL AVIV

When Gidon returned home Sunday afternoon, there was an overnight letter from his wife waiting for him. In it she told Gidon that she was staying another four or five days in Kuşadasi, that she had been thinking while she was away, and that she thought it best that one or the other of them file for divorce. She didn't want to hurt him but she was really in love with Hagai and wanted to live with him. She thought it might be best if she moved out, and moved in with Hagai while Gidon and she came to an agreement over a division of the property. As she had someone and Gidon did not, it would be better if the two children stayed with him. All these details could be worked out when she returned. She was sorry if this caused him any pain. But as things between them hadn't been all that good for years, this was probably for the best.

After Gidon read the letter, he did two uncharacteristic things. He found the whiskey bottle behind the corn flakes in the kitchen cupboard and poured himself half a tumbler. Then he went into his son's room and found a couple of cigarettes in a crumpled package underneath Geel's jeans in a drawer. He sat down on the couch. Drank the whiskey. Smoked the cigarettes. When that was done, he went into the kitchen and prepared dinner for his two teenagers.

## 79
*Sunday afternoon*
## THE SHEFELA

Yehuda was sitting next to Shmuel's bed. The sick man had been asking for him, and as soon as Yehuda arrived home Sunday afternoon, he hurried to see the dying man. The nurse who had been with him left the two men alone.

"Shmuel, I'm here," Yehuda called softly.

The man's eyes fluttered open. "I've been waiting for you," he said in a very weak voice.

"So now I'm here."

"I've been thinking while I've been dying. Big thoughts. Strange thoughts. I need to tell you."

"So, tell then, my good friend."

"The Jews are a very old people."

"Yes."

"Very old. They were always divided. But who kept the Jews from disappearing?" He paused.

"Who, Shmuel?"

"The *datim*, the religious, the ones you despise."

"I don't despise them, Shmuel. They are Jews."

"Listen to me, my friend, because I have little strength to elaborate my thoughts. I give you only bare bones."

"Speak."

"In every generation it was the religious who kept our people from disappearing—their stubbornness, their faith. But you know that. That's not what I want to tell you. It's about this other stream. In each generation they too were there. And this group disappeared into the *goyim*. Assimilated, we give it a fancy name now. But this is what's important. Those who disappeared, the assimilators, they brought something to the other peoples, something precious out of our blood and our inheritance into their blood and their hereditary stream." Suddenly Shmuel thrust himself upright and grasped Yehuda's arm in a tight grip. "Do you understand?" he turned feverish eyes toward Yehuda. "This is so very important, can't you see? All those Jews who melted into the other nations brought something to them, gave them something, God's gift, poured it right into their bloodstream. Their lives, those who left us, meant something. We must never forget them. In every generation. In the eyes of God. You see, don't you? In all the nations of the world, we Jews live too. We can never disappear."

"I see, Shmuel. Yes, I see. Now lie back. You should rest."

The man eased himself back onto his pillows with Yehuda's help. "Thank you, Yehuda. Thank you. It was important for you to understand. Yes, I needed you to understand before... Thank you." And Shmuel closed his eyes.

Yehuda rose up and called the nurse.

The next morning as Yehuda sat drinking his coffee, the nurse brought the news to him. Shmuel Rosen had died in the night.

## 80

*Sunday evening*

## THE GALILEE

"Come," a young man said to Mattie, "you have to dance." And he offered her his hand.

"But I don't know how to dance Israeli dances," Mattie said, with an apologetic smile.

"It's a hora, it's easy. I will show you. You must dance. This is a *simcha*, a happy celebration, the marriage of Netta to Allon. You cannot sit at the table, playing with your food."

She looked up at the blond young man—how old was he? Twenty?

"I've been watching you and it will not do."

"What won't do?" Mattie asked, amused despite herself.

"Not participating in the joy of this occasion. Do you want to give offense to your brother?"

"I don't think..."

"Your lady friend is dancing. Come." He took her hand and Mattie rose to her feet.

"Wait," she said. "I think I'd best leave these shoes here."

"Good," he said.

She kicked off her shoes and followed the determined young man to the circle that was dancing on the grass not far from where the tables had been set up.

It took only moments for her to master the steps.

The music was loud and the singing exuberant. As her feet accustomed themselves to the steps, Mattie felt something lift up out of her, some wraithlike person she no longer wanted to house, to give life to. Gone. Soon she was singing, not the words, but the melody. I'm free, she thought. I'm shedding skins. I'm shedding fears. I'm shedding sorrows. I can make choices, she thought. I can change. I will do that here. In Israel. At the edge of the world. In the center of the world. I can be my own creation. And the thought gave her an immense feeling of joy, and her bare feet pounded the ground and her shoulders lifted her into the air. She smiled at the young man who had liberated her.

Later the dances were disco, and she danced with her young admirer and with his friends and with her family and their friends. Even Beth could not keep up with her. "It's the wine," she told Beth, sitting down at the table next to her friend.

"I thought it was the haircut," Beth said.

"It's the wine, the haircut, and it's Israel," Mattie said, and rose when another young man came to ask her to dance.

## ☙81☙
*Sunday night*
## The Galilee

Mattie took a shower, then curled up in the armchair with a heavy book on her lap for a desk and a large sheet of stationary on it. It was late Sunday night, and Beth was already in bed, asleep. Her book on the Second Temple period was lying open across her chest, her glasses still in her hands. Mattie wrote:

Dear Doug,

Well, I promised to write you as soon as the wedding was over and give you an eyewitness report. First question and answer, yes, the bride did wear a traditional white wedding gown. It's up to the bride and her family if she is going to do that, even on a kibbutz. You see, the kibbutz allocates a certain amount of money for each wedding and the family can spend it anyway it wants. Though the wedding wasn't until evening, Elizabeth and I arrived late afternoon because the family wanted to take pictures. Afterwards, we wandered around Sde Gedalia. You were right, the settlement is extremely pretty, sitting halfway up a hill and surrounded by cultivated fields and orchards. Michael is terribly proud of the place. It's fairly old, as kibbutzim go, since it was founded in the thirties on land that was purchased from an Arab landowner. No doubt he told you all of this, too, so back to the wedding.

At half past seven in the evening there was an outdoor ceremony under a *chupah*, a square canopy, that was held up by four teenagers. The bride and groom stood under it with their mothers and fathers. There were no bridesmaids or ushers. The bridegroom wore a dark suit, no tux. Everybody else wore a range of clothing from party to just nice. The little white silk suit you helped me pick out seemed just right, but those high-heeled shoes were torture. Don't scold. I wore them the entire evening, except when I was dancing. And, yes, I really did dance. After the ceremony, there was a buffet dinner served outdoors with all sorts of foods and desserts—very Middle-Eastern, with a little German and Polish thrown in. Then after that there was dancing, half folk dancing, half modern Israeli rock and roll. There was a live band, made up mostly of kibbutz members. Ruth said that there were more than five hundred people at the wedding, mostly from the kibbutz of course, but others from various parts of Israel. Beth and I were the only ones from the States.

On Tuesday, we are moving over to Sde Gedalia for a few days. But before that, on Monday, we are going up to Caesarea Philippi with a friend we met on this trip. I'm not sure what I'll do after Beth returns to the U.S. But I'll stay on. Why not? There's much to see and I have a rather wild idea for a novel, part mystery, part mystical, that I want to develop. There's a wonderful place north of the Sea of Galilee that has an American restaurant and cabins to rent and even horses. It might be a good place to write for a while. You said I would enjoy this trip and I am, immensely. I can't think of why I took so long to come here. The country is fascinating, both old and modern Israel, the people amazing. I met Yehuda ben Yehuda, a famous poet-statesman, yesterday, and he was worth the whole trip. And, yes, you were right, Doug, the Israeli men are very handsome. . .

Mattie was about to cross out that last sentence, and then decided, what the hell. She signed the letter, "Love, Mattie, I'll write again soon." Then she added, "PS. I cut my hair. Quite stylish. You'll be impressed."

She addressed the envelope, slipped the letter into it, sealed it, then put it next to her purse. She brushed her teeth, put Beth's glasses and book on the table between them and turned off the light. Mattie was asleep a moment after her head touched the pillow.

## 82

*Sunday night*

## TEL AVIV

Gidon was slow to answer the phone. He had been in a heavy sleep, a boozy, dark sleep with menacing black dreams that fled away like insubstantial shadows the moment he picked up the phone.

"Fifteen minutes."

Gidon dragged himself out of bed and put on his clothes. He found some old coffee in the coffee pot in the kitchen. He swallowed it cold and went downstairs to wait for Dov.

In the car, Dov said, "I thought you would want to know about the house in Cana."

"Okay."

"What's the matter with you, you look terrible."

Gidon waved the question away. "Whose house is it?"

"It belongs to Mahmud's sister and her husband. His mother is now living with them."

"So what do you think?"

"The husband is a carpenter, an Israeli citizen, keeps his nose clean, as far as we can tell, hardworking, a family man."

"So?"

"The money could have been for them, or for them to pass on to someone else. We don't know. We're keeping an eye on them."

"Has it occurred to you that Jones might simply have been doing Mahmud a favor by bringing some cash to his mother?"

"Of course it's occurred to us. But we have to watch."

"Okay. So what do you want me to do?"

"Do what you've been doing, keep an eye on the women, get them talking, Jones in particular, and report to us. And try to keep them together. Jones went into Tiberias alone this morning."

Gidon raised his eyebrows questioningly.

"To the beauty parlor only. Lucky we had two men in the car. Not such a terrible assignment, this. A piece of cake for you."

He wanted to give Dov a smart-ass answer but his tongue felt like thick peanut butter and he was just too tired. He got out of the car without looking back. In his apartment, he stripped and crawled into bed to get a few more hours of sleep.

## 83

*Monday morning*

## THE GALILEE

At about eight-thirty Monday morning Gidon arrived at Kfar Hayam.

Mattie answered the door. "Come in," she said from inside the still dark room.

Gidon looked past her to Elizabeth.

Beth greeted him from her bed, propped up on her pillows. She reached over and turned on the lamp next to her.

"What's the matter, Beth?" Gidon asked coming to the foot of her bed.

"Headache, upset stomach," she replied and coughed into her tissue. "Too much party yesterday, or maybe the flu," she whispered hoarsely. "I hope you'll forgive me for copping out and I hope you'll go on without me. I'd hate to spoil the day for the two of you."

Gidon was silent.

"We could cancel if you like," Mattie told him.

Gidon looked over at at her. Beth saw him notice the changes in Mattie for the first time. He seemed almost disbelieving. That gave Beth a sense of satisfaction. And a tinge of regret.

Gidon turned back to Beth. "Perhaps we shouldn't leave you here alone?" The concern on his face almost made Beth change her mind.

"Of course you should," she waved her hand at them.

"I don't want the two of you hanging over me while I sleep."

"I think we should stay, Beth," but Mattie's voice was uncertain.

Damn it, Mattie, Beth wanted to say, take the opportunity. Instead she said, "Really, it's nothing serious. A day of rest and recuperation is all I need. How can I sleep if the two of you are hanging over me? Please don't change your plans. It will make me feel worse."

"Are you sure?" Mattie asked.

"Of course. What can happen to me here? There are hundreds of people about and a doctor in the kibbutz. Will you please go?"

Gidon spoke then. "She apparently would like to be alone for a while, Mattie." His voice sounded tired. "If you'd still like to go to Caesarea Philippi, I'm willing."

"Then, all right," Mattie said, and picked up a jacket and hat. "We'll see you this afternoon, Beth."

"Okay. Have fun you two."

After Gidon and Mattie had left the room, Beth glanced at her watch. Only eight-thirty. She rolled back on her stomach and was soon fast asleep.

## 84

*Monday morning*

## THE GALILEE

Gidon helped Mattie into the passenger seat of his car, slammed the door tight, then leaned in through the open window. "Will you excuse me a moment? I just spotted an old friend and I want to say hello."

"Of course," Mattie said. She watched him walk across the parking lot to a green car. He had a quick way of moving, a little catlike, she had observed, like a panther or, better yet, a jaguar. But today his shoulders seemed to droop, and the way he stood as he spoke through the driver's-side window radiated fatigue. Or something else. Disappointment. Mattie was too far away to hear the conversation, but she could see Gidon's profile and his face looked serious. He seemed less than happy about this day, which made her uncomfortable. It's Beth he's interested in, she told herself, and that's the way it is. There's nothing you can do about it. She reached up to whack her hair and found a handful of short waves. It gave her a momentary sense of panic. You'll be all right, she told herself. All you have to do is ask questions and be polite.

Gidon returned to the car, got in, started the engine without a word. They were soon out of the kibbutz and on a highway. Mattie, feeling like an unwanted burden, couldn't manage to ask Gidon anything, but after a while she squeaked out a few words. "We're heading straight north, aren't we?"

Gidon looked at her as if he were aware of her for the first time. "Yes, we're going to go north and then east toward the old Caesarea Philippi, now called Banias," he said over the drone of the engine. "It's one of the sources of the Jordan. There are three."

"Oh, really? And what are they called?" she asked him, misery lodging in her stomach like a stone.

"The Chatzbani, the Dan, and the Banias," he recited.

Then there was silence again. Mattie stared out of the window at the rocky barren hills with their reddish-brown soil. Limestone and volcanic, she noted. The first rain had come Saturday night. If more came soon, then the hills would rapidly turn green. She thought longingly of her own safe home in Big Sur.

Finally, Gidon spoke, "Do you know Beth's boyfriend?"

"I've met him twice," her words tasted dry in her mouth.

"What's he like?"

"He's very nice, bright, talented, very much in love with Beth."

"Would you say he's the jealous type?"

"I. . .I really couldn't say. I don't know him that well."

Gidon didn't respond.

Why had she come on this little tour with Gidon? Why hadn't she just canceled it when Beth became sick? Mattie looked out of her window at the limestone rocks sticking out of the ground, acres and acres of rocks. They reminded her of a cemetery, the one outside of Jerusalem, where everyone wanted to be buried for the coming of the Messiah.

After a time, they were traveling along the edge of a large and well-farmed valley. Mattie could no longer bear the silence. "Can you tell me what we are passing?"

"I'm sorry. Yes, of course. That's the Hula Valley. It was once a huge swamp. The pioneers drained it and a great many of them lost their lives in the process. Now it's one of our most fertile valleys." His voice sounded weary, his speech automatic. "Not too many miles to our left, in the hills, is the border of Lebanon and to our right, just beyond the valley, those hills are the Golan. There was almost daily shelling from 1949 until 1967, when we took it from the Syrians."

"Hard to believe," she said. What else was there to do except go on with the day. "It looks so peaceful." She reached for her hair and grasped a handful of air.

"The Syrians tried to divert the sources of the Jordan River. When they got close to Israel with their heavy equipment, we attacked. It's quiet now, for the most part. We grow cotton and apples here, some citrus, some avocado."

"You were in a war?"

"Yes, in the Yom Kippur War." For a moment his eyes lit up. What was it? Sorrow? Pride?

She kept talking, kept him talking. She couldn't bear the silence. "What do you think will happen to Jerusalem in this new peace plan?"

"I think Israel will never give it up."

"Not even for peace?"

"A body without a heart is not much of a body," he said, and Mattie noticed a shadow pass over his face.

A body without a heart. Was that what she had become since the death of her son and husband? Was she merely a body without a heart? An observant eye connected to nothing?

The car stopped then for a road check. Gidon produced some papers. Mattie showed her passport and the car was waved on. "They're very careful here," she said.

"The borders are nearby."

## 85

*Monday morning*
## THE GOLAN

Gidon turned the car to the east. This day was not at all the way he had planned it. He couldn't be in two places at once. Well, he had spoken to Paz who had kept watch most of the night. He had told him to stay on, to keep an eye on Beth. If she stayed in her room today, all should be well. Paz was a good man. Beth should be all right.

It was more urgent that Gidon get information from Jones. He had all day. Right now his head was hazy with fatigue. He had slept poorly the night before. Too heavily before Dov's call. Too lightly after. The note from his wife had left him first stunned, then elated, then angry, and finally numb. He couldn't sort it out yet. He had said nothing to his children except that their mother had extended her vacation, but from the looks he got, they knew something else was going on. How often had they seen their father drunk in the daytime? Well, he hadn't actually been drunk. He had apologized for having to leave them to travel north again for business. He hadn't counted on Avigail extending her trip, but he assured his two teenagers that their grandmother would be there again at night, as usual. He was fond of his mother-in-law, Dora. She was a warm and kind woman and his children adored her. He wondered how someone so *gemütlich* could have produced a daughter who was so cold and indifferent. But maybe it was the marriage that had made Avigail cold and indifferent. Maybe it was he. With Hagai she must be different. He felt a twinge of jealousy and then of anger. Hagai was welcome to her. Without question he could have her. So Geel would finally get what he wanted.

He pressed hard on the gas. The car took off and quickly passed two cars in front of him. That definitely felt good.

He glanced over at his companion who was hanging onto the strap above her door. Her body looked rigid, unrelaxed. He slowed the car down. He had a job to do, and he had better do it. What else was there?

"If we had continued north we would have come to Metulla, Israel's northernmost city. There used to be lots of shelling there before the Lebanon civil war. There's less now but there are often incidents."

"And yet people choose to live there?"

"Great climate. It's partly a resort town. Another resort is Mount Hermon. We're not far from there now. It's in the Golan Heights. We'll be in it's foothills when we arrive at Banias. Mount Hermon is a ski resort. It's 10,000 feet high and has snow most of the year. Israelis go as often as they can. There are no snow-covered mountains in Israel proper. Some scholars believe that Mount Hermon is where the transfiguration of Jesus took place." You could always become a tour guide, he told himself. "The other is in Israel proper. Mount Tabor. There's a monastery on the top of Tabor."

"I hope to see Mount Tabor while I'm here." Mattie's voice sounded hollow.

"It's very interesting." Why was she always so uneasy with him? Did she mistrust him or was it just attraction? Just. Amazing how. . .how modern and appealing a haircut could make one.

Gidon turned off the road and drove past an active

archaeological dig. "Here we are. This is our destination. The old city of Caesarea Philippi. There's a park here where we can walk and have a cup of coffee." He maneuvered the car into an empty spot, and then led the way toward the park. There were only two tour buses and a few passenger cars.

"There is a spring here called Banias, a corruption of the word Pan, or Panias. You have heard of the God Pan?"

Mattie nodded.

"Banias is one of the sources of the Jordan river. It comes from a deep cave. There is a pagan temple to Pan in the rocks. The trees here, if you are interested, are northern varieties."

"It's deliciously cool here," she said.

He watched her as she looked about. She seemed taken by the place. Again he noticed that when she was absorbed in something she was observing she forgot to be uncomfortable. Jones was a woman obviously happy to be in nature.

"Caesarea Philippi. This is where Jesus asked Peter who the people thought Jesus was," she said with a display of excitement, "and Peter answered, 'Thou art Christ, the son of the living God.'"

Beth might not be religious but this one was. Gidon wondered how someone so erudite could be so Christian. But Jones wasn't the usual kind of Christian. What kind was she? Should he try to find out? Was it germane to his task with her?

"Do you see those niches there, carved into the face of the mountain?" Gidon asked her.

Mattie looked to where he was pointing.

"They once had statues of the gods of the forest in them. That was during the Roman period."

"Something very appealing about that, isn't there? Gods of the forest, of all of nature. I should have liked to have seen them," Mattie said. Now that was a very uncharacteristic remark for a believing Christian.

The two walked around the lush park grounds and then came to a small restaurant.

"Would you like coffee?" he asked her.

"Yes, thank you."

He left her sitting outdoors staring at a stream that ran under the restaurant built on the bridge above it. Inside the small restaurant, Gidon put in a call to Kfar Hayam, to Beth's room. No one answered. He ordered two coffees and came back to find Mattie stooping to stare at something in the stream. Absorbed and relaxed, she looked quite pretty. Mattie rose when he called to her. And blushed at the sight of him.

"I just called Kfar Hayam. Beth doesn't answer her phone."

"Maybe she's asleep or maybe she's in the shower."

"We'll call a bit later. At lunch in Mas'ada." Beth not answering the phone made him uneasy.

"Masada?"

"No. Mas'ada is a Druze village in the Golan. If you're ready, we'll go on to see an old Crusader fortress, Castle Nimrod." He hadn't planned to take her up to that ruin but it was the right place for a little talk. If lucky, they might be all alone on top of that hill. His gut told him something was going on. And he was going to find out what.

## 86

*Monday morning*
### THE GALILEE

At 9:15 Monday morning Elizabeth Layton woke from a refreshing sleep. She showered, dressed, went first in search of some coffee, then entered the lobby of the guest house.

"I'm wondering if you can call over to the car service you use in Tiberias," she told the young woman at the desk there, "and find me a car and driver as soon as possible. I'd like to go to Safed."

The woman looked a little nervous. "It's very hard to get a car at the last minute," she told her, "but I'll try."

"Thank you. I'm going to go sit by the water. I'll check back in half an hour, okay?"

"That will be good," the girl told her.

When Beth returned to the lobby, the girl told her that she had been able to locate a car and that the driver would be there in thirty or forty minutes.

"And I have an envelope for you, forwarded from your hotel in Jerusalem."

Beth took the envelope. It was thick. She peeked inside. Good. It contained the fax from Paul Burrows, the one Beth had been expecting. She returned to her room to read it. She read it slowy, carefully deciphering Paul's tiny and somewhat shaky handwriting.

Dear Beth,

I have written you four long, long letters over these last several days and set each one of them aside, that's why I am so late in getting this off to you. My dear friend, I know myself. I can too easily become a pedant, too easily preach, too easily gush up information. But what good is it really? No matter what I tell you about the difference between a western and an eastern approach to karma, no matter how I try to convince you of my belief in an evolution of consciousness, I know, as much as I know anything, that in our times the freedom of the individual must be valued above all else. All the good hierarchies observe that dictum now.

You know that one cannot give his or her beliefs to another, nor his or her experiences. The road to an encounter with the spiritual world is a solitary one now. I can, however, give you a list of authors you might look into, men and women, whose words have meant much to me. And at least that will give you a context, a background, for what I am going to suggest you do now.

Begin to write. Start with where you are, with what you think you know. Start perhaps with the Crucifixion–two people, you and your daughter in that life–invented, of course, at first. And write from there. Perhaps through that marvelous imagination of yours you will write yourself into a closer encounter with that event and that time. Maybe the pictures won't be quite accurate, but they seldom are at the beginning because we clothe realities in images that are familiar to us from our present sense-perceptible life. But even if the pictures are not quite right, you might come closer and closer to the inner gesture, the inner core of those characters and maybe even the inner core of who you and your daughter were in that life. A good writer, at so many moments in the writing process, comes right up to the threshold and without too much drama crosses over it. You might find what you are looking for simply by doing what you do so well, by writing.

On another sheet, I have written a list of authors you might find interesting. I hope the list will be of some help. Don't be surprised to see the names of Ralph Waldo Emerson, Benjamin Franklin, and Gotthold Lessing there, alongside Rudolf Steiner, the theologians Emil Bock and Friedrich Rittelmeyer, and the Oxford scholar Andrew Welburn.

Of course, if you want to visit me when you return, I can lecture you for hours—or we can just get together and talk as old friends. I wish you good luck. And thanks so much for all those wonderful postcards you sent me from Europe. It means a lot to an old man to be remembered.

You know how fond I am of you. As is Annie.

Affectionately, Paul

PS. After much inner debating, I have finally decided to enclose one of the four preachy epistles. You can glance at it or, if it's too much, throw it away. P.

Folded up inside the envelope was a list of authors, and another letter. She put all the papers back into the envelope and the envelope into her purse. At 10:45, she stepped into a green Opal. A young man about thirty was at the wheel. Elizabeth told the driver where she intended to go and in moments they were driving out of the kibbutz and heading north. She thought about Mattie then, and smiled. She hoped her friend was making full use of the opportunity to get to know Gidon ben David better. Well, that was up to Mattie.

## 87

*Monday morning*

# NIMROD

Situated on one of the high spurs of Mount Hermon, the view from Nimrod was spectacular.

"But this is magnificent," Mattie said as she got out of the car.

They walked up to highest point of the hill where the remains of the castle fortress of the Crusaders lay.

"There was an important fortification here for thousands of years, long before the Crusaders came. The clear view tells you why."

Nature had long ago claimed most of the buildings on the hill. Gidon and Mattie were alone—no tour groups, no Israeli families or hikers, just the two of them. And that was good. He wanted her to feel the isolation, her vulnerability. That might get more truth out of her than sitting in a cozy restaurant full of people.

Gidon studied the woman absorbed now in looking at some wildflowers growing in the newly green grass between the fallen stones of the old fort. With her new haircut she was quite attractive. Of course, she had been pretty before, in an old-fashioned sort of way. Now she looked, well, chic, even trendy. He wondered what she would be like in bed? Cold like Avigail or warm as Corrine had been in Paris? Probably somewhere in-between. If he put a hand on her right now, however, she would probably faint. He had never met a grown woman so shy, unless she was talking about something that intrigued her. Hard to imagine her as a conspirator. Still, he had to know.

"Mattie," he called out to her suddenly, "can I ask you something?"

## 88

*Monday morning*

## NIMROD

Mattie looked up startled. For a few minutes she had almost forgotten he was there. "Yes, of course," and she stepped tentatively toward him.

"Sit down, please," he sat down on a large stone and motioned to a rock opposite him.

She came and sat as he had instructed. Their knees almost touched.

"You have a friend in the States called Mahmud Aziz." Gidon's blue eyes looked cool, impassive.

Those words stunned her. "Mahmud...But how do you know...?" Her heart began to thump loudly.

"What's your relationship to him?"

She was answering him even as she was experiencing a wave of shock and fear. "He's an old student of mine, a very gifted poet, very gifted."

"A student now?"

"No, not now. Just a friend."

"A lover?" Gidon's handsome face suddenly looked hard-edged, looked carved out of the rocks around her.

"I don't understand any of this. What do you want?"

"Just some information."

"Who are you, Gidon?"

"A friend, Mattie. Really, a friend. Please answer my questions and I'll explain everything to you later. Is Mahmud your lover?"

Mattie rose up quickly. She looked about her. Where was she to go? This old fortress was deserted. Empty grounds, empty castle, perhaps there were ghosts of knights, but they could not help her even if they wanted to. She was alone, high on a hill, with Gidon. Who was he? She felt Gidon's firm hand on her arm.

"It's better if you sit, Mattie."

She sat. "He's not my lover."

"Was he ever?"

"A few days, that's all. It wasn't right. He was too... too..."

"What, too Middle Eastern? Too what?"

Anger began to trickle through her chest, like a narrow rivulet. She stared at him coolly. "Too young. Too needy. Too political. The relationship just wasn't right. I have Jewish family here. Why do you need to know this?"

"Why did you bring a package into Israel from Mahmud Aziz and drop it off in Cana?"

She straightened up, her mouth fell slightly open. "How did you know? Was it George Hemmings? It was George Hemmings. He must have told you. You are a spy then, aren't you? You do work for Israeli Intelligence. Beth was right." The rivulet of anger was turning into a stream. "But what could you want with me, or Beth?"

He put his hand on hers for a moment, his voice softened. "I'll tell you what I can in a moment. But first, tell me what you brought in with you in that envelope."

"If you must know, I brought in two hundred dollars for Mahmud's family. He told me it was to help them buy a refrigerator. He promised me it was not for anything political, and not anything illegal."

"You believed him?"

She hesitated just a moment. "Yes."

"But you're not one hundred percent sure."

She rose up again, and this time walked away from him to stand staring out at the valley below them. "How can anyone be one hundred percent sure of anything? People can be very deceiving." She turned and looked at him coldly. And then back out at the valley. "Mahmud claims to be in love with me. He said he would do nothing to put me in danger." She then swung round and stared at him. "Did he? Am I in danger?"

## 89
*Monday morning*
## NIMROD

Mattie turned to stare at him, this time without blushing, without shyness, as if he were a stone to examine. "Did he? Am I in danger?" Gidon saw her eyes blaze and all fear and timidity disappear like mist burned off by the sun. "What do you want from me? What right do you have to question me like this?" She was angry. He had never seen her angry. "Have I broken any law? Have I harmed anyone?"

It was the wrong emotion but he found her amazingly attractive at that moment. She had a temper, no doubt she seldom lost it, but when she did it made her look like a Greek Fury, all storm and hair flying, except her hair was blond, golden. Then like a Nordic Goddess ready to do battle.

"I think I would like to be taken back to Kfar Hayam right now. If you don't, I'll report you to the American Consulate."

He laughed. He shouldn't have, but he did. He saw her eyes flame up,

"You can't keep me here. Why did you have to turn out to be. . ." And then she was sinking to the ground, sitting, clutching her knees, head down. And weeping.

He suddenly felt lousy. What was he doing? What the hell was he doing? There was no harm in her. Mattie was another of life's victims. No, that was unfair. Mattie was one of life's survivors. And maybe she was better at it than he. He believed her. Her story.

Gidon walked over to her, sat down next to her, and touched her hair lightly. She shook her head as if his touch were a fly.

"Mattie, I'm sorry. There's something going on and I think you should know about it. I really am a friend, Mattie, and I'm sorry if I frightened you. I just had to be sure about you."

She turned a tearful, furious face toward him. "You think I'm some sort of terrorist? Do you know how ridiculous that is?"

He smiled at her. "I do." He pushed the hair back from her wet eyes.

She stared at him imperiously, then her lips began to quiver and the corners of her mouth curved up. She started to giggle and then broke into laughter. It was a wonderful laugh, full and throaty. It was a laugh of release, of complete abandon. It was infectious and soon he too was laughing.

And then he was reaching for her, his hand moving around her neck. He drew her face toward his and kissed her. For a moment she was startled and then her lips softened and she kissed back. The passion of that kiss took him by surprise.

But he pulled away from her, brushed his fingers across her lips, her wet cheek, then he stood up and helped her to her feet. He couldn't read the expression on her face. She wasn't blushing. She wasn't looking away. She was merely staring at him.

He didn't have time to decipher it. "Come, let's get down to the highway. I want to use the phone."

## 90
*Monday morning*
## THE GALILEE

Sitting in the back seat of the car, on the way to Safed, thanks to Paul, she had a plan now. How modest he was. She had called him all the way from Jerusalem and had asked him profound questions. Of course he was chary of answering them. She remembered how he worried about being preachy. What a modest man he was.

But, of course, she was going to read the second letter he had enclosed.

She pulled out the thick pages and opened them up to stare once again at Paul's tiny hand.

Dear Beth,

I hardly know where to begin, you ask so many questions . . . Well, let me start by saying that your search for an understanding of reincarnation is not so very unusual today—though perhaps you were propelled by a more dramatic incident than most. The western human being was once kept from even having an inkling of past lives by the good spiritual powers. Western humanity had a special task to perform, just as eastern humanity once had in an earlier period. For the sake of this new task, at a certain moment in evolution, those spiritual beings retreated from the consciousness of human beings, allowing the human to struggle toward freedom—toward adulthood, one could say. But now it is time for a reconciliation. So as these same powerful spiritual beings once again approach humankind's consciousness, the gateway to that other world is reopening and with it, veiled memories of past lives flood through causing much confusion, much inner turbulence. Memories bubble up out of our unconscious, taking on strange forms, strange images, borrowed from the current life. Young children's memories are the purest, the closest to reality. So I wouldn't discount Alicia's remembrance as mere childish fantasy. Obviously, you are not. Or you wouldn't have rushed off to Israel. If it helps, then in my humble opinion, Alicia's memory likely points to a true event, to a remembered reality...

Beth finished the long letter then tucked it into her purse. It was as Paul had described it, full. Almost overwhelming in its implications. She closed her eyes and thought about what she had read.

## ⊰91⊱
*Monday morning*
## THE GOLAN

They had pulled into a gas station and Gidon was using the phone while an attendant filled the car with gas. When he returned, he was grim-faced.

"What's the matter?" Mattie asked.

"Beth was not in the room, and when I asked the girl at the desk, she told me that Beth had hired a car and had gone into Safed. Do you know anything about that?"

Mattie shook her head.

"What did she say about needing a day of rest?"

"She must be feeling better. What's the problem, Gidon?"

"I think she could be in danger. We have to head back, Mattie. I don't mean to alarm you, but I think Beth could be in trouble. I'll explain in the car."

## ⇥92⇤

*Monday afternoon*

## SAFED

Beth stood at the counter of the craft shop and stared at the earrings in the glass case. She pointed to a pair. Then, as the store clerk removed them for her closer inspection, Beth looked up and out of the shop window and caught sight of Paz, her driver, standing across the street watching the store. She sighed audibly.

Beth was glad that she had not attempted to drive to Safed herself. The old historic town was wrapped like a long scarf around the top of a high, steep mountain and it was hard to find one's way through it in a car and very hard to find a place to park. But Paz was familiar with Safed and he had found a parking place.

As she left the automobile, Beth told Paz that she would meet him back at the parking place in three hours. But Paz had insisted that he come along and keep an eye on her, that she would likely get lost in Safed and not find her way back to the car. Beth had argued with him for a while but when he suggested that he just follow at a discreet distance, she finally agreed.

Safed was largely a religious community. Here, old men and their students studied the kabbalah as they had for centuries. It was rumored that reincarnation was one of its tenets. The kabbalah was certainly interesting— what Beth had heard of it—but she had no hope of finding out about it while she was exploring Safed today. It was a secret study, only for those who were deemed capable, both by their knowledge and by their moral character.

However, Safed was also an artists' colony. Many artists experimenting in different media came here every summer, to work, and to sell their work. Safed was also a town where people had summer homes. It was high up in the mountains of the north where the climate was cool. With Paz trailing her at a respectable distance, Beth had roamed freely through the twisting and winding streets of the ancient town. It was almost November and many of the shops she had hoped to visit were closed. But this one with its marvelous hand-crafted jewelry was still open.

Beth held the pierced earrings made of green Eilat stone and silver to her ears. She was enjoying this day on her own. She had hardly been alone since she had arrived in Israel. She needed that space, her own company, needed to think, needed to just follow her own whims for a day. And she wanted to give Mattie a clear field with Gidon.

Beth purchased two pairs of earrings and left. She began to wander down streets looking for open shops. Paz trailed at a discreet distance. She found a shop selling sculpture, papier maché caricatures of famous people. She enjoyed the humor of the work, but bought nothing.

In another shop she found a lovely small vase which she purchased for her daughter Becky. She left, her packages tucked safely in her tote, and walked up a steep street and turned to her left. She was in an open square with a large outdoor kiosk. She knew where she was. The car was parked not far from here. She had been walking around for an hour and a half. Beth decided to get a sandwich and something cold to drink. She looked around for Paz to invite him for a light lunch, but didn't see him. That was odd. He had been behind her not more than five minutes ago. Well, perhaps he had gone to the bathroom. No doubt, if she sat still he would find her soon enough. If not, she would meet him at the car, in an hour and a half.

Beth entered the line at the kiosk, ordered a sandwich and coffee, then took it to one of the many tables on the other side of the busy street. She sat down and began to eat. She hadn't realized how hungry she was—she had eaten only a very small breakfast. She opened her purse to look for her notebook—she wanted to write down some of her impressions—but her hand closed over Paul's letter and she pulled that out instead.

> ...You've asked me about the events surrounding the life of Christ, and that is more difficult to write about than all your other questions. The union of the God with the man Jesus is perhaps the greatest of all spiritual-human mysteries. And humanity has barely scratched the surface of its significance. How could we? Our inner faculties have not as yet grown up to that task. But we can someday, and we will.

There was a man, an extraordinary man, called Jesus, prepared lifetime after lifetime (yes, reincarnation again!) to become the Christopherus, the bearer of the Christ ego. Then at the baptism in the Jordan he took into himself the Being of the Christ. And for three years the Christ moved ever more deeply into the soul sheath, the life organization, and finally the physical body of Jesus until he was completely man. And yet at the same time God. It was a unique event, no precedent for it in all the long evolution of humanity, never again to be repeated in the same way. The return of the God "in the clouds" is another matter altogether, misunderstood today. Gods or angelic beings had overshadowed great men before, but none had ever united so completely with a human physical body as had the Christ. It took great preparation, and a lofty, lofty spiritual being to accomplish it, and also a lofty human being.

And it was the Jewish stream, torn away from, and cleansed of, the pagan streams around it, that had been given that remarkable mission—to bring forth the Messiah.

That the Christ united with Jesus at the baptism and not at his birth is something that was known in the early centuries of Christianity and was later forgotten, or hidden from the common folk by the Church. This is a very long and deep story and I cannot put much of it in writing. If you care to visit me when you come home. . .

There is much that Christ did as a kind of prototype for what the human can become in the future. For humanity too is evolving toward godhood, toward taking its place in the angelic choir. There are nine hierarchies at present. In aeons to come, humanity will take its place as the tenth. That is why reincarnation is so important. All humanity partakes in evolution.

And we can talk in detail about just what this western approach to reincarnation really is when you return. It has to do with the times we live in and the changes in human consciousness, particularly the astonishing changes that have come about in this century. Perhaps that is why your experience in Chartres came with such power, a sort of wake-up call. John the Baptist said, 'Change your way of thinking. Repent.' You do seem to have a good guardian angel, my dear, who doesn't let you shut down. My prayers are with you, my friend. I hope something of what I have written will help you in some small way.

Love, Paul.

Beth sighed and put the letter away. How naive of her to think that her quest for proof of reincarnation was a simple one. Just let me know if it is true, she had asked of whatever powers were out there. One small memory would have done it. But nothing had happened. How could it? Still, she knew now what she was going to do next. It had come to her clearly after reading Paul's letter that morning as she sat in her room waiting for the car to come and take her to Safed.

Beth finished her lunch, then looked around to see if Paz had returned. She didn't see him. Well, if he lost her, that was his problem. As long as they both knew where the car was. And she had another hour and a half. She picked up her coffee cup to swallow the last drops, set it down, looked up and saw a young woman in her twenties weaving through the traffic toward her. She was waving and smiling at her. The woman had long black hair, and was wearing jeans and a T-shirt. A small knapsack was slung over one shoulder. Beth didn't know who she was. The young woman made a dash through the honking traffic and in moments was standing in front of Beth's table with a wide grin on her face.

"You're Elizabeth Layton, aren't you." It was a pronouncement not a question, and it was made in American English.

"I am," Beth said, smiling up at her.

"Forgive me for barging in on your privacy, but I so love your poetry! Imagine finding you here," she gestured broadly, "in Israel, in Safed, no less." The girl shook her head in disbelief. "Are you all alone?"

"Today I am. Won't you sit down, Miss. . .?"

"Jamie," she thrust out a hand which Beth took, then pulled out a chair and sat down. "My name is Jamie Fowler."

Not a Jewish name, Beth noted. "And what are you doing here, Jamie Fowler," and she in turn gestured widely, imitating the young woman's earlier gesticulations with a grin, "in Israel, in Safed?"

"Visiting, and isn't it fascinating? My dad's brother works in Israel and I'm on a sort of world tour after graduating Boston U last spring. My uncle's rented a house up here for weekends and vacations. My aunt's a potter. So Safed is marvelous for her. And a good place to get away to. I can't believe it's really you. I studied you in American Contemporary Poetry and loved what you had to say, your stuff on women particularly. And I came to a reading you gave at the 92nd St. Y in New York." She was bubbling with enthusiasm. "What brings you to Israel?"

## 93
*Monday afternoon*
## SAFED

A few buildings down the street, tucked into the shadows of the doorway of a closed shop, Paz watched the two women with interest. Layton had been followed to Safed, of that he was sure. But that car had disappeared and then suddenly there had been a different one, with two men and a young woman, following Layton when she left the last shop. The young woman had gotten out of the car not far from the kiosk where Layton had purchased her lunch.

He couldn't hear what the women were saying but from the body language of the two he was sure that they had never met before. They spoke for about fifteen minutes and then the two women stood up and started down the street together. Paz pulled back deeper into the shadows as they passed by him and when they were several yards away he followed them.

They were heading downhill. After walking about five minutes along the busy, shop-lined street, they turned left into a narrow residential street. Paz hurried after them. He entered the street in time to see the two women go into a house halfway down the block. He was about to follow them when he heard the screech of a car in the main street above him. Two men leapt out and as he whirled to meet them, they grabbed him by the arms and held him fast.

The man to his right said to him. "Easy does it. You've gone far enough. It's best if you don't follow the women any farther."

## 94

## *Monday*

## THE GALILEE

"But that doesn't make any sense," Mattie said, after she had heard Gidon's story. "Why would anyone want to follow Beth?"

"I thought you might tell me," Gidon said. Gidon was driving awfully fast and she was hanging on to the strap above her side window, her eyes never leaving the road.

"How would I know, Gidon?"

"Every time I've been with Beth, every time we've been together, we've been followed."

"Well, maybe it's you they're following."

"No," he shook his head emphatically.

"It just doesn't make sense."

"Could it be someone her boyfriend hired?"

"Eric? Is that why you asked me if Eric is a jealous type? That's a crazy idea. Of course not."

"Are you sure?"

Mattie thought about it for a moment. "Well, I can't be sure, but it's just not true to his character."

"How well do you know him?"

"Not too well. It just doesn't sound like him."

"Obsessive people do strange things. Do you believe her story about why she came to Israel?"

"Of course, I believe her story. Don't you?"

"Someone is following her, Mattie, and has been following her since she got off the airplane. If it's not her boyfriend, and she really did come here spur-of-the-moment to try to resolve some religious problem, do you have a better idea?"

She just shook her head. "Do you?"

"Kidnapping."

"Kidnapping?" Mattie's voice slid up an octave. "Who? Why?"

"Terrorists. Because she's a public figure and a kidnapping might get a lot of attention. . ."

"But why?"

"To throw a monkey wrench into the peace process."

Mattie was silent, then asked, "Arabs? Jews?"

"It could be either?" Gidon reached over and patted her hand. "It's just a possibility, Mattie. Don't get so worried. There could be another explanation."

"Why shouldn't I worry?" Mattie flung the words at him. "You're worried! Just who are you, Gidon?"

"I'm who I said I was, Mattie. I represent a consortium of collective settlements trying to sell their stuff abroad. Times are very crucial now in Israel and everyone helps out where they can. I've been drawn into this because I befriended Elizabeth on the plane. And because I know people in high places."

When they arrived at the outskirts of Safed, Gidon pulled out of traffic. "Slide into the driver's seat," Gidon told Mattie as he opened the car door. When she hesitated, he said to her, "You can drive, can't you?"

Mattie nodded. She was momentarily paralyzed.

"Then slide over," Gidon ordered.

Mattie slid over. She automatically reached down and adjusted the seat.

Gidon climbed into the passenger's seat. "Drive. I'll direct you."

So Mattie pulled out into traffic.

"Just follow the flow of traffic unless I tell you to

turn. But drive slowly." He reached into the glove compartment and to Mattie's alarm pulled out a handgun.

Gidon saw her consternation. "Don't be afraid, I'll only use it if I have to. And I do know how to use it." And then he stopped paying attention to her and her concerns. He was carefully scrutinizing the sidewalk and the streets, obviously looking for Beth.

Mattie could feel the adrenaline rush through her. She concentrated on her driving, turning when Gidon said to turn and driving straight when he asked that of her. Fear fueled her excitement and made her high.

"Stop, stop," Gidon called out after they had been circling for about fifteen minutes. Mattie eased out of traffic.

"It's Paz' car," Gidon told her, and he got out to look inside it.

When he returned, he said, "Let's go."

"Who's Paz?" Mattie asked, as she pulled back out into traffic.

"Beth's driver, a young man that I pray is with her right this minute or I'll break his neck," Gidon said. "Okay, let's see if we can find them." And he directed Mattie as she drove slowly through the side streets, pulling out now and then into the main traffic. Ten minutes later, they were on the principal road, when Gidon shouted, "Back up, back up. It's Paz."

And Mattie backed up. Cars honked. People on the sidewalk yelled but Mattie, red-faced and determined, backed up the car and turned into the side street where Gidon had spotted Paz sitting on a curb. She parked the car halfway on the sidewalk as she had seen other cars do.

## 95
*Monday afternoon*
## The Galilee

Paz was on his feet and waiting when Gidon leapt out of the car.

"Why are you here? Where's Layton?"

"In a house down the street," and Paz motioned with his head.

"What's she doing there?"

By now Mattie was out of the car and standing next to them.

"She went there with a woman she met in the streets."

"In the streets? And you let her?"

"I followed. Don't get excited."

Mattie interrupted. "What's he saying? What happened? Can you please speak in English?"

Without skipping a beat, Gidon slid into English, "Whose house is it?"

Paz shrugged, and answered in English. "Some American's."

"Why the hell haven't you found out? Why haven't you gone after her? What kind of training are they giving you guys these days?"

"She's in a house?" Mattie asked. "Why? How did it happen?"

But Paz was looking at Gidon coolly. He gestured with his head to a black car parked down the street just beyond the house. "You see that car. There are two men in that car, big men, probably armed, and they have suggested I wait patiently for Layton. She should be out, they said, in an hour." He glanced at his watch, "Which is in about fifteen minutes."

Gidon stared at the car. He could vaguely see two shapes through the windshield.

"Why didn't you go for help?" he asked Paz.

"And if they moved her when I was gone. . .? It was best to give them the hour and see what developed. If she had been kept longer, I would have gone for the police."

"No way to get out the back?"

"The yard of the house backs up onto a sheer hill. This street is the only way out."

"She's in a house?" Mattie said. "Oh my God."

"Are you going to be all right?" Gidon asked Mattie. She nodded.

But he wasn't looking at her, he was looking down the street.

"What are you thinking?" Paz asked him.

"They didn't let *you* in, okay. Let's see what happens if *I* walk down to the house and knock on the door. Which house is it exactly?"

"Six houses from here on the left."

"If I get in and I'm not out in half an hour, do what you think is right. No matter what happens, wait at least half an hour. Mattie, you stay with Paz."

"Are you sure?" And she surprised him when she said, "I know how to use a gun."

Gidon gave her a wry smile. "I'm not taking a gun." And he gestured with his chin at the black car waiting down the hill.

## 96

*Monday afternoon*
### SAFED

Gidon strode downhill to the house, walked up to the front door and knocked loudly.

After a moment, a woman, apparently a domestic servant, opened the door. "Can I help you?" she asked him in Hebrew.

Just as he was about to answer, he heard footsteps. As he turned to look, the two men who had been sitting in the car came up behind him.

"Edie, nothing to worry about. We'll take care of this," one of the men said to the woman in American English.

Gidon felt an arm on his elbow and another on his shoulder.

"Go in, Mr. ben David."

And Gidon entered the house, with his two escorts behind him. He saw the woman called Edie disappear through a door at their left.

"Wait a moment, please," Gidon was instructed.

One of the men walked to a door at the back of the entry hall in which they stood, knocked and went in. In a moment, he returned and said, "Go in."

Gidon entered a room made dark by the blinds closed against the afternoon sunlight. Neither of the two men followed him. The door was closed but not locked. It was a small living room, with a sofa, several chairs and tables. He walked over to the window and pulled the blinds. The windows opened onto a garden with a small building at it's end. The garden was filled with flowers and pottery. Gidon turned when he heard the door open.

"What do you think of my garden, Gidon? That building is the studio where my wife works. She's a potter. But the garden is mine." The man was about Gidon's age, medium height and with dark hair.

In the shadowy light, Gidon couldn't see them, but he knew the man had bright blue eyes. "Robin Fowler. Well, well."

"You look good, Gidon." The speech was soft but precise. "Come sit down." He motioned to a chair opposite the sofa. Gidon took it. Fowler came forward, holding a half-smoked cigarette, and sat down on the sofa. "Kept your weight down," Fowler said, and took a drag of his cigarette. "I heard you had gotten out of this business."

"That's right."

"I haven't seen you since East Germany, how many years ago?"

Gidon shrugged. "What are you doing in Israel?"

"Working. At the Embassy. Two years now."

"You're at the American Embassy? Doing what?"

Fowler put out his cigarette stub in an ashtray, and lit another one, then offered the pack to Gidon.

Gidon shook his head.

"You never did smoke, did you? One of the few Israelis from the old days who didn't. I'm an assistant to the American Ambassador."

Gidon smiled at the euphemism. "Well, that's a demotion for someone of your talents."

Fowler laughed. "A nice, easy job. Benefits. Regular hours. Time for the family. Occasional travel. And a chance to come to Safed on my days off and on holidays."

"Nice place."

"One of the perks. My wife's a professional potter, so we come up when we can. She a little more often than I. There's an artists' colony here, you know."

"I know. I understand a friend of mine came to your house a little less than an hour ago."

"Yes, my niece brought her here for a visit. We had coffee and a nice little chat."

Gidon's eyes narrowed. "Where is she now?"

"She's visiting my wife's studio in the back of the garden. I'll call her after we have our little talk."

"What's there to talk about? The old days? I'll tell you about my children if you tell me about yours?"

Fowler laughed. Gidon had liked him when the two had worked together in East Germany on some joint venture between the Americans and the Israelis. The two of them had done a lot of drinking and whoring together in Berlin when they had had a little time off. An American father and a Mexican mother accounted for Robin's bright blue eyes and straight black hair, still full. He wasn't a tall man but he was powerfully built, handsome, a man women went for.

"Tell me why the Israelis are so interested in Elizabeth Layton. You want tea or coffee? Something stronger?" He got up and went to the door.

"Coffee."

He opened it and called to someone, then came back and sat down again.

"Interested is too big a word," Gidon said. "It began as a mild curiosity. When Layton suddenly changed her flight to America for a flight to Israel, the wheels started turning. At any other time probably nothing would have happened. But in these days when everybody is on the alert, we got curious."

"Understandable."

"I happened to be on the plane with her..."

"Chance?"

"Pure chance. So the powers that be decided to put me next to her. I think our curiosity would have quickly diminished if she had not been followed from the airport. It was not our boys, so it must have been a couple of yours?"

Fowler began to laugh. "And if you had not been on the plane sitting next to her and if you had not driven her to Jerusalem that evening, we probably wouldn't have followed her."

Gidon stared at him.

"We knew your people were looking into her when she changed her reservations. You know how we Americans love to watch the watchers. We were alerted here, so we had someone at the airport, just to see what was what. We knew you were seated next to her on the plane, that you had been placed next to her deliberately. We saw you come out of the airplane and go through customs together. We saw you drive her to Jerusalem when we know you live in Tel Aviv. So we followed you. We were very curious to know just why Israel Security was so interested in an American poet."

"You were worried?"

Fowler grinned. "So, was it Security or some rogue Israeli group? Our country has some stake in this peace process, I'm sure you realize."

It was Gidon's turn to laugh. "My old bosses would have dropped out after my initial report but for the fact that someone was following her. So we decided to put our people on her to see what was up."

There was a knock on the door and Edie came in with a tray of coffee and some cookies. She set it down without saying a word and left the room.

Robin Fowler poured the coffee.

"And Hemmings, how does he fit in?"

"He's not important, an American businessman who does small things for us on occasion. He happened to be in the country."

"A courier?"

Fowler just smiled. "Our people are pretty busy now too."

"What did you say to Layton?"

"I asked her why Israeli Security was accompanying her all over Israel?"

"And what did she say to that?"

"She looked at me as if I had lost my senses."

"So you told her about me."

"Did I mess something up?"

"The lady has a lover. I'm not it."

"Too bad. What about the other one?"

"Mathilda Jones? What about her?"

"Are you satisfied that she only brought in a little cash for a friend's mother?"

"You know her friend?"

"We know him. We know also that today Mahmud's brother-in-law bought a new refrigerator in Haifa and that he and two cousins hauled it back in one of the men's truck."

Gidon just shrugged and took a swallow of the still hot coffee. The adrenaline was draining out of him. A comedy of errors. He began to laugh again and Fowler laughed with him. "If people knew how many silly, comical screw-ups there are in Intelligence," Gidon said, "they would probably think twice about allocating any money for this whole silly business."

Fowler gave him a wry smile, "Well, not always silly business."

Gidon acquiesced, "No, not always silly business. So, can I collect my American terrorist?"

"Are you sure she'll be happy to see you?"

Not at all sure, Gidon thought.

And then there was a loud rap on the outside door and in a moment a white-faced Edie came in. "There's a man at the door who threatens to call the police if I don't take him to a man called Gidon ben David, right away."

"Let him in, Edie, by all means let him in."

## ≈97≈

*Monday evening*

## THE GALILEE

The sun was low in the sky somewhere behind them. The Sea of Galilee, where they stood, was calm. Small waves rubbed up against the shore and melted back into the darkening water. Gidon was waiting for Beth to say something, but she had turned away to stare out at the sea. She was angry at him, and it hurt. She seemed unwilling to give up that anger. Still, he waited, hoping. He had sent Paz home alone from Safed, then had driven the two women back to their guest house. Both he and Mattie had tried to explain to Beth all that had gone on since she had first set foot in that airplane bound for Israel, but Beth had barely responded. She had asked a few questions, and then had shut down.

When they arrived back at the guest house, Gidon asked Beth if she would take a walk with him. He wanted to talk to her. At first he thought she was going to say no, but Mattie had said to her, "He deserves a hearing, Beth. That's the least you can do, in all fairness." So Beth had come. They had walked toward the sea in silence. Her anger and her hurt were held in front of her like a shield. She wanted, obviously felt she needed, protection from him.

"Beth, I'm sorry. Really, if you've been hurt in any way in all of this, I'm sorry." He knew his words sounded feeble, pat, a clichéd excuse.

She didn't answer him but continued to stare across the sea.

"Beth, please yell, or strike out at me or something. Don't just give me the silent treatment."

Still no answer.

"You think that you were nothing but a job I was doing. And that I'm the world's best actor, and nothing that moved between us was real." It was a statement. His voice was flat, tired. My God, he was tired.

Her voice, when she finally spoke, was low and filled with pain. "I don't know what to take away from all this, Gidon, what to make of all our conversations, the days we shared, anything. What reality was I living in, Gidon, when you were so obviously living in another?"

"Everything I said when we talked was true."

She turned on him then and raised both fists and shook them at him. "Fine, good, everything you said. But what about all those things unsaid, all your suspicions, all the things you kept from me, what about them? If I was in some sort of danger, shouldn't I have been told? You didn't tell me because you weren't sure of me, didn't trust me, thought I might be some sort of Mata Hari."

And now he had a hard time answering her. "Let's walk a little," he said, and he touched her arm. They began strolling along the beach. "I can't give you an easy answer, Beth. I can't deny what you just said. Can you understand if I tell you that I was two men every time I was with you? There was that man doing a job for his country. But that's not the man that met you on the plane, the one who drove you to Jerusalem, and that's not the man who spent the day with you in the desert and took you to see ben Yehuda, that's not the man who found you so attractive that he forgot sometimes to be the other man. I can't explain this any better. I had a little crush on you,

Beth. You're an extraordinary lady, and though I know you're in love with another man, I would like to be your friend. I want you to think better of me than you do now. Our conversations, about life, religion, poetry, have meant so much to me. . ."

She didn't answer him but he knew she listened and he could feel the air change between them, the tension leave. After a few moments she said, "Let's sit," and she motioned to a bench beneath some trees facing the water.

He wiped the damp bench with a handkerchief and they sat. Beth reached down and picked up some pebbles and began to throw them one by one into the sea.

"Yes, I understand how it's possible to be two people at the same time. Strange, but of all the things you've said tonight, that makes the most sense to me. And now I'm thinking that if I hadn't been followed from the airport, we might never have met a second time. And that would have been a terrible loss." She turned to him and she smiled. "Thank you."

"For what?" he reached out to take her hand. She didn't pull it away. He wound his fingers through hers.

"For worrying about me, for wanting to keep me from danger."

He grinned. "You know, I really am out of that work. Chance pulled me in again."

"Maybe destiny."

"You believe in destiny?"

"That's why I'm here."

"I know." He leaned over and kissed her on the mouth. It was a soft, yielding mouth. "That's just a kiss between friends who are making up after a misunderstanding." He let go of her hand then. "What are you going to do now?"

"Well," he saw that she couldn't quite look at him yet.

"I'm going to spend a few days at Sde Gedalia with Mattie and her family. And then I'm going to come back here or perhaps stay in one of your parents' cabins and I'm going to write."

"You've given up your quest?"

"Oh...no. That's a way to pursue my quest, to move into those times through writing poetry. After all, a writer writes. I'll rent a car, go back to some of the places where Jesus walked and taught. I'll soak up the atmosphere of your country. I'll read and study. And write."

"And Eric? How will he take the delay in your return?"

"I think it will be okay with him, when I tell him I'm beginning a new book of poetry centered here in Israel. I'm going to send him a fax tomorrow morning to tell him of my plans and to tell him..." she didn't go on.

With only a modicum of sadness, Gidon said, "...that you agree to the marriage."

Beth nodded. And turned to look at him.

"He's a lucky man." Gidon stood up. "Now let's go collect Mattie, and I will take you both out to dinner to celebrate the end of our mystery. Then tomorrow I will help you move over to Sde Gedalia."

## 98
## *Tuesday*
## Tel Aviv

His mother-in-law, Dora, and his two children were still up when Gidon arrived at his home Tuesday evening. He did as he had planned. He sat them all down, and read Avigail's letter to them. After Gidon had finished, Geel burst into tears. He rose quickly and ran into his room and shut his door. Gidon, stunned, was about to go after him.

"Let him be," Dora warned, her own eyes full. "Let him have his privacy."

Gidon nodded and walked over to the window to stare out at the damp, hot night. Rinat came over and stood next to him. She reached for his hand and he took it. When he looked at her, he saw silent tears running down her face. He took her in his arms and held her.

"Come," he finally said to her, "let's make tea for everyone. Grandma sent cookies, her American oatmeal ones."

## 99
*Tuesday evening*
### THE SHEFELA

Tuesday evening at dinner, Malkah said to Yehuda, "So, are you going to tell me what is going on, or are you going to stay silent for the rest of your life?"

So Yehuda told his best friend the beautiful and terrible dream he had had while visiting David and Sharone. He told it slowly, describing every detail. He had gone over and over it in his mind a dozen times so he could recall every part of the dream.

"I feel, my Malkah, like I have failed some big test. An angel looked at me, showed me something, everything, and I failed. I couldn't give him the right answers... no, I didn't want to give him the right answers."

"And what are the right answers, Yehuda? The whole world is in trouble? We know that. We read the newspapers. We watch TV. We aren't isolated. We have done, and you in particular, Yehuda, what all people should do, we have worried about, and taken care of, our own. If everybody did that, the world would be a better place to live in."

"You think so, *ketzeleh*?"

"I think so."

"I think," he told her, stirring the salad in his plate around and around, "that if everybody took care of themselves and of their own, the world would be worse than it is now. More hatred. Endless wars. Everybody would be fighting everybody for the same piece of land, for the same opportunities."

"So maybe there have to be winners in the world and losers. It's the way it has always been. Why should it be different now?"

"Someday it all has to end or what will be left? And who will be left?"

"So what are you saying, Yehuda, Israel was a mistake? It shouldn't have happened?"

"No, no, never. That I'll never believe. We had no choice. The world didn't want us. We had to have a state of our own or we would have disappeared, like Shmuel's second stream, all of us. We would have died out, melted into the world. The world would have liked that better. No, this land had to be."

"So what are you saying then?"

He sighed. "This is the wrong conversation, Malkah. This is not what I'm talking about."

"Good, what are you talking about?"

"I'm talking about the old angel."

"Why are you always talking about the old angel and never about the young angel?"

"What?"

"It's always about the old angel, your concern. But there are two angels in your dream. And one of them is quite happy with you. Why don't you pay attention to that one instead of the other one? After all, he is an angel too."

Yehuda sighed and was silent for a long time. Malkah ate her salad and watched Yehuda toy with his.

"Yehuda, eat. You don't eat since you came back."

Dutifully, Yehuda put a few bites of the salad into his mouth and went on thinking. Malkah buttered a roll and put it on Yehuda's plate.

Finally Yehuda said, "There are good angels and there are bad angels. If you believe in angels, there are good angels and there are bad angels."

"And do you believe in angels, *ketzel*?"

"If not angels, at least in dreams, *ketzeleh*."

## 100
*Wednesday*
## NEW YORK

Eric arrived in New York early Wednesday evening from Los Angeles. He was tired and very glad to be home, but the trip had been rewarding. He had negotiated for three pieces of sculpture for the Barry Museum and for a video installation, a favorite of Mrs. Barry's.

He dropped his suitcase in his bedroom and went into his home office to see if he had any faxes. There were several, most were business related, but he was looking for one special one. And there among the pile of slippery paper was the one he was looking for. He extricated it and carried it into the kitchen. He took out a bottle of beer from the refrigerator, opened it, sat down at the kitchen table, and read the message. "Dear Eric, Welcome home. I hope I've timed this correctly and that this letter is waiting for you when you return from L.A.! I'm spending a few days with Mattie at Ruth and Michael's kibbutz. You have that number and address. On Friday I'll be moving over to a cabin I've rented, where I intend to be on my own to write. . ."

Eric felt the disappointment rise up like a tide in his chest. She was staying on. Stop it, he warned himself. You told her to take all the time she needed. He took a swallow of beer and continued reading.

". . .I have an idea for a series of poems bubbling around in my brain and I need to take notes, look hard at the area and sites, mostly in the north of Israel. I'll rent a car and go around to some of the sites I've already seen, but this time I'll take copious notes. No, I haven't found the answer to my quest. I understand now that I was naive, expecting experience to just drop out of the heavens, but I do think I can write my way toward such an experience. I'll explain this all when I get home..."

Eric sighed audibly. But at least she was writing. And that was good. That was great. "...I hope to gather material, take notes, begin some of the poems, then come home and write and write. After we get married..." It took some minutes before Eric could move his eyes away from the word *married*. "...some time in the winter (I do think winter is a wonderful time for a wedding)..." He stared, mesmerized by the word *wedding*. "...I would love to come back to Israel with you, manuscript in hand, and take you to all the places that you should see and also the ones that moved me..."

Eric stopped reading, put his glass down. Wait, he told himself. Read that again. And he did, then went on with the letter. "...I love you more than I can say. I need about ten days or two weeks, and then back to you and back to an exciting writing project. And back to plan a little wedding. Love, Beth."

Eric read the note over and over. There were tears sliding down his cheeks but he was grinning.

## 101
*Thursday*
## NEW YORK

### FAX TO ELIZABETH LAYTON FROM ERIC HALSEY, BARRY MUSEUM, NYC

Dear Beth, I love you. A new book of poems about Israel, how intriguing. I love you. How about a February wedding and a month-long honeymoon in the spring in Israel and anywhere else you want to go? Did I tell you I love you? Stay as long as you need. But not too long or I'll have to come fetch you. I love you, Eric.

## ~102~
## Wednesday, Thursday, Friday
### THE GALILEE

The three days Beth and Mattie spent with Michael and Ruth were full and pleasant ones. They toured the kibbutz. The couple gave a small reception for them in their rooms. On Wednesday they visited Haifa. Thursday they spent touring some of the digs in the surrounding area. They visited the eerie catacombs of Bet Shearim, a town that was once the seat of the Sanhedrin, the highest religious and judicial body of the Jews after the destruction of Jerusalem in A.D. 70. They looked at the remarkable mosaics in the old town of Zippori, now a National Park.

On Friday they drove into the Golan to visit another Talmudic Village, called Katzrin with it's remarkable synagogue. They toured the Golan, went to it's museum, and Michael spoke eloquently about why he was for the peace initiative but not for giving back the Golan. They drove up to the heights where Syrian guns had once shelled the valley below. That evening they dropped Beth's things off at one of the cabins run by Gidon's parents, had dinner in the Silvers' restaurant, and then Michael and Ruth took Mattie back with them to their kibbutz.

Beth was alone to work at her writing.

## 103
*Saturday*
### ISRAEL

Early Saturday morning, Mattie took a bus from the town of Afula to Tel Aviv. Gidon met her at the bus station, and they headed out of town, in his car, for a day in the desert. He took her to Qumran. He took her to Masada. He took her then to the hill where he had talked to Geel only days before and where once in his youth he had come camping alone to decide on the direction his life was to take. They carried blankets up from the car, a thermos of hot coffee that they had purchased in the restaurant at Masada and a thermos of water.

They were all alone on the hill. While the afternoon sun slowly slid down the western sky, they talked. Gidon spoke about his marriage, his children, the breakup. Mattie talked about her own marriage, the loss of her parents, the simultaneous loss of her husband and child. And how because of the losses, she had allowed her life to narrow down. As she spoke about it, words she had not spoken in years, she began to cry. She wept and wept, and Gidon held her. Then they made love, wild, passionate, needy love. And then they talked again. Gidon talked about his work, his restlessness, the uncertainty of where he was heading, the future of the country, his own personal future. Mattie spoke about her childhood, her parents, Doug, her large family, her cabin, living alone, her love of nature, the need for poetry in her life. They drank coffee and made love again. This time it was tender, comforting, satisfying love. It was dark. They were huddled together under the blankets, staring up at the blazing stars in the sky.

"I can't imagine anything more beautiful, more real then a desert," Mattie said.

"Do you like it? I love it myself. I always come to the desert when I need to think things through. It's clean, unadorned. Your soul feels stripped naked."

"And restored."

He reached for her hand beneath the blankets and squeezed it. "Mattie, I don't know what I can offer you," he began.

"Shhh," she shook her head vigorously making the short, blond hair ripple like waves. "No one is asking for anything. I'm too old to ask for anything."

"You're not . . ."

Mattie let go of his hand and pulled hers out from under the blanket and touched his lips. "I'm past nest building and child rearing, past worrying about need. Whatever will be, will be. Let it alone, Gidon."

"What a strange creature you are, Mattie. I love your poetry. And the body's not bad, either." He leaned over and kissed her lips, then leaned back on his elbows.

She looked at him, barely able to make him out, but drawing with her forefinger the lines on his face. "This is what I'm learning here in Israel. I'm learning to live without certainty, to meet whatever the day has to offer, and to dance in the fire of life without fear, without any guarantees."

Gidon sat up. "Israel does that for people. It brings out the hidden capacities in them, wakens in them skills and a courage that few knew they had. Maybe that's why God chose this tiny land for his people. Maybe that's why we've fought so hard for it over the millennia. Israel changes you."

Mattie reached up and pulled Gidon's face down toward hers. "And change is good, Gidon, change is very good."

## 104

*Early November*

## The Galilee

Each day, of ten days, Beth rose early, worked for an hour, then went to the restaurant for a hearty breakfast. She returned to her room worked for another few hours, then after a light lunch she climbed into her rented car and headed for some sites around the Sea of Galilee or back into Nazareth and Cana. She took copious notes, wrote drafts of poems, sometimes first lines, or fragments, sometimes only ideas. She was writing about present Israel, herself in present Israel thinking about the time of Christ. She was also reaching back to that time, writing from many voices, most often a woman's. She was writing loosely, not fixing anything, reaching, reaching for that other woman...

Late afternoon and evening, she read the books she had purchased in Jerusalem about the period around the time of Christ. She read Josephus' Jewish Wars and then drove out to look at the sites he had described. She was at peace, happy, anxious, and tense, as one is when one is in the throes of creativity. A character was forming in her mind, a young woman who lived in Nazareth at the time Jesus lived there, a friend of Mary's. Many poems would be told from the young woman's point of view. And on that fateful Passover celebration, she would be among the company that had gone up to Jerusalem. She would have witnessed the Crucifixion. What would that have been like? Beth didn't know yet. She would do what she could do now in the Galilee, spend a few days in Jerusalem before she left the country, and then become a fixture in the large public library in New York City, researching that era. Later she would go up to Gloucester, Massachusetts and talk to Paul.

Beth was falling in love with the Galilee. The rains had come and the land was beginning to look renewed. It was as beautiful here and as restorative as the desert was depressing and deadly. Perhaps those feelings did stem from another time, from another incarnation. If so, she was going to build on them, build them into the character she was writing about. After all, didn't people live more closely with their native environment in those days than they did now? Yes, she was making a beginning. And if she could sense something of her destiny through the writing, well and good. If not, she would have a book of poems out of it, and at least a growing closer to a world and a land that had not interested her before. Maybe that's what the whole experience in Chartres was about. Maybe this too was destiny. She was led here to this country. And she was writing.

## 105

*Early November*

## TIBERIAS

Mattie met Beth at a restaurant in Tiberias.

"So it's happened," Beth said to her after they had ordered.

"Does it show?" Mattie grinned.

"Yes, absolutely. Is it all right?"

"It's... it's fine."

"What do you want, Mattie?"

"The amazing thing is—nothing, Beth. Whatever is, is. And whatever comes of it, will come of it."

"Good God, you're starting to sound like an Israeli!"

And they both laughed.

As they were drinking their coffee, Mattie said, "I have an idea for a novel."

"Yes, I know. You told me that."

"I want to know how you feel about this, Beth, before I proceed."

"That's ridiculous. Why should you need my approval?"

"Because I don't want you upset, thinking I've appropriated your idea."

Beth looked at her curiously.

"Remember I told you that people reincarnate with the same circle of friends...?"

"Right... oh, my God. You think you were here, too. Oh, my God!"

"Well," Mattie felt taken aback, "it's possible, and the more I've moved about this country, the more possible it seems."

"Oh, my God!"

"Beth, stop saying that."

"But, Mattie, this is marvelous. You're going to do a novel and I a book of poems. But that's marvelous." And she leapt up out of her chair, came round the table to hug her friend.

"You're not angry?"

"Angry? Why on earth should I be angry? I'm thrilled," Beth said, plopping back into her chair. "Suddenly this is not so lonely a road. We can share the results of our research. We can study together, visit Paul when you return to the States. When are you coming back to the States? Not too soon, I hope. Give this thing with Gidon a chance. Oh, my God, Mattie, this is wonderful!"

And Mattie just nodded and burst into tears.

## 106

*Early November*

## THE SHEFELA

On a Friday morning in early November, Gidon received a call from his uncle. Yehuda wanted to talk to him. It was important. Could he come down tomorrow, on the Sabbath. Gidon agreed.

He was in Yehuda's kibbutz by noon, had lunch with him and Malkah, and then Yehuda spirited him away to his office.

Yehuda sat behind his large, messy desk, looking small in his oversized swivel chair. Gidon sat opposite him.

"I have a proposition for you, Gidon." Elbows on the desk, he clasped his folded hands to his mouth, and looked thoughtfully at Gidon.

"What kind of proposition?"

"Work. I want you to take on the coordinating of a new little project of mine."

Gidon raised his eyebrows.

"I have lined up a few important men who will lend their names to the project, and also their money. Sir Isaac Greene in London, Samuel Stein in Detroit, Robert Margolin in New York." Yehuda mentioned the names of three very wealthy Jews who were great friends of Israel, and who were also admirers of his.

"That's quite a group."

"There'll be more. And not only Jews, I hope."

"Oh, so what's your project?"

"I want to open up a museum in Jerusalem?"

"Another museum in Jerusalem?"

"Not just another museum, Gidon, a world museum. A great museum that will be centered in *Ir Shalom*, the city of peace, the city from which three great religions have gone forth."

"Go on."

"I want to establish a World Holocaust Museum."

The surprise that must have registered on his face, Gidon could see, gave Yehuda a sense of satisfaction.

"Why not? We tell the world to remember. To remember what the world has done to the Jews, and so we have our own Holocaust Museum. But to remember only the sufferings done to the Jews is not enough to remind people that only peace makes sense in a tumultuous world. I want a museum to rise up in our land, in our holy land, that is a memory for all people. I want to see a museum built to commemorate all the terrible wars and cruelty that has gone on in the world, for all peoples."

"The city isn't big enough for such a monumental project."

"You are right. I agree with you." Yehuda nodded solemnly at him. "So therefore I propose a museum dedicated to the twentieth century, with a little looking back into the end of the last century. Two great wars and the Russian Revolution that killed millions, upheavals in China, in Korea, Vietnam, Cambodia, the Shining Path in Peru, Bosnia, half of Africa and Asia coming out from under colonial rule, Afghanistan, South America. Name a country. There have been, and still are, atrocities and cruelties, and we must remember them, all of them. Not just our own...which we must do, must never forget. But the rest of the world, too, has suffered. And we Jews, who understand this, must spearhead this, must bring it about, this world memorial, this world remembrance."

There was silence. Yehuda watched him. Gidon stared back.

"Okay, all right," Yehuda said. "I don't think a museum is going to change the world. I don't think a museum is going to bring world peace. I haven't turned senile. But it is a gesture."

"You want to make a gesture?"

"Before peace, before love, the gesture. . ."

"Who said that?"

"I did. In some poem or other. So?" Yehuda asked.

"It's an interesting idea. You can raise the money?"

"You know I can. A few phone calls."

"What does this have to do with me?"

"I want you involved. You know a lot of people. You know this terrible world. You've been places that you still can't talk about. You can speak to people, you can make connections. You could even administer the whole thing. With my advice, of course."

"Uncle, you're eighty-five years old, this is a huge undertaking for you. I thought you retired from public life."

"I will only give advice. I will only talk, make phone calls. I do it now. Why not?"

"You're not satisfied that you've done enough in your life?"

"Let's say, I want to do this for someone."

"For whom?"

"My secret. A good angel."

"It must be a very good angel. But, Uncle, what do I know about this, about museums, about any of this?"

"You know people, how to manage people, how to get things done. And besides, I'll be here to help you."

"I've got a job."

"You don't like that job. Now that you are getting a divorce... yes, yes, I know. You can't keep news like that secret. Now that you are getting a divorce you need to alter your life. Try something useful for a change."

"Uncle, you're incorrigible. Let me think on it."

"So you like this new poet?"

"You've heard about that also?"

"Of course."

"I like her very much."

"That's a beginning. My advice to you, my child, think with your heart. It's about time."

"I'm trying Uncle. Believe me I'm trying."

## 107

*Mid-November*

## TEL AVIV

The night before Beth left for the States, Mattie and Gidon took her out for dinner in Jerusalem where she had just spent three days. They went to a fish restaurant recommended by David and Sharone.

Over dessert, Mattie asked her, "How is it coming?"

"It's too early to say, I have lots of material, lines, partial poems, drafts, ideas, but I need to do more research when I get home, and more writing, lots more writing. And then come back. It's hard to talk about, but I feel like barriers are falling away. However, I need to learn more, to know more before I come back. And how is it going with you, Mattie?"

"Still looking, still thinking, taking notes, just ideas, nothing clear yet. But I definitely am going to do it."

"Good," Beth said.

"What?" Gidon asked.

"A novel," Mattie said. "I can't talk about it yet. The Muse will disappear."

"Writers are a peculiar lot," he said, and looked at her with affection. Then grinned at Beth.

Beth turned to Gidon. "I spoke to Yehuda the other day," she said, "he told me about his museum and the job he offered you. Are you going to do it?"

"I'm still thinking. It's not going to solve anything, not going to make peace happen. It's not very important, really. . ."

"But Yehuda says it's a gesture."

"And gestures have to be made," Mattie said. "It's a moral stance..."

"For my uncle, very important. He's gone after this like an adolescent after his first love."

"And for you, Gidon?" Beth asked.

"It means a big change, a leap into an area where I don't have expertise. I think Yehuda wants me so the project will stay in the family and he can retain control. He's got an amazing list of people and even some governments that are willing to help get this thing off the ground. It might be too big for me. But maybe some small position in the whole thing."

"Think big," Mattie said. "Don't be afraid."

He grinned at her and gestured toward her with his head. "I'm now getting advice from a former recluse on how to be a man of valor."

"Change or die," Beth said. "That's what Mattie said when she came here. And I guess we've all taken that advice to heart."

They all laughed, and then reminisced about their times together until the restaurant was ready to close. Mattie and Gidon took Beth back to the hotel, collected her suitcases and drove her to the airport for a very late night flight. At the security check-in there were hugs and a promise of letters.

"Gidon, I've finished this poem while I've been in Israel. It's dedicated to you." She thrust an envelope in his hand. And then Beth was walking away, through the security, and toward the lounge.

In his car, Gidon opened the envelope, and read the poem out loud to Mattie:

What Kind of People
*for Gidon ben David*

You slice the air with your finger
twenty kilometers as the crow flies
and say, "The Syrian-African rift."

Standing on a roof
in East Jerusalem, we gaze
past the Herodian stone
city rushing down
hill to the bleached
Judean Desert
below.

"The abyss," I say, "the quick drop
into Hell."
"Solitude," you say.

The achromatic sands drift
toward the horizon and swallow it.
I ask, "What manner of people
did this wilderness shape?"
"Yes," you answer.

We try to find the great salt sea
where it drinks down the hot sky.
"Is it ugly?" you ask.
I ask, "Is death?"

I see the rain stop
at city's edge and there
where the crow lands
the Jordan falling helpless

into the Dead Sea. And John
baptizing. *"Change
your way of thinking,"* he says.

"The self dissolving, melding
into the ether," I say.
"The potent strength of the self," you say.

Out beyond the thumbprint of blue
the white chalk wilderness waits.
"The heart dry, parched
as St. John's bread," I say,
"History wears away like a dune."
You say, "My people begin again."

John says, *"Prepare you the way
through the wasteland
of the soul. Make straight
the path of the I am."*

"No tree, no grass, little water, unadorned
as a poor bride. What kind
of people was forged here?" I ask.

"Yes, yes, what kind of people?"


As Beth stood in line to board the plane, she thought, I wonder who I'll sit next to on this plane?